THE HORSE TRADER'S CHILDREN

Both David and Kate had grown up in Scotland believing Edward Gardiner to be their true father. They knew no lack of love from this man who had wed their mother when she was pregnant by another, and who had then used her dowry to further his driving ambition.

Now David was in London, trying to change from a raw country lad into a gentleman. And Kate had followed him there to become involved with John Law, the fashionable rake and gambler, who was David's rival in everything from winning women to conquering society.

Unprepared by their upbringing, brother and sister plunged into a devious and dangerous world . . . driven by the rebellious spirit they had inherited from their still-beautiful mother . . . struggling to avert scandal and uphold the honor of the rough-and-ready horse trader who was their father in name . . . and plotting desperately to subdue the wrath of the powerful nobleman who was their father by blood. . . .

WILD HARVEST

Great Reading from SIGNET

WILD HARVEST

by
Allison Mitchell

A SIGNET BOOK
NEW AMERICAN LIBRARY
TIMES MIRROR

PUBLISHER'S NOTE

This novel is a work of fiction. Names, characters, places, and incidents are either the product of the author's imagination or are used fictitiously, and any resemblance to actual persons, living or dead, events, or locales is entirely coincidental.

SIGNET TRADEMARK REG. U.S. PAT. OFF. AND FOREIGN COUNTRIES
REGISTERED TRADEMARK—MARCA REGISTRADA
HECHO EN CHICAGO, U.S.A.

SIGNET, SIGNET CLASSICS, MENTOR, PLUME, MERIDIAN AND NAL BOOKS are published by The New American Library, Inc., 1633 Broadway, New York, New York 10019

FIRST PRINTING, JULY, 1983

1 2 3 4 5 6 7 8 9

PRINTED IN THE UNITED STATES OF AMERICA

In memory of my friend and mentor,
Eden Hughes

Chapter One

1

Inveraray, Argyll, Scotland
July 11, 1673,

The redheaded, fair-skinned Highland lass was, he judged, about sixteen. There were three of them after her, chasing her around the inner courtyard. They were encumbered by breastplates and sword belts. They weren't young, either, but what really was slowing them down was that they were tired. The bastards who had fought them here, who had made a fortress of three stone farm buildings had been tenacious. They'd fought his men from noon, and the last of them hadn't died until fifteen minutes ago, with the sun already sinking from the sky.

The rebels had had no chance of winning, or even of running. They had known they had only two options, to surrender or to die, and they had chosen to die. They had taken sixteen of his men with them. Their deaths, and the deaths of his men, had been unnecessary, and John Maitland, Duke of Lauderdale and Lord High Commissioner for Scotland, was heartsick and furious.

He stopped to watch the chase. He was fifty-seven, a tall man, broad-shouldered, pale-skinned. His hair, once golden blond, was now thin and faded. His beard, once as blond as his hair, had long turned gray. He was dressed like his men, in a breastplate over a tunic, trousers, and a helmet, battered and bent. There was a wide leather belt around his waist, holding a sword and a dirk and a brace of flintlock pistols. His tunic was stiff with dried sweat, and his head hurt from the weight of the helmet. His face was streaked with dried sweat and dirt.

The Duke of Lauderdale, who was a friend of King Charles II, as well as the crown's senior officer in Scotland, was not expected to leave Holyroodhouse Palace in Edinburgh to personally pursue rebels through the Highlands. There were younger, less important men available, and expected, to do that. The king had heard, of course, that Lauderdale went into "the field." The king was pleased at Lauderdale's devotion to duty, which he logically thought meant that Lauderdale was willing to leave the comforts of Holyroodhouse Palace and put up with the discomfort of a tent pitched somewhere in the Highlands, if that was what it took to properly command the forces supressing the rebellion.

The king would not have approved had he known that not only was Lauderdale incapable of staying where he belonged in Edinburgh, but also that once in the field, unlike his peers in the upper echelons of the nobility serving the crown, he was unable to sit astride a horse protected by a troop of cavalry and order his men into battle from a faraway hill. Had he known that John Maitland, Duke of Lauderdale, led his men into battle and fought as hard, and certainly as well, as any of them, he would have ordered him to stop.

In his reports to the king, John Maitland never mentioned his personal participation. It was not a lie. He referred to "your Majesty's forces." If the king did not think of the Duke of Lauderdale as part of his forces, that was, of course, the king's privilege.

The girl had no more chance of getting away, John Maitland thought, than her father or her brothers—or whatever the hell the men who had made his men kill them were to her—had had to escape. Her capture and rape was inevitable, simply a matter of time. He thought, approvingly, that she was nimble of foot and mind. She was making his men look like clumsy horses' asses as they tried to grab her. But, he thought, eluding them that way was not going to do her any good. It would be worse for her when they caught her. The realization bothered him.

Lauderdale started to walk across the courtyard again, hoping that when he got to the house, the last of the bodies would have been removed, the blood washed from the floor, and there would be water waiting for him, and clean clothing.

The duke wanted to be clean when he buried his men. He didn't know why that seemed important, but it was. As a fitting place to bury them was important. He had just come from selecting the place where his men would be buried: a place near the top of the hill, a spot large enough to lay his men neatly to their final rest in four rows of four. The nineteen Argyll rebels would be buried in one grave, side by side, just outside the stone barnyard wall, where for a very long time their grave would remind whoever finally took over this farm that rebellion against your rightful king was inevitably paid for with your life.

He was almost at the house when they caught the redheaded lass. She screamed. Not a scream of terror, he thought, but of surprise and perhaps of rage. He turned to look. A fourth soldier had joined them. Probably, he thought, that's how she had been caught. She had not been expecting the fourth man, and the fourth man had caught her.

Two of them had her wrists, holding them to the ground. A third man was holding her legs. As he watched, the fourth soldier straddled her, squatted on her stomach, and ripped the neck of her dress. The girl spat at him. The soldier straddling her hit her with his open hand and shifted his body so that he could rip her dress further.

Her breasts were firm, he saw, with small pale-pink nipples.

"Hold!" John Maitland said. His voice was deep, and

he was sure the men had heard him, but the soldier squatting over the girl didn't stop what he was doing and none of the others looked his way.

"Hold!" he said again, raising his voice so there was no chance for them to pretend they had not heard him.

Now they all looked at him. A couple of them were simply curious. The other two had anticipated what he was going to say next and wore looks of disappointment and, he thought angrily, a hint of defiance.

"Chain her," he said levelly, "and bring her to me."

The four soldiers didn't move.

"Immediately," he said, "God *damn* your souls!"

Then he turned and walked on and went in the house.

There was no question in his mind that he would be obeyed. In the field, he commanded as a captain, or even a sergeant, commanded. Disobedience was punished on the spot, with a gloved fist. He was still able to knock a man unconscious with his fist, or break his jaw, and his men knew it.

In his mind, it made for more efficient discipline than what was provided by the King's Regulations, parading the troops to watch one of their number tied to a tree or a wagon wheel and lashed by the sergeant major.

When he went inside the house, the bodies were gone and his servants were just about finished washing the blood from the room where he would spend the night. He saw that his bedding had been laid out on the stone floor.

There was only a table in the room. What other furniture there had been was broken up for use as material to bar windows and doors by the men who had chosen to defend this place. He thought the only reason the table was intact was that it was too heavy to break up easily. It would take sawing, and they probably hadn't had a saw.

He took off his helmet and set it on the table.

"Get me a chair," he said to one of his servants. "If there's none left, then bring me an oak box."

"Right away, milord," the taller, the senior, of his servants said, and hurried from the room.

John Maitland rubbed the angry red marks on his forehead where the leather strapping inside the helmet had ground sweaty dirt into his skin. He had six leather-bound oak boxes four feet long, two feet high, and a foot and a half deep. Three of the six packhorses in his train carried the boxes, two to a horse. The remaining packhorses carried his tent, which he would not need this night, and his clothing, and his tableware. The pack train was a half a mile away.

He walked up to the other servant, a young man, more a boy. About as old as the redheaded girl, he thought, and turned his back to him. The servant undid the latches and thongs of the breastplate, and when the duke had shrugged out of it, took it from him and set it on the table.

"Is there wine?" the duke asked. "Here, I mean?"

"Yes, milord," the young servant said, and went to his bedding and returned with a small, squat, clay wine jug.

"And soap?" he asked.

"Yes, milord."

"I should have told him to bring the pack animals," he said.

"I'm sure he will, milord."

The duke looked carefully at the stone floor, and when he could not make up his mind, dropped to his knees and lowered his head. The stonemason had indeed known his craft. The floor sloped toward the door, but so slightly that you really had to look close to see it. He was pleased. He would be able to take his wash in here. He did not think it seemly to be seen naked before his men.

He sat on the table and pulled the cork from the wine jug and drank thirstily from it. He raised his right leg straight out, a signal for the servant to pull his boot off, then unwrap the binding from around his feet. The binding had twisted and left angry red marks on his foot. He held his left leg straight out and the servant removed the left boot and the foot bindings.

He stood on the cool, smooth stones on the floor. They felt good against his hot feet.

There was a knock at the door.

"Come!" he ordered.

It was the soldiers with the girl. Her wrists and ankles were now circled with iron rings two inches wide and fastened with locks, and connected with a chain. A length

11

of chain connected the ankle and wrist chains and another chain was fastened to the right ankle restraint. The chains, he thought, had been intended for men, not girls. One of the soldiers held on to the chain and two others each held one of the redheaded girl's arms.

He looked around the room. There were two narrow windows cut in the stone wall. He gestured at them. The soldier holding the loose end of chain threaded it through the windows and then fastened it to itself with another lock.

"That'll do it," he said. The soldier handed him a key on a large brass ring for the locks. Then he bowed and backed out of the room.

He looked at the girl. He could see her breasts again, with their small, pointed light-pink nipples. The way she was chained, she could not raise her hands and wrists high enough to pull her torn dress closed.

He turned his back on her and stepped out his pants, then pulled the sweat-stiff tunic over his head. The servant climbed onto the table, and when he nodded, slowly poured water on him. When he was wet, he dipped his fingers into a clay bowl of lye soap and rubbed it over his body until it made bubbles. He rubbed a lot of the lye soap on his forehead, where the leather of the helmet strap had rubbed his skin, and a lot on his feet, where the bindings had twisted, and a lot under his arms, where he had a tendency to develop a painful rash from chafing.

When he was satisfied, he motioned for his servant to pour water on him again. It took eight bucketfuls before he was free of the soap. He dried himself and put on scent, which stung his skin. There was the smell of blood on him, sick-sweet, and he wanted the scent to overcome that.

He dressed, with the servant helping him, in a clean tunic and breeches, and then sat on the table and allowed the servant to bind his feet. The other servant returned, leading four soldiers carrying two caskets.

"I could not find chairs, milord," the servant said apologetically.

The duke nodded and motioned impatiently to show him where to arrange the caskets at the table.

"You," he said to one servant, "get me a list our dead, and their homes. And you," he said to the other one, "see if we are ready for the funeral service. Get the dominie."

They bobbed their heads in unison, said, "Yes, milord," and left the room.

"Who are you?" the girl asked as soon as they were gone.

He was surprised that she would have spoken to him. He looked at her. He saw again her small pink nipples and, for the first time, the tuft of red hair at her groin. Another minute, mistress, he thought, and that trooper would have been in you. And after him, the others. He wondered why he had stopped them. The women of the vanquished belong to the victors.

"John Maitland, mistress," he said dryly. "Duke of Lauderdale."

"The betrayer of the Duke of Argyll," she said. "His murderer."

"The former Duke of Argyll betrayed his king, mistress," he said. "He was *executed* for his treason."

"You'll burn in hell for your treason," she said.

"Whom, mistress," he asked, half-angry, half-amused, "do I have the honor of addressing?"

"Mary MacPhee," she said, proudly, defiantly.

His eyebrows went up. One of the most dangerous rebels was Brian MacPhee, Master at Arms to Lord Davies of Icomkill.

"Your father is Brian MacPhee?" he asked.

"Until you murdered him here today," she said.

"You and I, mistress," he said, "can both find solace in your father's dying as a soldier."

"You are his murderer," she insisted.

"I am Lord High Commissioner for Scotland," he said patiently. "Your father died as a rebel against Charles, his king."

If Brian MacPhee had fallen here today, he thought, it explained why they had fought so long and so well. And it meant that one of the rebels' better leaders would fight no more.

13

"If you would identify your father, mistress, I will see that his grave is marked."

That would, he thought, accomplish two things. She would not identify someone else as her father, so he could be sure that Brian MacPhee was indeed dead. And he could bury him with the honor to which his valor at arms entitled him.

She thought it over for a moment, a long moment, before replying.

"Yes," she said simply.

He walked to her and looked at her chains. If he removed the manacles, he thought, and held on to the chain that now held her to the windows, that would be enough. She could not run away. If she tried, he could upset her by pulling on the chain.

"I am not surprised that you stare shamelessly at my nakedness," Mary MacPhee said coldly.

He had not been doing that, and the accusation angered him for a moment. Then he thought that he probably had indeed been "staring shamelessly." He was certainly aware of her body.

He unlocked the chain and removed the manacles from her wrists. Then he led her from the room and the house with the chain fastened to the manacles at her ankles. Like a wolfhound, he thought, on a lead.

She stood by the edge of the mass grave he had ordered for the rebels, and pointed out a red-bearded body with a sure hand. Then she returned the hand to keep her torn dress closed over her body.

"Take that one," he said to the troop commander, Captain William Law. "And bury it separately, and mark it 'Brian MacPhee, Master at Arms to Lord Davies of Icomkill, rebel, killed here this day by forces of his Majesty's Lord High Commissioner for Scotland.' "

Captain Law, a tall, rather handsome young officer, nodded his acceptance of the order.

"That explains a lot, doesn't it, milord?" Law said.

Law, the duke thought, was a good man. He was an Edinburgher, and a wealthy one. His family had owned the brewery for centuries. It had not been necessary for him to purchase a commission. Most men of wealth, with

young wives—in Law's case, a pregnant young wife—
would have been happy to let other men serve their king
by suppressing the rebels. But Law had purchased a
commission as a lieutenant three years before, and had
earned rather than purchased his captaincy. It was a
pity, the duke thought idly, that his father had died. He
had asked for permission to resign his commission so
that he could take over the brewery. He would have
made a good professional soldier.

"Yes," the duke said, "it explains a good deal." He
smiled at Law and then led the girl back into the building.
There was food laid out on the table now.

"Sit and eat," he ordered.

"As I wait to bury my father?" she asked defiantly.

"Your father is dead," he said. "You are alive. Eat or
not, and be damned."

Mary MacPhee thought that over and then sat down
and picked up a quartered roasted chicken and ate it
with unconcealed hunger.

"What are you going to do with me?" she asked when
she sensed the duke's eyes on her.

"I haven't decided," he said. "Legally, I can hang you."

"Legally!" she snorted.

"I could turn you back over to the soldiers," he said.

"Or you could pleasure yourself with me yourself," she
said.

"Yes," he said. "That, too."

"Do what you will," she said. "I don't give a damn."

The dominie appeared, in a clean white vestment with
a cross embroidered in gold on it. Beneath the vestment,
the duke saw that his tunic was dirty and torn.

"We are ready, your Grace," he said.

"All right," he said.

"God will bless you, your grace, for saving the girl
from the men," the dominie said.

"He saved me from the men for himself," Mary MacPhee
said. The dominie's eyebrows went up, but he didn't say
anything. The duke glowered at Mary MacPhee.

What in God's name is wrong with her? Doesn't she
know what a mess she's in? Or does she want me to rape
her?

15

"We will ask the Good Lord to receive our men into heaven first," the duke said solemnly to the dominie. "And then the rebels."

"Whatever your Grace wishes," the dominie said.

"*I'll* not ask God's mercy on your murderers," she said.

The duke looked at her, amused and touched.

"You must look on my men as I have chosen to look on your father," he said finally. "As good men in error."

She offered no further resistance and stood stoically at the end of the chain by his side as the dominie said the service over both grave sites. It was dark by the time they had finished with the rebels, and when he led her back to his room, a fire had been lit and there were candles on the table as well as wine jugs and his daily ledger.

He removed one ankle manacle so that she would no longer have to hobble. One manacled ankle chained to the table would be enough.

"I have to relieve myself," she said.

He handed the chain to his servant.

"Take her outside and bring her back," he said.

When she was gone, he sat on a casket and made the entry in his daily ledger. He entered the names of all his fallen men, the location of their grave site, and an account of the battle, including the notation that Brian MacPhee had been leading the rebels. And then he wrote a personal note to the king, telling him that Brian MacPhee, one of the most dangerous rebels, had fallen to forces commanded by Captain William Law.

There was a chance, a small chance, that King Charles would be in a good mood when the note arrived (normally communications from Lauderdale reminded him only of the cost of suppressing the rebellion) and would be disposed to show his pleasure. The duke thought it would be a nice thing if Captain Law could return to civilian life as Sir William Law. Knighthood would cost the king nothing, and Law deserved it. But what was likely to happen is that if the king did anything at all, it would be to give Law a grant of land, from land forfeit to the crown as property of proven rebels. Law, the duke decided, didn't need any land, so that's what he would get. Three hundred acres of barren Highland, to pay taxes on.

While the duke was working, his servant returned the girl to the room. Somewhat impatiently, the duke raised his eyes from his ledger and gestured for the girl to be chained to the leg of the table.

He became aware that the servant was waiting to be dismissed for the night.

"You can go now," he said.

"Thank you, milord," the servant said. "Rest well, your Grace." The duke watched him leave the room, then returned to the letter he had written to the king. He folded it, dipped wax from the candle on it, and sealed it with his ring.

When he was finished and had put the ledger and the letter away, he looked for Mary MacPhee. She was sitting with her back against the wall, asleep. Her dress was hanging open, exposing her breasts. He went to his bedding and took a skin and walked over to her. He looked at her again, this time shamelessly. She had, he thought, the perfect breasts of youth.

He felt a stirring at his groin.

"Is it to be now?" she asked. She had woken up.

He threw the skin at her face and stormed back to his bedding. He sat on the bedding and pulled off his boots and unwound the wrapping around his feet. Then he pulled off his tunic and breeches, and lay down, pulling two sheepskin robes over him.

He tried to sleep, but his mind's eye was full of her pink-nippled breasts and the tuft of red hair at her middle, and the smooth, firm white belly above it.

The servant had left a candle burning on the table. It would be enough light, he thought, to look at her again. To make up his mind what he wanted to do.

When he rolled over, she was awake and looking at him.

He threw the sheepskins off him and stood up.

He went and stood over her. He had an erection. Her eyes kept dropping to it and then rising to glare at him.

He went to his bedding and got the key and unlocked

17

her manacles. He grabbed her wrist and led her to his bedding.

"Are you going to fight me?" he asked.

"What good would that do?" she asked.

"Take that off," he ordered. His voice was husky.

She shrugged out of the dress.

The perfection of youth, he thought. Much too fine to be wasted on the soldiers.

He put his hands on her shoulders and forced her back down onto the sheepskins.

She screamed once and whimpered a lot, but after he got going, she forgot she hated him and let herself go, and it was everything he had fantasized it would be and more.

2

In the morning, there was blood on the sheepskins.

"Is it your time?" he asked, somewhat repelled.

"It is the mark of a virgin," Mary MacPhee said.

"You could have told me that," he said. You old bastard, he thought.

"Would it have mattered?" she asked.

"No," he said after a moment. "It would not have mattered."

"Now do you hang me? Or turn me over to your soldiers?"

"No, Mary," the duke said, his voice tired and surprisingly emotional, "never that."

3

Mary MacPhee rode with John Maitland, Duke of Lauderdale, His Most Britannic Majesty's Lord High Commissioner for Scotland, for five weeks. When he was busy, he manacled her ankles and left her in the company of one of his servants. Otherwise, unmanacled, covered in one of his tunics, she was at his side on the march, or at table, or, alone, naked with him.

The duke knew what was wrong with him. He was an old man. Old men liked young girls. It had something to do with nature. She made him feel young again. He

18

worshiped her body, reveled in the smell of her, the softness, her surprising passion, took a wild pleasure in stopping in the middle of it, so that she would suck in her breath and hold it while her hand searched desperately for his organ, to grab it, to put it where she wanted it.

He allowed himself fantasy. He was like Attila the Hun, or El Cid in Spain, or the leader of a Roman legion; not a civilized Englishman, close personal friend to his king. He had won the enemy's virgin in battle, and taken her and tamed her for his pleasure.

An old man, he told himself, should be allowed a fantasy.

But eventually, the time came for him to return to Edinburgh, where he would not be Attila the Hun, but John Maitland, Duke of Lauderdale, who was Lord High Commissioner; and nearly as importantly, where there were the Duchess of Lauderdale and Lady Alice Maitland, their daughter, nearly twice as old as Mary MacPhee.

Captain William Law, he decided, would have one more duty before being allowed to take off his uniform. Technically, his application for permission to resign his commission would have to be acted upon by the Minister for War, acting on the advice of the Lord High Commissioner for Scotland. What would really happen was that the duke would send the Minister for War a letter saying he had granted Law permission to resign "in the best interests of his Majesty's government for Scotland," and that would be the end of it.

But before Law went home, he would do the duke one more service, above and beyond the call of duty.

The duke dispatched Captain Law and a guard of six to take the girl to the Highlands. He gave Law a letter for the Lord High Sheriff in possession of Lord Davies of Icomkill's confiscated estates instructing him that Mary MacPhee was to receive her father's confiscated property and telling him that he would be personally grateful if a marriage to a good man could be arranged for her.

"He's a thieving bastard, William," John Maitland said. "So you had better tell the Lord High Sheriff I am doing this because I admired her father as a soldier. And that I want a detailed report of what he has done."

19

"Forgive my asking, Milord," Captain Law replied carefully, "but will you be wanting to see her from time to time?"

John Maitland resisted the temptation.

"I want this young woman married well, Law," he said. "To a responsible tradesman, or a craftsman. Who will respect her for the devout Christian woman she is. Do I make my point?"

"Yes, milord," Captain Law replied.

John Maitland gave Mary MacPhee a purse of gold.

"It makes me feel the whore," Mary said, hefting it in her hand.

"You were taken against your will," John Maitland said.

She raised her eyes and looked at him. "At first," she said.

There was an exquisite feeling of loss the next morning as she looked down from the horse at him, saying nothing, and then as she rode away; and he knew that he would never again touch her body, or taste it.

4

Edward Gardiner, of Anstruther in Fife, on the northern shore of the Firth of Forth, came into the presence of the Lord High Sheriff more curious than frightened by the summons. He was a short, fair-haired, barrel-chested man of twenty-three. He had a square, freckled face with blue eyes that were usually amused but sometimes could turn to ice. He was on the Lord High Sheriff's rolls as "Horse Breeder & Farmer."

"I had hoped to see you before this, Gardiner," the Lord High Sheriff said.

"Your Excellency will understand that I had three mares foaling," Edward Gardiner said. It was a statement of fact, not an apology.

"Gardiner, this is Captain Law," the Lord High Sheriff said.

Gardiner bobbed his head in respect. He knew who Law was, both as an officer close to the Lord High Commissioner and as Law the Brewer.

"The foaling went well, I hope?" Captain Law asked.

"Aye, your Excellency, it did."

"You have a reputation as someone who knows horses," the Lord High Sheriff said.

Edward Gardiner met the Lord High Sheriff's eyes.

"Aye," he said.

"And as someone loyal to his king," Captain Law said.

"Aye," Gardiner said.

"Tell me, Gardiner," the Lord High Sheriff said. "In your heart are you Presbyterian or Episcopal?"

"I take neither side," Gardiner said.

"I asked, 'in your heart'?"

"And if my answer does not please your Excellency?"

"It is between us, as men."

"I wonder what Christ himself thinks about the killing that's done on both sides in His name," Gardiner said.

"How is it you've not married?" the Lord High Sheriff asked.

"I have trouble feeding this mouth," Gardiner said.

"I have need of a reliable source of mounts," the Lord High Sheriff said. "For my own service and for that of the Lord High Commissioner."

"I am not large enough, your Excellency, for the favor of that size a trade."

"All the man will have to do is buy horses, and see that they are rough-broke, and deliver them here," Captain Law said.

"To buy, a man needs money," Edward Gardiner said. "And then to gather the animals and feed them and rough-break them, he would need more money."

"Money can sometimes be arranged," the Lord High Sheriff asked. "I am a little surprised that you aren't a hell of a lot more interested."

"I will not go to the moneylenders," Edward Gardiner said. "Better a dozen animals that are mine than two hundred in my name, but liened to some moneylender."

Captain Law chuckled understandingly. He liked this fellow's simple honesty.

"Perhaps you could find a woman with a dowry that would keep you from going to the moneylenders," the Lord High Sheriff said.

Gardiner laughed. He had finally come to understand what the Lord High Sheriff was up to. He, or maybe Captain Law, had a female relative to marry off, probably a widow. There were a lot of widows around who had lost their men in the fight over who, Presbyterian or Anglican, would tend to the immortal souls of Scotland.

She would have some money. Gardiner decided that the woman would be the widow of one of Law's men. Law had pots of money. He was going to pay the dowry. As a matter of conscience. The idea was, Gardiner thought, that he would use the dowry money to buy and rough-break horses. The Lord High Sheriff would see to it that they were bought for the service of the government. A good price would be paid, more than the animals were worth, less than would cause questions by the Lord High Commissioner's office here or the Keeper of the Purse in London. The profits would be secretly split between them.

He is interested more in me as a single horse trader, Edward Gardiner thought, than a horse trader who happens to be single.

"What did I say that makes you laugh?"

"How old is the widow you have in mind, your Excellency?" Edward Gardiner asked.

The Lord High Sheriff was pleased at how well Gardiner's mind worked. "She is not a widow," he said. "She is the daughter of Brian MacPhee."

"I don't know him," Gardiner said.

"He was a rebel," Captain William Law said. "Killed last month."

"He was in the service of Lord Davies of Incomkill? That MacPhee?"

"He was master at arms to Davies of Incomkill," Captain Law said. "And to answer your question, she's sixteen."

"And she has a dowry, and your friendship, though her father died a rebel? What's wrong with her?" Edward asked.

The Lord High Sheriff didn't answer. He knew the answer would occur to Gardiner.

"Whose bastard is she carrying?" Gardiner asked coldly.

22

He thought he knew. Why else would Captain William Law be involved.

"I understand she was held prisoner for a month, as the Lord High Commissioner finished his campaign," the Lord High Sheriff said levelly.

"No, thank you, your Excellency," Edward Gardiner said.

"I must have been misinformed about you," the Lord High Sheriff said.

"Probably," Gardiner said.

"I was told that you were a shrewd trader," the Lord High Sheriff said. "A shrewd trader would not turn down a deal until he had carefully looked it over."

"I have no intention of taking to wife a girl who's been a soldier's slut for a month," Gardiner said angrily. "Not if you set me up as remounter by appointment to the Royal Army."

"She is not what you seem to think," Captain Law said.

Gardiner looked at him, afraid to speak his mind.

"The child she carries is not mine," Law said, reading his mind. "And she was never a soldier's whore."

"An officer's whore, then?"

"She was held by an officer, yes," Law said.

"Why don't you see for yourself what damage has been done?" the Lord High Sheriff asked. "She's really a bonnie lass."

"Thank you, no," Gardiner said.

"I would consider it a courtesy," the Lord High Sheriff insisted coldly.

Gardiner waited a full thirty seconds before he nodded his head in agreement. He was in no position to refuse the Lord High Sheriff. Perhaps he could think of some way to get out of this. That was unlikely but possible. What was sure was that he was in no position to say nay to the Lord High Sheriff and Captain Law.

5

Mary MacPhee Gardiner stood by the table in the kitchen of her husband's cottage. She looked around the room, reminding herself that it was now to be her kitchen.

It was sparsely and roughly furnished, but it was cleaner than she had expected it to be.

She looked down at her hands and for a moment covered her face with them. Then she shook her head and took her hands away. She lowered her left hand to her groin and touched the leather bag of gold coin hanging there from a thong around her waist.

She was going to have to find someplace to hide that before he wanted his way with her. It was her escape from this, if it didn't work out. If he beat her, or worse (her father and brothers had beaten her, and she had learned that you lived through a beating), treated her as a whore, she was going to run.

Mary had thought that option over carefully. If she ran, she would run first to Edinburgh, where she would somehow arrange to see John Maitland. He was a good man, and if he knew that she was carrying his child, he would help her. Or he would have her hanged. One of the two. Being hanged was preferable to a life married to a man who thought he had bought a whore.

She heard the door open behind her, but did not turn around. She heard him slide the latch home.

"So," he said. She did not reply. "There is some bread," he continued. "But it is doubtless stale. And if it hasn't spoiled, there is a joint of mutton. And there is cheese. And water. Cheese and water don't spoil."

"Nor does tea," she said. "Would you like tea?"

"There is no fire," he said.

"I will lay a fire," she said.

"There's wood," he said. He was standing behind her, so close she thought she could sense the warmth of his body. "Enough to start a fire. I will get more."

"There's no coals," she said.

"I have a blacksmith," Edward said. "He was here yesterday. Perhaps there are coals from his fire. Otherwise, I'll have to go to the Douglass's. Over the hill."

"Would you rather have cheese and water first?" Mary asked.

"Let me check his fire," he said.

She sensed him going away from her, and then she heard the sound of the latch and the creak of the door opening. When she was sure he had gone, she raised her skirt, untied the leather bag with the gold, and hid it in a pewter mug on the mantel over the fire. Then she dropped to her knees and arranged the wood in the fire.

"Out of the way!" he called, so cheerfully that she turned in surprise to look at him.

Smiling, he came across the kitchen with a shovelful of glowing coals.

"Terry," he said, "he's the blacksmith, must have stoked his fire just before he left, so's we'd have fire when we got here. He's a good old bastard."

He dumped the coals into the fireplace and she took a small hearth shovel and arranged them so the wood would catch. She took a long time to make the fire, but finally there was nothing left to do, so she stood up and then moved the kettle on its wrought-iron hooked arm over the fire.

"I didn't mean to use the word 'bastard,' " he said.

She turned and faced him.

"It is a perfectly proper word," she said.

"I was thinking," he said. "There ought to be another word. I mean, there's a difference between what happened to you and what happens to some slut who lifts her skirts to every man."

She did not reply.

"Was it very bad for you?"

I can seek his sympathy and tell him that it was.

"I would rather not talk about it," she said.

"The bastards!" he said, and then he smiled. "You see what I mean? The way I used the word then?"

He is a good man.

"Can you read, by any chance?" he asked. It was a surprising question.

"Yes, I can. And write."

"Oh," he said, obviously disappointed. Then he said, "If you couldn't, I was thinking that I could teach you."

"I can read and write and do sums. "But I am not a very good cook."

"I wouldn't know the difference," he said.

"What is going to happen when the bastard comes?" Mary asked.

"I was thinking about that, too," he said. "I mean, there is no reason anyone has to know. Sometimes women don't go the whole nine months."

"It won't be yours," she said.

"Is the child Captain Law's?" Edward Gardiner blurted.

"No," she said.

"But you won't tell me whose?"

"It isn't important," she said.

"If Law knows, others will know."

"Law will not say anything," she said. "He gave me his word."

"And you trust him?"

"Yes," she said.

"But you won't tell me?"

"No," she said, softly but firmly. "I will not."

"All right," he said after a pause.

"I asked about you," Mary said. "When it comes."

"It won't know it's a bastard," Edward Gardiner said. "Do you feel you would have to tell it?"

"You'll know the difference," Mary said.

"You want this to stand between us?"

"What other way can it be?"

"I was thinking, as we rode from the church," he said, "that it's not like we were already married and you were carrying another man's child. It's more like you were widowed. You follow my thinking?"

"No," she said.

"I mean, if you were a widow and I married you, the decent thing to do would be to treat the child as if it were mine."

"Could you do that?" she asked.

"I have something to say to you," he said. "It is hard."

"We had better say these things now."

"Yes," he said. "I had decided, before the High Sheriff brought me to see you, that I was going through with this."

"I see," she said.

"There was the money," he said. "I need the money. I can make my trade two, three times as big as it is now if I have money to buy animals."

"I understand," she said.

"And. And I must tell you this. I thought it would be better to have a steady woman than to do what I do. What I did. I don't mean to do for me, I do for myself very well. I mean in the bed."

"I understand," Mary repeated.

"And I thought there was probably something wrong with me, for I was not like the other lads I grew up with. I never could tell much of a difference between one woman and another. So I figured that it wouldn't make much difference about you, either. I have to tell you this, I mean no insult."

"I understand," Mary said.

"I wish you would not keep saying that!" he said.

She nodded her head, in acceptance of the order.

Edward Gardiner was red in the face, and Mary wondered why her saying "I understand" over and over had made him so angry.

But he was not angry.

"And then I saw you," he blurted. "Standing against the wall, looking at me out of those eyes of yours, and I knew that nothing was wrong with me, that the reason I hadn't gone daft over a girl before was because I had never seen a girl like you before."

There was a defiant look in his eyes for a moment, and then he flushed even more and looked away.

"The tea is here in the cupboard," he said. "And the cups. And the water is near hot enough."

Mary went to the cupboard and took out the tea and the pot and two cups and set them on the table.

"I like a little honey with my tea," Edward said. "There's a mug of it where you found the cups."

She set the gray clay pot of honey on the table.

"So what I was thinking," he said, grabbing her arm so hard it hurt her, "was that the way it was, was that because of what happened to you, I was getting a girl I could never otherwise get, and that there was a chance for us to put everything that happened to you behind us. I can pretend, I can make myself believe, that I put that child in your belly."

Mary looked into his eyes and then put her hand to his

hand, where he was painfully holding her arm, and pried his fingers loose. He dropped his head.

"I'm a bloody goddamned fool, as I know full well," he said.

Mary went to the fireplace, took the pewter mug down, and turned it over and spilled the leather bag with the gold into her hand. Then she went to the table and set it before him.

"What's this?" he asked.

"Gold," she said. "I was holding it back from you."

"Why would you do that?"

"In case," she said, laughed, and then finished, "you turned out to be a bastard."

He hefted the bag in his hand.

"There's some money in here," he said.

"Yes," she said.

"The father gave it to you?"

She didn't reply.

"It had to be an officer," he said. "If he could afford to give you this,"

If I tell him it was the Duke of Lauderdale, she thought, he's liable not to believe me. And it is better, anyway, for him not to know for sure.

She nodded, and that seemed to be enough of an answer to satisfy him.

"And why are you trying to give this money to me?"

"Because I want to show that I trust you," she said.

"You're burning your bridges behind you," he said.

"Yes."

He pushed the leather bag away from him. "I don't want your gold. I could not take it."

"It's all I have to give you," she said.

"What we'll do is put it away for the child," he said. "And when he's grown, we'll give it to him." He looked at her, then blurted, "And money's not all you can give me, if you've a mind."

Mary felt her face flush. "I'll see if the pot boils," she said.

She went to the fireplace and took a rag and picked the kettle from the hook. She sensed again that he was standing behind her. She stood rigid. After a long time, she felt the very gentle brush of his fingers on her upper arm. She let her breath out and, moving very slowly, leaned back, so that his chest was pressing into her back.

"You're so *uncommonly* beautiful!" Edward said, very softly, as if to himself.

6

On April 18, 1667, during a late snowstorm, after an eight-hour labor, Mary MacPhee Gardiner was delivered of a son. He was a large and healthy child, and that explained, her husband thought, how big her belly had been. An hour after the boy was born, Mary MacPhee Gardiner was delivered of another baby, a smaller infant, a girl.

It was strange and wondrous the way God and nature worked, people said when they saw the babies in their crib. The girl, who was christened Catherine, was red-headed and dainty like her mother. The boy, who was christened David, was (except for his blond hair, which would probably change color later) the spitting image of his father.

Chapter Two

1

Holyroodhouse Palace, Edinburgh
June 12, 1679

Edward Gardiner, purveyor of horses by appointment to King Charles II's Lord High Commissioner for Scotland, accompanied by four handlers and two members of his family, was delivering mounts today.

He had brought with him eighty-three rough-broke horses intended for the use of the crown: a very few very good animals intended for the Lord High Commissioner and for the Lord High Sheriff themselves, but most of them intended for the troop of Horse Guards who served the Lord High Commissioner both as a symbol of his close relationship to the king and as a highly mobile force to maintain the peace.

Gardiner had brought the animals overnight from his breeding farm, stopping for the night only when it was too dark to see and getting up from the ground at first light to continue. It was near midday when they came down from the Pentland Hills and approached Edinburgh Castle. They stopped near the castle to tie the bridles of the animals together, in train, four long trains of twenty horses each.

Riding in the dust at opposite ends of the column were two youngsters. The casual observer would have taken the smaller of them, bringing up the rear, to be a slight young boy. The young boy, riding bareback with an ease that comes only to those who have learned to ride before they could really walk well, was dressed in hand-me-down clothes and hat that more than likely were discards of the larger boy riding at the head of the column with the serious face of a boy aware he is discharging a man's responsibility.

David Gardiner, at twelve, was a large boy. His face and arms were browned by the sun. He had a full head of unruly, thick, sun-bleached hair. He was somewhat phlegmatic, people said, like his father. The two were seldom seen apart. David Gardiner had begun to trail in his father's footsteps from the time he could walk. From the time he was three, most of his tears and temper tantrums had come when he was denied permission to go somewhere his father was going.

He looked nothing at all like the smaller child riding the high-stepping Arabian mare at the rear of the column. The smaller child's skin was pale and freckled. The hair that peeked out of the oversized hat was bright red. The hands that held the mare's reins were thin and soft, as opposed to the muscular square hands of the already broad-shouldered boy.

There was a good reason for this: the smaller child was not the larger one's little brother, but instead his twin sister.

Catherine Gardiner was not supposed to be with her father and her brother and the rough-broke horses. She had been expressly ordered to remain behind. Not only did her mother need her to help around the house, she had been told, but she might as well start understanding right now that she was a girl, soon to be a young woman, a young *lady*; and young ladies did not go along with the men when they were delivering animals and would have to spend at least one night, and maybe more, sleeping on the ground.

Catherine—Kate—Gardiner had not argued with her parents when the speech had been delivered. She had not even responded to the smug look of masculine superiority on her brother David's face. Nor had she wept. She had simply walked out of the house and gone down to the near field, to carry the Arabian mare a carrot.

Kate had been put astride a shaggy-haired pony from the Shetland Islands at eighteen months, and by the time she was ten, she had a better seat bareback than most men had in a saddle. And she knew that she was good around animals, that she could move them where she wanted them, calm them when they were excited, even break them, just about as well as David could.

Moreover, she knew that her father knew this. *He* had no objection to her going along to deliver the animals to Edinburgh. He objected only because of that "you're soon to be a young woman" argument delivered by her mother. It wasn't really even that. He objected only because her mother objected. Kate had long before learned that her mother most often got what she wanted from her father. Not by arguing with him, but generally by doing what she wanted to do and then smiling at him when he found out about it.

If it worked for her mother, Kate had decided, it would work for her, too.

The worse that could happen was that she would be whipped. The question was whether going to Edinburgh was worth risking a whipping. In the end, she decided it would be.

Two hours after her father and her brother and the handlers had led the animals down the road, Kate wrote a message to her mother on the slateboard in the kitchen. She didn't want her mother to worry that she had been hurt. Her mother had two worries about her: that she would fall from her mare somewhere, and that she would be carried off by gypsies. Kate fell more often walking than she did from a horse, and the only gypsies she had ever seen looked like poor and frightened people, but telling her mother this had not changed her mother's mind.

Her mother, if she disappeared, would think the worst. It was better to let her know, Kate decided, and wrote: "Gone with Father & David."

That said everything that had to be said.

Kate and the Arabian mare made better time, of course, than her father and the others had made, but when she finally caught up with them, they were still nearly a four-hour ride from the farm.

That meant it was too far and too late in the day to send her back. Her father would not want her on the pike alone after dark. And he couldn't spare a man, even David, to go with her.

"I'd beat you here and now, girl," Edward Gardiner said. "But I'm so mad with you, I'm afraid I'd kill you. But don't think you're getting away with this. A beating when we're home is the least you can expect. You think about that from now until we get back. And don't think you'll be turned loose in the market, either."

She thought there was at least as much chance that she would escape a beating as that she would get one. And the one advantage she could see in being a girl was that when she was beaten, she never got it as bad as David. David didn't get beaten often, but when he did, his father generally gave him a good thrashing.

Both of them were hardheaded, Kate thought, and alike in other ways. David aped his father's movements when he walked and the way he nodded his head. People said that was because as he grew older, he came to look like his mother. He had, they said, acquired his mannerisms and character from his father and his looks from his mother. That was fortunate; it could have been the other way around, which would have made him an ugly man of high character and a sometimes flaming temper.

Just before they got to the city itself, Edward Gardiner got them all together and gave them a speech. The strange sights and sounds of the city might likely startle the animals, he said, and he had no intention of losing a valuable animal to a broken leg within sight and smell of the money he would get for them.

"I'll take the lead," he said. "I want David to ride up and down the file, and the others to ride in it. Kate, you ride in the tail. If they break, I think they'll run from the city. And you're good at calming them."

Kate hoped that one of them, a couple of them, would spook and try to run away. Then she could catch them, calm them down, and save them, and her father would have to consider that when it came time to punish her for coming along when she had been ordered to stay at home.

She was, in fact, a little disappointed that nothing whatever happened as the procession made its way down the Castle Hill ridge into Lawnmarket and then down High Street and the Canongate to the stableyard at Holyroodhouse Palace, where they would turn the animals over to the Lord High Sheriff's master of horses and the handlers under him.

She wondered if her father was still mad enough at her to carry out his threat that she would not be allowed to go to the market. Soon after they had taken the animals into the remount station, Kate knew that there would be an hour and a half free to explore the wonders of High Street and Lawnmarket. Their father, if things went the way they usually did, would be having lunch inside the palace. Or so both Kate and David hoped. Something could go wrong, but normally, when their father delivered rough-broke animals to the Lord High Sheriff's master of horses, he was invited to take lunch with the Lord High Sheriff himself.

It was a polite fiction between them. David and Kate were told by their father to stay with the handlers. Their mother didn't want them running free and alone in Lawnmarket, where David would see things he shouldn't and Kate was liable to be stolen by gypsies.

But as soon as Edward Gardiner disappeared into the palace, Kate and David would head for the market, to eat, which was not the same thing as "running loose." And if on their way to eat they happened to stop to watch jugglers or trained bears or even to throw the dice in a penny game of hazard, neither was that "running loose." They were always back in time to be there when their father returned from taking lunch with the Lord High Sheriff, and the only question their father ever asked them was, had they eaten. And they always had.

Bringing the half-broke animals to the Lord High Sheriff's stables had been something Kate had been doing since she was a little girl, something she had really looked forward to, and something she was unwilling to give up just because she was old enough to have started to grow in the chest and was about to "become a young woman."

She was relieved when she saw the Lord High Sheriff's master of horses come out of the palace to examine the animals. That meant, for sure, that her father would be asked to eat in the palace. Even if the Lord High Sheriff himself wasn't there, he would eat with the master of horses.

But there was a major change when the near-ritual invitation for Edward Gardiner to have lunch was extended. This time the invitation had included Kate and David.

"You're sure?" Gardiner, surprised, asked the master of horses. "About the kids, I mean?"

"I was there myself, Edward."

"And he said, 'bring the kids'?" Gardiner asked disbelievingly.

"If you have to know, Edward," the master of horses said more than a little smugly, "it was his Grace himself who said it."

"The duke is in there?" Edward Gardiner asked. The master of horses gestured to the flagpoles flying atop the ramparts at the main gate to Holyroodhouse Palace. The Union Jack, the cross of Scotland's Saint Andrew superimposed on that of England's St. George flew there on one pole, signifying the presence of the king's Lord High Commissioner for Scotland. Beside it flew the flag of John Maitland, Knight of the Garter and Duke of Lauderdale, Lord Thirlestane, Marquess of March, Baron Petersham, and Earl of Guilford. Lauderdale was still not only the most powerful man in Scotland, but the second or third or fourth most powerful man in England.

Without Lauderdale's approval, Edward Gardiner knew

well, the Lord High Sheriff would not have been able to arrange his appointment as purveyor of horses to the crown. He had met the old man a half-dozen times—in other words, had been allowed to make his bow and been privileged to have his Grace ritually inquire as to the health of his good wife and family.

But he had never before been commanded to table.

"Indeed, he's there," the master of horses said. "And his Grace hisself said it; you are to bring the kids. When the High Sheriff said you was here with the draft of animals, his Grace said he would like to see you, and then the High Sheriff said he wouldn't be surprised if you had your kids here with you, and then his Grace hisself said, 'If Gardiner has the children with him, Foster, be good enough to tell him I would be pleased to receive the lot of them.' That's exactly what he said, Edward."

"All I want you to say in there," Edward said to his son and daughter as they waited in the great hall of Holyroodhouse Palace to be received by John Maitland, "is one of three things: 'Yes, your Grace'; 'No, your Grace'; and 'Thank you, your Grace.' You understand that?"

Both the Lord High Sheriff and the Duke of Lauderdale were old men, and David and Kate were rather disappointed with the both of them. And were made a little uneasy by the way the duke stared at them.

"How old are they now, Gardiner?" the duke asked.

"They was twelve in April, your Grace," Edward Gardiner replied.

"The girl's a little small, isn't she? Anything wrong with her?"

"I think, your Grace, that she takes after her mother. Her mother is a small and dainty woman, your Grace."

"Yes," Lauderdale said. "The lad looks healthy enough."

"Yes, your Grace," Edward said. "Large and healthy."

"And bright?"

"Yes, your Grace, the wife has taught the both of them to read and write."

"Ah, yes, your good wife. I presume all is well with her?"

"Yes, your Grace."

"Please be good enough to convey to her my best wishes," the duke said.

"She will be highly honored, your Grace."

"You have other children, do you not?"

"No, your Grace. Just these two."

"These two look like enough," the duke said.

"Yes, your Grace," Edward said. "Sometimes more than enough."

The duke frowned.

"You are a fortunate man, as I am sure you appreciate, Gardiner. With a good wife and two fine children like these."

"I am grateful to God, your Grace, for His many blessings," Edward said. "And for your Grace's many kindnesses."

"You have received at my hand only what you have earned," the Duke of Lauderdale said, and then motioned to Kate and David to come to him.

David seemed rooted to the ground. Kate grabbed his hand and led him to the duke. She made what she hoped would be a curtsy, and that made David remember to bow his head.

The duke reached into his purse and handed each of them a shining coin. It was so shiny, David thought, that it must be brand-new. But there was a date stamped on it, 1644.

"Is this new or old, your Grace?" David asked, looking at the old man.

"Both," the duke replied. "It was made a long time ago, but it has never been in use."

"Oh," David said, accepting the explanation. He turned the coin over. The back was stamped with a picture of a city, and below it, the word "OXON."

"A man named Thomas Rawlins engraved the die," the duke said.

"The what?" David asked, forgetting to append "your Grace."

"The die, the thing that impressed the picture and the lettering."

"I thought a die was what you used to play hazard," Kate said.

"Hazard? You know what hazard is?" the duke asked.

"I know," Kate said, suddenly aware she had inadvertently confessed a sin.

"And you play hazard, do you?" the duke asked. "And sometimes throw crabs?"

"Sometimes, your Grace," Kate confessed in a faint voice.

"And does your father beat you when he catches you?"

"He's never caught me, your Grace," Kate said. "He's caught my brother but he's never caught me."

The duke laughed out loud, so hard that the laughter turned into racking coughing.

"Would you like to have that gold coin?" the duke asked finally.

"What would I have to do?" David asked suspiciously.

The duke laughed aloud again, and again was racked with a coughing spell.

"Would you, my Lord High Sheriff," he asked, "say that the boy takes after his father?"

"Indeed, I would, milord," the High Sheriff replied.

"If I give you the double crown," the duke said, turning to Kate, "I don't want you risking it at hazard."

"No, your Grace," Kate said.

"What that is, lass," the duke said, "is an uncirculated coin. It was first minted in 1644, the first engraved coin. It's a perfectly good coin, and you could spend it, if you wanted. But it will grow more valuable with age. You understand?"

"I think so."

"When you get home, give it to your good mother and ask her to keep it for you until you are older."

"Yes, sir," they said in unison.

"And be good enough to extend to your mother my regards," the duke said.

When they got home, and their father told their mother what had happened, it was enough to make her mother forget her vow to beat that little bitch within an inch of her life.

"And you won't believe what the duke gave them," Edward said. "Take a look at this, will you?"

He gave Mary the two golden coins.

She examined them carefully.

"I hope you remembered your manners," she said.

"She looked like something dragged through an alley," Edward said, "but she behaved."

Her father had not, Kate noticed, mentioned her confession about playing hazard.

"These coins are yours," Mary said to her children. "I'll put them in your father's strongbox for now, but you can have them when you're older. And for the time being, if you want to look at them, you can ask me and I'll get them out for you."

Edward Gardiner told his wife that the Lord High Commissioner had sent her his regards.

"What did you think, David," Mary asked, "of the Duke of Lauderdale?"

David told her that he seemed a very old man and that he coughed badly.

"He's really not the entire bastard some people would have you believe," Mary said. "I'm sorry he's old and sick."

"I liked him," Kate volunteered.

"Because he gave you the coin?"

"No, I just liked him. He wasn't what I expected."

"What I think would be very nice," Mary said, "would be if you were to put this coin away, and keep it, and give it to your son, David, and your daughter, Kate, and tell them that you got it from the hand of John Maitland, and explain who he was. And then your children could pass it on to their children, and on and on."

"That's a nice idea," Kate had said, not meaning a word of it. "It's too nice to spend."

She had already figured out that when her mother had decided on something, as she had about what was going to happen to this coin, there was no point in either arguing or pleading. Since she wasn't going to get to spend it, she might as well be agreeable and say that keeping it for her daughter was a nice idea. After all, she had not gotten the beating she expected.

2

It turned out that that three-day trip to Edinburgh was the last one Kate Gardiner was to make. For a long time there had been talk about "getting a little place in Edinburgh." There were a number of arguments in favor of it, some personal and some, most important, concerning the business.

Edward Gardiner had a good business the way it was, breeding and buying animals for sale to the government and to a few private people. And he wasn't, he said, a greedy man, determined to kill himself in the hungry pursuit of the last halfpenny. But on the other hand, it seemed beyond argument that if he had a place of business in Edinburgh, he could do more business. People in Edinburgh in need of animals were not about to take a day and a half's ride into the country to see if Edward Gardiner had something to sell. Not when there were a dozen horse traders in Edinburgh, and not even because he had earned the reputation of having fine horses at reasonable prices.

If he had a place in Edinburgh, someplace where he could stable a dozen or so animals, the business, he knew, would come to him. That meant buying, or taking a long-term lease on, a building for a stable, and finding someplace for him to live while he was in the city.

It was not an impulsive move. It had been talked about so much that Kate had lost interest. The idea of living in Edinburgh, where there was always something going on, instead of at the farm, where the only thing that happened was church on Sunday and infrequent visits to or by other people very much like themselves, seemed like a dream. And since dreams didn't come true, she lost interest when she overheard her parents talking about it.

And then, all of a sudden, it happened. Kate and David were left behind to "watch over things" while their parents went to Edinburgh. Mary went two or three times a year to Edinburgh with her husband, to shop for cloth

41

and other things needed for the house, and just, she readily admitted, to see some life.

When she came back that time, she was more excited than usual. Her face was flushed with excitement.

"Your dad has bought a place off the Lothian Road," she announced as she came through the door. "And we're all going to live there!"

David was not excited about the move. Edinburgh was a fine place to go to every month or so, but after a day or two he had enough of the crowds, the smell, and even of the fascinating sights at the marketplace. He would have preferred to stay on the farm and do what a farmer and a horse breeder did.

"You're going to go to school," Mary said to him, and when she saw the look on Kate's face, added, "the both of you. I've taught you all I can."

"I can already read and write and do sums," David protested. "I don't need school."

"I'll tell you what you need and don't need," his mother snapped. "Just who do you think you are?"

The house on the farm off Lothian Road was larger and grander than Kate would have dreamed.

"Your father was afraid it was too grand," Mary told her daughter, "but I told him that he was going to have do more than say he had the best animals in Edinburgh; he was going to have to look as if he did. And I told him that it was long past time for you and David to have your own rooms."

There were four rooms upstairs in the house, three bedrooms and a small room her mother appropriated for a sewing room, because there was good light in the windows. Downstairs was larger. There was a sitting room, a dining room separate from the kitchen, a pantry and a washroom, and small room off the entrance foyer that Edward Gardiner took for use as the place where he would offer customers a cup of tea or something stronger.

They had brought a wagon load of furniture with them from the farmhouse, but it was immediately evident, even to David, that, except for their parents' bed and chest of drawers, it wasn't right for the new house.

The first thing they had to do, her mother said, was

find nice things for the sitting room and Edward Gardiner's office. That was business. Furniture for the other rooms would have to wait. For now, Kate was to sleep on the floor of her room. The only furniture in it was the washstand and mirror from the room she had shared with David at the farm.

Just about every afternoon, Kate hitched an animal to the wagon, and she and her mother drove Princes Street to the old-furniture sellers', looking for "decent" things for the sitting room and her father's office, provided they could be found at what her mother considered to be a "right" price.

One piece at a time—a chair here and a lamp there—they furnished the house. It was getting time, and Kate knew it, when it would be her turn to get a bed and a chest of drawers and maybe even a carpet for her room.

But then her father had an idea that took all their available cash. He had long ago learned that if he took the most handsome animal he had, put a fine saddle and a thick wool saddle blanket on it, and saw to it that the animal was freshly curried and had his hooves freshly blacked, and then rode it around town and tied it up before a good restaurant while he went inside for a mug of ale, enough times to make it worth his while, some man would see the animal and make him an offer for it.

He was also able, Kate noticed, to get a better price for the animal by pretending reluctance to sell his "personal" horse. A horse, the buyers reasoned, that was good enough for one of the better horse dealers to claim as his own had to be something better and worth a good price.

It followed, his father said, that if that worked for a riding horse, it would also work for a carriage horse. A well-turned-out, docile, good-looking horse pulling a nice carriage driven by a horse trader's wife would be something worth a premium price, too.

"That means we'd have to buy a carriage," Mary said. It was a statement of fact, not a complaint.

"Maybe I can pick one up reasonable," Edward replied, "and work it over, so that it would be nice."

Even a carriage in need of major refurbishing cost a lot of money, and with what they had to pay the bank on the loan for the house, there wasn't much of that around. Kate continued to sleep on the floor, and David and her father spent long hours at night stripping the paint from the body of a landau carriage her father had bought "reasonable" at an auction, and replacing rusted metal parts, and finally painting the whole thing with coat after coat of black India shellac, so that it glistened and shone.

Kate and her mother made a new top for it, out of canvas, and their fingers and the heels of their hands were often bloody and black-and-blue from the effort of forcing the needles through the canvas with a saddle-maker's leather pad.

When that was done, there remained one thing, Edward Gardiner said, "to complete the picture."

"Now what?" her mother asked, exasperation in her voice.

"You get yourself and the girl some fancy clothes. Well, maybe not fancy. But dignified."

"You don't like the way I look?" Mary challenged her husband.

"You look fine to me. But I want you to show off horse and carriage," he said.

"I'll get some material," she said.

"No," Edward said.

"Well, then," Mary said, "I'll see what I can find in the market. Sometimes, there's stuff not too bad worn."

"No, what you'll do is go find a seamstress and have her make you up a dress. Two dresses. And if she's not too dear, for Kate, too. And hats for the both of you."

"You don't buy dresses for thirteen-year-old girls," Mary announced bluntly. "The way she's going, she wouldn't wear it a dozen times before she grew out of it."

"Buy her one," Edward said. "I tell you, this is business."

"You're making me feel like a fancy woman," Mary said. "Where do you expect me to go all fancied up, anyway?"

"I want you to go shopping every day," Edward said. "You don't have to buy much, but go to the expensive markets and stores and make sure they know who you are, in case someone should ask about the horse."

When the dress came from the dressmaker, it was the most beautiful one Kate had ever seen. It made her look, she thought, like a young lady. Maybe there was something to be said for becoming a young lady after all.

When David saw her in it, he rolled his eyes and stuck out his tongue and grabbed her hand and planted a kiss on the back of it. What he really did was spit out a sticky lump of the honeyed almonds he had been chewing.

She kicked him on the shin, remembering at the very last moment what her mother had said about it ruining a man for life if he was kicked where Kate really wanted to kick him.

The very next morning, she and her mother, all fancied up, got in the glistening carriage behind a beautiful three-year-old jet-black mare and went shopping on High Street. They bought bread at one store, some strawberry jam at a third, and were on their way to a dealer in wild fowl when the most astonishing thing happened.

There were a number of carriages along High Street, from little two-wheelers and small landaus like theirs to really fancy carriages with drivers and footmen. And as they were headed down High Street to see if they could buy a brace of duck at a reasonable price, a goods wagon rolled across the street in front of them and they had to stop.

And then a really fancy carriage, with a driver and a footman in front, pulled up beside them and stopped. In the back was a tall, good-looking gentleman and a tall, good-looking young gentleman. The first thing Kate thought was that the young gentleman (her assessment of him was based on the way he was dressed; almost exactly like the man with him, who was probably his father) looked as bored as she had ever seen anyone look. Then she thought that he was really beautiful. He was the most beautiful young man she had ever seen.

It occurred to her that that was the first time she had ever looked at a young man and noticed what he looked like that way. Previously, she had judged them with David as the criteria. They were as old, or older, than David; smaller or larger; more or less funny-looking. This one was beautiful.

He gave her a look first of curiosity and then of impatience and turned away. She felt her face flushing.

And then she saw that his father had put his hand to his hat and tipped it.

Why, she wondered, would a perfect stranger tip his hat to her mother? Was that the way people like that behaved? Kate stole a look at her mother to see if she had noticed. She had noticed, although she was ignoring the man. Kate knew that she had noticed because her mother's face was red with embarrassment.

Just as soon as the goods wagon got out of their way, with a very unladylike, very loud clucking noise and a flapping of the reins, Mary urged the black mare into motion. Obviously, Kate decided her mother did not like strange men tipping their hats to her. Kate wondered why. It seemed like a compliment.

When they came out of the wild-fowl merchant's store, Kate carrying two ducks in a basket, the man who had tipped his hat and the beautiful young man were getting out of their carriage. He even, Kate noticed, had a walking stick like his father.

And the father tipped his hat again to her mother, and this time she could not ignore him, for he addressed her by name: "Mistress Gardiner, I believe," he said.

"Captain Law," her mother said, and Kate wondered what in the world was wrong with her mother. She could never remember ever having seen her so ill-at-ease before.

"May I present my son, Mistress Gardiner?" the man said. "This is my son John."

"Madam," the beautiful boy said, and bent over in a bow as he swept his hat from his head. "I am honored."

"And this, I presume, is Miss Gardiner?" the man said, and smiled at Kate.

"This is my daughter, Catherine," Mary said.

Kate remembered that she was expected to curtsy; she could not remember precisely how low to curtsy, and it was awkward and humiliating. Captain Law, whoever he was, didn't seem to notice.

"She has," Captain Law said, "if I may be permitted to say so, inherited a good deal of her mother's beauty and charm."

The beautiful boy didn't miss her awkwardness. Not only did he not bow to her and kept his hat on his head, but there was an undisguised look of amusement on his face.

"You are very kind, Captain Law," Mary said.

"I haven't been called 'captain' in a very long time."

"It has been a very long time since we saw each other," Mary said.

"Yes," he said. "May I say that the years have treated you more than kindly?"

Her mother didn't reply.

"I understand that your husband has gone into business here in the city," the man said. "Would you be good enough to extend to him my best regards."

"Certainly," Mary replied. "It was good of you to speak to me, Captain Law."

"My pleasure, Mistress Gardiner," he said, and tipped his hat to her again. "It was nice to make your acquaintance, Miss Gardiner," he said to Kate.

He started to walk away. The beautiful boy tipped his hat to Mary Gardiner and looked right through Kate.

"Madam," the beautiful boy said.

His name, Kate remembered, was John. John Law.

"Who were they?" Kate asked as soon as they were in the carriage.

"Oh," her mother said. "Someone your father and I knew a long time ago."

"But *who* are they?"

"Don't concern yourself about it," Mary said.

"I'm not concerned, just curious."

"Curiosity killed the cat," her mother said. Then she pointed to a sign nailed to the wall of a tavern: LAW'S BEERS & ALES. "See that?"

"Yes," Kate said. "What about it?"

"That's who they are. That's the brewer."

"Where did you and Father meet him?" Kate asked, impressed.

"During the rebellion," Mary said. "Before you were born."

"But how?"

"We're going to drive past St. Barbara's School," Mary

47

said, changing the subject. "We won't go in today, but I got directions to it, and I want to see where it is."

Damn, I thought she'd forgotten about that school business.

3

Kate didn't get to go, that year, to St. Barbara's School, although after she had a little time to think it over, going seemed to be a much better idea than it had at first. If a girl were to grow up and marry a fine gentleman, she decided, it would be better if she had an education so that she would know how to behave like a lady and would not embarass her husband.

It was money again, and being a girl again. Her mother explained it to her. Her father had been right, as he usually was, about being able to make more money by coming to Edinburgh. But for the time being, they were going to be a little short of money.

Kate asked out loud what she was thinking. If her father was making more money than he ever had, why were they short of it?

They had to pay for the new house and the furniture, her mother explained, and there were extra wages because there were more men working for the firm, and Edward Gardiner had to put out more money to buy more stock, which meant that he had to buy more feed.

"So, for this year, there's just enough money to send David to school," her mother told her. "An education is more important for a boy than for a girl, as you know. But your father tells me that if things go as well next year, there will be enough money for you to go to school, too."

That made perfect sense, Kate decided: David, who hated school and who could have made himself really useful all day in the stables, was being forced to go to school, whereas she, who was absolutely useless around the house except as an unpaid maid and who really wanted to go to school and learn how to be a lady, couldn't go.

The whole family returned to the farm in the very

early spring. There was the foaling, of course, and her parents wanted to be there to help with that, and there was more. Her father wanted to gamble on his ability to judge horseflesh. You could buy a colt at birth, to be separated from his mother at weaning, for a lot less than you could buy a colt at weaning. If the colt died before it was weaned, that was the problem of whoever owned it.

Edward Gardiner believed that he could tell which newborn colt was going to make it to weaning often enough to risk buying them. And there were even cheaper newborn colts available, those whose dams had died or were sick or who for some reason had rejected them. Mary was really skilled in feeding orphaned colts.

For that matter, so was Kate. She was near as good as her mother. What they fed them was cow's milk with honey and malt, and part of the secret was in making them walk. If you just let them lie in the stable and fed them, they'd more often than not die. But if you made them walk, for some reason that kept them alive.

When Edward and Mary Gardiner, on saddle horses but leading a wagon, went out into the Highlands to see what colts they could buy and keep alive, they left David and Kate behind them at the farm.

That's where Wanderer was born. He was out of Bonnie Bell by Kelso, both fine Arabians, and Bonnie Bell dropped him at three o'clock in the morning on what they later remembered was their fourteenth birthday. There was some trouble with the delivery, because he was a big colt; Kate was really afraid for a while, because the mare was covered with sweat and there was a lot of blood. But David got Bonnie Bell through it all right, and by the time their mother and father returned from the Highlands, Bonnie Bell was on her feet again and the colt suckling hungrily.

He was hardly a month old the first time he made his way through an opening in the fence and went wandering, and he did it twice again in the next two months.

"By rights," Edward told them, "we should geld him. That calms them down."

"I wish you wouldn't," David said. He wouldn't want that done to him.

"There's always a market for a reasonably gentle stallion," his father said. "He's not mean, nor even wild. He just likes to wander, is all. We leave him here, he'll get away again. We better geld him."

"Take him to the city," Kate said. "He can't get through or over that fence."

"You know what it would cost to feed him and his dam in the city?" Edward asked.

"Less than it would cost if we lost him," David argued. "And we get for him what I think we can get for him."

"We'll have to think about it," Edward said, and walked out of the barn.

Brother and sister smiled at each other. They knew what was going to happen. The colt was not gelded, and they took him and Bonnie Bell back with them to the city, and he was named Wanderer.

And once they got him in the pasture and yards in the city, Wanderer never tried to run away again. He spent most of his time hanging his head over, or sticking it through, the fence to look at the house to see if either David or Kate was headed in his direction.

There was enough money for Kate to enroll in St. Barbara's School, and she went there every morning. It wasn't what she thought it would be. She thought she would really learn something interesting. But what they taught her was needlework, which she already knew about and didn't like, and there was a daily class in religion. And then there was one called "God's Sacred Mystery," to which she had really looked forward. It wasn't what it sounded like at all. It was a nun, talking about where babies came from. When Kate told some of the city girls how it was with horses, they didn't believe her.

Every once in a while, she caught a glimpse of John Law, or thought she did. Every time he saw her, he looked right through her. It was, she thought, because she still looked too young. But that was changing. The way her front had grown in the past year was astonishing. She was always catching some young man staring at her. Sooner or later, she thought, John Law would notice. Why should he be different from the others?

4

By the time Wanderer was a year old, it was generally conceded by anyone who saw him that he was an exceptional animal. He was beautiful, for one thing; smart, for another; and, at least around David and Kate, very gentle.

David had been around horses too much to say that he loved one of them. Only fools and females loved horses. And even if he was a fool and suspected that Wanderer was about as fond of him as he was of the horse, thinking about that would be foolish, for Wanderer could never be his horse. For one thing, his father was in the horse-breeding business, not a country gentleman or a member of the nobility who kept horses for pleasure, the way ordinary folk kept canaries in cages. Wanderer was a horse they were just waiting for the right price to sell, and it was foolish to think about anything else.

There had been good offers for him from the time he was six months old and showing the signs, in his forequarters and the depth of his chest, of what he was going to become. David's father had turned down all of them, saying that if they were offered so much now, they would probably be offered a lot more later.

Sooner or later, of course, Wanderer would have to be sold, so there was no sense in paying any more attention to him than to any other animal in their stock. But there was something special about Wanderer. There were some horses who seemed friendly and even affectionate, and Wanderer turned out to be one of these. There were some horses who took to the bridle without a fuss, as Wanderer did, and there was nothing special about that, either. Nor was Wanderer the first stallion in recorded history, or even in David Gardiner's experience, who didn't buck once when his first rider mounted him, just stood there a little nervously, as if making up his mind, and then turned his head to look up at David on his back, as if asking him what was expected of him.

He was fast, too. Really fast. David knew that once it got around the swells and the aristocrats just how fast Wanderer was, an offer for him would be made that even

patient Edward Gardiner would jump at. So there was no
sense in getting emotionally involved with a stupid
damned animal, especially since as the son of a horse
breeder, you should know better.

For his sixteenth birthday, David had high hopes that
his father would give him a fowling piece, for his father
had often told him that at sixteen you stopped being a
boy and became a man, and a good fowling piece seemed
to be sort of a symbol of manhood. The shotgun he was
using was old and battered, the lockwork unreliable.
And there was something else, he thought, it wasn't as if
the gun would be hung over the mantel and just looked
at. All summer and whenever else they were out there, it
would be used like any other tool around the breeding
farm. In a year or less, he would be able to bring down
enough birds and hare, and maybe even, if he was lucky,
deer and stag, to more than pay for the double-barreled
fowling piece he had looked at so often and so longingly
in the windows of MacWheeler & Shaw, Gunsmiths, on
Tailor's Row.

On the morning of his sixteenth birthday, however,
the only present he found outside his bedroom door when
he opened it was a small package that held a leather
purse with a clever arrangement of its straps so that it
could be carried around his shoulder and also, by rear-
ranging the straps, hung from a saddle.

It was a fine purse, he told himself, and he reminded
himself that now that he was sixteen, he was near a man
and should expect the kind of gifts adults gave each
other, like the fine purse, not some kind of a toy. And
certainly not a double-barreled fowling piece from Mac-
Wheeler & Shaw.

The proof that he was now considered near a man
came at breakfast, when his father told him that after
he'd run the regular weekly check of the stone fence, he
should throw a saddle on Wanderer and bring him to
"the office."

A month before, Edward Gardiner had decided that
what he needed was a place of business in town. The
farm off Lothian Road was fine for what it was, but he
needed an office in town, as well. A lot went on, he said,

deals he had missed, because he was way to hell and gone out here on Lothian Road, and not where things happened. He had rented a store on George's Street.

"I think he's throwing money down the well," Mary had told her son. "But I have been wrong before."

"We're finally going to get him off the books," his father said.

"Somebody local?" David asked, succeeding, he thought, in hiding his unhappiness.

"There's a father about town with a son he thinks would look elegant on an animal like Wanderer," his father said. "He's probably giving him the horse just so that people will know he can afford it."

"That's a terrible thing to say!" David's mother snapped.

"Terrible or not, it's true," his father said.

David did not have the heart to ask for specifics, but he suspected that Wanderer's new owner might very likely be the brewer's son, John Law. He didn't know Law, but he had been around Edinburgh long enough to be familiar with the folklore: John Law was the apple of his father's eye. All he had to do to get something was ask for it.

He had heard two different fathers of his friends, when asked by their sons for something, respond with the question, "Who do you think you are, John Law?"

At least, he thought, if it was Law, Wanderer would be well cared for. Not by John Law, but by grooms in the employ of his father.

After breakfast, he threw a saddle on Wanderer and rode him slowly around the outer stone fence of the farm off Lothian Road, sliding off his back half a dozen times to replace stones in the fence that somehow had become displaced. Once, when he was struggling to lift an unusually large piece of stone, Wanderer leaned his head down and rubbed his soft nose against David's neck. David had to remind himself that he was sixteen and near a man, and men didn't cry about stupid damned horses.

It was near midday when he rode up to the office in town and tied Wanderer's reins to the hitching post. He refused to let himself dwell on the fact that he had probably just ridden Wanderer for the last time, but he did take a little extra time to pat his neck and gave him a large lump of sugar, instead of a small piece. There was no telling when his new owner would think to give him sugar.

Then he went into the office. His father was standing up, leaning on the wall beside his tall desk.

"Took you long enough," his father said. "I've been waiting."

"I rode the fence and came directly here," David said sharply.

"And that's all you've got to say?"

"All I've got to say about what?"

"The sign, for one thing," his father said.

"What sign?"

"How many signs do we have?" his father asked dryly.

David went outside to look at the sign, wondering what he was supposed to say about a sign. It was a perfectly ordinary sign, white painted wood, on which was painted EDWARD GARDINER, DEALER IN HORSES. It had been hanging from a post by the lane to the farm on Lothian Road, and his father had taken it down and brought it to the city the day the office had been opened.

But it was gone now. What was hanging in front of the office was a brand-new sign, carved from white oak, with its letters painted in gold:

EDWARD GARDINER & SON
PURVEYORS OF FINE HORSES
BY APPOINTMENT TO H.R.H. CHARLES II
BY APPOINTMENT TO THE DUKE OF LAUDERDALE

His mother had been after his father for a long time, for years, come to think of it, since he had received the first warrant of appointment to the Lord High Commissioner, to advertise that fact. It would mean business, she said. His father, while always agreeing with her, had never seemed to get around to it.

Now he had gone whole hog. David wondered why. And then he knew. He had waited until David was sixteen, a man, or almost, so he could add "& Son" after his name without looking foolish. David's eyes watered over. And it got worse when he looked at Wanderer and saw that Wanderer was looking at him out of his great brown eyes, his ears up in curiosity and expectation that he was about to be ridden again.

Well, that was over. What his mother said about there being a price of pain to be paid for every joy was true. The price of his becoming a man, of having "& SON" up there on the sign was the pain of knowing that purveyors of fine horses couldn't grow fond of animals and had to sell them when the price was right.

He ran his hand over Wanderer's hard, warm nose and then went into the office.

"I don't know what to say," he said to his father.

"You could try, 'Thank you, Father,' " his father said.

"Thank you, Father," he said, and the two looked at each other for a moment, and then David forgot that he was now sixteen, and went to his father and hugged him.

After a moment, his father's arms went around him and in a gruff voice, Edward Gardiner said, "I've had my troubles with you, but on the whole, you're a damned good lad and I'm terrible proud of you, David."

And then, almost at once, both of them were embarrassed about the emotion and they broke apart.

"I suspect that you'd better be about delivering Wanderer," his father said, and taking his kerchief from his trousers pocket, started to blow his nose as he walked out of the office and down the street.

David wiped the tears from his eyes after a moment and walked to his father's desk and took out the large stock ledger, carefully opened it, and flipped through the large pages until he found Wanderer's first entry.

"18th April AD 1681. Out of Bonnie Bell by Kelso, sire, a male colt. Appears healthy."

His eyes lost their focus again when he remembered the day Wanderer had been foaled; then he thought of the way the stallion had looked at him several minutes before. He wiped the tears away again and put his finger to the line under the disposition column, where it said, Sale Price and Sold To.

Under Sale Price it said, 1/1/1, which meant one pound, one shilling, one pence, and was something they wrote in the books when for some reason there was no real price, but they needed a figure for the bookkeeper and the tax collector. His father, David decided, had probably bartered something for Wanderer. Aware that he had been purposefully avoiding looking at the end of the line, where the new owner's name would be written, he did so now. What it said under Sold To was David Gardiner, Esq.

Chapter Three

1

The "sporting set" of Edinburgh—which Mary called the "wastrels" and Edward called "the ticks" because they did no work, but rather lived by sucking the blood of decent working people—gathered on Sunday afternoons in Holyrood Park, a five-square-mile area near Holyroodhouse Palace. Specifically, they gathered on the south shore of Dunsapie Loch, where there was near a quarter-mile of straight and level land where horses could be raced.

There were other diversions: taverns and restaurants set up under the trees from the backs of wagons, hazards tables, tumblers and jugglers, and carriage loads of fancy women chaperoned by their madams, who thus were able to combine an afternoon in the outdoors for their girls with a bit of discreet advertising. It was understood that the fancy women would not leave their carriages and mingle with the "respectable" ladies who came to the loch to watch the races.

The primary entertainment on the shores of Dunsapie

Loch was horses. There was a never-ending parade of immaculately turned out "gentlemen," including some with a legitimate claim to that appellation, on immaculately turned out animals, riding alone or in pairs, tipping their hats to ladies and sometimes to fancy women in their carriages.

The excuse for the gathering at Dunsapie Loch was the races. In a sense, these were informal, simply the testing of one gentleman's horse against that of another. But over the years, a protocol had developed and custom had the force of regulation.

There were generally two kinds of races, one-way and return, and sometimes a third, a double, two trips up and down the shore of Dunsapie Loch, which made the race nearly a mile.

David had known about the races as long as he could remember, and on several occasions, when he and his father had been in Edinburgh delivering animals over a weekend, he had gone to the shores of the loch with his father. But when they had moved to Edinburgh, his father had decided that a respectable businessman who hoped to enjoy the trade of the respectable class in Edinburgh should not be seen often, or at all, at the loch.

One of the first things that had popped into his mind when his father had given him title to Wanderer was that he could now go out to the loch on a horse that was not only quite as good as any other animal to be found there, but that was his. On three occasions, when he was certain in his own mind that his father would not learn about it, he had gone out there. It had been an entirely satisfying experience to be there, and on Wanderer. Wanderer seemed to sense that he was being appreciatively eyed, and moved with the grace of a dancer.

On his third Sunday-afternoon visit to the loch, once he had seen enough to understand the protocol of the racing—and more important, the protocol of the betting on the races—he had made his first wager.

A small, well-put-together, somewhat nervous piebald mare was being raced against a horse not unlike Wanderer—that is to say, a large, young, and somewhat ungainly stallion. There was no question in David's mind that the mare could take the stallion over the short haul, but he thought it was entirely likely that when the stallion understood what was expected of him in the double that they were to run, it would settle down to running, and that his greater stride and endurance would see him win.

When the odds were announced, three-to-one in favor of the mare, David put two shillings on the stallion, aware that if he lost that meant he would not be able to stop by one of the wagons and have a Law's Old Pale Ale, for the two shillings was all the money he had.

The stallion took the race by three lengths, and never had a mug of ale tasted quite so delicious. In what he thought of later as a moment of weakness, he showed his winnings to Kate when he got home, and told her what had happened. The first suspicion that he was making a mistake in telling Kate came almost as soon as he started telling her about it. There was a peculiar look in her eye, and he wondered if she would betray him to their parents, let them know that he had been both at the loch and gambling.

But that wasn't what she had in mind.

"I want to go with you the next time," Kate said.

"No, you don't," he said. "It's no place for a girl."

"If it's no place for me, it's no place for you," Kate countered.

"That's not what I meant," he said. "What I meant is that Mother and Father would never let you go."

"I want to go out there," she said.

"You tell me how I can take you there, and I'll take you," David said, convinced that the problem had been solved.

"If you're going to race Wanderer, David," Kate said, "I want to be there to see it."

"I'm not going to race Wanderer," David replied, looking at her in surprise. It had never entered his mind to enter one of the races, even though every time he had gone there, he had been on Wanderer, and from the time Wanderer was a year old, he would have been able to make a good show.

For one thing, he didn't have that kind of money.

Placing a two-shilling wager with one of the men who called themselves turf accountants was one thing. But under the protocol, you couldn't enter your own horse and then wager two shillings with a turf accountant. Those were side bets. The protocol required a wager between the gentlemen who owned the animals, and the smallest wager David had ever seen made was a pound.

He was very much aware, furthermore, that his father and mother devoutly believed that gambling was a sin. More important, horses could be hurt racing. He would have been no more able to explain to his father an injured horse—either one with a pulled tendon or one that had to be destroyed—than he would have been able to explain his burning down one of the barns. Their horses were for sale, not for sport.

"Who do you think you're fooling?" Kate asked.

"I swear, Kate," David said. "I have never even thought about racing Wanderer."

The way to deal with the situation, which meant the way to deal with Kate, David decided, was to stay away from the loch for a couple of weeks, so that she would forget all about it.

The next Sunday, however, when they came home from church, he learned that Kate not only had not forgotten about the loch, but had come up with the solution to the problem of getting herself out there.

"Aren't you going to change out of your good dress?" Mary asked her daughter as they started to prepare the noon meal.

"I'll put an apron over it," Kate said. "After we eat, David's promised to take me riding."

"I said no such thing!" David said.

"We're going to hitch that sorrel mare Father took in trade to the carriage and ride through Holyrood Park," Kate said.

"I don't want you going out there," Mary replied instantly. "Wherever did you get such an idea?"

"It's a good way to show off the mare," Kate said. "And we'll tie Wanderer to the carriage, to make sure people notice us."

"I'm not going out there with you," David announced flatly.

"What were your plans for the afternoon?" Edward asked.

"I didn't have any," David confessed.

"Now that I think of it," Edward said, "it's a good idea. A very good idea. You're always after me about taking you out there, David. I don't think I should be seen there, but there's no reason you shouldn't. There's no reason at all anyone should think there's anything wrong with a young man taking his sister out there for a ride on Sunday afternoon. The best young people in Edinburgh go out there sometimes." And then he smiled at David. "And if you're there with her, I doubt that you'd do anything I wouldn't approve of."

"I don't want to take her out there!"

"You'll go," Edward ordered. "By your own admission, you have nothing else to do anyway, and maybe we'll find someone to take that mare off our hands."

And so David and Catherine Gardiner, in their Sunday-best clothes, rode out the lane from the farm onto Lothian Road in the glistening carriage, David driving, Kate beside him in gloves and a hat, and with Wanderer, saddled with the best saddle and a brand-new white woolen saddle blanket, tied behind them.

David had learned from a man who had been there that it was actually true that the savages in India made a practice of drowning female babies at birth. At the time he'd heard it, he had been shocked. Now it seemed as if the Indians really had some good ideas.

By the time they got to the loch, however, he had calmed down and was able to see the bright side of the situation. He was here, after all, and with permission. He also had six shillings. If he came across another situation like the one that had earned him the six shillings, he just might be able to make a little money.

Kate was fascinated with everything. David took great delight in telling her just precisely what the half-dozen fancy women whose matched pair, carriage, driver, and clothes she admired, did for a living.

He got out of the carriage and told her he was going to

get a beer and asked if she wanted a cup of tea or something.

"Get me a glass of wine, please," Kate said.

"Don't be silly," he said.

Kate took a hand from her muff and handed him a coin.

"I'll pay for it, don't worry," she said.

He glowered at her.

"Please, David," she said.

"Damn," he said, and went to bring her a glass of wine.

When he came back, she announced there had been a race in his absence.

"That's why everyone comes here," he said. "Because of the races."

"Wanderer could have taken him easily," Kate announced.

"Don't reveal your stupidity," he said. "Wanderer could also break his leg in the trying."

"You know that's not true," she said.

"What I do know, missy," David snapped, "is that I'm not going to risk getting Wanderer hurt for a shilling or two!"

But the seed of temptation had been sown, and it sprouted when David was forced to acknowledge that there were very few horses being raced here today that were as fast as Wanderer. Possibly none. Probably none. And it was clear that Wanderer wanted to race. He whinnied and danced all around when he saw the other animals lining up, and once he went back on his hind legs, to the length of his reins, when a half-dozen came galloping back to the starting line.

But it would be absolute insanity, he told himself, to risk injuring the animal just to make a couple of shillings.

"I admire your horse, sir," a voice said to him.

David turned to see who was speaking to him. It was a young man several years older than he, on a well-set-up black stallion. The horse, who had a white blaze on his nose and had a lot of Arabian in him, was beautiful, and David paid more attention to him than he did to the young man.

"Thank you," David said. "I admire your animal, too."

It was only then that he recognized the young man. It was the brewer's son, John Law.

Kate had had no difficulty whatever in identifying him. More important, she thought, he had recognized her. He had tipped his hat politely to her. The last time she had seen him, he had looked right through her.

"Might I be so bold as to inquire who owns your animal?" John Law asked.

He is John Law, David decided. I have just been complimented on Wanderer by the son of probably the richest man in Edinburgh.

He noticed that John Law was dressed like a member of the aristocracy and that he affected their manner of speech.

"He's mine," David said.

"I don't believe I have the honor of your acquaintance," the young man said.

"My name is Gardiner, David Gardiner."

The young man did not reply. He looked down at Kate, obviously waiting for an introduction.

"And this is my sister, Kate," David finally said.

Catherine, damn you, Kate thought.

"Miss Gardiner," the young man said, bowing to her again.

"I believe our parents are acquainted," Kate said.

David looked at her as if she had lost her mind. Then he decided that he had been wrong. Despite the clothing and the aristocratic manners, this could not be John Law. If Kate said that their parents knew this fellow's parents, they did, and that eliminated any chance of him being the brewery-owning Law's son.

"I thought for a moment there that you were the brewer's son," David said without thinking.

The young man raised his eyebrows.

"You know who I mean," David explained. "John Law."

"But I am," the young man said. "Does that somehow bother you?"

David looked at him for a moment before replying.

"What bothers me is that I seem to have made a horse's ass of myself," he said finally.

At that moment Kate could cheerfully have choked her brother.

"Not at all," John Law said. "I do that myself all the time."

"You do?" David asked, chuckling.

"Most of the time, according to my father," John Law said with a wide and disarming smile, "I'm a wastrel. But the rest of the time, I'm what you said you were. Does your father say that about you?"

"No, as a matter of fact, he doesn't," David said.

"How lucky for you," John Law said dryly.

David smiled at him, somehow ill-at-ease and for some reason not liking John Law.

"We must put such unimportant things to one side and concentrate on important things," Law said. "For example, the most important thing I have thought all day is that the only horse here which appears as if he might give Emperor a fair run is yours."

David replied with what he had been thinking.

"He might at that," he said.

"Well, then, shall we have a go at it?" Law asked with a smile.

"I don't race my animal, thank you," David said.

"You don't race him?" Law asked incredulously.

"It doesn't seem worth it," David said. "The risk, I mean, to the animal, for a couple of shillings."

Law looked at him thoughtfully. "For a shilling or two," he said. "Obviously, you're correct. But the solution to that problem is obvious. I have no intention of racing Emperor for a shilling or two, either. 'Make the wager worth more than the horse,' is the rule I usually follow. How does a couple of double crowns strike you?"

"I don't have that kind of money," David confessed. "And I don't think I'd have the courage to wager it if I did."

"Then wager the horse itself," John Law replied. "If you lose, *when* you lose, you already have the means to get home without him." He gestured at the carriage. "I will," he added, "exclude that saddle from the wager."

He means it, David thought. Again, he said what he was thinking.

"I think you're crazy," he said.

Law's eyebrows went up as if in disbelief.

John Law looked at him thoughtfully for a moment, considering the insult and what to do about it. Then he nodded his head and smiled.

"And *I* think," he said, "that you know your animal, as good-looking as he is, is not very fleet. And I admire, I suppose, your strength of character to admit that. There are fools out here who would lose their animals for the sake of their pride."

"Well, I'm not one of them," David said.

"Pity," John Law said, "I would have really liked to part you from that animal."

Then he tipped his hat to Kate, smiled at her, and rode off.

When he was out of earshot, David turned to Kate. "Damn. If I'd have had the money," he said, "I think I'd have put it up just to put that bastard in his place."

"Do you mean that?" Kate asked, and the way she asked it made him look at her curiously.

"Yes, I mean it," he said.

"And you think that Wanderer could take his stallion?"

"You know as well as I do that he could."

"Then bet him," Kate said.

"Put up Wanderer? Are you out of your mind?"

Kate reached into her muff again and came out with a small leather purse.

"There's two double crowns in there," she said.

"Where did you get two double crowns?" he asked, not believing her. He opened the bag and there were two golden double crowns inside.

"I had a birthday, too, you know," she said.

He had, now that he thought of it, wondered why Kate hadn't sulked on their birthday when he'd gotten Wanderer and all she'd gotten was a leather-bound chest, a hope chest to be filled with linen for the time when she would marry.

"I couldn't let you wager that money," he said, and handed the bag back to her. "It's for when you marry."

"It's my money," Kate insisted.

"No."

"Then borrow one of them from me," she said.

He didn't understand what she meant, and it showed on his face.

"I'll loan you one of the double crowns," she said. "You can pay me back when you get it, a little at a time. And then we'll each bet one double crown against John Law's Warrior."

"I've got a little over a pound, all together, I could give you right away," David said. He smiled at her. "You're sure, Kate?"

"I'm sure," she said, and put the bag back in his hands.

"I'll go find the bastard," David said.

He had trouble finding him and was afraid for a while that Law had become bored and left the shores of the loch, but thirty minutes after he'd started to look for him, he found him. Law was about to race his black stallion, on a return race, against a sorrel.

David watched the race with interest. Law's stallion won, but not with as much of a lead as David would have thought. Wanderer was faster. It wouldn't even be a fair wager, David thought. How could it be fair if you knew you were going to win?

But what was worse than sinning, he decided, would be losing, and the way you kept from losing was to know what you were doing. He walked Wanderer up the shore of Dunsapie Loch parallel to the path on which the racing was done, carefully studying the course. He was not at all surprised with the conclusion he drew that there was practically nothing hazardous at all about the racecourse. It was dirt, there were no stones that he could see, and it was level.

If he could get John Law now, after having turned him down before, into a race for two double crowns, five minutes later, he and Kate would be a two double crowns richer, and the only cost would be his having to walk Wanderer for a few minutes to cool him off. There was absolutely no question in his mind that Wanderer could handily beat Law's stallion.

He saw where John Law was walking his stallion to cool him, and caught up with him.

Law seemed surprised, even annoyed to see him. "I

suppose it is too much to hope," he said, "that Satan has taken possession of your soul and that you are going to wager your horse against mine, so that I can take both home with me?"

"I'll race you for two double crowns," David blurted.

Law's eyebrows rose. "*Two* double crowns?" he asked. "Doubtless, you have them with you?"

The tone of his voice made it plain he thought that to be highly unlikely.

David fished the leather purse out.

"I take your word for it, of course," Law replied. He looked thoughtful for a moment, and then asked, "A one-way sprint? A return? Or a double?"

"A return," David said, aware that he hadn't even thought about that.

"Which tells me that you think you can overcome your beast's slowness in getting up to speed by running a return," Law said. "But that you don't think he has a mile's endurance."

"I'll race you over a mile," David said. "If that's what you want."

That, he realized, was a mistake. That had been anger talking, not common sense.

"A double, that is to say, a mile, it is then," Law said.

"And if I had more, I'd bet more," David said. He was suddenly painfully aware that Satan himself must have whispered that in his ear. The proof of that seemed to be he wasn't nearly as worried, as terrified, as logic told him he should be. He now very much wished he hadn't started this whole business at all. And then, in rapid succession, he had several other very uncomfortable thoughts. First he thought that he apparently did not have the backbone to resist temptation. When temptation was placed in his path, he jumped right into it. And dragged his sister down with him, which was really rotten. And then he had two other really painful thoughts. Kate had placed the temptation in his path. She was the one with the money. Her wedding money.

"Good Christ!" David said aloud.

"Yes?" Law asked. "You said something?"

"No," David said, and managed a smile. He had said

nothing. But he had *thought* something and thinking it was bad enough. The two crowns Kate had weren't her birthday present to be saved for her marriage. They were the double crowns they had been given by the Duke of Lauderdale at Holyroodhouse Palace.

His sister was insane. Females got that way. She was insane for taking those coins, but what he had done was worse. He was the one who was going to be blamed for what had happened when he lost the race. And that would be fair, he thought. He was supposed to take care of his sister, keep her out of trouble, not help her get in worse trouble.

He couldn't force himself to think what would happen when, eventually and inevitably, it came out that the two double crowns they had received from the hand of the Lord High Commissioner for Scotland himself had been wagered, and lost, on a horse race.

"Let me cool him down a little more," Law said. "And then we'll have a go at it."

David forced a smile on his face.

"Anytime you feel ready," he said in what he desperately hoped sounded like a confident tone of voice.

Law's idea of cooling off his stallion, David saw, was walking him up to others of the sporting set, all of whom seemed to know who he was, informing them of the race, and making bets with them. He was wagering, David saw, an incredible amount of money. The smallest bet he heard him make was for a pound, and most of them were for a crown, and many for a double crown. Law wasn't much older than he was, but he apparently had access to large amounts of money.

And Law was confident, even gaily confident, which just about destroyed David's own confidence. If Law was willing to wager all that money, he knew something David didn't. Had he purposefully held back his stallion so that David would underestimate the stallion's speed?

For the ninth or tenth time, David desperately wished that he had never come to the shore of Dunsapie Loch at all. He wished there were someway he could simply disappear. It was quite clear now that he was going to lose, and that meant he would have to give Law the uncirculated gold double crowns that he and Kate had received from the Duke of Lauderdale and that they were supposed to give to their children.

There was a feeling in his stomach, as they went to the starting line, as if he had swallowed a two-pound rock. He thought that it was practically indecent that the sun should be shining so brightly, and the birds singing, and the grass be so green, and the water sparkling in the loch. He was in bad trouble, and things should not be so pretty.

Kate had driven the carriage up to the starting line, and she waved happily at him.

Goddamned foolish female!

Starting the race didn't take any time at all, and even that got him in trouble. The man who stood between the horses and explained the rules was a customer, maybe even a friend, of his father's. Now his father, no matter how this turned out, was going to find out about it practically right away. There wouldn't even be time to search for some way to replace the damned double crowns in his father's strongbox.

"I'll raise my hand, holding a kerchief," the man who knew his father said. "I'll call, 'ready,' and if you're ready, you make a sign. Then I'll call 'set,' and finally 'go!' I'll drop my hand when I do that. You know where the end of the course is. The race is two returns. You both understand that?"

"Of course," Law said. "Just make sure everyone who will owe me money is here when I come back."

David just nodded.

The man stood to one side, and before David really knew what was happening, the race had started. John Law got ahead of him at the start—six, eight, maybe ten lengths ahead of him before they got to the end of the first straightaway. Wanderer didn't seem to understand what was expected of him.

On the way back to the starting line, David reduced the distance between himself and Law to four lengths, but Wanderer turned wide before starting up the lakeshore path again, and David was unable to get closer than four lengths before it was time to turn again.

He was going to lose. There was no question about that. God had turned a deaf ear to his desperate prayers for a miracle.

"Goddammit, boy, run!" David shouted as they made the turn. He kicked Wanderer with his heels.

And Wanderer began to run faster than he had ever run before. His strides were enormous and his pace smooth. In an incredibly short time, he had pulled beside Law's black stallion and then was pulling ahead. He seemed to be still picking up speed.

And then they were across the finish line. The miracle had happened. He had won. He slowed Wanderer down and looked over his shoulder to see what had happened to Law. For the first time, he thought that the reason Law hadn't caught up with him was because his stallion had stumbled or something else had happened to him.

But Law was still astride his stallion. And when he came close to David, he did not, as David expected him to, rein his animal in. He kept galloping. He took his hat off, waved it, and kept on going.

There was laughter, and even applause, from the spectators, and David was immediately convinced that somehow—he had no idea how—he had been made a fool of. He was tempted to just ride over to where Kate, confused by Law's galloping away, was standing in the carriage, tell her to shut her mouth and ask no questions, and lead her and the carriage off.

They had not lost the wager, so he would not have to give away the double crowns. No harm had been done. The obvious thing for him to do, he decided, was just take Kate home and put the whole incident gratefully behind them. He would have a long talk with Kate and make her aware how close they had been to going over the cliff's edge, make sure she understood that they should never get involved in something like this again.

But that noble resolve quickly dissolved, to be replaced with anger. He had wagered in good conscience, and he wanted his money.

He slid off Wanderer's back and walked back to the spectators. He was vain enough to thoroughly enjoy getting slapped on the back by some of the sporting set and to have hands offered for him to shake. Finally he found the man he was looking for, the man who had started the race and who knew his father.

"Well run, David!" the man said, and shook his hand. "What's your father asking for him?" The man patted Wanderer's neck.

"He's not for sale," David said, and then he blurted: "Where did he go? John Law, I mean?"

The man looked at David with understanding in his eyes.

"A gentleman," he explained, "pays his gambling debts the very next time he sees the man he wagered against."

"I don't understand," David confessed.

"Since young Law kept on going, he didn't see anyone he wagered against, did he?" the man said.

"Oh," David said, now understanding.

"Well, you've nothing to worry about. The next time you see John Law, he'll have your money."

"Thank you," David said, and forced himself to smile.

That was going to be a problem. Since he was never coming back out here again, how was he going to be able to see John Law so that he could get his money?

He'd think of something. He *was* going to get that damned money somehow.

Kate caught up with him as he was walking Wanderer down the path to cool him.

"I told you we'd win," she said.

"Just shut up, Kate, will you?"

"Give me the money," she said. "I want to see it."

"I don't have it," he said.

"Why not?"

"I'll tell you later."

"Tell me now," she said. "You didn't get weak knees at the last minute, did you, David, and not bet all of it?"

"I wish I had," he said, and then he told what the man had told him.

He thought that she would have trouble understanding it and that she would probably be angry because she didn't have the money. He thought she would certainly wonder if John Law was trying to cheat them out of it.

But she didn't.

"Well, give me the duke's double crowns anyway," she said. "They'd kill us if they knew we took them."

"If you know that, Kate, then why did you take them?"

"Because I wanted to bet on Wanderer," she said. "And it was the only money I had."

"You could have told me," he said.

"If I had told you," Kate said, "you wouldn't have bet it."

"Christ, I really feel sorry for the man who winds up married to you," David said.

"I've already cost him two double crowns," Kate said.

"What the hell is that supposed to mean?" David asked. And then he understood her. "You're really out of your mind," he said. "If you think that John Law . . ."

She shut him off.

"I'm hot and sweaty," she said. "And I'm going home. Make sure you don't lose the double crowns."

Then she snapped the reins and the mare pulling the carriage broke into a trot, and she left him.

2

By suppertime the next day, Edward Gardiner had the essential details of David's having raced Wanderer on the shore of Dunsapie Loch, and he was, as David predicted he would be, furious.

He hadn't learned some of the specific details, such as the amount of the wager, which would have opened the question of where David had come by two double crowns, and he didn't choose to think that Kate knew what was going on, much less that she was a willing participant. But he knew enough to be furious.

Even if David was too stupid to know that the likes of him had no business wagering with the likes of John Law, Edward Gardiner railed at his son, he should have had enough sense to know that Wanderer was a valuable animal and could easily have been hurt badly, even to the point where he would have to be destroyed. If he had half the sense he was born with, he would have known that only a goddamned fool risks the only thing he has in the world worth more than the clothes on his back in a goddamned horse race.

Moreover, he had humiliated his family. He had humiliated his mother before her friends at the church, for having a son who committed the sin of gambling, and did it in public. He had humiliated his father before his friends and business associates for having a goddamned fool for a son, a son stupid enough to risk an animal like Wanderer for a couple of shillings, betting against the brewer's son who, any damned fool would know, would have the finest horse his father's money could buy. And he had probably ruined his sister's good name, once and for all, by taking her with him, where every wastrel in town could see her and draw the logical conclusion that she was the next thing to a fancy woman.

"I'll have the money, David," his father said.

"What money?" David asked, momentarily confused.

His father slapped him on the face, then went to David's garderobe, and through his clothes, until he found David's cache of money.

"Six goddamn shillings!" Edward Gardiner shouted bitterly. "Six goddamn shillings. You risked that animal for *six goddamn shillings!*"

And then David was sure that his father hadn't heard about the two double crowns. It didn't seem that correcting him, telling him the wager had been for fifty times that much, that after the race he and Kate had been two double crowns richer, would do any good. That would bring up his taking the double crowns from the strongbox.

David had early decided to take the responsibility for Kate's having taken their coins from the strongbox. It was not entirely a noble sacrifice. He had considered what his father's reaction would be if he told him that Kate had encouraged him to make the wager and handed him the double crowns to make the bet with. From the time he could remember, he had been told that he was expected to look out for his little sister. His father's rage would in no way be diminished if he learned that Kate had been involved; probably the reverse. He would be held responsible for leading his sister down the sinner's road.

They went from David's bedroom to the horse barn, where Edward leaned his son against a stall door and whipped him with a two-inch-wide cinch belt.

"Until I tell you different, you'll be either here, or at school, or at the store," his father said. "Not only are you not going to run free anymore, but if you ever go near the loch or the swells again, by God, David, I think I'll kill you."

Mary MacPhee Gardiner came to David's room that night and rubbed tallow and some sort of herb dressing on the angry red marks the cinch belt had left on David's back and legs, and told him that he should think that if his father didn't love him so much, he wouldn't have been so upset about David getting off on the wrong path.

An hour after she left, just as David was about to drop off to sleep despite the pain, Kate sneaked into his room.

"I owe you for not telling on me," she said. "And I'm sorry I got you into this, David."

"Forget it, Kate," David said. "I should have known better than to have listened to you."

"You could have told on me," she insisted. "And I thank you because you didn't."

"I told you, forget it," David said.

"What are you going to do about getting our money?" Kate asked.

David rolled over on his side, wincing at the pain.

"I don't know how just yet, Kate," he said with great determination, "But don't you worry, I'll get your goddamned money from that bastard for you."

"You've got no cause to be angry with John Law," Kate said, and walked out of his room.

3

It was two months before Edward Gardiner turned his son loose from his confinement to the farm, school, and the office. David had several times considered sneaking off to seek out John Law and collect the wager, but in the end decided against it. For one thing, the only place he knew to look for Law was at the loch, and he was unwilling to risk going there. He felt sure that his father had asked whoever had told him that he'd been there the day of the race to report if he ever saw him there again. He did not want to run the risk of defying his father that brazenly, as much because he wanted to regain his father's respect as from fear of another beating with the cinch belt.

And there was a practical consideration, too. The races at Dunsapie Loch were held only on Sunday afternoons, and on Sunday afternoons, after church, David was regularly, as part of his punishment, required to work around the farm, with his father periodically checking on him.

But eight weeks after "what happened at the loch," Edward Gardiner decided that his son had been punished enough. As they were spooning their bread pudding after the Sunday meal, he turned him loose.

"If you think you can be trusted not to get yourself, or your sister, into some scrape," he said. "Why don't you put the double hitch on the carriage and hitch up those sorrels and take a drive through town and show them off?"

David was not thrilled at taking a drive in the carriage with Kate, but he realized that he was being at least partially pardoned, and in no position to turn down the "suggestion." By the time he had changed the hitch on the carriage so that it could be drawn by the matched set of sorrels, he had concluded that, probably within a month, the restrictions on his movements would be sufficiently relaxed so that he could start looking for Law after school and on Saturday afternoons, when he was not required to be working. He was determined to get the money he was owed. God knows, he thought, he had by now earned every halfpenny of it, and he hadn't had a halfpenny to call his own since his father had taken from him the six shillings he thought David had won in the race.

No sooner had they turned off the lane onto Lothian Road and headed toward town than Kate revealed what she had on her mind.

"Elm View is two miles out from Burchfield, between Burchfield and Murchiston."

"That's nice," David said sarcastically. "What's Elm View?"

"Elm View is the Law house," Kate said. "I asked around at school."

He took her meaning then. "And you want me to drive you there, right?"

"I want my double crown," Kate said.

David thought that over a moment.

Why not?

Elm View turned out to be an enormous house, red sandstone and brick, just barely visible from the Murchiston Road down the double row of ancient elm trees from which it had apparently drawn its name.

As they drove up to the circular pebbled drive in front of it, two footmen came half-running down the stairs to meet them.

"We're here," Kate announced, giving her arm to one of the footmen to get out of the carriage, "to see Mr. John Law."

She posed the footmen something of a problem. To their practiced eye, she wasn't what they thought of as a young lady. On the other hand, the carriage, and especially the matched sorrels, had not come from some public livery. They were beautiful, expensive, well-cared-for animals.

And the young master had some strange friends.

"I will see, miss," the elder footman said, "if the young master is at home. Would you care to wait inside?"

"Please," Kate replied. "Thank you so much."

Kate's eyes widened when they went inside the house. It wasn't as large as Holyroodhouse Palace, the only other mansion she had ever been inside, but she immediately decided it was more elegant. And this was a private house, she thought, not one owned by the king.

David, she thought, looked uncomfortable, unhappy, but determined.

They were left standing in the foyer; one of the footmen remained with them while the other announced again that he would see if the young master was at home.

John Law came down a wide flight of stairs a minute

or two later. He was wearing only an open-collared shirt, trousers, and boots, but Kate thought he was the most elegant young man she had ever seen. She felt her heart beat when he gave them first a smile of recognition, and then, she thought, a smile of approval when he saw her.

"Well, what a pleasant break in an otherwise incredibly dull afternoon."

He meant what he said. He was home and just about bored out of his mind; after a series of unfortunate wagers on one thing and another, he could not go out to Dunsapie Loch because he didn't have the cash to pay off a number of wagers.

That was obviously what these two were doing here. He owed them money and they wanted it. It was really in quite bad taste for Gardiner to show up here without an invitation, but it seemed likely that he needed the money he was owed, and had not, quite by accident, run into John Law since the race.

"Let's go to the upstairs sitting room and have a glass of wine," John said, already wondering exactly how he was going to put it to his father that he needed some money to pay a debt of honor. William Law had only recently delivered another of his speeches about absolutely refusing to give him any more money than he was already getting, and that if he insisted on gambling, he would just have to learn to gamble with what he had been given and not expect to be handed money as if his father were the chancellor of the exchequer and John the crown prince.

The redhead, John thought as he followed her up the stairs and watched the movement of her hips, was exquisite. Pity about the brother. He would have loved to give her a tumble, but David was obviously a prime example of lower-class brothers who considered it their charge from God Himself to see that their sisters went virginal to the marriage altar.

John took them into the upstairs sitting room at the head of the stairs and rang for the butler.

"Would you please bring us tea," John said when the butler appeared, "and I think some wine." He looked at David Gardiner. "Or would you prefer a beer?"

"I'd like a beer, thank you," David said.

"And a bottle of beer," John said. "And do you know where my father is?"

"In the library, sir," the butler said.

"Thank you," John said.

He waited until the tea, an ornate display of breads and cheeses and preserves laid out on silver platters, had been rolled in and until the wine had been opened, poured, and served before excusing himself.

"I won't be a moment," he said. "I have to have a word with my father."

When he was sure that John was far enough back down the stairs to be out of earshot, David Gardiner said, "He probably has to get our money from his father."

When there was no response, he looked around for his sister. Kate was halfway through a door leading out of the room.

"Where are you going?" David asked.

"I'm going to have a look around," Kate said.

"You're crazy," David said.

"I'll be back before he is. When you hear him coming up the stairs, give me a whistle."

"Kate, goddamn it . . ." David began, but she was gone. David took a swallow of his beer.

Kate found herself in a long, rather narrow corridor. She thought there were more chairs in this corridor than there were in her parents' house. One of the doors leading off it was ajar and she went to the crack and peeked through.

All she could see was a wall of books, and then she heard a voice and recognized it as John Law's.

"Might I have a word with you, Father?" he said.

It took her a moment to understand what was happening. John had indeed, as she thought, gone down the stairs to the library to see his father. But the library was two stories tall and the door she was looking through opened onto a sort of a balcony.

"I was just about to send for you," another voice, an older voice, said.

"Oh?" John asked.

"Who are those young people I saw drive up?"

"Their name is Gardiner. They're brother and sister."

"They're twins actually," John's father said.

"Oh, that's right, you know them. The girl said something about you knowing their parents."

"What are they doing here?" William Law asked.

"As a matter of fact, I suspect that David Gardiner rather hopes that I will pay him the money I owe him."

"You've been gambling with him? Good God, I despair of you."

"I raced Warrior against him," John confessed. "I should have known better than to run against the son of a horse trader, I suppose, but the fact of the matter is, I didn't, and I owe him a bit of money."

"I want you to stay away from them, John," William Law said. "And I want you to understand that this is not something I am suggesting; I mean it."

"They seem to be perfectly nice, decent, people . . ."

"They are," Captain Law said. "And I don't want to see them hurt, and simply being around you, that's liable to happen."

"I have the strangest feeling that you're quite serious," John replied.

"I am absolutely serious," William said.

"My God, Father, what are you saying? Who are they? Bastards of a prince of the blood? Of old Lauderdale himself?"

"Why did you say that?" William Law asked coldly. "About Lauderdale, I mean?"

"My God, I hit it right on the head," John said triumphantly. "Now that I think about it, I'm not surprised. The girl has the same look in her eyes. As if viewing the world from Mount Olympus."

"Shut your goddamned mouth, John!" William Law said furiously. "Don't ever again mention Lauderdale in the same breath as the name Gardiner."

"What's so special about them?" John, irrepressible, said. "There are Lauderdale bastards scattered all over Scotland . . ."

Kate had crept onto the balcony so that she could see as well as hear what was going on. She peered down to the main floor of the library in time to see William Law slap his son as hard as he was able, with the back of his hand, so hard that John fell against a library table.

"Now do I have your attention?" William Law demanded furiously.

"Yes, sir," John said. He touched his hand to his mouth and then looked at it. There was blood on it.

"How much do you owe him?" William Law asked.

"Four crowns," John said.

"Thank God, you lost," William said. He opened a drawer in the table, took out a leather bag, and spilled coins from it. He handed two of them to his son. "Pay him," he said. "And get them out of here. And then stay away from him. From them. You especially stay away from the girl."

"Shall I throw them out?" John asked. "Or have the servants do it?"

His father hit him again, and Kate saw that his face was white.

"You will treat them with perfect courtesy," William said. "And if you see them on the street, you will tip your hat to them and, if necessary, exchange a pleasant word with them. But aside from that, you will stay as far away from them as you can. If they come in someplace, you will leave. Can I make it any clearer?"

"No, sir," John Law said.

"And you will put any connection between them and the Duke of Lauderdale from your mind, do you understand?"

"Yes, sir."

"Believe me, John," his father said, "you cannot afford to have Lauderdale annoyed with you, much less angry."

"I thought he was a good friend of yours," John said very carefully.

"He is," William said. "This conversation is closed. I suggest you return to your guests."

Kate hurried back to the sitting room and was demurely sipping her tea when John came back up the stairs.

It was absolutely incredible to think that she and David were bastards, much less bastards of the Duke of

Lauderdale. But that was what John Law's father had as much as said.

It seemed even less credible, if that was possible, when they got home and she looked at her mother and father. Her mother was a young woman and the Duke of Lauderdale was an old man. Kate knew that she could never mention what she had overheard to David.

Once, a month or so later, when she heard from David that John Law had been sent to school in London, she had another thought: perhaps William Law was her father, and he had just brought the Duke of Lauderdale into it so that he wouldn't have to admit that to his son.

But then one day, she and her mother met William Law on High Street, and they stopped to chat; she watched her mother with him, looked into his eyes, and knew that he couldn't possibly be her father.

It didn't really matter, Kate finally concluded. Even if Edward Gardiner wasn't her real father, he had been her father as long as she knew, and she couldn't ask for a better one. What did matter was that John had been sent away from Edinburgh and that she would probably never see him again. Or not until he was married and she would see him from a distance, riding in a carriage with his wife and children.

That really hurt, and sometimes she dreamed about it. She thought that after a while she would get over it. Or him. But she didn't.

Chapter Four

1

August 15, 1685

The whole idea of David going off to school in London had come out of the blue about six months before. David hadn't at first known what to think, much less what to do, about it. He had been a little surprised, but not especially worried when the headmaster had called him in and told him to ask his parents when it would be convenient for the headmaster to call on them.

He hadn't been in trouble in school and couldn't imagine what the headmaster wanted with his parents. His father gave a credible explanation when he relayed the message.

"He wants money, that's what he wants. Now that you're near finished, he wants me to express my appreciation by giving the school money."

"Are you going to give him any?" David asked.

"More than I want to and less than he expects to get," Edward said.

But a contribution to St. Michael's Parish School was not what the headmaster had in mind.

"Your David, Mr. Gardiner," the headmaster said, "has an unusually fine mind. He hasn't done near what he's capable of at St. Michael's."

"I'm indeed sorry to hear that, and sorrier still," Edward had replied, "that you have to come here, Father, and bring it to my attention. But I'll tell you this: for as long as he's there, I'm sure you can look forward to an improvement."

"Oh, Mr. Gardiner, you misunderstand me," the headmaster had said. "David has done everything we've asked of him. What I'm saying is that he has the mind to do more than we were able to give him."

"Forgive me, Father," Edward said, "I don't think I quite understand you."

"What I mean to say is that, given the right kind of education, there's no end to what he could do with his life."

"Are you by chance," Edward had challenged suspiciously, "thinking of David taking Holy Orders?"

"No," the headmaster said. "Sadly I have concluded that God has not elected to call David to Holy Orders."

"Then," his father said, visibly relieved, "exactly what *is* it you're talking about?"

"I would like you to consider—just think about it, there's plenty of time to make a decision—to *consider* sending David to St. Peter's."

"I don't believe I'm familiar with St. Peter's," Edward confessed.

"It's in London," the headmaster said.

There is about as much chance of Father sending me to London to go to school, David had thought, even if I wanted to go, than there is of Kate becoming Queen of England.

"London," Edward Gardiner repeated.

"St. Peter's offers our brightest lads an education in commerce and banking, as well as in the sciences," the headmaster said. "They accept only the brightest lads. Young Law, the brewer's son, has been going there for two years now."

"Well," Edward had said levelly, "I'm pleased that you think my son is bright, and I will consider sending him to London, to St. John's—"

"St. Peter's," the headmaster corrected him.

"St. Peter's," Edward corrected himself. "So that he can study banking and, what was it you said, 'commerce,' with young John Law."

For about thirty seconds, David thought, until you're gone and out of earshot and won't be able to hear him laugh out loud.

But the headmaster had succeeded in planting the idea, and Edward Gardiner had not dismissed it out of hand. Exactly what had made him decide in favor of the idea (of which his mother had immediately approved) was beyond David, but there were several possible explanations.

The business, after they had moved to town, had been more successful than anyone had dreamed it would. In just a few years, Edward Gardiner & Son had changed from being one of many horse dealers into being the second or third in size, and possibly first in prestige, of them all. And David knew that his father relished his role as a successful businessman. Only a successful businessman would be able to afford sending a son all the way to London to study banking and commerce.

That was probably part of it, David decided; another part of it, one of the reasons his father had offered for sending him, was that as the business had grown, so had the paperwork. It had been necessary to hire a bookkeeper when the work overwhelmed Mary. There was something in Edward Gardiner's makeup that made opening his business secrets to a stranger unpalatable. David could learn to run the books and other things about business that it would be good to know.

If David had been asked, he would have preferred to be sent out to the breeding farm when he was finished with school, to be given charge of that. But he wasn't asked, and finally his father made up his mind and went to call on the headmaster to tell him he had decided David should go to London.

That seemed to settle it for a while, but a month after

that, the headmaster came to call. Somewhat embarrassed, he announced that there had been a letter from the headmaster of St. Peter's School, regretfully informing him that it had been impossible to accept David for the next year. That, David thought, would be the end of the idea.

But by then his father had decided he was going to go to London to school, and he wasn't willing to give up on the idea. There had been a line in the letter from the headmaster of St. Peter's that gave him a little hope. The letter had said that they would put David's name on a waiting list if that was his father's wish, and went on to say: "Applications accompanied by letters of recommendation from prominent persons of course receive attention."

The only prominent people Edward Gardiner knew well enough to ask for the favor of a recommendation were William Law and the Lord High Sheriff. Edward Gardiner suspected that William Law would not like the notion of David going to the same school as his son, so there was no point in asking him. But the Lord High Sheriff was a possibility. Over the years, he had always been willing to do Edward a service if he could, and he might be helpful here. Edward went to Holyroodhouse Palace and asked him.

The Lord High Sheriff was both surprised to hear what Edward wished for his son, and noncommittal about doing anything specific about a letter of recommendation. Disappointed but not really surprised, Edward was for several days convinced that he had somehow overstepped the line between a businessman and a high official of the crown. A week later, however, the Lord High Sheriff sent for him, and when he went to his Holyroodhouse Palace, showed him a copy his scribe had made of the letter he had sent to St. Peter's School in London:

Reverend Sir,
   His Grace the Duke of Lauderdale, H.M. Lord High Commissioner for Scotland, has commanded me to inform you that he would be pleased if you were to act favorably upon the application by

Edward Gardiner, Esq., of Edinburgh for the en-
rollment of his son, David, at your school.

James Foster
H.M. Lord High Sheriff for Scotland

The letter from the headmaster of St. Peter's School,
announcing that room had been found for David for the
next class, had come within the month. Edward Gardiner
thought that it had been a very nice thing indeed for
Foster to use the duke's name that way. The duke more
than likely wouldn't remember David at all.

When it came close to the time he was actually to
leave, David carefully brought up the question of taking
Wanderer with him to London, riding him there instead
of going to London by boat. He didn't really need a horse
in London, he knew, but he didn't like the thought of
leaving Wanderer behind.

His father surprised him by readily agreeing not only
to his taking Wanderer with him to London, but also,
when David pressed his luck and asked, to his taking a
string of buy-trade-sell animals with him as well.

David had not even been sure about being allowed to
take Wanderer, and if he was a betting man—which, he
thought, indeed he was—he would have offered odds that
his father would have decided it would be best if the
other animals remained in Scotland, to be sold or traded
by Edward Gardiner & Son, Purveyors of Fine Horses.

There *had* been a speech, less a speech than he expected,
but a speech: Wanderer, Edward Gardiner told his
eighteen-year-old son, had been a gift and was his to do
with what he willed. And, his father had admitted, the
seven other animals were *morally,* as opposed to *legally,*
David's as well. Under the law, his father had told him,
until David reached his majority, he couldn't legally own
any property, whether horses or the shoes on his feet.
Everything he thought he owned was legally his father's
property.

"Now, I'm not that kind of a father, and you know I'm
not," Edward had told him. "But you're going off alone,
and going far, and when you don't know what you're
about, you had damned better understand the law.

Whether or not it makes any sense, the law is the law, and the law is that you're a minor and can't own property on your own."

"Yes, sir," David had said. He had long ago learned not to argue with his father.

"So what I'm telling you, David," his father said, "is that if you start your horse trading, you're going to run into lads such as yourself, who believe that the animals they have are theirs to do with what they will. And you're going to run into the *fathers* of those lads, who, if you make the usual sharp bargain with them that you seem to do so often, are going to run the nearest sheriff or bailiff or constable and remind *him* of the law: that since boys can't own property, they can't barter or sell it, and that any deal you have made isn't any good."

"Yes, sir," David said again.

"Now, what I think you should do," the old man's speech had continued, "is get rid of every animal but Wanderer. Sell them, not trade them, just as soon as you can get a fair price. You're soon going to find out what feeding them is going to cost you in London. I'm sending you to London to St. Peter's, not to trade horses. I expect you to devote your time to your studies, not to thinking about trading horses."

"Yes, sir," David said.

"Now, I don't want to sound a braggart," his father had told him. "But God's truth is that we're not simply horse traders anymore. Not that there's a thing wrong with horse trading; it fed your mother and me when you were wee, but we made more money lately buying and selling grain, and tack, and wagons and coaches than we made from selling horses. And you're going to have to know about business when the time comes for you to take over."

"Yes, sir," David had replied.

"I know what you're thinking, David," his father had said. "That picking up some quick money talking somebody into or out of an animal is a lot better than planning a business. But just because you've had good luck so far doesn't mean it will go on forever."

David had no reply.

"Or betting on them," his father had said. "Don't think I haven't known about that."

When he'd raced Wanderer against John Law's black stallion on the shore of Dunsapie Loch two years before and his father had told him that he didn't want him going back to the races at the loch, David had said he wouldn't go back—and he had not gone back. But there were other places around Edinburgh where people raced horses, and he had not felt honor-bound to avoid them.

"I've only wagered when I was sure," David had replied. "If you're sure, it's not really a wager."

"You can never be sure," his father had said. "But I don't think you're going to believe that until you lose badly."

"It's been my money I've put up," David had replied, not defiantly. "And I have more now than when I started."

"I'm not going to be a hypocrite and tell you that wagering your pocket money is a sin that'll see you burn in hell. There are worse ways a young man can spend his time than with horses. But what I am telling you is that when you take over the firm, you'll be responsible for your sister, your mother, and for the people we hire. You get into the habit now of wagering a lot, you'll keep the habit."

David had bit off the reply he was about to make.

His father had noticed. "Say it," he had said.

"I'm so far ahead. And when you yourself trade for a horse, what is that but a gamble?"

The reference had been really to David's success with his buy-trade-sell string of horses, and the money they represented. Several weeks after he had gone to Elm View and collected his double crown from John Law, he had been at the Craigmillar Fair with his father. His father had been offered, and rejected, a horse because he thought the animal's bloated belly meant he was blown. David had gathered his courage and argued with his father, announcing the only thing wrong with the animal was that it had eaten wet oats and was gassy.

"You're not putting up your money, so it's easy for you to say that."

"If I had the money, I'd buy him," David had argued.

"But you don't have the money, so all you're doing is talking."

"Loan me the price, and I'll pay it back," David had said.

"How?"

"I'll work for somebody on Saturday afternoons and Sundays after church."

"When the animal dies, you'll pay this back working for me on Saturday afternoons. No son of mine will work for another, or on Sunday."

He had given David the two pounds he needed to buy the horse.

The horse, after first blowing up so bad his father thought they might have to pierce his stomach with a hollow tube, finally started passing an incredible amount of wind and within a week was as sound as he could be.

Two weeks later, David had traded him to an innkeeper for a mare in foal and twelve shillings. He reduced his debt to his father by one pound on that transaction. Six weeks after the mare had dropped her foal, he traded both for a yearling and a pound to boot.

There followed a number of transactions, some taking place in the same week, some taking place three months after the previous trading. In two years, after scrupulously paying his father for all the feed and the other costs of maintaining the animals, David owned, in addition to Wanderer (who as a stallion had earned him a total of three crowns covering other people's mares), another stallion, untried, two mares, a gelding, and had nineteen pounds four shillings and sixpence in his leather pouch.

He had been worried at first that his father would order him to stop his horse trading, especially after he had, six months into his trading career, traded a sound mare for a gelding and two pounds. The gelding had almost immediately come down with paralyzed hindquarters, from thread worms, and had to be destroyed.

His father had even been something like sympathetic, rather than scornful. "You just paid for an expensive lesson," he had said. "Thinking you were a better judge of an animal's physical condition than you are. But if you learned the lesson, it was worth twice what you lost."

It was from his father that David learned, several months after the racing incident, that William Law had sent John to London, to St. Peter's School. He had never spoken to David again after the day they'd gone to his house, although David had seen him a half dozen times on the street. David realized he was being snubbed, and since he thought his hands had been clean in their relationship, was angered. He had told his father truthfully that he didn't much care what happened to John Law.

In addition to permission to take his buy-sell-trade animals with him to London, Edward Gardiner gave his son something else, something David didn't expect, and with an admonition for the sake of God not to tell his mother.

"You never need one of these," David's father had said, pushing an object wrapped in an oily cloth across the table to him, "until you need one badly."

Inside the cloth was a pistol, from MacWheeler & Shaw, Gunsmiths, Tailor's Row, Edinburgh.

David had looked at his father in surprise.

"You can threaten a man with a sword or a knife," his father had said. "But you should never raise this to a man unless you plan to shoot him, and you should never plan to shoot somebody unless you are prepared to kill him."

When David set out from Edinburgh to London, the pistol was in a saddlebag, out of sight, but available should he need it. There were footpads and robbers about, although not nearly as many as David's mother felt there were. The sight of a young man, even one as large as David was, traveling alone and leading four horses behind a fine-looking stallion might be a temptation to them.

David rode slowly from Edinburgh, through Midlothian and Peebles counties to Tweedsmuir. In the Traveller's Rest in Tweedsmuir, he sold the untried stallion and one of the mares to a traveling jewelsmith, taking gold coin instead of the jewels he was offered, and assured it was a bargain he would regret for the rest of his life not having taken.

The next day, he got only as far as Moffat, for it rained all day; the rainwater mixed with the clay in the soil of the road and made it slick, and the going was slow. The rain stopped during the night, but the road didn't really dry until late the next afternoon, by which time he was in Ecclefechan, near the border.

He put up overnight there, rather than trying to make the border by nightfall, and left a call for first light, so that he could make up the time the rain had cost him.

He crossed the border near Gretna Green, and by noon had passed the ruins of the old Roman wall and started to ride down the last slope of the Cheviot Hills toward Carlisle.

There was little traffic on the road. Often, for hours, he saw no one. And then he became aware that a lone horseman, on a high-stepping mare, was behind him, gaining slowly and steadily on him. When he grew closer, David saw that he was a gentleman, with a large feather rising high from the crown of a wide-brimmed hat. As he got even closer, David saw that he had long, carefully combed hair and a full mustache with waxed tips.

Finally the mustachioed dandy on the high-stepping mare passed him.

When he drew abreast, he rose in his stirrups, swept his hat from his head, and made David a low, mocking bow.

David nodded, not knowing what to do about the mocking bow. It was only after he was out of sight that David could identify him. The mustache had thrown him off.

The mustachioed dandy was John Law. Remembering that John Law was at St. Peter's, it seemed now not surprising that they should meet on the road, since they were both bound for London to do the same thing. David had thought of looking up John Law once he got to London. Now, he would not have to waste that time. It was perfectly clear from John Law's attitude that he wanted nothing to do with David Gardiner.

2

Rochdale, England
August 28, 1685

Thirteen days after John Law had passed David Gardiner on the road, David reached a road sign that announced that London was three miles, or no more than an hour away.

The sign did not please him. As eager as he was to get to London, to have the long trip done with, the closer he got to London the less chance there would be of finding a good place to leave his animals.

David knew full well how much livery owners charged— what, in fact, Edward Gardiner & Son charged—to stable an animal in Edinburgh, and obviously the prices in London would be at least as much. Even if he had good luck in buying and selling animals, the price of boarding them in London would wipe out any profit he could reasonably expect to make.

What he needed was a farmer willing to board the animals at a decent price, on a farm as close as possible to London, so that he get to it whenever he had a day or a weekend free. He had been looking for such a place since he'd started out this morning. He needed a place no more than three hours away from London, and better less far than that, a place where it looked safe to leave the animals. He hadn't found what he wanted and had been growing more than a little concerned.

The sign announcing the distance to London seemed to make it official that he wasn't going to find what he needed.

But then, a hundred yards past the sign, down a lane between stone fences, he saw a collection of outbuildings and a farmhouse that made him think his luck had changed. From the highway, it looked well-tended, and he thought he might have found, just after giving up hope, what he was looking for: a clean and decent place where he could board his animals, and at a reasonable price. In any event, it was worth a look.

He nudged Wanderer with his knee and the stallion turned into the lane between the stone fences.

The closer he got to the buildings, the more he liked what he saw. The fences were in good repair. David believed what his father believed: that you can tell what kind of a farmer a man is by his fences. And the whole farm gave the impression of being well-looked-after. Most of the farms he had passed had been untidy and dirty. England was apparently no different from Scotland: Clean, decent, well-kept farms weren't common in Scotland, either.

He saw, and was pleased to see, that the horse barn was unusually large. That meant there was a good chance the farmer would have room to accommodate seven extra horses.

The farmer himself, when he appeared, was a tall, muscular man of forty or so, and was as clean and tidy as his farm.

David took off his hat and nodded at the man.

"Good day to you, sir," he said.

"Maybe I can save your time by telling you I'm not in the market for any animals," the farmer said.

"Well, that's a pity," David said. "For I'm always willing to sell, if the right price is offered. But that's not why I'm here."

"Then you're buying? You're bound for London, and if I'm willing to practically give them to you, you'd be willing to take some of my animals off my hands."

"If you were willing to practically give them to me," David said, smiling, "I would take some animals off your hands. But I don't think you're the kind of man who gives things away."

The farmer laughed.

"Then what is it you're after?" he asked.

"I'm looking for a place to board these animals."

"That you've found," the man said.

"Presuming the price is right," David said.

"Naturally," the man said. He laid his hand on the stallion's neck.

"I could offer you a fair price for this one," he said.

"Naturally," David said. "That's the only one not for sale."

They laughed together and the farmer put out his hand.

"My name's Thomas Ward," he said.

"Gardiner," David said. "David Gardiner."

"You're a Scot?" Ward asked.

"You can tell because you think I talk funny?" David asked.

"I didn't say that," Ward said.

"That's how we can tell when a man's an Englishman," David said. "At home, I mean."

Ward smiled at David and then walked down the line of horses, examining them quickly and expertly. "You've got some nice animals."

"For which I'd be happy to take a fair price," David said.

"What's a Scotsman doing so far from home?" Ward asked. "If you don't mind my asking?"

"I'm being sent to school in London," David said. "To St. Peter's."

"We're an hour from London," Ward said.

"I saw the sign."

"And you deal in horses and go to school, is that what you're telling me?"

"That's it."

"For how long were you planning to board the animals?"

"Until they can be sold," David replied.

"You're a bit young for that sort of thing, aren't you?"

"My father's a horse dealer," David said, as if that explained everything.

"Maybe we can work something out," Ward said after a moment. "Would like to see the barns and stables?"

The farmer called for his wife, and she appeared: a plump, clean, but unsmiling woman.

"I'll be at the barn," Ward said. "If the kettle's not on, would you put it on?"

Ward's wife said nothing, just stared suspiciously at David.

"My name is David Gardiner."

"Are you buying or trying to sell?" Ward's wife asked.

"Boarding," David said.

The woman snorted and walked back in the house.

"I am, mistress, grateful for your hospitality," David called after her.

"She'll do that way," Thomas Ward said to David. "But I'll be surprised if there's not tea and something to eat on the table when we come in."

David smiled his understanding. Ward gestured for him to walk to the barns.

David looked through the horse barn for five minutes, Ward trailing along after him.

"And do you find my barn satisfactory?" he finally asked.

"I find it clean and well-cared-for," David said.

"You've been around horse barns before," Ward said to him.

"I told you," David said. "My father raises horses."

"You did say that," Ward said. "But I can't help but ask myself, What is a Scottish horse farmer doing outside London with a string of horses?"

"I told you that, too. I'm being sent to school."

"You're near a man," Ward said bluntly. "Too old to be a schoolboy and too young to have a string of animals like that."

He hadn't been called a liar, but the next thing to it. David controlled his temper by reminding himself that his father, under similar circumstances, would have behaved in very much the same way.

Ward saw the anger and softened the question: "If I'm to keep these horses," he said reasonably, "I have the right to know if they're yours."

"We haven't come to a price yet," David said.

"We will. You know what it's worth to board a horse and look after him well, and so do I. I'm neither dishonest nor greedy. My price'll be a fair one. *If* I'm satisfied about you. I'm not accusing you of anything, but I think you'll have to admit yourself that you look somewhat young to have this many animals, and to have them so far from where you say is home."

"I've got bills of sale for these animals," David said.

"I'll have a look at them, then, if you don't mind," Thomas Ward said.

David took the bills of sale from Wanderer's saddlebag and handed them over.

After Ward had carefully examined them, and was satisfied, he looked at David and asked, "You didn't take offense?"

"My father would have done the same," David said. "In Scotland, they as often hang the man in possession of stolen animals as they do the man who stole them."

Thomas Ward nodded and then quoted his price to board the animals. It was less than David had been willing to pay, and he accepted immediately.

"You know as well as I do," Ward said, "when you have a number of animals, adding a few more doesn't cost so much."

Then he motioned for David to go to the farmhouse.

David decided that he had found a good place for his horses. He liked Ward.

"We've struck a deal," Ward said to his wife after he'd led David into the house. "Mr. Gardiner will be leaving his animals with us."

"He doubtless paid in advance," Mistress Ward replied.

"No," her husband replied. "I was about to tell him I expect to get paid by the week."

"In advance," Mistress Ward said.

A startlingly pretty girl appeared in the room.

"I wondered where you were," Ward said to the girl.

"I'll tell you where she was," Mrs. Ward said. "She was sneaking around the horse barn, listening to you, that's where she was."

"I was not," the girl protested, but her flushing face gave her away.

"Anyway, Mr. Gardiner," Thomas Ward said, "this is my daughter . . ."

His daughter, red with anger and humiliation, fled into the kitchen.

Ward laughed and then corrected himself, "What you *saw* was my daughter, running away."

"She's just a girl," Mistress Ward said pointedly.

"They're about the same age, I'd guess," Thomas Ward argued.

"She's just a girl," his wife insisted.

"Sally!" her father called.

There was no answer.

"Sally!" he called again.

Still no answer.

"Leave her be," Mistress Ward said.

David sensed that she didn't like him, and he wondered why.

"Damned if I will," Thomas Ward said. "Sally, dammit, come in here!"

Reluctantly, the girl came into the room.

"This is Mr. Gardiner," Thomas Ward said. "He'll be boarding some horses with us."

Sally made sort of a curtsy, but refused to look him in the eye.

"Hello," David said.

"Usually," her father said, "she's eager to meet young men."

Sally fled again.

"What did I say?" Ward asked.

"You never know," David Gardiner said to her father, man to man. "I have a twin sister, and I never know why she does what she does."

"You shouldn't have said that about her being eager to meet young men," Mistress Ward said. "You embarrassed her."

"How?"

"Thom, she's just a girl," Mistress Ward said. "And you embarrassed her in front of him."

The way she pronunced "him" confirmed to David that he had somehow gotten on the wrong side of Mistress Ward. He took some satisfaction in remembering that his mother sometimes acted the witch when some of his friends talked to Kate, or for that matter just looked at her.

There was one way, he thought, that he could please her. He took out his purse and insisted, over Thomas Ward's objections, on paying two weeks' board for the animals in advance. But even that didn't seem to please

Mistress Ward, only reluctantly satisfy her that he hadn't come to swindle her husband.

"You'll have a bite to eat before you go," Mistress Ward said. It sounded more like a royal command than an invitation.

"Thank you, ma'am," he said.

"It's in the kitchen," she said.

The "bite" turned out to be a huge, farmer's midday meal. And the startlingly pretty girl, whose name he remembered as Sally, sat down at the table with them, which at first pleased David. But the pleasure soon dissipated. The girl's reaction to him was not hostility, but something more painful. She ignored him.

After they had eaten, Thomas Ward told him that Sally had been taught to play the lute and ordered his uncomfortable daughter to fetch the instrument.

David was pleased. Now he had an excuse, when she was playing, to look at her. She was uncommonly comely, he thought, and had a sweet personality to boot. But her father interfered with that, too. She had only played two tunes when he took the instrument from her hands and began to play it himself. He was, David quickly heard, a really skilled player, but he would have much preferred to have Sally play, so that he could look at her.

"I'd better see about putting the animals in the fields, or wherever you want them," David said after half an hour or so. "And be on my way."

Thomas Ward got to his feet and handed the lute to Sally.

"If they've been on the road that long," he said, "they'll appreciate a stall in the barn. I'll show you."

As they finished backing the animals into stalls and filling buckets with oats, Thomas Ward had a thought. "Where will you be in London?" he asked. "In case I have to get in touch with you?"

"I don't know. But as soon as I get a room, I'll give you the address. Or send it out."

"If you don't have a place to stay," Thomas Ward said, "you'd better spend the night and ride in first thing in the morning. It'll be dark and you don't want to be alone in London without a place to stay after dark."

"That's more than decent of you," David said.

"Not at all," Ward said. "I'm doing it to annoy the wife."

"How so?"

"She seems to have gotten the idea that you've got eyes for Sally."

"I don't think so," David said.

"You don't know her," Thomas Ward said.

"My father told me one time that the best way to keep sons from chasing after girls was to give them sisters," David said.

"And you've got a twin sister? Is that what you're saying?" Ward said, laughing.

"Yes, sir," David said.

Now why did I say that? The truth is that I think Sally Ward is the best-looking girl I've seen in a very long time.

Chapter Five

1

When Sally Ward woke early she immediately climbed out of her bed and pulled her nightdress over her head. She was long-legged and slender and fair-skinned, and she thought the only thing wrong with her body was her breasts. At first she had worried that she would never grow any at all; then when they had started to grow, she was afraid they would never grow large enough; and now, at seventeen, she was afraid they would never stop growing.

Young men, and men not so young, when they thought she wouldn't notice (and sometimes without caring about that) stared at them. She had heard that was supposed to be flattering, but it made her uncomfortable.

She went to the windows and opened the wooden blinds wide enough to let light into the room, then went to her wash table and dipped a cloth into first the water, then the soap she had helped her mother make special for them. They had used less lye than normal, and picked over the ashes to be mixed with the lard to get rid of every last unburned chip, and then had let the mixture "mild" longer in the root cellar before adding to it the final, special ingredient: rose petals crushed in a pestle. Sally made suds with the washcloth and soap and then sniffed them for the rose smell before she began to wash herself.

When she was finished, she took a fresh-washed cloth six inches wide and eight feet long and wrapped it around her chest and back, tucking the end in, binding her breasts. She was going to see their young guest, David Gardiner, today and she was willing to put up with the constriction and the chafing of the band if that's what it took to keep him from staring at her the way the bulls stared at the cows across the fence.

Sally put on a blouse and a skirt, and sandals, wrapping the thongs around her ankles. Then she went back to the windows and opened the blinds wide, so that she would have light to brush and braid her hair.

Sally had come to understand several things about life generally and young men in particular. She was a farmer's daughter, and she had known since she was five or six about animals, she-animals and he-animals and what they did together that resulted in colts and calves, puppies and lambs, and for that matter even chicks and ducklings. She had understood about the way God had arranged for living creatures to reproduce long before she really understood that in God's great scheme, things weren't really much different for men and women.

Or for boys and girls, as her mother had made clear to her, when Sally was about twelve, in a long, rambling, and somewhat bitter speech on the occasion of her first menses.

Men, her mother had told her, were no better than bulls or stallions. They had one thing on their minds, and as a bull would batter down the strongest fence to get at the cows, as a stallion would leap a tall fence to get at the mares, so would the human male do whatever was necessary to get at, and satisfy his animal urges with, a human female.

It was both woman's duty to God, Sally's mother told her, and in her own self-interest, to deny them the satisfaction of their sinful lusts. In marriage, it was somewhat, but not much, different; but marriage was a long time away for Sally, and bridges need not be crossed until one came to them.

At the time, Sally's reaction had been mingled surprise and disgust. She had seen the mares whinny in pain when the stallions covered them, and she had no intention whatever of having something as disgusting as that happen to her. She was surprised that her mother thought it necessary to warn her.

As she grew a little older, however, she was surprised to find that it was rather pleasant to have young men look at her, at her body, and obviously find it satisfactory and worthy of their approval. She knew, too, that she was judging young men, finding one more attractive than another. That was obviously the devil at work, as her mother had warned her he would be, putting temptation in her path.

Not, of course, that she would have been willing to let any of the young men of her acquaintance do to her what the stallions did to the mares. She wasn't even sure she would permit one of them to do that to her after she was married. It was just that there was something *interesting* in having young men prance about her, flaring their nostrils, so to speak, and sometimes actually digging their toes in the dirt, the way stallions pawed the ground.

When she was about fifteen, Sally had also come to understand that the interest in her being displayed by some young men was not only because she had a rather comely face and a firm young body. There was a practical aspect involved. God had seen fit to reward her mother (or was it punish?) with only one successful pregnancy. She had been with child four times, but the only child to live more than several days was Sally herself.

What that meant was that her father's farm would one day pass to her. Or, more specifically, to the man she was married to. When young men (or for that matter, the parents of young men) looked at her, they were seeing not only a comely seventeen-year-old, with healthy teeth and a body that suggested it would bear healthy young with no trouble, but also the farm and the farm animals and the farm buildings.

If a marriage could be arranged, the successful suitor could at first expect a substantial dowry, and ultimately, possession of the farm itself. It was, she thought, as if she were being forced to buy a husband. There was something about that she didn't like, even after she looked around and found that was the way things were done.

Her parents, Sally had come to understand, were interested in a husband for her as much for what he would do for them as he would for her. They naturally had their old age to think about. Since there were no sons who could be expected to take care of them, they had to look for a son-in-law who could and would.

That complicated the rules of husband selection somewhat. It practically eliminated poor boys with families. A poor boy with a family would naturally feel it was his right to support *his* family with the farm he had inherited through his wife. Women had no rights in property; property was held by their fathers and husbands, and sometimes their brothers.

The ideal situation, so far as Sally's parents were concerned, was for her both to marry young and to marry a second or a third son of a prosperous farmer, who would have no responsibility to his parents and no rights to his parent's farm. He would move in with the Wards, and Sally would bear him a son; the son would grow to maturity, and the farm would be turned over to him. He would have an obligation to take care of his parents and his grandparents, and everything would be taken care of.

It had never entered Sally's mind, except as a fantasy, that she might marry someone who was not a farmer, someone who lived in the city, someone of higher social position. She had never had, for one thing, the occasion to be around young men who were not farmers.

She had seen what she thought of as as elegant young gentlemen, like David Gardiner, either riding past the farm or sometimes buying horses from her father; and though she had found several of them very interesting, she was very much aware that elegant young gentlemen did not marry simple farmer's daughters. But it was possible, easy, and a bit exciting to dream of what it would be like to be Mistress Somebody, a fine lady with a house in town, and servants, and fancy clothes, and a carriage with a coachman and matched grays—a fine lady who did not have to bake bread or wash clothes or, when one of the hired men was down with a chill, be expected herself to take a shovel to the manure in the stables.

It would be nice, Sally thought, if someday, some fine and elegant young gentleman would see her, be stricken by her, find out who she was, and come calling at the farm to get to know her, and then to ask her father for her hand.

But what was *going* to happen, she knew, was that she would continue to be examined by young farmers in just about exactly the same way as they would examine sows and mares and heifers. And eventually, one of them would speak for her, and if he met her father's approval, she would be married off to him. Exactly, she thought, as a mare was turned loose in a field with a stallion.

2

Sally came into the horse barn that morning a few minutes after David himself had first gone there.

Her hair, he saw, had been neatly braided, and the braids pinned to her skull over her ears. He had a sister, and he knew how long braiding hair took, which meant that she had been up for some time. Last night her hair had not been braided.

And last night, he thought, her breasts had been far more evident under her blouse than they were this morning. She had obviously bound them. That act puzzled him and aroused his curiosity. But he had never been quite able to bring himself to ask Kate why she sometimes did it, whether to give the teats support or because of some notion of modesty or fashion. He had personally found Sally's chest far more interesting last night than it was now.

"Good morning," Sally said.

"Good morning," he said, getting to his feet. He had

been kneeling on the earthen floor of the horse barn, repacking his bags, Wanderer peering curiously out of his stall.

"What are you doing?" Sally asked.

"Packing my things," he said, gesturing to the cases.

She seemed, he thought, much more in control of herself this morning than she had yesterday.

"Can I help?" she asked.

"Not unless you want to carry all that to London for me," David said.

"I'll have to ask my Dad," Sally said.

He looked at her in confusion, not at first understanding her reply. He had been making a joke and she had taken what he said seriously. And then he understood. She saw the problem—that there was no way he could load Wanderer down with two fairly large cases and ride him to London—and thought of the solution—riding into London with him, so that she could bring a pack animal back to the farm before he had.

"I wasn't really asking that," David said. "What I was thinking was that I'd have to keep the pack animal, that sorrel, with me in London until I could arrange to bring her back here. But since you brought it up, do you think your father would let you ride in with me?"

"We can ask," she said. He nodded, and she went on. "My father sent me to fetch you for breakfast."

To David's surprise, Thomas Ward readily agreed to having Sally ride into London with David.

"I wasn't thinking about your things," he said. "But that makes it an even better idea. What I was thinking, when I woke up, is that I know a good, clean, cheap tavern where you could stay for a day or two, until you find something permanent, and that I'd have Sally ride with you to show you where it is and have a word with the tavern keeper."

"You could as easy draw him a map and send a note along with him," Mistress Ward protested.

"But then he'd have to board the pack animal until he could come back out here," Ward explained.

"That would be his problem, wouldn't it?" Mistress Ward said.

"The girl will go with him," Ward said firmly. "If they leave here within a half-hour, she can be back by midafternoon."

"Unless she's set upon by bandits," Mistress Ward said.

"Or stolen by gypsies," David offered. "That's what always worries my mother about my sister."

"I didn't think," Mistress Ward said, "David Gardiner, that you'd dare mock me under my own roof."

Then she did something that surprised David. She smiled at him.

3

They left the Ward farm just after seven, Sally riding astride a small but well-set-up piebald, David on Wanderer leading the sorrel mare laden with his cases. It was quarter to eleven, and they were riding down a wide, well-traveled, muddy road through a wooded area when Sally Ward reined in her piebald mare within sight of a palace.

David, who had fallen slightly behind, rode up beside her.

"What's going on?" he asked.

"We're now in London," Sally said. "Father said I was to point out landmarks to you so that you could find your way back."

"And that's a landmark?" David asked, nodding toward the palace.

"That's Buckingham Palace," Sally said. "Formerly Buckingham House." She pointed straight ahead. "The Thames River is that way," she said, and then pointed to the left. "When you come back, you'll be coming from there. And you know where we came from. Can you remember this, do you think?"

David looked around, turning in his saddle, to lock the crossroads in his mind.

"Yes," he said, and then went on to ask, "Is that where the Duke of Buckingham lives?" He turned again in his saddle to take a better look at the palace. He was a little disappointed. There were finer buildings in Edinburgh.

The palace where he'd met the Lord High Commissioner for Scotland was far more imposing.

"That's what the king bought for the queen. My father told my mother he heard at the fair that the king paid Buckingham twenty-one thousand pounds for it."

"Twenty-one thousand pounds?" David asked, demanding confirmation.

"My father said, 'I guess if you want to get a woman out of the house, money is no object.'"

David laughed and looked at Sally. Their eyes met and, for a moment, locked; and then, her face reddening, Sally averted her eyes.

"The Duke's Arms," she said, "where we're going, is down this way."

She touched her heels to the piebald and headed toward the Thames.

4

John Law came down the stairs from the second floor of the Duke's Arms, entered the public room, and walked up to the bar. At twenty-one years of age, Law was tall and thin, with a large narrow nose and dark eyes set in deep sockets. The result, a young woman of his acquaintance had once told him, was that he was "hawklike." He had not been offended. Law believed that there was something not unappealing about his looks, and that he would far rather look like a hawk than, say, a robin. Or a cow. There was something to be said for looking like a bull, but most people who resembled the bovine family, he thought, resembled cows, not bulls. They looked plump and placid.

In the opinion of John Law, who as someone about to commence his third and final year at St. Peter's School in London quite naturally thought of himself as a gentleman of some experience, wisdom, and culture, the Duke's Arms left a very great deal to be desired.

In point of fact, the sole redeeming grace of the Duke's Arms was that he could, in his current unfortunate financial condition, afford it.

The man at the Bank of London, his father's correspondent, had been very polite and very firm. He was empowered to pay John his allowance on the first of every month, and looked forward to doing so. But since this was not yet the first of the month, he obviously could not pay the allowance. Neither could he make John a loan. Captain William Law's instructions on the subject of loans were quite specific: there were to be none.

John had arrived in London three days before, happily anticipating a trip to the bank to get some money. His purse, which had held nearly fifteen pounds when he'd ridden out of Edinburgh, now held one shilling more than one pound.

Some of the money had gone for his traveling expenses, and eight pounds had been stolen from his wallet by a rather plump blonde who had shared his bed in one of the villages along the highway with a willingness he now recognized was primarily based on her belief that as soon as she got him to sleep, she could help herself to the contents of his wallet.

He had not discovered the theft until the next evening, when he opened his wallet to pay for a room in the next village. By then, of course, it had been too late to do anything about it. Even if he spent the next day riding back to the village, she would have been gone and he would have found himself explaining to a disapproving village constable that he had been robbed by a whore whose name he could not remember.

He had not been left entirely without funds. He had his emergency money, two pounds, in the tip of his boot, and that had been enough to get him to London with a shilling more than a pound. He had been rather smug about that, in the naive belief that once he explained the loss of his money (the buxom whore became a man wearing a naval uniform who shared his room in the story he told the banker), the banker would immediately advance him the funds he needed to get an apartment.

The only thing the banker gave him was advice and a credit recommendation: the King's Arms offered clean accommodation at reasonable rates, and under the circumstances, he was prepared to inform the tavern keeper that John was going to come into money as of the

first of the month. The credit had been forthcoming, once
John agreed not to take his horse from the Duke's Arms'
stable until his account was settled.

If he had come to London by ship, of course none of this
would have happened. And he would have come by sea if
it were not for a small flaw in what otherwise he thought
had proved to be a splendid physical makeup. To his shock
and chagrin, it had turned out that he was unusually
vulnerable to *mal de mer*, as the French put it. When he
had arrived in Edinburgh the past July, aboard the *Prince
Charles*, after a nine-day voyage from London, he had
taken a solemn vow that he would never again set foot
on anything that was floating in a body of water larger
than Dunsapie Loch.

He had been wrong in believing that a larger ship (the
Prince Charles was enormous, carrying more than one
hundred passengers) would be less vulnerable to the movement of the sea than smaller ones. The reverse had
proved to be the case. He had been sicker aboard the
Prince Charles than he had been on his three other
voyages on smaller ships between Edinburgh and London.
On the *Prince Charles* he had fallen to *mal de mer* within
three hundred yards of land in the Thames estuary, and
he had been sick until ten minutes after being helped
ashore in Edinburgh.

That left him two options vis-à-vis returning to London.
He could go by stagecoach or he could ride alone. The
prospect of approximately two weeks in the confines of a
lurching coach in the company of six or eight complete
strangers had been nearly as horrifying to him as the
thought of going aboard another ship. He had sent his
luggage by ship and set off alone on horseback.

The proprietor of the Duke's Arms saw the young man
looking down his nose at his bar and display of goods and
glowered at him.

"What can I get you?" he asked.

"I suppose a beer," Law said. "If you please."

The tavern keeper went to a barrel and pumped a
mugful of beer and set it before John. Then he turned
and took a piece of slate from under the bar, his account
of John's indebtedness, and marked the beer down on it.

John Law raised the mug to his lips and took a swallow. He grimaced when he tasted it. Someone had apparently used spoiled hops.

The tavern keeper glanced at him at that moment, as he returned the slate to its place.

"Something wrong with the beer?"

"I think there was something wrong with the hops," John Law announced professionally, trying to be both helpful and polite.

"You're a brewmaster, no doubt?" the innkeeper said.

"I know something about brewing, yes," John replied.

"And ye don't approve of that?"

"As a matter of fact, no," John said.

The innkeeper went to him, picked up his mug, drained it without taking it from his lips, wiped his lips, and belched with evident pleasure.

"You're right," he said sarcastically. "It's undrinkable. What'll you have instead? Water or whiskey?"

"Whiskey, please," John said. He congratulated himself for controlling what could have been an unpleasant scene.

The tavern keeper put an inch and a half of whiskey in a cup and set it before John. Then he took out the slate again and recorded the sale.

The whiskey was as raw as the beer had been bitter.

John Law reminded himself that he had come into the public room to eat, not to drink, and also that there was nothing whatever he could do until the first of the month, two days hence, when he would get his money, settle his slate, claim his horse from the stable, and ride, forever, away from the Duke's Arms.

"I think," he said to the tavern keeper, "that I would like something to eat."

"Go sit over there," the tavern keeper said, pointing to a table against the rear wall, "and I'll have the missus fetch it to you."

"Thank you so kindly," John said, and bowed to him.

The tavern keeper cleared his throat and spat on the floor.

The beef and kidney pie served five minutes later was cold and tough. Law was convinced the innkeeper had served it cold on purpose. He probably didn't know how bad it tasted. But there was, of course, nothing he could do about that either. It was either eat the coagulated greasy mess or go hungry.

In two days, my period of purgatory will be over.

He had taken two spoonsful of the pie when he saw David Gardiner come into the public room of the Duke's Arms. With him was a surprisingly attractive blond girl. The tavern keeper smiled broadly at them, an act of which John would not have believed him capable, and then called for his wife.

The wife came from the kitchen and kissed the girl, and the tavern keeper then drew a mug of the bitter beer and handed it to David Gardiner.

David Gardiner hadn't yet seen John Law, and Law was relieved. He wanted neither Gardiner's company nor for Gardiner to see him here, at all, and particularly in the present embarrassing circumstances.

It had nothing to do with his father's having told John to stay away from the Gardiner twins. That prohibition, like other parental prohibitions, had been left behind in Edinburgh.

It was, John thought, an extraordinary coincidence, an unfortunate one, that he would run into Gardiner again, after having seen him on the road less than two weeks ago. He wondered what Gardiner was doing in London.

When he had seen Gardiner on the road, he had at first thought that he would perhaps have the chance of meeting someone like himself, a gentleman, with whom he could share the trip.

What he'd gotten instead, of course, was Gardiner. First he'd recognized the horse as Wanderer, the horse who'd taken Warrior on the shores of Dunsapie Loch. Then he recognized the animal's rider, and the hope that perhaps Gardiner had sold the animal (which was really much too good an animal for him) died. And so had the idea that he had found a traveling companion.

He had not spoken to Gardiner as he rode past, and had then believed that would be the last he would see of him. Gardiner was already much farther from home than Law had expected to see him.

Both horse and owner had matured, John judged, the horse for the better. That had triggered a line of thoughts about the red headed twin sister. If her brother had turned more or less into a man since he'd last seen him, it would naturally follow that the girl, who his father had clearly implied was the bastard of the Duke of Lauderdale, had matured, too. She had been exquisite at sixteen or so. What was she like now?

It was, of course, possible, he thought, that she had gone the other way, that her youthful beauty had already started to degenerate into lower-class coarseness, as often happened. The way her brother had been sitting on his fine horse, as if the magnificent stallion were hauling a manure wagon, that was a distinct possibility. The brother, Law thought, was absolutely devoid of class. He had brought what inarguably was an elegant horse down to his own plodding, cowlike level.

It was also possible that the exquisite redheaded girl had been married, and was a mother. Or twice a mother. Those sort of people married off their daughters early, and once married, they bred like rabbits. It would be a pity if that were the case with the girl. He had thought of her often—for unknown reasons, probably, he had finally concluded—because he had been denied a shot at lifting her skirts by his father. His father had been dead serious about the risks of somehow annoying the Lord High Commissioner for Scotland through association with the Gardiner twins.

He had never spoken to either of them again, after the day they had come to Elm View to collect the wager. He had seen the boy, David, several times, but had been able to avoid having to talk to him, and he thought he had seen the girl, Kate, several times, riding in a carriage with her mother.

That was understandable. With the exception of the Sunday afternoons at Dunsapie Loch and the streets of downtown Edinburgh (and of course, a lower-class tavern like the Duke's Arms), their paths would never cross. Not even at horse sales. The Law family bred their own animals, both draft horses to pull the beer wagons, and saddle and carriage animals for their own farm. When they had animals to sell, they sold them to their friends, and when they, rarely, bought animals, they bought them the same way. They did not deal with horse traders, so there had been no chance to see any of them that way. And socially, of course, they would never have met anywhere.

Probably, he thought, if he had stayed in Edinburgh, he would have run into them somewhere, sometime. But he had been sent off to London. He still wasn't quite sure why. It could have been for the *official* reason—that is, the one announced to the family at dinner. The official reason was that he was being sent to St. Peter's so that he would be better equipped to run the business when the time came for him to do that. The way his father had put it was that he was being sent to London to school so that he would be better able to meet his obligations to the family, to the family business, and to their loyal army of employees. *Noblesse oblige*, so to speak.

His mother might have accepted that, but his sisters certainly had not. There was no question in their minds that he was being sent off to school to get him away from undesirable companions. That was a legitimate possibility, but then, if that was true, there was a question of the identity of the "undesirable companions." Were they the people with whom he gambled and drank, or were the "undesirable companions" David and Kate Gardiner, because of their somewhat mysterious, even intriguing relationship with the Duke of Lauderdale?

Whatever the reasons, he had been sent to St. Peter's. And in the long run, it had turned out all right. Because it was such a sacrifice, to be away from the family and the brewery, and because his father had somehow acquired the notion that student life at St. Peter's was monastic (a misimpression John was careful not to correct), his father had seen fit to ease his pain with a reasonable allowance.

He had recently begun to have doubts about that, too. He had begun more and more to appreciate his father's subtlety. It had occurred to him that it was quite possible that his father knew all about his life in London, which was not at all monastic, or ever scholarly, and that the allowance was intended to make him content in London, so that he would not try to come home. That opened, again, the question of why his father wanted him away from home.

It had gone no further than idle curiosity. Being away at school had a number of positive advantages. In the two years he had been at St. Peter's John Law had learned a great deal, much of it having very little indeed to do with the operation of a brewery. The truth of the matter was that he was really going to hate to finish St. Peter's, which he would at the end of this year, and have to return, for the rest of his life, to Edinburgh.

Immediate upon entering the public room of the Duke's Arms, David Gardiner proved the validity of John Law's judgment of him as someone utterly devoid of good taste: the first thing he did was take the mug of the execrable ale the tavern keeper offered him, gulp it down in two drafts with obvious relish, belch loudly and with even more evident pleasure than the innkeeper, and then immediately hold up the mug in request for another.

And then the innkeeper pointed in John Law's direction.

I should have known that I would not escape meeting him. Everything else has gone wrong. Why should this be different?

David smiled broadly and happily and walked across the room to John's table.

"Hello," he said. "I'm glad to see you again."

"I can't imagine why," John said.

The smile on David's face weakened, but did not go away.

"First, I thought you'd have another of whatever you're drinking on me," he said.

"Thank you, no," John said. "If you wish to please me, go away."

The smile now vanished. "I don't see how I can," David said reasonably.

"My dear chap, all you have to do is turn around and walk in the direction whence you, uninvited, came."

"Our innkeeper tells me that we're to share a bed," David said.

"Never," John said.

"But that's what he said," David said, with the clear implication that that was the end of the discussion.

At that point, John remembered the first run-in he had had with the tavern keeper: "I can give you a bed," the innkeeper had said, after he had read the note from the man at the Bank of London.

John Law had not completely understood what the innkeeper was saying.

"Splendid!" John had said. "I much prefer a bed."

The innkeeper had shown him to a small, dark cubicle with one window opening upon the stable yard, and then told John Law that if it was necessary to put someone in the bed with him, as well it might be, he would be charged slightly less. The first disagreement they had had was over that. Law did not wish to share his bed with a complete stranger, and the innkeeper would just have to put anyone who came after him in with someone else. He was not interested in a reduced price.

"I'm an innkeeper," the man had replied. "If there's room, I makes it available. Money ain't the only thing."

"And what will you take to have me in here alone?" John had asked.

"I told you, it's not the money, it's the way I do things here," the innkeeper had said. "You're free to leave if you like."

There was nothing, of course, that he could do about it. The Duke's Arms had been reluctant to offer him credit, even with the Bank of London as a reference. It was unlikely that another tavern would do the same.

And now the person he was expected to share his bed with was David Gardiner, who would obviously figure things out immediately and relish the thought of seeing him existing on credit.

"What will it take to have you go away?" John asked.

"I'm not in the habit of sleeping with strangers, either," David said, his face fixed, his voice level. "But these people are doing me a favor—"

"A favor?" John sarcastically interrupted him.

"And I don't intend to hurt their feelings," David said with finality. "They're putting me in with you, so that's the way it's going to have to be."

John looked past David to the bar, where the innkeeper, a pleased look on his face at the discomfiture he had caused Law, his arms crossed on his chest, was watching the exchange.

The bastard, John thought, would like nothing better than to throw me out of here.

He looked up at David with as contemptuous a look as he could muster.

"I may have to share my bed with you in this hovel," Law said, "but otherwise, please spare me the displeasure of your company."

David turned red in the face, and for a moment John thought that he might have gone too far and that the horse dealer's son was going to have the effrontery to take offense, perhaps even assault him.

But all he said was "Right," and turned on his heel and walked back toward the innkeeper at the bar.

5

"Right," David said, his face red. There was a terrible temptation to spill the contents of his beer mug into John's lap, but, with an effort, David contained it. The tavern keeper was a friend of the Wards', and he didn't want to embarrass them, or Sally, by getting into a fight ten minutes after he had walked into the tavern.

"You know him?" Sally asked.

"He's from Edinburgh," David said. "But he's not what you could call a friend."

"What he needs," the tavern keeper said, "is a boot up his ass."

"William!" the wife said. "Not in front of Sally."

"Sally's heard that word before," the tavern keeper said.

"Can we get something to eat?" David asked, to change the subject. "Sally's got to get started back."

"We'll put some beef and kidney pie back in the stove," the wife said, "while William helps you with your things."

Ten minutes later, having taken his cases to the room, David came back into the public room and saw that Sally was now sitting at the table where John Law had been and that plates had been laid out for both of them.

He wondered, idly, momentarily, where John had gone, and then he sat down beside Sally and picked up a spoon.

Thirty minutes after that, he was astonished at how sorry he was to see Sally ride off on the piebald. There was something strange about that girl. She made him feel comfortable, like he felt with his sister, and excited, like when he happened to accidentally get a look down a girl's dress.

He would, he decided, get back out to the Ward farm just as soon as he got things in order around here.

The tavern keeper and his wife had the vaguest information about St. Peter's School, only a notion that it was somewhere in the neighborhood of the Inns of Court. They drew a map for him, and he got on Wanderer and went looking for it. He found it, not without difficulty, but when he finally got to it, the only information he got was that the headmaster would probably be free the next morning.

It was three o'clock in the afternoon. He thought that by then Sally should be back at the farm. He started back for the Duke's Arms and then changed his mind. There was nothing there but a public room, and a room in which John Law had made it clear he was anything but welcome.

He decided to explore the city and rode around for two hours, getting himself hopelessly lost. But he was amused by that, rather than frightened or even annoyed, and he rode around for another hour before finally asking for directions.

It was dark when he finally got back to the Duke's Arms and got Wanderer unsaddled, rubbed down, fed, and into his stall. Then he went into the public room, where he took a small table by the door to the kitchen and ordered his supper. It was a plate of boiled beef and cabbage, satisfyingly hot and much tastier than the beef and kidney pie had been. When he finished the first plate, he ordered another, and another mug of ale.

Two workingmen, carpenters or joiners, to judge by their scarred hands and the smell of fresh-cut wood they carried with them, came in and had their mugs of beer. Then they took out a deck of playing cards and began to play slamm. David watched them play and was not surprised when, after a while, they asked if he wanted to join them. Slamm was a simple version of whist, a game played often at fairs and trading days, and he had been playing it since he was a small child.

When he received a friendly smile from first one of the men and then the other, he knew that he was about to receive an invitation to play, and that shortly after he accepted, there would follow a compliment on how well he played the game, and shortly after that a friendly suggestion that they make the game a little more interesting by making small wagers.

David's expertise in the game was not limited to a rather comprehensive understanding of its rules and the strategy of play. He had learned that from Terry, the blacksmith, who had been with his father since before he was born. He had also learned that there were people here and there who found it interesting and profitable to entice people who looked innocent or stupid, or both, to play, and to play for money. And he had also learned that if these people really believed you were stupid and innocent, it wasn't really hard to separate them from their money, rather than the other way around.

If you have half the brains you were born with, David told himself, you will ignore that game. You will ignore those people. You will do what is smart, namely, have another mug of ale and then go upstairs and go to bed.

"That's whist, isn't it?" David asked, the next time one of the village men looked his way and smiled.

"Nah," the village man said. "This is slamm. Ain't nearly so hard as whist. Come over and watch, if you're of a mind, and we'll show you."

Old Terry's voice seemed to be in his ear as he moved to the next table: "The secret, Davy boy, is to keep them thinking that what you have is dumb luck. When you keep winning, you got to look as really surprised as they are. And don't be greedy!"

He had become aware, as the rules of slamm were explained to him and as they began to play, that across the room John Law had come into the public room. He was sitting at a table with some relatively well-dressed men, probably local merchants, and they were talking, not playing at cards. He knew that Law had seen him, but there wasn't even a nod of recognition.

Ten or fifteen minutes later David became aware that John Law and the men he was sitting with were involved in a loud discussion on the merits of Scotland having its own parliament, rather than sending its own representatives to the House of Commons in London. John, not unexpectedly, was rather passionately taking the side of an independent Scottish parliament. The volume of their voices had grown so that much of the discussion was clearly audible through the public room of the Duke's Arms.

And five minutes after he first became aware of the argument, David was not really surprised when the loud voices turned into shouts, nor even when the table was knocked over and he saw John Law preparing to defend his position with his fists. He thought that a well-delivered punch to Law's rather prominent nose would probably do wonders to teach him a little humility.

But it instantly turned from a heated argument in which there was the danger of blows being struck between two adversaries into something much more ugly. FIrst of all, David was more than a little surprised to see, John Law knew how to use his fists. He skillfully ducked the powerful punches thrown at him, and using his left hand with precision, he managed to land two punches to his opponent's face.

Someone almost as skilled as David's father had obviously taught John how to box. But he had taught John to be a puncher, to deliver a few hard punches. Edward Gardiner had taught his son a different style of fighting. He believed that it was better to land a half-dozen relatively light punches on your opponent's face than it was to wait for an opportunity to land a heavy blow. Heavy blows had a way of missing and leaving the man who threw them exposed to a counterpunch. Still, David thought, John was doing much better than he would have thought.

David was a little surprised the fight had not been stopped by the friends of the man Law had now punched three times, and so hard that the man's nose and mouth were bleeding. He probably had some loose teeth, too, David thought.

But what happened was nasty. The friends, instead of trying to reason with the man taking the beating, or even to grab him and hold him so that he couldn't continue a fight he was losing, grabbed John Law's arms and held him while the third man punched him hard, three times, twice in the face and once, very hard, in the stomach.

That was unfair, David decided, but then again, John had more than likely said something really arrogant, something insulting in both content and tone of voice, that had angered all of them; probably he had deserved what he got. Lying on the filthy floor of the public room of a dirty country inn with his breath, and probably his supper, knocked out of him would provide the lesson in humility.

But when they let loose of his arms and John Law, grabbing his stomach, fell to the floor, they didn't stop there. They started to kick him.

"That's enough!" David called out, without thinking.

He spoke loud enough to get their attention. They all looked at him, ignored him, and then resumed kicking the helpless, agonized John Law.

"Enough, by God!" David said, getting to his feet.

"Mind your business, lad, or we'll give you some of the same."

David rushed across the room and grabbed the nearest of the three men. Before the man grasped what was happening to him, David had twisted his arm up and behind his back.

"Tell your friends to stop," David said in a harsh whisper, "or I'll pull your arm out of your shoulder!"

He pushed up on the man's arm hard and far enough to cause him genuine pain, but not hard enough to do any damage.

The man yelped. His friends looked at him, and at David.

"That's enough," David said, "unless you want me to pull his shoulder joint!"

121

They stepped away from the man on the floor.

"Let him go," one of them said.

David let the man go after a moment, and then started to squat over the curled-up body of John Law on the floor. As he dropped to his knees, John coughed and then threw up. David hastily started to come out of his squat. He sensed, rather than saw, the chair that one of the men, holding it in both hands, had tried to hit him with. He dropped to one side, and the chair smashed into the overturned table and shattered.

Without thinking what he was doing, David punched the man who had tried to hit him with the chair, sending him flying backward. Then he balled his fists and prepared to defend himself. The three men formed a half-circle and started to stalk him. David backed away, toward the door to the kitchen, wondering why the innkeeper didn't come to his aid.

And then John staggered to his feet.

Before David could open his mouth to scream a protest, Law had unsheathed his sword, and for a terrible moment David thought he was going to run the sword through the back of the man nearest him. The blade flashed as John jabbed with it. But it was a short jab, not a lethal thrust, and it was directed not at the man's back, but at his buttocks.

The man screamed and clapped his hands to his rear end. His face turned white when he felt the blood, and his eyes widened when he brought one of his hands, sticky with blood, and then the other before his face for confirmation.

"All right, you bastards!" John said angrily.

The other two turned from David to look at him and the blood on the hands of the third man. Now they began to retreat, with Law stalking them, David thought, as a cat stalks a mouse. Law forced them into a corner.

They were all white-faced now, and terrified, and begging for their lives.

David somehow understood that murder or even serious bodily harm was not on John's mind. There was something in his face, a faint smile, that told him Law was more amused than angry.

When he got the three men into a corner, John put the tip of his sword between the abdomen and the leather suspenders of the largest of them and sliced the suspenders in half, one at a time. As the man's trousers began to fall, the fop raised the tip of the sword to the man's throat and kept him from trying to catch them from falling.

The largest man wore no underclothes. The under-trousers of the second man were ragged and tattered, and the underclothes of the third man, whom Law had pinked in the buttocks were startlingly red with blood.

"Now get out of here, you bastards," John ordered, indicating the front door with his sword. They began to move slowly, then broke into a run. Then John turned to David and bowed just as mockingly as he had bowed to him on the road.

"One would have thought," he said wickedly, "that one so large would have been better equipped, wouldn't one?"

David smiled. With his trousers down at his ankles, the large man's "equipment" had been in sight. David had noticed in surprise at how small it was.

"Obviously," John went on, "there is something to the old wives' tale that a man's equipment reflects the size of his brain and not his brawn." He waited to see David's reaction to this, and then when he saw the smile, went on, "With all due modesty, I have found that to be true in my case."

"I was afraid you were going to kill him," David said.

"Oh, no," John said, mockingly solemn. "Someone told me there is a law against that."

David guffawed.

"I now stand in your debt, Gardiner," John said. "Perhaps you would be good enough to join me in a glass of whiskey?"

David was on the edge of telling him what he could do with his glass of whiskey, but John was grinning infectiously and David was unable to resist returning the smile.

John put his arm around David's shoulders and led him to a table beside the overturned table.

He snapped his fingers. "Innkeeper, bring whiskey and glasses."

The tavern keeper looked dubious. David nodded and smiled at him, and the tavern keeper brought a gray clay bottle, two pewter mugs, and a pewter water pitcher to the table.

"Well, Gardiner," John said, now bubbling with camaraderie, "what brings you to London?"

"I'm here for the same reason you are," David said. "To go to school."

"Is that so?" John asked, wondering how David had come to know that he was in school. "Where?"

"St. Peter's," David said.

Wait till Captain William Law hears about that, John Law thought, and then: Oh, my God, he's going to be an embarrassment, if he announces, as he's damned likely to, that we're "old friends from back home."

"Are you really?" John said.

"When I saw you," David said, "I thought maybe you'd sort of show me around."

"Delighted," John said, forcing a smile.

Twenty minutes later, as he was painting a picture of life at St. Peter's designed to point out the vast chasm between first- and third-year men, and how one was expected to associate with one's classmates, three uniformed men marched officiously into the public room of the Duke's Arms.

The smallest, fattest and oldest of the three had corporal's stripes on the sleeve of his coat, a saber hung from a strap over his shoulder, and the royal coat of arms, in the form of a large brass pin, on both his coat and his hat. The other two men carried six-foot-long pikes, with a strange-looking blade at their tips.

"I'm the corporal of the watch," the corporal announced officiously. "What's been going on here?"

The innkeeper, to David's relief, gave a dispassionate and factual account of what had happened. David was painted as a peacemaker who had stopped the three local men from doing serious harm to John Law. The three local men were described as drunk and looking for trouble, who fought unfairly. John Law, the innkeeper said, could have easily killed all three of them if he had been of a mind.

David thought that would be the end of it, but the corporal took his sworn duty to uphold the peace, as spelled out in the King's Ordinances, quite seriously. As he saw the situation, there had been a brawl in a public place; there had been damage to property (the smashed chair); there had been bodily injury (to John Law, when the men had kicked him on the ground, and to the "rear end of Tom Hainey"); and, most importantly, a deadly weapon had been in play.

"Now, don't be an ass, Howard," the tavern keeper said. "I told you if this one had wanted to hurt them, he had his chance."

"When I am about the king's business, I'll thank you to call me 'corporal' and to treat my office with due respect," the corporal said.

The matter clearly required the decision of a senior officer of the watch, the corporal then announced, and until that happened, John Law would be placed in custody.

"You'll give me your deadly weapon, please, sir," the corporal said to John Law, "and please come with me."

"You're going to arrest me?" John asked, in surprise.

"Not arrest, sir," the corporal said, "that's for the officer to decide. Detain is what I'm going to do to you."

"And if I don't decide to go along with you?" John asked angrily.

"Then that would be resisting a lawful officer of the crown, sir, and I would have to use what force would be necessary."

"Go with him, John," David said, laying a restraining hand on Law's arm.

Law looked at him for a good thirty seconds before he made up his mind. There was something in Gardiner's eyes and the tone of his voice that made him consider that he was in deeper trouble than he at first thought he was.

"It's something to talk about when we're old and gray," John said. "How on the eve of your education, when I was supposed, as a final-termer, to set you on the right path, I was hauled off to jail."

He stood up and handed his sword with a sweeping, mocking bow to the corporal.

"My deadly weapon, sir," he said, and then went to the two watchmen with the pikes and held out his wrists. "Chain me!" he said.

No one in the room but David saw the humor.

6

David half-expected that John Law would be turned loose sometime during the night, and when he didn't return to the Duke's Arms, he became concerned about him. Telling himself that Law's problems were of his own making didn't seem to do any good. He was also forced to remind himself that John had gone off to jail peacefully at his urging. He had been, in a sense, a Judas sheep.

David woke very early and went down to the public room. The breakfast offered him by the toothless crone in the kitchen was what was left from the beef and kidney pie he had had for the previous day's midday meal. David Gardiner, who had been raised on his father's farm and was not about to eat something like that for breakfast, went into the kitchen and bribed the crone to boil him four eggs.

While he was eating them, the tavern keeper, yawning and breaking wind, came into the kitchen.

"You're up early," he said to David.

"I'm worried about my friend," David said.

"Your *friend*?"

"My mother knows his family," David said. "What's going to happen to him?"

"Well, in about an hour, they'll send the wagon round and haul him off to Broadmoor Prison."

"He hasn't been tried yet!" David protested. "Or for that matter, charged with anything."

"I guess the officer of the watch asked for a cash bond," the tavern keeper, obviously speaking with the expertise of someone who had dealt with the watch often, said. "Unless they can post a cash bond, they hold them at Broadmoor. Until they decide what to do with them."

"Well, why didn't he post it?"

" 'Cause he don't have no money, is why," the tavern keeper said. "He's living here on the slate until the first of the month. The bank says he's got money due him then."

"Well, I can't see him going to jail for what happened," David said, as much to himself as the tavern keeper. "What do you think the bond would be?"

"A lot. Five pounds. Maybe more. That would depend on the watch officer, probably."

David thought that lending John ten pounds to keep him out of jail would be the neighborly, the *gentlemanly,* thing to do. He realized, smiling to himself, that he had a somewhat less noble motive. It would be amusing to see the arrogant Mr. John Law in a jail cell.

David took a half-dozen hard-cooked eggs and a half loaf of bread and set off in search of the jail. It turned out to be two rooms with their windows bricked shut (except for two openings, each the size of one brick) in the rear of one of a row of brick houses three blocks from the Duke's Arms.

The watch on duty said that the officer was asleep, but that he would let David into John Law's cell and then go fetch the officer. He told David that Law was in one cell, the others from the brawl in the other.

John was sitting on the stone floor, resting his back against the wall. He smiled with pleasure when he saw David. "You've arranged to have me freed!" he said.

The watch corrected that misimpression by slamming the door behind David and then locking it.

"I brought you some breakfast," David said. "He went to get the officer."

John immediately took one of the boiled eggs and started to crack it. "I am starved," he said. "I haven't had anything at all to eat since noon yesterday."

"You didn't miss much at the Duke's Arms," David told him. "Breakfast was yesterday's lunch, served cold."

"Good God, that's what I mean. It was terrible at lunch, and absolutely inedible last night," John said, delicately breaking off a piece of the bread and putting it in his mouth.

David, who had been served boiled beef for the evening meal, didn't argue the point.

"I wonder when they're going to turn me loose?" John wondered aloud.

"When you post the cash bond."

"What cash bond?" John asked, apparently genuinely mystified.

"The cash bond you have to post to keep from going to Broadmoor prison," David said.

"You're serious, aren't you?" John asked after a moment. "Didn't they tell you last night?"

Law shook his head, no. "To tell you the truth, I had a few words with the officious little bastard who was in charge last night."

"You don't fight with the watch," David said. "What's the matter with you?"

"How much of a cash bond?" John asked, ignoring David's remark.

"Somewhere from five to fifteen pounds, I understand," David said. He saw John's face fall.

"Say, listen, Gardiner," John said, "I would normally be far more reluctant to ask this, but since we're going to be seeing a lot of each other in the future . . ."

"We are?" David asked innocently.

"I mean, we'll both be at St. Peter's."

"From what you said last night, we'll hardly see each other at all."

"Not in school," John qualified. "But after school. On weekends. On holy days. Dinner, that sort of thing."

On the very same day, David thought, that pigs will fly.

"I came here to loan you your cash bond, Law," David said. "You can stop trying to charm me."

Chapter Six

1

William Law was in the north settling room of the brewery when the messenger came to him. There were eight huge vats in the north settling room. Nearly identical, they were made of oak, banded with iron, and each of them had a capacity of just over 2,100 gallons of brew. William Law had come to "North" at the request of the brewmaster, and he had just confirmed the brewmaster's judgment that six of the eight vats required immediate replacement. Not repair, not overhaul—replacement. They were old, nearly half a century old, and they were just worn out. Rotten.

For a number of reasons, replacing the vats, especially all at once, was going to be very expensive. The brewery had its own coopermaster, and he had a staff of four. If it had been possible to replace the vats one at a time, the brewery could have put on some extra hands to work the oak under the coopermaster's skilled eye, taking one vat, and only 2,100 gallons of settling capacity, out of production at one time. Over a year or so, the vats could have been replaced, one at a time, without causing a major disruption in the flow of product.

129

But that wasn't going to be possible. These vats were going to have to be taken out of service as they were emptied, which meant at the rate of at least two, and more likely three, a month. There was no way the coopermaster and his staff were going to be able to keep up with their regular work and build new vats at the same time.

That meant they were going to have to just forget maintenance of the ten-, twenty-, and eighty-gallon beer and ale kegs used for retail trade, so that the coopermaster could get right on the new settling vats. And that meant he was going to have to go outside the company and buy God alone knew how many kegs of doubtful quality at God alone knew what outrageous price.

And since he would have both the old kegs, which, though they required a cooper's attention, were too good to discard, and the new kegs he would have to buy, that raised the question of storage. You just couldn't stack the damned things somewhere. They had to be washed and then filled with water; otherwise the oak would dry and shrink and the kegs would be useless. Where the hell was he going to find room to store two or three thousand kegs?

"Excuse me, Mr. Law," a man from the office said to him. He hadn't noticed him coming up, and he was startled.

"Yes? What is it?" William Law snapped, more curtly than he intended.

"There's an officer here to see you, sir," the man from the office said.

"I've no time," William Law said. "Tell him I'll be in the office later."

"He insists on seeing you, sir," the man from the office said. "He's from the Borderers."

The Borderers, correctly the King's Own Scottish Borderers, was the main body of troops assigned to reinforce the authority of the Lord High Commissioner for Scotland. William Law had once been Captain William Law of the King's Own Scottish Borderers. It was his regiment, and he never forgot—and neither had the half-dozen colonels who had succeeded to the command of the regiment since he had left it.

He was routinely invited to major social functions of the regiment, it being understood that he would most often send his regrets and invariably, with his compliments, a case of brandy for the officer's mess, a twenty-gallon keg of Old Pale Ale to the sergeant's mess, and an eighty-gallon keg of beer to the other ranks' mess.

William Law was sorely tempted now to run the officer off, to have the man in the office ask him the date of the upcoming affair, and inform him that Captain Law would be pleased, since the press of other business precluded his accepting the invitation, if the colonel commanding would accept a small token of his unfailing devotion to the regiment along with his regrets.

But he could not. The officer had been sent to see him, and it would be difficult for him to have to return and report that he had been unable to get to see Captain Law.

"All right," Law said. "Send him over here."

The officer who appeared in the north settling room five minutes later was a tall blond young man of, William Law judged, about twenty or twenty-one. He carried his polished helmet in the crook of his left arm, and he had his right hand on the hilt of his sword. His black leather boots, a flap of which rose above his knees, glistened. His white trousers and his blue tunic were well-tailored. He was freshly shaven. William Law, late captain of the Borderers, approved of the subaltern's military bearing. And the thought ran through his mind again, as it often did, that perhaps what he should have done for John was purchase a commission for him in the Borderers.

William Law had become a man in the Borderers, and it was likely that the Borderers would have turned John into a man, too. The difference, of course, was that he had been in the Borderers during wartime. His time had been occupied with warfare. In peacetime—and say what you would about his methods, John Maitland, Duke of Lauderdale, had brought peace to Scotland—there was little for a young officer of the Borderers, particularly one with a little money, to do but get in trouble.

The subaltern saluted Law, and this, too, pleased him. The Borderers saluted only soldiers, not civilians. But here, so far as they were concerned, once a Borderer always a Borderer.

"Good afternoon," William Law said.

Subaltern Frazier stood to attention as he spat out with military precision his message: "Sir, Subaltern Frazier presents to Captain Law the compliments of his Grace the Lord High Commissioner for Scotland, sir!"

Maitland, Christ, now what?

"Thank you, mister," William Law said. "Will you be kind enough to pass on to his Grace my own compliments?"

"Sir," Subaltern Frazier went on as if he had not heard Law, "his Grace commands me to inform Captain Law that his Grace would be pleased to receive Captain Law at five this afternoon at Holyroodhouse Palace, sir."

"Please inform his Grace," William Law replied, "that I would be honored to attend his Grace at his convenience."

"Sir, thank you very much, sir," Subaltern Frazier said, and saluted. "By your leave, sir," he said, and then without waiting for a reply, did a perfect about-face and marched stiffly out of the north settling room.

Law was at first annoyed that he would have to give up whatever else he had planned for the rest of the afternoon, so that he could go home and change into clothing suitable for the occasion and have himself driven to Holyroodhouse Palace. And then, when he asked himself, "What suitable clothing," he realized he had other cause for concern: the command had not included an invitation to dine. That left the question whether to wear dinner clothing or simply formal clothing.

If it had been Maitland's intention simply to see him, Law decided, he would have been invited to dinner. Over the years, he had dined a dozen or more times a year with Maitland, sometimes alone, sometimes as one guest among fifty or a hundred others. And he had had the Lord High Commissioner to Elm View four or more times a year and had ritually issued invitations to dinners he knew Maitland would decline.

When they had campaigned together, Captain William Law had seen enough of Maitland's capriciousness, and knew enough about his power, to stay as far away from him as he reasonably could. Those close to the duke could profit from Maitland's reflected power, and unless they were both careful and lucky, incur his displeasure. Law had left the Borderers—which was to say, John Maitland's intimate immediate circle—very much aware that he had been extraordinarily lucky to have been so close to the fire so long without having been burned, and he had very carefully put as much distance as he felt he safely could between himself and the duke over the years.

He had, he thought, succeeded. Around Edinburgh, he was known as someone who had been at Maitland's side during the rebellion and who enjoyed the Lord High Commissioner's favor. That had been valuable. And he had, he thought, developed a relationship with Maitland himself that was as safe as he could make it. He saw the duke only rarely, and under conditions unlikely to trigger the duke's temper and his sometimes incredibly vicious vindictiveness.

Perhaps, he thought, before he turned his mind back to the problem of the damned rotten settling vats, the period of peace was about to end. Either he had done something (he couldn't imagine what) that annoyed Maitland, or, more likely, Maitland wanted something from him.

He would not know until he faced the duke, and there was no sense tormenting himself about it.

2

Subaltern Frazier, who had delivered the command to attend the duke, was waiting at the main guard post to Holyroodhouse Palace when William Law's carriage drove up to it. Law had decided at the end that it would be best not to presume an invitation to dinner and had put on a formal suit, without decorations or sword. The duke, he remembered, was prone to fury when he thought that someone was presuming on his good nature by, for example, thinking he had asked them to table when all he wanted was a brief word with them.

He had guessed wrong. The first thing Subaltern Frazier said to him after Law's footman had helped him from the carriage was,

"Sir, I believe it is his Grace's intention that you take supper with him."

"I shall offer his Grace my apologies for my dress," Law said.

Goddammit, everything has gone wrong today! What next?

Frazier led him through the palace, which was an office building as well as the Lord High Commissioner's official residence, to the duke's private apartments on the third floor.

The duke was with the Lord High Sheriff, and the two old men had obviously been at the bottle.

"Good Christ, Willy," the duke bellowed, "it's good to see your ugly face!"

"Good afternoon, your Grace," William Law said, bowing formally. "I very much appreciate the honor of attending you."

The duke was often informal with his underlings, which was to say every living soul in Scotland, but it was an awesome mistake to believe he was encouraging reciprocal informality.

"How are you, Law?" the Lord High Sheriff said.

"Very well, milord, thank you," William Law replied, bowing to him. "Might I inquire into the state of your Lordship's health?"

"Old, Law, old," the Lord High Sheriff said. He got to his feet.

"Get Captain Law something to drink, Frazier," the duke said. "Then put the Lord Sheriff into his carriage and come back here."

Subaltern Frazier picked up a clay gallon jug of whiskey and filled a glass half full and handed it to Law. The common clay jug was out of place in the elegantly furnished apartment.

"Did you know, Willy," the duke asked, "that the worst thing you can do to whiskey is decant it like wine?"

"No, my lord, I had not," William Law said.

"It's the truth," the duke said. "The man who made that for me told it to me as the gospel."

"That's very interesting, milord," William Law said.

At least, he seems to be in a pleasant drunken state. He easily could have been in an unpleasant one. Pray God his mood doesn't change as he gets drunker, which, certainly, he shall.

"To your Grace's very good health," William Law said, and raised his glass.

"When you're my age, Willy," the duke said, "you are never in very good health. You are either sick ... or sicker."

"I'm sorry to hear that you're not feeling well, milord."

"I haven't felt well in ten years," the duke said. "I am beginning to suspect that the dominies are right about the wages of sin."

The duke went to the clay gallon jug and picked it up, as if to refill his glass. But then he gestured toward the door with it.

"What did you think of him?" he asked.

"The Lord High Sheriff, milord?" William Law asked, confused.

"*No*, Willy," the duke said impatiently. "Frazier."

"He seems to be a fine young officer," Law said.

"Bring back memories, did he? I remember you, Willy, as a subaltern."

"Yes, milord, he did."

"God forgive me," the duke said. "I miss those times. I sometimes wish I'd fallen then. That would have better than this, dying an inch at a time. You ever miss those times, Willy?"

"Yes, milord," William Law replied truthfully. "Sometimes I do."

"I often think that I would have rather spent my life as a soldier," the duke said. "Do you ever think something like that, that you would have rather been a soldier?"

"Sometimes, milord," William Law said. Then he added, "Often, to tell the truth."

It's probably going to be all right. All he wants to do is

tell war stories. That's behind the summons, and nothing else. I have been foolish again.

"You don't know who he is, do you?" the duke asked, and then answered his own question: "Of course not, how could you?"

"I don't follow you, milord," William Law said.

"You remember Davies, don't you? Davies of Icomkill?" the duke asked, looking at him intently.

"Yes, milord, I do," Law said. "That was a long time ago."

"I hung him," the duke said. "As a traitor."

"I remember, milord," Law said, and he did in fact remember. They had hung Lord Davies of Icomkill from a balustrade of Icomkill Castle. He had died cursing them all, vowing they would burn for eternity in hell fire. William Law took another deep swallow of his whiskey.

"This is very nice, your Grace," Law said, about the whiskey.

"A little fellow makes it. I don't suppose he makes two hundred gallons a year, but what he does make is good. If you're hinting you'd like a bottle, forget it."

"I had no such thoughts, milord," Law said. "I offered only an observation."

"We never caught Lady Davies," the duke said. "The king wanted her beheaded. She was more traitor than her husband."

"I remember, milord," William Law said.

"She had been a Frazier," the duke said. "Did you know that?"

Jesus Christ!

"No, milord," William Law replied, keeping his voice level. "As a matter of fact, I did not."

"I really hated to hang Davies," the duke said. "Some of those bastards, I enjoyed hanging. But Davies was a man, Willy, a soldier. He didn't know what the hell he was about. He gave his word, to lay down his life, if that's what it was going to take. And when it came down to that, he didn't beg for his life."

"I remember the day, milord," William Law said softly.

There was a knock at the door, and Subaltern Frazier

returned. He appeared hesitant a moment and then took up a position at the door, his hands folded on the small of his back.

"Were you aware, lad, that Captain Law here served with your regiment?" the duke asked him.

Frazier came to attention before replying, "Yes, your Grace. I knew that."

"As improbable as it may look now, lad, the two old men before you once wore helmets and rode out and killed people for God and country. And we were pretty goddamned good at it, too, weren't we, Willy?"

"I like to think so, milord," William Law said.

"You're goddamned right we were," the duke said. "We killed all the enemy, and raped all his women, and burned what was left. Isn't that so?"

The turn the conversation was taking was beginning to alarm William Law.

"For God and country," the duke went on bitterly. "And that's what young Frazier's dreaming about. Going off someplace to kill people and rape their women, isn't that right, Frazier?"

Subaltern Frazier was distinctly uncomfortable. Law was afraid for him.

When he didn't reply, the duke snapped, "I'm talking to you, Mister Frazier."

"I hope to loyally serve the king wherever sent, your Grace," Frazier finally said.

"And to kill his enemies, right?"

"If that is necessary, your Grace," Frazier said.

"And rape the enemy's women?" the duke pursued.

Subaltern Frazier was white in the face.

"And rape his women, I asked?" the duke said rather nastily.

"I would hope that I would never do that, your Grace," Frazier said finally.

"Never? You don't like women?"

"Rape is a sin, your Grace," Frazier said.

Law sipped his whiskey, waiting for the duke's response to that.

"You know why he says that, Willy?" the duke asked him.

"Perhaps, your Grace," Law said carefully, "because that is what he has been taught."

"*No*," the duke said, impatient with Law's answer. "For two reasons. First, he's never had the blood of battle surge through him. When that madness is on a man, Jesus Christ Himself would throw the nearest available woman on her back."

He paused for breath and looked between Law and Frazier.

"And there is another reason," the duke said, and laughed nastily in his throat. "And that is because he doesn't have to rape any woman. They take one look at that firm young body and that elegant uniform, and they're on their backs with their legs spread before he can unfasten his breeches. Isn't that right, Frazier?"

Frazier looked uncomfortable.

"That, milord," Law said, "I confess, is one of the reasons I often remember my service with a sense of loss."

"You're goddamned right it is," the duke said. "Tell me, Frazier," he challenged. "If I didn't have you here, wouldn't you be trying to get under some female's skirts this very minute?"

"Yes, your Grace," Frazier said, because he understood that was the response the Lord High Commissioner for Scotland wanted. "I believe that I would."

"You're goddamned right," the duke said. "Goddamned right. So go to it, Frazier. Go out and have youself a woman. And enjoy it. Where you're going, they're fat and covered with lice, and three months after you pleasure your first one of them, you'll have the French pox."

Frazier looked both confused and frightened.

William Law decided to take the chance. "You heard his Grace, Mr. Frazier," he said. "You are dismissed."

Frazier, a look of enormous relief on his face, snapped to attention. "By your Grace's leave?" he asked.

"Get the hell out of here and have your fun," the duke said. "On your way, tell somebody to bring Captain Law and me our goddamned supper."

3

The Duke of Lauderdale, juice from the rare rib of beef dripping down his chin, lifted his eyes to William Law.

"He's being seconded to the minister for war, going to Hanover as aide to Neville," the duke said. "To keep an eye on George Louis."

"I don't think I understand, milord," William Law confessed.

"George Louis is going to be King of England one day," the duke said. He looked at Law and added triumphantly, "You didn't know that, did you?"

"No, milord, I didn't," Law admitted.

"He's married to Sophia," the duke said. "Sophia Dorothea."

Law desperately searched his memory for a better identification of Sophia, and in a moment it came to him: Sophia Dorothea was the daughter of the Duke of Brunswick-Lüneburg.

"I see, your Grace," William Law said, hoping that was sufficiently noncommittal. He had no idea why the duke was telling him all this.

"From what I hear," the duke said as if the information pleased him, "Sophia's been under every male over fifteen at her court."

Law was reminded again that there was another side to John Maitland, Lord High Commissioner for Scotland. He was the Duke of Lauderdale, and as close to the crown as any man in England or Scotland. What Law had allowed himself to forget was that that meant he was as deeply involved in the international intrigues of the British crown as he was with the affairs of Scotland.

"At the moment, she's bedding the Graf von Königsmark," the duke said with something close to relish. But then he seemed to remember who he was talking to. "But that has nothing to do with Frazier."

"Forgive me, your Grace," Law said. "I'm confused."

"We're talking about Frazier," the duke said impatiently. "What about him, milord?"

"Having him with Neville in Hanover is a good place

for him for the time being," the duke said. "Neville belongs to me."

"I understand, milord," Law said, although he understood nothing.

"But it would be better for him if he were more than a subaltern," the duke said. "You know that, Willy. You were a subaltern when I met you."

"Indeed I was, milord," Law said.

"He doesn't have the money. It took their last farthing to buy him the commission as a subaltern in the Borderers."

"I understand, your Grace," William Law said. He was now reasonably sure that he was about to be asked for money. That had happened once or twice over the years too. And Law had believed the duke had not diverted the money to his own purposes. For one thing, he was enormously wealthy. It was just that, sometimes, situations arose when it would have been awkward for him to personally provide money that was needed for some purpose.

Such as, Law thought, giving the son of a man the duke had hung, but whom he had admired, a suitable nest egg to buy a decent commission in the Borderers. And to provide him with enough money to live decently while seconded to a political assignment in the Hanoverian court.

As if reading Law's mind, the duke said, "What the lad needs is a little money."

"I believe, milord, that funds can be obtained to get him started on the right foot when he goes to Hanover," William Law said.

The duke glowered at him. He had not been finished with what he had planned to say.

"Hold your mouth, please, sir, until I have finished," the duke said.

"I beg your Grace's pardon," Law said.

"I was saying what that lad needs is a little money," the duke said. "Such as he might come into through a dowry." He paused. "You take my meaning, Willy?"

"Money and a wife, milord?"

"Otherwise, he would be very alone in Hanover," the duke said.

"I take your Grace's meaning," Law said, and wondered if he was being ordered to offer up both a dowry and one of his daughters. The thought made him nearly ill. Was one of his daughters about to be taken from him to marry Frazier and then to go off to Hanover? William Law had heard about the personal lives of the nobility to have long ago concluded that he was the most fortunate of men. He had as much money as he needed—more, in many cases, than some members of the nobility, and none of their responsibilities.

"Gardiner," the duke said, "the horse trader. He's done well for himself, hasn't he?"

"Yes, your Grace, he's done very well."

Gardiner? Now what does he have in that devious mind of his?

"Well enough to send one of the twins to London, to school," the duke said.

"The twins" Law noticed, not "*his twins.*"

"I didn't know about that, milord," Law said.

"The matter was brought to my attention by the Lord Sheriff," the duke said. "He reported to me that the lad was unusually bright, according to the headmaster of his school. I had the Lord Sheriff inform the headmaster of St. Peter's that I would be pleased if he would take the boy, and he was kind enough to admit him."

The duke was obviously proud of his bastard son.

"I wasn't aware of this, your Grace," Law said.

"Your boy is at St. Peter's, isn't he, Willy?"

"Yes, your Grace, he is."

"Perhaps they will come to know each other," the duke said. "In any case, that settles the future of the boy. Now, it seems to me that if Gardiner can afford to send the boy to school, he should be able to come up with a dowry for the girl large enough to purchase her husband a commission—say, a captaincy in the Borderers—and have a bit left over."

"I'm sure that would be the case, milord," William Law said.

"I would be very pleased, Willy," the duke said, "if you were to come to me in the near future, and tell me that *was* the case."

4

It had been impossible for Edward Gardiner not to be aware of William Law over the years. Law's Brewery, which of course meant William Law, was as much a part of Edinburgh as Holyroodhouse Palace. And Edward Gardiner had never been able to put entirely from his mind that William Law knew that Mary MacPhee had David and Kate in her belly when he married her. He was able to put it away, so to speak, in a far corner of his mind, but he was not able to get rid of it.

It wasn't that he didn't think of David and Kate as his kids. God knows, he couldn't love them any more if they had been his. And God hadn't seen fit to give him and Mary any others, and sometimes he thought that was another of the mysterious ways in which God worked. It was possible that if he and Mary had had other children, he might have made a distinction between them and Kate and David. So God had solved that problem by not giving him and Mary any more.

After they'd moved to Edinburgh, of course, he had often seen William Law. They met on the street and at the bank, and every once in a while, the Law family— William, his wife, and their girls—would drive up to St. Paul's Church on a Sunday morning for worship services, and he saw them there.

And William Law had always smiled when he saw him, and tipped his hat, and if he was close, offered his hand and called him, "Mr. Gardiner."

But he didn't know Mr. William Law. He didn't expect to. There was a wide social and economic gap between them, near as wide as that between him and any member of the nobility.

Edward Gardiner was, therefore, both surprised and a little worried when William Law invited him to his club for lunch. He'd gone to the bank to arrange for the payment of some money owed him by the government to his tax account. He'd learned that once he'd assigned money due him from the government back to the government, he didn't have to worry about the government paying him in time so that he could pay the taxes. That saved him a lot of interest money. Doing so had pleased him. It made him feel that he had really learned how the wiser, more experienced businessmen conducted their affairs. From that, it was not entirely vanity to think of himself as an experienced businessman.

He'd met Law, who had been in the office of the general manager, at the bank. When Law saw him and their eyes met, David Gardiner had nodded to him, expecting the same in return. But Law had said something to the general manager and then quickly come out to the main room to offer Edward Gardiner his hand.

"I'm glad I ran into you, Gardiner," Law said. "I was about to take a chance and stop by your office to see if you were in."

"It's always nice to see you, Captain Law," Edward Gardiner had replied. Law had never been to Edward Gardiner & Son, Purveyors of Fine Horses, and Gardiner wondered why he had intended to now.

"There's something I'd like to talk over with you," Law said.

"I'd be happy to talk to you, sir," Gardiner said, "at your convenience."

"Good, good," Law said. "Kind of you. I don't suppose, Gardiner, that you're free for lunch today?"

"As a matter of fact, I am," Edward Gardiner said, and immediately regretted it. He had by then concluded that Law wanted something from him, that he either had horses to sell (which seemed most likely, considering how friendly he was being) or wanted to buy something. Under those circumstances, he should have been a little reticent.

"Well, then," Law said, "how about my club at the noon hour?"

Edward Gardiner was aware that the man he dealt with at the bank was now looking at him, being invited to take lunch with William Law at his club.

"What club is that, Captain Law?" Edward Gardiner asked.

Law's smile flickered. "The Borderers," Law said. "Do you know where it is?"

"Right by the cantonment, right?" Gardiner asked. He was aware that he had just managed to look ignorant. He should have known what Law's club would be. The Borderers, whose members either were the officers of, or who had served at one time in, the King's Own Scottish Borderers, was the most prestigious gentleman's club in Edinburgh. And they called Law "captain" because he had been a captain in the Borderers. What other club would he belong to?

"Right," Law replied. "If I'm not there when you get there, just give the man my name, and he'll take care of you."

"Thank you, Captain Law," Edward Gardiner said. "I look forward to it."

He was mildly annoyed with himself for having been so impressed with being invited to take lunch with Law at the Borderer's Club, with his man at the bank hearing it all, that he had forgotten to play a little hard-to-get.

Edward Gardiner timed his arrival carefully so as to be ten minutes late. He didn't want to get there before Law did. The Borderer's Club was as elegant as he thought it would be. There was a flunky, a retired sergeant of the regiment wearing all his medals, at the door of the building.

"Excuse me, sir," he said, "would you be Mr. Edward Gardiner?"

"I am," Edward Gardiner said.

"Captain Law asked me to look out for you, sir," the old sergeant said. "He sent word round that he'd be a few minutes late and that we was to make you comfortable till he got here. If you'll come with me, sir, we'll get you a little something to help your appetite."

He was led into a dark-paneled bar room, furnished with leather-upholstered chairs. Oil portraits of the king, the Lord High Commissioner, and of half a dozen former commanders of the regiment hung from the walls, separated by flags, swords, armor, and other military items.

The old sergeant showed him to a chair facing another over a small table.

"If this would be satisfactory to you, sir," he said, "I'm sure the captain will be along in a bit."

"Very nice," Edward Gardiner said. "Thank you very much."

He recognized some of the men in the room. He took the chance of nodding his head, and was nodded to in reply. The man he nodded to didn't seem surprised to see him in here.

You've come a long way, Edward Gardiner, from the farm. Even if he has invited you here to get a better deal in a business situation, you're here. Dad would have never believed it.

Without his having to order anything, a boy served Edward Gardiner a tray with a glass and two small bottles on it.

"Shall I mix, sir?" the boy asked.

"Please," Edward Gardiner said. The boy half-filled the glass with what was apparently whiskey and then started to pour water in it.

"Say 'when' if you please, sir," the boy said.

"When," Edward Gardiner said quickly. He didn't like any water at all in his whiskey.

"Thank you, sir," the boy said, and left.

Edward Gardiner sipped his whiskey, reminding himself that gentlemen in a place like this probably did not drink their whiskey the way he liked his, all at once.

Captain William Law arrived a few minutes later.

"Oh, there you are, Gardiner," he said, obviously pleased to see him. "Have they taken care of you all right? Have you been waiting long?"

"I just got here, as a matter of fact," Edward Gardiner replied, pleased that he had known enough not to show up on time and look eager.

Law put his hand above his head and snapped his fingers. The boy almost immediately appeared with a tray like the one he had served Gardiner.

"And you'd best bring us another dram," Law said, "while you're about it."

"Very good, Captain Law," the boy said.

"Do you like the whiskey?" Law asked.

"It's first-rate," Gardiner said.

"We have a man in Dunfee who makes it for us, and for no one else," he said. "It's a blend of several whiskeys. Some for strength, some for flavor."

"It's first-rate," Gardiner repeated.

"If you're not just saying that, Gardiner," Law said, "I'll have them send some round to you."

"Oh, that would be very kind of you," Gardiner said.

That settles it: the day William Law sends whiskey around to Edward Gardiner, he wants something from him.

"My pleasure," Law said.

I wonder if he's going to feed me lunch first or tell me what he wants from me?

"Your club is an interesting place, Captain Law," Gardiner said. "As well as an elegant one."

"We like to think it's comfortable," Law said. "I don't know about elegant."

Edward Gardiner suddenly had the feeling that Law was waiting for someone, or something. He kept looking toward the door.

And then a young Borderers officer, a subaltern, came into the room and headed for their table.

"Captain Law, sir," he said. "With the Lord High Sheriff's compliments." He handed Law a large envelope.

"How are you, Frazier?" Law said as he laid the envelope on the table.

"Very well, thank you, Captain Law, sir," the young officer said.

"Pull up a chair, Frazier," Law said, "and have a dram with us."

"With respect, sir, I believe the Lord High Sheriff expects me right back," Frazier said.

"You tell him that I asked you to have a drink with me and another old friend of his, Frazier, and I'm sure he will understand," Law said. It was polite, Edward Gardiner saw, but it was also an order. There were, he thought, very few people in Edinburgh who dared risk annoying the Lord High Sheriff, and he was sitting with one of them.

"Thank you, sir," the young officer said. "Very good of you, sir."

"Mr. Frazier, may I present Mr. Edward Gardiner?"

"How do you do, sir?" Frazier said, and offered Gardiner his hand.

"Mr. Gardiner and I are very old friends," Law said.

Why the hell is he saying that?

"I see," Frazier said somewhat uncomfortably.

"And he is also an old friend of the Lord High Sheriff," Law said. "I think I already told you that."

"Yes, sir," Frazier said.

"None of which, I am sure, Mr. Frazier, is half so much of interest to you as what you may already know."

"And what is that, sir?"

"That he is the father of one of our more spectacular Edinburgh beauties."

"Yes, sir," Frazier said, really surprising Edward Gardiner. "I've seen Miss Gardiner around town."

"You know my daughter?" Edward Gardiner asked.

"I know who she is, sir," Frazier said. "I don't have the privilege of her acquaintance."

"Perhaps we can remedy that," Law said.

Edward Gardiner was to remember later that he had had the thought before Captain William Law had brought the subject up.

A fine-looking young man, he'd thought. He'd make a fine match for Kate. And it's not impossible. If he's that old, and a subaltern—subalterns were usually no more than fourteen or fifteen—that means he doesn't have the money to buy a higher commission.

"I would be honored to be introduced to Miss Gardiner," Frazier said.

I wonder how I would go about arranging that? Edward Gardiner thought. Maybe I could bring it up to Captain Law, somehow.

When their waiter came to announce that their table was ready, Subaltern Frazier, Edward Gardiner noticed, had barely touched his drink; he thought that was a good sign.

"Give our respects to the Lord High Sheriff, won't you, Frazier?" Law said as they all stood up. Frazier shook hands with both of them, and his grip was firm. Gardiner liked that.

The food in the dining room, Edward Gardiner thought, was nothing special. Nice, but nothing special.

"He's a nice lad, didn't you think?" Law asked as he cut a piece of broiled fish with his fork.

"He seemed to be," Gardiner said.

"He's the son of Davies of Icomkill," Law said softly but matter-of-factly.

"I thought you said his name was Frazier," Edward Gardiner said, and then had another thought. "Wasn't Lord Davies hung and his property confiscated?"

"Yes," Law said. "I was there when Lauderdale hung him."

"And does he know that? The lad, I mean?"

"I don't know," Law said. "Possibly. Very probably." He met Gardiner's eyes. "He's obviously a bright chap. Perhaps he has already learned that all one can do in sad circumstances is try to build something on the ashes."

"Aye," Edward Gardiner said. "There's no point in harboring hate."

"And often, as you yourself have learned, some very fine things come from some very unfortunate circumstances," Law said.

"I'm not entirely sure what you mean, Captain Law." Gardiner was fairly certain that Law was bringing up, tactfully, what had happened between them when he had married Mary MacPhee.

"You and Mistress Gardiner have built a very good life for yourselves," Law said. "Isn't that true?"

"Aye, that's true," Gardiner said.

"You have two children any man could be proud of."

"Aye."

"A son in school, and a daughter who has already caught the eye of that young officer."

"Captain Law," Edward Gardiner said. "As you have just pointed out, you know what I am. And what I am is a man who's not skilled at fencing with words. I would be very grateful to you if you would tell me what it is you want from me."

Law looked at him a moment and then chuckled. "I know what you are, Edward Gardiner, and I respect you for it. Do you suppose that you could bring yourself to call me by my Christian name and afford me the privilege of calling you by yours?"

Gardiner did not reply. He had the feeling he was floundering. Law put his hand out to him.

"Edward?" he said. "Can we be friends, Edward? I'd like that."

"I suppose we could," Gardiner said, and with a genuine effort, managed to add, "William."

"Now, we can talk openly," Law said. "We have more in common than you would think."

"And what would that be?"

"We both have children, near adult," Law said. "And in that you're ahead of me, I think. From what the Lord High Sheriff tells me, you can really be proud of your son."

"Aye," Gardiner began, and forced himself, "William, I can. My David is a fine lad."

"Between you and me, Edward, mine is spoiled rotten," Law said.

"He's a fine-looking lad," Gardiner said. "I've seen him."

"And one day, I pray, he'll settle down. But at the moment, whenever anyone mentions his name to me, I hold my breath until I hear what he's done."

Now, I think I know what he's after. He's heard David's at St. Peter's, and he is tactfully going to tell me he doesn't want the two of them together.

"If they meet in London," Law said, "and perhaps we should see that they do, perhaps some of your son's stability would rub off on mine."

Damn! I was wrong about that, wasn't I?

"David *is* stable," Gardiner said.

"What, if you don't mind my asking, are your plans for the girl?"

"Oh, I suspect that before long, some father will come looking for a dowry," Gardiner said.

"And if a lad doesn't have a father, then a friend might

149

come to see you on behalf of a fine young man?" Law said.

And then Edward Gardiner knew, finally, what it was all about.

"I suppose that's why we're having lunch?"

"Yes," Law said simply.

"Who? Frazier?"

"Yes."

"You're looking out after him?"

"In a manner of speaking," Law said. "He has other people, some very important people, interested in his future."

"What sort of a future can he have in the Borderers as the son of a hung traitor?" Gardiner asked.

"His father was the traitor, not the son," Law said. "And it has been arranged for him to be seconded to the minister for war."

"I don't know what that means," Gardiner admitted.

"He's going to be sent to the court of the Elector of Hanover, as aide-de-camp to Lord Neville."

"Oh," Gardiner said, as he tried to figure out what that meant.

"The problem is that he's only a subaltern," Law said.

"How old is he?" Gardiner asked.

"Twenty-one."

"I thought he looked a bit old for just one pip," Gardiner said.

"If he were a captain, say, he would be a lot better off. As a captain, he could start to really build a fine career for himself in Hanover. It's even possible, I suppose, that at some time in the future, the king might restore his lands and title. It's happened before."

"What do you think a captaincy in the Borderers would cost?" Gardiner asked.

"A thousand pounds," Law said.

"My God, that much?" Gardiner asked, shocked.

Law did not reply for a moment, then said, "Edward, if that's out of the question, I have reason to believe that others interested in Frazier's welfare . . ."

"It's not the money," Gardiner said. "It's the thought of

Kate going off, she's still a girl, to Hanover. To a royal court. She's just a farmer's daughter, so to speak."

Law started to say something, then stopped.

Gardiner caught him. "I raised her as my own, Captain," he said curtly.

"With God as my witness, Edward," Law said, "I was about to say you're a hell of a lot more than a farmer. And so is your wife."

"Then why didn't you?"

"I think you know why," Law said simply, meeting Gardiner's eyes.

After a moment, Edward Gardiner realized William Law was telling the truth.

"Then you'll believe it's not the thousand pounds that makes me hesitate," he said.

"That is a decision you would have to make as a loving father," Law said.

"Does the boy know anything of this?"

"No," Law said.

"How could we get them together, to see if they liked each other?" Edward Gardiner said.

"People learn to like each other, Edward," Law said. "People with something in common."

Edward Gardiner looked at William Law and asked himself again if Law were really Kate's father. The reference was to Kate's conception. There was nothing of Law in Kate. Then, who?

He forced the question again from his mind. It would be a good marriage for Kate, a much better one that he could arrange for her. A thousand-pound dowry would buy for him only the son of a businessman such as himself. If he went through with this, it would buy Kate the son of a lord, even if he had been hung as a traitor. It would buy her the chance to be married to a man who might have his land restored. And his title. He knew that he could do no better for Kate. And the final duty of a father to his daughter was to try to see that she was married as well as possible.

"How could we get them together, William?" he asked.

"I think my wife would be pleased to have you and Mistress Gardiner to Elm View for a dinner," William Law said. "And your daughter. I'm sure Frazier would like to come, too, if he knew your daughter was going to be there."

"I would be grateful to you, William," Gardiner said.

Chapter Seven

1

Captain William Law sat at one end of the long, elaborately set table. Along the sides of the table, to his immediate right and left, were Mary MacPhee Gardiner and Subaltern Thomas Frazier of the Borderers. Edward Gardiner and the eldest Law daughter sat beside Mrs. Law at the other end of table. Scattered between them were two other young officers of the Borderers, the colonel commanding and his wife, and the other two Law girls, and Kate Gardiner.

There was no coincidence at all, Kate thought, that she was sitting beside Subaltern Frazier. His name had been mentioned a half dozen times to her in the week since they had received the surprising invitation to take dinner at Elm View.

He was not, she was honest enough to admit, quite what she expected. For one thing, he was better-looking than she had expected he would be. While she hadn't actually put it into words, it was clear to her that they had been invited to Elm View so that she could meet a young man. Or the other way around, so that a young man could meet—perhaps examine was a more accurate word—"the Gardiner girl."

Frazier was more of a gentleman than Kate expected. She expected some outstanding farmer, some son of a businessman, who had somehow managed to come up with the cash to purchase a commission in the Borderers, and was now looking for a wife. Since he was examining a horse farmer's daughter, Kate had decided that he was not in a position to examine the daughters of those who were higher placed in society, because real young ladies would not be interested in him.

John Law's sisters were fascinated with Thomas Frazier. The oldest one stared at him, Kate thought, as if he were the realization of her dreams. And it was obvious to Kate that Thomas Frazier was a good deal more at home in surroundings like these than she and her mother were.

Whenever she looked at Thomas Frazier, he flushed, which Kate found rather appealing.

The food was quite good—roast beef, roast venison, and roast lamb—served by half a dozen waiters assisted by as many maids.

And then there was an unexpected guest.

Kate saw the butler, his face showing his concern, come into the dining room from the entrance foyer and make hurriedly for Captain Law. He bent over him and whispered in his ear, and Law immediately got to his feet and walked out of the room. Kate glanced at Mrs. Law. She seemed surprised to see her husband doing what he was doing.

And then the double doors to the dining room flew open. The butler stepped inside.

"His Grace," the butler announced, "the Lord High Commissioner for Scotland, the Duke of Lauderdale."

The officers of the Borderers got quickly to their feet, the colonel commanding so quickly that he knocked over his wineglass. The ladies took a little longer to get out of the chairs, but everyone was standing when the duke actually walked into the room.

He was not dressed for dinner.

"Keep your seats," the duke said with an impatient

wave of his hand. "I'm imposing and I know it, and I don't want to ruin your dinner."

"Your Grace is always welcome at our table," Mrs. Law said.

Kate started to take the duke at his word, to sit down, but she noticed that no one else had, so she straightened up.

A waiter came running up with a chair and stopped when no one told him where to put it. The duke walked along the side of the table to the head, with Captain Law following beside him. He looked around for the waiter, as if, Kate thought, he knew he would be there, and motioned for him to put the chair beside Captain Law's place.

"Pray, I said, be seated, madam," the duke said to Mary MacPhee Gardiner.

Mary, her face red, sat down. Some of the others at the table followed her example.

Another servant arrived with a place cloth, and behind him a maid with silver, and behind her another maid with plates and glasses. The duke impatiently waved away the waiter and the first maid and took a goblet from the hands of the startled second maid.

He was, Kate saw for the first time, quite drunk.

"I'll not be eating," the duke said, and sat down and reached for the decanter of wine before William Law's place. He poured his glass full and then looked down the table and saw that some guests, including the colonel commanding the Borderers, were still on their feet.

"Pray be seated," he repeated impatiently. "I said that I didn't want to ruin your dinner."

Then he turned to Mary MacPhee Gardiner. "Mistress Gardiner, I believe?" he said.

"Yes, your Grace," Kate's mother said. Her face was red.

Then the duke looked directly at Kate. His eyes, she saw, were rheumy and bloodshot.

This is my father? This drunken old man?

The duke did not speak to Kate. He spoke to Thomas Frazier. "So this is her, is it, Frazier?" he asked.

155

"Your Grace?" Thomas Frazier asked. His face was blood-red.

The duke snorted. "I suppose I have spoken too soon," he said. "I have a tendency to do that."

There was no reply to that from anyone.

The duke took a healthy swallow of his wine, and although the glass was not empty, reached for Law's decanter and filled it. He looked directly at Kate, and then nodded his head, as if in appreciation of what he saw. Kate averted her eyes.

"Colonel," the duke called to the colonel commanding the Borderers.

"Your Grace?"

"Do you know who you're eating with?" the duke asked.

"I believe so, milord," the colonel said, uneasily.

"Does the name Brian MacPhee mean anything to you?" the duke asked.

The colonel looked uncomfortable. After a moment, he confessed, "I'm afraid not, Your Grace."

"He was master at arms to Lord Davies of Icomkill," the duke said.

A very strange look came over the face of Thomas Frazier. Kate wondered what it meant.

"That was a very long time ago, your Grace," Captain Law said. He looked as uncomfortable as Thomas Frazier.

"You're right, Willy, it was," the duke said. "But I remember brave men."

"He was a brave man, your Grace," Captain Law agreed.

"Like his lord," the duke said. "Did you know, Willy, that Mistress Gardiner is the daughter of Brian MacPhee?"

"I did not, milord," William Law said.

Kate saw that he was lying. And she saw that Thomas Frazier looked intently first at her mother and then at Kate, and then back at the duke.

"By the grace of God," the duke said, "and with the considerable help of the Borderers, those bad days are over."

"Your Grace had more than a little to do with that," Captain Law said.

The duke waved his hand impatiently and looked right

at Kate. "Did you know, miss, that your grandfather was a warrior?"

Kate met his eyes. "My mother does not talk of such things, your Grace," she said.

"Women do not talk of war," the duke said. "But they damned well like soldiers better than other men. Isn't that right, Mistress Law?"

Mistress Law fixed a smile on her face. "My husband was once a soldier, your Grace," she said.

"And a damned fine one Willy was," the duke said.

"Thank you, milord," Captain Law said.

"It's God's truth," the duke said a little thickly. Then he turned to Thomas Frazier. "Isn't that what you're hoping, Frazier?"

Thomas Frazier colored again. "Excuse me, your Grace?"

"Now that you've seen this one," the duke said, pointing at Kate with his wine goblet, splashing some onto the tablecloth, "aren't you hoping that she likes soldiers better than other men?"

"Yes, milord," Thomas Frazier said softly. And then he looked at Mary MacPhee. "I hope so very much, milord."

"Goddamn right," the duke croaked triumphantly.

Kate was aware that her own face was flushed.

"Now I've got her blushing," the duke said. "I didn't intend that."

He turned to Mary MacPhee Gardiner. "I didn't intend to embarrass your daughter, madam," he said.

"I'm sure my daughter has taken no offense, your Grace," Mary said.

"I've been drinking," the duke explained. "It helps the stiffness in my joints sometimes. And when I heard that Willy was introducing Frazier to a girl, I wanted to have a look."

"We are honored by your presence, your Grace," Captain Law said.

"One of the reasons I've always liked you, Willy," the duke said, "is that you're incapable of lying convincingly."

He drained his glass and pushed himself to his feet. "I have no business here," the duke said.

"Your Grace," Law started to protest. The duke shut him off with a wave of his hand and marched out of the room. At the door, he stopped and looked at the table as if he was going to say something. But then he turned again and was gone.

There was silence at the table for a moment, and then Captain Law spoke. "Thom," he said, amusement in his voice, "perhaps at some time in the future, when you recall when first you met Miss Gardiner, you will also recall that the duke was at table. Not for long, but at table."

It wasn't that funny a remark, but hearty laughter filled the room.

A moment later, Kate felt a touch on her sleeve. She turned to find Thomas Frazier looking at her.

"Miss Gardiner, to the extent for which I am responsible for that, I am deeply sorry."

"Don't be silly," Kate said. "There's nothing to be sorry for."

"Might I," Thom Frazier asked, visibly afraid that he would be refused, "dare to call upon you at your home?"

That's not what he's really asking, and he knows that I know it. Is this the man with whom I will spend my life? Whose children I will bear?

She met his eyes and then looked at her mother. And then she looked back.

"That would be very nice, Mr. Frazier," she said.

2

"I want you to understand, Gardiner," John Law said as he and David walked back to the Duke's Arms from the jail at the watch station, "that your kind loan is as safe as money in the bank."

David chuckled. "I'm sure that you will regard it as sacred an obligation as you would a gambling debt," he said.

"Precisely," John said automatically, and then he caught the droll tone in David's voice. "You're mocking me," he accused.

"Not at all," David said. "I'm just hoping that I won't have to go looking for you the way I did the last time you owed me money."

"Oh," John said, remembering, and being embarrassed, "that."

"That," David said.

"Put your mind at rest," John said. "First thing in the morning, we'll go to Threadneedle Street."

"Threadneedle Street?"

"The Bank of London is on Threadneedle Street," Law explained impatiently. "Where, despite your dark fears to the contrary, you will be given the money I owe you, just as soon as the bank opens."

"Splendid," David said wryly.

"There is one small problem."

"No!" David mocked him. "*One* small problem? And what would that be?"

John looked at David with his expressive eyebrows raised. "You're mocking me," he accused.

"A little," David cheerfully admitted. "What's the one small problem?"

"It's one hell of a long walk from our lodgings to Threadneedle Street."

David laughed. "And you don't have a horse? That's no problem. I will ride slowly beside you."

"I have a horse," John said tartly. "The bastard at the Duke's Arms is holding him as security against what I've got written down on the slate."

David laughed and shook his head.

"You find that amusing, doubtless?" John said.

"What the hell happened to you?" he asked. "What has reduced you to the Duke's Arms, with your horse being held against your slate?"

"If you must know, I was robbed," John said.

"Really?" David asked, no longer mockingly. "On the highway, you mean?"

"Not on the highway," John said.

"Where then?"

"By a whore in one of the villages." If he laughs at me again, I'll punch him.

David laughed. But there was something about the way he laughed, a look of understanding, perhaps sympathy, in his eyes that kept John's anger from rising.

"I thought it had to be something like that," David said. "Was she worth it?"

"To tell you the truth, I don't remember," John said.

"Wouldn't the bank give you any money?" David asked.

"Not a farthing," John said. "On orders from my father. They were kind enough, however, to put in a good word for me with our innkeeper."

"I would have thought you would have had a place to live, at the school, or an apartment," David said.

"I gave up the apartments I had," John said. That isn't precisely the truth. The damned landlord refused to renew my lease. Just because of the alleged damage to the wall and his damned chest of drawers. If I had known he was going to make me pay for that, and then throw me out, he'd not have gotten a halfpenny.

"Why did you do that?" David asked. "Didn't you think you were coming back?"

"If you must know," John said, "I was thrown out."

David shook his head and smiled. "I can't imagine why anyone would think you were anything but a very desirable tenant," he said dryly.

He does have a rather droll sense of humor; there is more than a small spark of wit behind that dull farmer's face. "The man at the Bank of London is looking around for an apartment for me."

"Oh," David said, "I don't have any idea even where to look for a place to live."

I know what he's thinking. But it would obviously be quite impossible to share lodgings with him. "What I was about to suggest, Gardiner," John said quickly, "is that since you have been kind enough to advance me the funds to keep me out of jail, and since tomorrow I will have funds, perhaps you could see your way clear to—"

David interrupted him.

"I'll loan you enough money to clean your slate and get your horse back—"

"Very kind of you," John interrupted David.

"If you will do me a service," David continued.

"Certainly," Law said. "What?"

Good God, I hope he's not going to use the loan as a wedge to get me to share lodgings with him.

"I'd like you to show me around London," David said. "And I've got to go by the school, and you can take me around there, too."

"Certainly," John said, forcing a smile. "My pleasure."

"And maybe you could help me find a place to live myself," David said. "You know the town."

"I'm sure you'll have no trouble whatever finding something suitable," John said.

"Someplace not too expensive," David said.

"Naturally," John said.

The rest of the day went far more pleasantly than John would have dreamed possible.

The first thing they did was go to St. Peter's School. John was dumbfounded when the headmaster actually apologized to Gardiner for not being available the day before. And then went on to tell John that he would consider it a personal service if he would see that Gardiner was comfortably settled. On his own arrival at St. Peter's, all he'd gotten from the head was a curt nod of the head.

And the tour of London was actually quite pleasant. Their first stop was a tavern, where they, in Gardiner's words, "took aboard victuals for the upcoming journey." That meant two mugs of ale.

They stopped regularly, every half-hour or so, and took "victuals aboard," and by the time it began to grow dark, were pleasantly tight.

"I'm drunk," David said.

"You don't look drunk," John assured him.

"There's proof positive," David announced solemnly. "I'm never generous when sober. And I just decided to buy you a dinner."

"I'm flattered," John said. "Anything but the fare at the Duke's Arms."

"I found out that they're serving the same thing tonight they served last night," David said. "And I don't think I could face that again."

"I know a fine place for roast beef," John said.

"Lead on."

"But inasmuch as you have been so generous to me, I insist that you be my guest."

"Splendid," David said. "I was hoping you would say that."

I'll be damned, he tricked me into that. He is a good deal more clever than he at first appears.

The tavern to which they went was on the bank of the Thames, aboard a barge tied permanently to the bank that catered to riverboatmen and the butchers who came to select their wares from animals sent down the river for sale in London.

They ordered first some beer, and then their meal, and went to the rear of the barge to watch the river traffic while their food was being prepared.

"I understand," John said, "that your father's close to the Duke of Lauderdale."

"Where'd you hear that? Close to the Lord High Commissioner? He sells him horses, is all."

"Oh," John said. "But he does know him?"

"For that matter, I know him," David said.

"You do?"

"When I was a kid, we were called in front of him, and he gave Kate and me a double crown. One each."

"What for?"

"Damned if I know," David said.

"But, then, your father does know him?"

"I don't know how to answer that," David said. "The duke knows who my father is. It goes back to the rebellion, I think. My father never talks about it. And, as I say, we've been selling horses to the government for as long as I can remember."

And then he thought of something else.

"I think I know what you're talking about," he said. "The reception I got from the headmaster."

"It was unusual."

"He made the same mistake you're making. Thinking I'm close to Lauderdale."

"Where would he get that idea?" John asked.

"What happened is that I had trouble getting into St. Peter's, so my father went to the Lord High Sheriff, who he does know—he has lunch with him, things like that—and the Lord High Sheriff did my father a favor and used the duke's name to get me in."

"How do you mean?" Law asked.

"He wrote a letter saying it would please the duke if I was accepted; but I think he just did that. I mean, I wouldn't be surprised if the duke didn't know anything about it."

I'll be damned, John Law thought. It's true, all right, that he's the duke's bastard. The High Sheriff wouldn't dare use the duke's name unless the duke knew about it. And my father, who rode with the duke, would not have dared to ask him for a favor like that. He's the duke's bastard, all right, but I'm quite sure he has no idea that he is.

"How's your sister?" John asked.

"How's yours?" David asked.

"I beg your pardon?"

"Why are you so curious about my family?" David asked.

"There's no reason to take offense," John said. "Forgive the question."

Half a beer later, all passed in silence, David said, "My sister is fine. All right?"

"Would it offend you if I said you're the first twin I ever knew?"

"Why should it offend me?"

"I'm curious. I mean, was it tough to leave your sister?"

David thought that over before replying. It was tougher than he thought it would be. "Well, I'd have had to leave her sooner or later," he said. "She's about old enough to get married."

"Somebody told me that twins think the same things at the same time," John said.

"Well, I never know what she's thinking," David replied. "And I would hate to think she could read my mind."

"I wonder what causes it? Twins, I mean."

What he was thinking was that it was incredible that this bull-like phlegmatic character was the twin of the exquisite, fiery-eyed redhead. He had another thought, which pleased him. Perhaps he would get to see more of her in Edinburgh now that David was in school with him. Once he told his father that Lauderdale himself had arranged for David to get into St. Peter's, perhaps the prohibition against associating with them would be relaxed.

He realized that was a foolish thought. His father would never condone his association with bastards, the duke's or anyone else's. He was going to have a fit when he heard that David Gardiner had also been sent to St. Peter's.

He might even take me out of school. Or would that offend the duke?

There was a more immediate problem, John Law thought. While there was going to be money at the bank tomorrow, it was no longer going to solve all of his financial problems. Not by half.

If he hadn't had to borrow the money from David for his cash bond, all would be fine. But if he repaid David that, and he was going to have to, there would hardly be enough money left to make it through the month.

Unless there was some way to not have to pay Gardiner back.

He had seen him playing at cards in the public room at the Duke's Arms, just before the argument he had been in had gotten out of hand.

"What say, once we've eaten, that we go back to the Duke's Arms?" John said.

"Suits me."

"I saw you playing at cards, didn't I?" John asked.

David nodded.

"We could have a go at that," John said. "Are you a very good card player?"

"Better than you, I would guess," David said.

John thought: If there is nothing easier to pluck than a rooster who believes he's good at cards, it is a rooster who's been drinking ale all day. It will not be at all hard for someone of my skill at slamm to win back the money I owe, and very possibly a pound or two besides. I will, of course, leave him enough money to make it through the month.

John learned that night that there was something in David Gardiner's makeup, both his bulk and something about the way his system reacted to alcohol that gave him a tolerance for drink beyond anything John thought possible. And he had incredible luck with the cards he was dealt. When they finally quit for the night, John owed David a total of twenty-seven pounds sixpence. That represented the fifteen pounds David had loaned him to make up the difference between what cash John had with him and the amount of his bond, and what Law lost to him before he realized that he was the one whose judgment was befuddled by the ale.

David was not offended because John had shamelessly tried to take advantage of what he thought was his innocence and ignorance. He had expected that sort of thing from someone like John. The aristocracy and the people his father called the "swells," those commoners who had risen high in government service or who had grown wealthy in business and mimicked the dress and manners of the nobility, found nothing wrong in taking unfair advantage of their social inferiors.

"The thing to do, David," his father had told him, "is pretend you don't notice. And then, when they're not paying particular attention to you, do the same thing to them."

David, even in the most intense horse trading, had not been able to consciously cheat his betters. And since he had learned his honesty from his father, he doubted that his father could cheat, either. But because the aristocracy and the swells (and John Law was certainly a swell) believed that God had ordained them to be smarter all around it was often easy to get the better of them honestly, with all the cards laid out on the table.

The card game with John was a case in point. It had never entered John's mind that the son of a horse dealer would be able to read the cards and figure the odds better than he could. He simply believed that since he was richer, it obviously logically followed that he was smarter.

For his part, although the problem of paying the debt had yet to be faced, John was not disturbed that he had been unable to part the horse dealer's son from his money. For one thing, as a sportsman he believed that there were occasions when the cards simply went against you, when the most skilled gambler simply could not win, and this session had obviously been one of those occasions. For another, it had been a pleasant surprise to find in David someone who seemed to understand something of the game beyond the simple distribution, by chance, of the cards. He had found it rather amusing to learn that beneath David's pleasant and guileless face there seemed to be hidden peasant's shrewdness that had brought to the game a challenge he had not expected.

But there was the problem of paying off the money he owed him. What to do about that?

When all else fails, tell the truth.

"I find myself, Gardiner," he said as they rode toward Threadneedle Street, "in an embarrassing position."

"You don't have enough to pay me off," David said.

"As a matter of fact, yes."

"You were the one who wanted to play cards," David said. "And you were warned. I told you that I was probably a better player than you."

"You did say that, yes," John admitted.

"Well, I'll do what the Duke's Arms did," David said. "Keep your horse as security, and then you can pay me whenever you get the money."

"I was thinking that perhaps we might come to some other arrangement," John said.

"Such as?"

"If we were to take an apartment together, it would be cheaper for the both of us."

"What about what you owe me?" David asked.

"I'll give you some now, and the rest later." And in the meantime, I will play cards with you again, and this time I'll not so much as sniff a cork.

"It's an idea," David said.

"Yes, or no?"

"We can give it a try, I suppose."

The effrontery of the man! John thought.

David decided that he had rubbed the salt in enough. "To tell you the truth, John," he said, "I was going to suggest that myself. I'm full aware that I have the manners of a farmer and am going to be out of place here. I was thinking I could learn from you, if we lived together."

"Give me two weeks, Gardiner, and you'll have the manners of the Duke of Buckingham," John said.

Actually, he thought, it wasn't all that bad an idea. It might be amusing to do something with Gardiner. To give him instruction in manners and dress, to turn him, if not into a gentleman, which would be difficult if not impossible, but into a tradesman with some class.

He admitted that there was a certain element of self-interest in this notion. Gardiner would of course be grateful to him, and one never knew when it would come in handy to have someone like Gardiner, someone with the strength of a bull and, John Law was sure, doglike devotion, in one's corner, to be summoned forth as one needed him.

The problem, John thought, would be to maintain the proper distance between them. He didn't want a brother, or really close friend. What would be nice, if it could be arranged, would be to keep Gardiner very much aware of his inferiority and grateful for the privilege of making himself useful.

3

The Bank of London's man who handled the accounts of Law's Breweries sent John Law to see a three-room apartment in an old building three squares from St. Peter's School. David Gardiner, as he felt he was expected to, bargained with the landlord about stable space and feed, in case he should have to buy another animal; and about the charges for a maid to clean the place; and about the price of wood to heat it when the fall came; and about the price for the apartment itself. The final price agreed upon—for maid service, animal boarding, fuel, and the apartment itself—was far less than the price the banker had told John Law was the minimum the landlord would accept.

There was an initial euphoria, brought about by the apartment itself and the mutual unspoken realization that if, as it was said about husband and wife, "two could live as cheaply as one," it was also true of two bachelors. Each realized, and each decided it best not to mention it to the other, that they would be living better, and for less money, than if they had found separate places to live.

David thought of this as a matter of saving money that he could then invest in horses, and John thought of it as having available to him sufficient funds for the amenities of life without having to go deal with that stingy bastard in the bank.

They also saw in each other traits of character that had not before been visible. John, David decided, was not entirely the foppish swell that he at first appeared to be. He did have some good qualities. David, John decided, wasn't really as dull as he looked; he had a droll sense of humor and he could handle himself, and well, in unpleasant situations. He would be a handy chap to have around when such situations inevitably arose during the next year.

They both came to conclude that good luck had brought them together, and that together they could look forward to spending the next year more pleasantly and more comfortably than they could have alone.

The euphoria lasted about a week.

They fell out over the maid, the services of which John had told David were absolutely necessary to gentlemen and whom he had ordered up from their landlord. The maid turned out to be a firm-breasted Irish girl of not quite sixteen, who wore her long light-brown hair in braids curled and pinned over her ears.

John believed that expecting sexual services from the servant class was as much the right of their employers as expecting them to sweep the carpets. The first time he saw Alice-Mary, he decided that he would give her a quick tumble in the sheets as soon as the opportunity presented itself—in other words, as soon as he could get her alone in the apartment.

It was his belief that while there was no question that she would let herself be had (in fact, would probably welcome the opportunity to pick up a little gift of a shilling), there was something about her that made him think she would not be willing to do so publicly—in other words, if David were in the apartment when he made his move.

She would be willing to be make the beast with two backs with David Gardiner, too, of course, but not by the two of them together. He understood that it would be a *bit* awkward for her to go to confession and confess that she had been tumbling with her employer, but that it would be *really* awkward for her to go and tell the priest behind the cloth that she had been taking both of them on.

He waited, therefore, until David had risen early their first free Saturday to ride back out to the Ward farm to see about his horses. There was a fair scheduled, David had told him, and he thought he might try to sell some of the animals. That meant that David would be, John thought, when David told him good-bye, gone all day for sure and probably until late into the night. The good-looking blond girl John had seen David with was at that farm, too, even if David had carefully avoided mentioning her.

"Make lots of money," John said, and rolled over and jammed his pillow under his head and went to sleep thinking of what Alice-Mary Cullen would look like without her clothes.

The whole thing had gone very badly. For one thing, Alice-Mary Cullen had not been as willing to take off her dress and get into his bed as he believed she would be. At first he had thought she was simply playing hard-to-get, that with servant class shrewdness, she had decided that the greater the reluctance she displayed, the larger a gift she could reasonably expect afterward.

Under some circumstances it might have been an amusing game to play, but John was in no mood to play games that morning. For one thing, it had been a long time between tumbles, and that had made him eager. For another, he'd put away his share and then some of brandy the night before, and brandy always seemed to make him randy in the morning. He was in no mood to play her game, and when she insisted on playing it, it had been necessary for him to remind her of her station in life and his.

If she expected to continue in his employ, he told her, getting very generous pay indeed for little work (he and

Gardiner ate almost all of their meals in taverns, and there was almost no kitchen work at all for her to do), she would have to be reasonable. Once he had pointed that out to her, she tried one final ploy, tears, which angered him. He was angry because she had had the nerve to try tears and because she insisted on making it clear that the only reason she was going to let him have his way with her was because her job depended on it.

John much preferred the kind of serving girl who was rather flattered when her employer was gracious enough to give her both a tumble and then a little gift afterward.

And once he had gotten her dress off and gotten her in bed, she had kept up the tears and the sobbing and it had been necessary for him to slap her to get her to stop. After that, she had been as responsive as a wet rag.

And then, before he was finished with her, the door opened and David marched in, wearing first a look of disbelief and then a look of pious disapproval, as if he were chairman of the local chapter of the Royal Association for Servant Chastity. When Alice-Mary Cullen saw him, that set off a fresh series of howls.

Pursuing the matter to its logical (he would have thought inevitable) conclusion was now clearly out of the question.

John Law rolled off Alice-Mary onto his back and swore bitterly.

Alice-Mary Cullen, still howling, got out of bed, pulled her dress on, and fled from his bedroom. John could hear her talking to David, but he could not hear what they were saying.

Several minutes later, David came into the room. The look on his face, that billboard of a face, showed what he was thinking.

"I gave her a pound," David said, "And told her that you were drunk and that it would not happen again."

"You gave her *how* much?"

"A pound."

"You're mad," John said.

"I hope you are drunk," David said. "I would hate to think you would do something like that sober."

"Something like what? Giving her a tumble?"

"I am a very simple man," David said. "I only do that with girls who want to do it. And I believe it is a sin to take advantage of your inferiors."

"You self-righteous bastard, you!" John exploded.

"You're disgusting!" David said self-righteously.

"Get your self-righteous ass out of my sight!" John shouted, found his brandy bottle on the floor by the side of his bed, and threw it at David. The cork was gone, so even though David neatly caught the bottle, he was sprayed with some of its contents.

John saw the rage on David's face, and more than just a little alarmed, wondered what would happen next. When David marched angrily across the room to the bed, John had a moment's fear that David was going to throw the bottle at him or perhaps even hit him with it. But that was not what David had in mind.

He leaned over John and put his ham of a hand on John's throat, pinning him to the bed. Then he poured the rest of the bottle of brandy onto John's crotch.

For a moment, there was a not unpleasant, cool sensation at his groin, and John laughed at David's idea of revenge.

David got off the bed, threw the empty bottle across the room, and started for the door. He had almost reached it, and John was still laughing, when the burning started. John's entire midsection, but especially his private parts, seemed suddenly to be on fire. He howled with the pain.

David turned and grinned from one ear to another.

"You wanted hot balls, you got hot balls!" David said with absolutely infuriating self-satisfaction. And then he went out of the room.

Hopping in pain, John went to the pitcher on the washstand and poured the water, awkwardly, on his groin. The burning momentarily diminished, but quickly returned. John returned to the bed and rubbed himself hard with the bedclothes. That didn't work either. Swearing, he ran into David's room and poured the water from his washing pitcher over himself, and then dried that off on David's bedclothes.

He would, he decided, kill David. He would knock him to the ground and batter his head on the floor.

But David was gone from the apartment.

John managed to stay angry all that day and the next, and to plan in finite detail how he would deal with David when he returned to the apartment on Sunday. David was not a gentleman, so it would be both unfitting and unfair to resort to the sword. The thing to do to him was box him. David, like most other young men of his class, more than likely believed he could "handle himself" with his fists. So far as people like David were concerned, John was convinced, "boxing" involved trading blows with an opponent, the winner being the man who could stand up longest. Since he was so large, he had probably done well in that kind of fighting and would probably be unwilling to quit until he was no longer in any condition to fight.

John took pride in his own boxing, the philosophy of which was not to trade battering blows with your opponent, but to stay out of his reach and wait for the opportunity to land a really good blow, a haymaker. He was absolutely sure that he could have taken on the three men in the Duke's Arms that way, one at a time, had they not ganged up on him and held him.

What he would do, he decided, was give David a really good beating. He would humiliate him by bloodying his nose, boxing his ears, perhaps even loosening a tooth or two, meanwhile dancing about him untouched. And when he was sufficiently humiliated, he would forgive him. The point would have been made, and punishment would have been rendered, both for the brandy on his groin and for the humiliation he had suffered.

Starting about one o'clock Sunday afternoon, John prepared for the encounter. The arena, he decided, would be their sitting room. Since the breaking of lamps and furniture would accomplish nothing, he removed breakable objects from the tables and moved the more fragile items of furniture out of the room. He debated with himself for a long time before deciding to roll up the carpet.

David, he was sure, would return before nightfall. He waited for him from five o'clock, and didn't give up until seven-thirty, when hunger got the best of him. One of two things was true, he decided: either the magnitude of what he had done had finally gotten through to David, and he was afraid to come home; or more likely, he was spending the night at the farmer where his animals were boarded, primarily because he had been invited and it saved him the price of supper and breakfast, but also because of the pretty girl.

John went to the tavern two squares away where they had already become regulars. He would have a piece of beef and some ale, and perhaps with a little bit of luck he would find one of the serving maids in a friendly mood. In addition to everything else, David had deprived him of sexual gratification, and that undeniable hunger remained.

When he pushed open the half-door to the rear of the tavern, he found not one but two serving maids obviously receptive to masculine attention. One of them was sitting on David's lap and the other was standing beside David's chair, pressing her body against him as she drank from his mug of ale.

David smiled broadly when he saw him. "That was quick!" he said.

"I beg your pardon?" John asked icily.

"I don't think it's five minutes since I sent the boy to stable Wanderer and to see if you were home," David said.

"Is that so?" John replied.

"I just now got back," David explained happily. "And, oh, what a nice day I had."

"You don't say?"

"There was an army of people at the fair who just had to have what I had to sell," David went on.

That meant, John realized furiously, that David had made himself some money. He was at poverty's door, and the farmer's son was rolling in money. If possible that made him even angrier.

"David," John asked, keeping his voice under control with a mighty effort, "do you suppose that I might have a word with you in private?"

David gestured elaborately with his eyes at the girls. "Won't it keep?"

"I would be very grateful for a moment of your time right now," John said.

"Sure," David said magnanimously. When he unseated

the girl on his lap, he patted her backside happily. She giggled in pleasure.

"In the alley, if you please, my dear fellow," John said, gesturing for David to precede him out a side door.

"I hope this isn't going to take long," David said.

"Not long, I'm sure," John said. He followed David through the door and then closed it behind him. They were in a narrow alley paved with cobblestones.

"How much do you need?" David asked, taking out his purse.

"I'll be goddamned!" John exploded. "I didn't bring you out here to borrow money. I don't want any of your goddamned money!"

"Splendid," David said, and put his purse back in his waistband.

"Defend yourself, Gardiner!" John said, raising his fists in the correct position. His left arm was extended, elbow down, balled fist held at the level of the chin; his right arm, elbow down, was held close to the chest, with the balled fist near and to the right of the chin. His knees were bent and his left foot was forward.

David looked at him and laughed out loud. "What?" he asked.

"Defend yourself, sir!" John said firmly.

David assumed the same, correct boxing stance, but made a mockery of it and put a mockingly stern look on his face.

John bounced around him on the balls of his feet and threw his first punch. With maddening ignorant luck, David, at the last instant, pulled his face out of the way and counterpunched. Incredible luck was with him again, for the punch (actually a slap) connected with John's face.

"Defend *yourself*, sir!" David said mockingly.

John told himself that anger had got the best of him, throwing his timing off. He waited a long time for the right time to strike a proper blow. And precisely the same thing happened the second time as had happened the first. David dodged his blow and landed another slap on John's cheek, just hard enough to make John's eyes water.

174

"*Defend* yourself, sir!" he called again, laughing.

John threw another punch and got slapped again.

This time, his ears rang and his eyes watered so badly he had to wipe them.

"You want to tell me what this is all about?" David asked, and then, remembering, answered his own question. "Oh, the brandied balls!" he said, and then laughed heartily.

John lost his temper. He threw himself at David in a rage. David stepped to one side and then caught John from the back, pinning his arms to his side. He was incredibly strong, John realized, as his most strenuous efforts to break loose failed.

"Now stop it," David said conversationally. "You're going to hurt yourself."

That incited John to even more furious exertion, but he was as securely immobilized as he ever had been.

He could feel the vibrations of David's laughter against his back.

"If you stop," David said, as to a small child, "you can have your pick of the lassies inside."

John struggled some more.

"And if you don't stop," David went on, "I'm going to rub your face in the gutter."

"You would, too, you bastard!" John said furiously. And then he too was laughing. At first he was furious with himself, but he could not resist the urge to laugh.

David let him go.

"Who taught you to box, you bastard?" John asked.

"My father," David said.

"I don't think I'd like your father."

"That's all right. He wouldn't like you, either."

They smiled at each other.

The door was now open, and the girls, relieved to see them smiling at each other, smiled happily.

"What was that all about?" one of them asked.

"We were deciding how to divide you up between us," David said.

"And what did you decide?" she asked coyly.

"That you throw the dice," David said. "The winner gets me."

4

"I am surprised," John said to David as they walked through the muddy streets of London shortly after dawn the next morning, "at the depth of your hypocrisy."

"Now what are you talking about?" David asked.

"That was you, wasn't it, in the next room, making all those groans of joy?"

"I thought gentlemen don't talk about things like that."

"And I thought you were head of the chastity league," John said.

"Whatever gave you that idea?" David asked, chuckling.

"That very convincing demonstration of moral outrage when I was having at the maid."

"Alice-Mary," David supplied her name.

"The way you leaped to the defense of Alice-Mary's virtue," John said. "I would have laid good odds that you violently disapproved of tumbling generally."

"Didn't you have a much better time this night when—I forget her name—was willing?"

"We are talking about you," John said, turning aside the question.

"I don't think you should take advantage of people who are weaker than you," David replied. "There are two kinds of girls: the kind we just left, who you can tumble, and the Alice-Mary type, who you shouldn't."

"Why, for God's sake, not?"

"Because she couldn't say 'no' to her employer. Speaking of surprise, I was surprised to find that you were determined to take her even after she told you no."

That triggered the memory of Alice-Mary's tears, and having to slap her, and of her making it quite plain that she was repelled by him, not overcome. The memory was unpleasant, so John changed the subject.

"And what about the blond farmer's daughter? Is she the kind you tumble or not?"

"I'd rather not talk about her, if you don't mind," David said. "She's not that kind of a girl."

"Good God, Gardiner! Don't tell me you're serious about her."

"She's a nice girl," David said. "I thought so the first time I saw her, and the proof came over the weekend."

"In other words, you *are* smitten," John said.

"All right," David said, red-faced, after a pause.

"And your idea of bliss is a cottage in the Highlands somewhere, with this farmer's daughter by your side, holding your hand with one hand and a string of brats with the other?"

"My sister, Law, is a farmer's daughter."

"That's different," John said.

And it's really different, for she's also a duke's bastard.

"Sally Ward is as nice a girl as my sister," David said solemnly.

"I'm sure she is," Law said mockingly.

"If you keep this up, John," David said, surprisingly softly, "I don't think I'd be able to hold my temper."

The strange thing is, John thought, that I don't want to laugh. That's fortunate, because I would hate to have David come at me after he'd lost his temper.

"Is this affection known? Is it reciprocal?" he asked more seriously.

"Of course not."

"Then aren't you taking a lot for granted?"

"If I want something, I'm usually able to do what's necessary to get it," David said.

The odds are that this boyish infatuation will pass, but for the moment, he's obviously dead serious.

"Well, I wish you luck, if you are serious," John said. "I'd like to meet her sometime."

"I'll take you out there with me sometime," David said.

"Thank you, David," John said, and smiled gratefully at him.

If I hadn't handled that, as I did, with great skill, it would have meant the end between us. I wonder why that would have been important to me? I certainly wouldn't have backed away from a confrontation like that with anyone else I know. And while it is quite obvious that I would rather not have David angry with me, I think that it is the end in itself, rather than because I am a bit afraid of him physically. The conclusion to be drawn is that I value his friendship and don't wish to lose it. How odd!

So their friendship was saved, through what John thought of as his generosity, his willingness not to laugh at David or to tumble the farmer's daughter.

It rather quickly evolved into a relationship like that between brothers. There was an unspoken bond between them: the apartment was their home and they took care of each other. But they came from different backgrounds, had different personalities, and spent less and less time with each other.

Law had gone to Christ Church School in Edinburgh. He had come to London prepared for St. Peter's School and had had two years to learn what was expected of him—in other words, the minimum work he had to do to get by. It gave him no trouble, and he did not have to spend long hours in study as David did (because he thought it was expected of him, not because he was slow; John no longer thought of David in any way as backward).

The generous allowance John got weekly from his father through the Bank of London, even after making payments on his debt to David, permitted him to accept the invitations that came his way because of his father, and to spend much of his time with his peers, the three dozen or so others in the last year or two of school whose families supported them as generously as he was supported.

John was invited out for dinner two or three times a week, and habitually remained behind in the tavern on the nights he ate there when David returned to the apartment to prepare for the next day's classes.

David's allowance from home was modest. Edward Gardiner had begun life as a poor man and simply did not believe it would have been right to give his son enough money to be "idle" while away at school. He gave him enough money to live, but not much more. He knew, of course, that David would be dealing in horses and would make money at it, but he reasoned that dealing in horses would take time, and even if he made money, he would not have the time to be "idle."

It did not occur to either of them that anything would be permitted to come between David and his schoolwork.

David was not jealous of John's way of life, nor was he surprised or hurt when the aristocratic young men who were John's friends called at the apartment to issue invitations that did not include him. He was not an aristocrat and he knew it. Despite his father's relative affluence, and his status as a purveyor by appointment of fine horses to the king, his father was a farmer, and it logically followed that he was a farmer's son, nothing more.

It was not his lot in life to be invited to dine in fine houses, or even to go off on a round of the taverns or gambling houses or sporting houses with young men whose fathers were peers of the realm, or for that matter, successful brewers. Perhaps *his* son, if he were able to build Edward Gardiner & Son into what his father dreamed it could be, could come to London like John Law, with a pocketful of money and a man at the Bank of London who would make introductions for him.

And on just about every other weekend, sometimes every weekend, there was Sally. Sometimes, he thought he saw pleasure in her eyes when she saw him coming down the lane to the farm, and more than once, he had caught her looking at him thoughtfully. As if, in other words, she was wondering if he was to be the man in her life.

Chapter Eight

1

John Law had been in London nearly six weeks before he got to go to Crockford's Club on St. James's Street. The problem of course was money, as it usually was. He had first had to pay David Gardiner back the money he owed him, the money David had loaned him to pay his jail bond and the money he had lost to David before he learned that David was a better card player than he could imagine.

The jail bond money was, of course, lost. He could have gone to court over the matter, taken his chance that the magistrate would have believed his version of what had taken place, and gotten his money back. But it was possible that he would have been found guilty of "brandishing a deadly weapon" (he had, of course, pinked that bastard in the arse), and that would have meant a fine.

The logical thing to do was simply forget that money, count it as spent, and spare himself the mess, and probably the notoriety, that would go with a trial. But there had not been enough money waiting for him at the Bank of London to repay David in full, which meant that he had to repay him a little each week. The man at the bank had been ordered not to advance him any more except in the case of emergency, and it was his definition of an emergency that counted, not John's.

So he had to wait until the next month's allowance was paid before there was enough money to go to Crockford's. David had turned a deaf ear to his request that he be allowed to stretch out the repayment of his debt over a longer period—say, six months, at least four.

"Not on your life. I need my money." David had laughed at him.

There were now two pounds in his pocket as he rode up to the front entrance of Crockford's a few minutes before nine o'clock. A whale-oil lamp burned on either side of the white double doors of the four-story red-brick building. A boy of about eight, his feet wrapped in rags against the unseasonable cold of the October night, who had been sitting on the sidewalk, resting his back against the building, jumped to his feet. He went quickly to the door and rapped the knocker twice, and then he went to reach out for the reins of Law's mare.

"Evening, sir," he said.

Law didn't respond, but after he had swung out of the saddle and adjusted his sword belt, he reached into his vest and came up with a twopenny piece, which he handed to the boy.

"Inside, now," he said to him. "Not tied to the stable rail."

"Yes, sir," the boy said.

By the time Law reached the double doors, the left one had been swung open inward and a short plump man of forty-five in butler's dress and a short white wig was bowing to him.

"Good evening, Mr. Law," he said.

That he recognized him both flattered and surprised John. He hadn't come to Crockford's, London's most prestigious gambling club, since the previous year, and he had only been here three times before, and then only as a guest of the Honorable Vernon Gripshaw, not on his own.

He thought that through. Crockford's was an efficient operation. They probably made it their business to learn about the people who came through their doors. They had made inquiries about him and had learned he was a Law, of the Edinburgh brewing Laws. That entitled him to some special attention, he thought, providing they didn't know that it wasn't until tonight that he could afford to come back.

" 'Evening," Law replied to the man at the door, and turned his back to him so that he could remove his cape. Then he turned and handed him his hat.

"Nasty out there tonight, for this time of year, isn't it, sir?" the footman said.

"Cold as a witch's teat," Law agreed, and went first into the drawing room of the mansion. There was a bar set up on a table, with a serving man behind it. The man inclined his head in question as Law approached.

"Cold as a witch's teat out there," Law repeated. "What do we have to warm me?"

"Just the thing, sir," the serving man said. He picked up a pewter mug and filled it with the steaming contents of a silver pitcher. Then he took a knife, cut a chunk of butter from a pound square on a silver plate, dropped it in the mug, and finally used the knife to stir the steaming liquid until the butter had melted and dissolved.

"There you go, sir," he said. "There's nothing better than hot buttered rum against a chill."

Law nodded and carefully sipped the drink. There should be, he thought idly, some way to get hot buttered rum from a mug without burning your lips.

He looked around the drawing room. There were perhaps twenty people in the room, a half-dozen women, the rest men. He knew a very few of them by sight, and when his eyes met those of people looking in his direction, he made the rudiments of a bow. The women were all tarts.

He had been told of the protocol: ladies did not go into the drawing room, and tarts did not enter the gaming rooms. Law had often thought wryly that some of the ladies he had seen upstairs in the gaming rooms probably had their skirts lifted as often as the tarts, and that some of the tarts acted more ladylike than the ladies.

Several of the tarts were more than attractive, and he

thought that if luck was with him, he could probably end up the evening with one of them. But it was a bit early for that. First he would see if he could make a little money.

Carrying the still-too-hot-to-drink mug of rum with him, he went out of the bar room back into the foyer and then up the wide staircase to the main gaming rooms on the second floor.

There were two main gaming rooms: one to the right and one to the left at the head of the stairs. The one on the left was the card room, holding a dozen tables at which ladies and gentlemen sat, playing mostly at whist. To the right was what he thought of as the hazard room, although it also held two wheels of chance. One of the wheels of chance was in use; the other, and the men who tended it, stood idle.

The wheel of chance was a circular board, around the circumference of which nails had been placed at regular intervals. The wheel was marked off into thirty-eight pie-shaped segments, numbered from 1 to 36, plus 0 and 00. A pointer on top, fixed with a piece of spring steel, rested against the nails.

One of the two attendants stood by the wheel, giving it a good spin when it was time to play. The wheel would spin for a moment, and then come slowly to rest, with the spring steel pointer at the winning number.

A long, narrow table stood before the wheel, marked off in numbers corresponding with those on the wheel, except the wagering board did not have space to place a wager on 0 or 00. Most of the players stood to play, but there were four chairs for ladies.

Ladies played at the wheel of chance, which, if the pointer came to rest on the number you selected, returned thirty times your w ger. It was possible, in other words, to lay ten shillings on the wager board and pick up fifteen pounds.

The practice of final-year students at St. Peter's School introducing first- or second-year students to Crockford's as part of their cultural education was a long-standing custom. It was forbidden by school authorities, but that served only to give the practice a certain allure and did nothing to stop it.

When he had first come to Crockford's, John Law had played the wheel of chance, primarily because he understood the rules of play after he'd watched two or three spins of the wheel. He had felt obliged to stand apart from the other second-year men with him, who stood around nervously with their mouths hanging open at the display of sin and wickedness.

His attempt at *savoir faire* had not been entirely successful, for it had quickly become apparent to him that only boys, old men, and women played the wheel of chance, and that the sophisticated men he was trying to ape almost never did.

But he brazened it through and he'd had a spot of beginner's luck, winning three times in the first twenty spins of the wheel. He had been so thrilled at winning forty-five pounds in less than an hour that it had taken him another thirty minutes to realize that the really important figures were the odds.

It had come to him as a dazzling revelation that luck had very little to do vis-á-vis winning and losing at the wheel of chance. It was, instead, quite clearly, for those who had eyes to see, a question of percentages.

There were thirty-*eight* (counting the 0 and 00) numbers on the wheel, not thirty-six, as there were on the wagering board. Since it was impossible to place a wager on 0 or 00, that meant there were two chances in thirty-eight, or one in nineteen, that one had no chance whatever of winning. (Or, he computed mentally with his newly acquired understanding of percentages, courtesy of the business figuring classes at St. Peter's School, more than 5 percent. That obviously explained where Crockford's made its profit.

And as he had stood there on his first night, he understood that Crockford's was greedy, and not content with a 5-plus-percent advantage over its members. That 5-percent figure would apply only, he realized, if they paid off thirty-six times the winning wager. They weren't paying off thirty-six, they were paying off *thirty*.

He had to figure the odds, the percentages again, and

it took him a moment or two to do it. Without pen and paper (or that fascinating device the instructor had shown him, from China, a system of beads that one slid up and down wires to make computations) it was impossible to compute with precision the percentage, but in his head he could do it close enough. Crockford's was paying off, *if* you won, only about 80 percent of the wager.

The odds, completely ignoring what luck one might have regarding where the wheel stopped, were five-to-four in favor of the house. Only a fool, John Law realized, would play the wheel of fortune, and he was no fool.

He had then, that first night and on his three subsequent visits last year, moved to the hazard tables, studied how they operated, and tried to compute the odds there. Hazard was played with two ivory cubes, the sides of which were marked with dots, each dice having a side marked with one spot, two spots, and so on through six.

If when one rolled the dice, two sides with one spot on each came up, this was called "crabs" and the dice thrower lost.

There were other rules, complicating the game, and it was obviously going to be impossible, without the Chinese calculator, to compute them. So on his first night at Crockford's he gave up trying and wagered the money he had won with beginner's luck at the wheel of chance. He lost almost all of it and vowed that *that* would never happen again.

The Monday after his first visit to Crockford's, he had bought both dice and a Chinese calculator and spent long hours trying to compute the odds on hazard. He was not very pleased with the initial results of his computations. It had seemed at first that the odds were just about even. If that were so, it would be a game of chance, and he didn't think that hazard was really a game of the simplicity of flipping a coin.

On his next visit to Crockford's, he had studied the operation of the hazard tables far more carefully than he had ever studied anything else in his life. He quickly saw that not all of the bets were between the dice shooter and the house, or between spectators and the house about what the dice shooter would throw. There were bets made *between* spectators, and any bet went that was accepted by both parties. Wagers between shooters and the house, and between spectators and the house, were rigidly codified, to the advantage of the house.

But the business of wagering *between* spectators, John Law saw, opened up a whole new avenue of gambling, one that had to do with people's behavior as much as it did with the chance way the dice came up with numbers.

It was as plain as the nose on his face that people became excited when they were in a winning streak (and wanted to believe they couldn't lose) or in a losing streak (and wanted to believe their bad luck simply could not continue). And he had no doubt whatever that this phenomenon could be applied to his benefit. It was simply a question of deciding how it could be done.

The first thing to do, obviously, was to become a member of Crockford's, so that he could go there whenever he wished, rather than only when some final-year man was graciously disposed to take him as a guest. John Law quickly learned that while there were probably two thousand members of Crockford's, joining their ranks was very difficult.

He wondered why, and figured that out, too. There was no way, short of sending thugs, that Crockford's could collect gambling debts. Membership was therefore restricted to those who were likely to pay what they owed and pay it shortly after incurring the debt. More important, as gentlemen, members of Crockford's were liable for the gambling debts of their guests.

It took him several months to have the man at the Bank of London say the magic words—"he's good for his debts"—to the management of Crockford's, and John was frankly surprised that he did it at all, until it occurred to him that there was probably something in it for him, from Crockford's, to send them someone who could be expected to lose at their tables.

It had been the understandable concern of the man at the Bank of London who had arranged a membership at Crockford's for young Law that Law, like other young men of his position, would promptly lose more at the wheels of chance, or more likely at hazard, than he could afford to.

"I'm doing this only as a special service to you, John," the man at the bank had said, trying, John thought cynically, to sound paternal. "Your father, as I'm sure you will appreciate, would certainly hold me responsible if something unpleasant were to transpire at Crockford's."

"I give you my word as a gentleman," John had replied.

"I'll meet you halfway," the man at the Bank of London said. "I will recommend you for membership if you give me your word you will play there only with cash in hand."

"Agreed," John had said. He had no intention of getting himself in a position where he couldn't pay a debt. That was the one sure way of having himself ordered home at once. What he was after was the privilege of going to Crockford's whenever he wished, rather than waiting to be asked as a guest.

The man at the Bank of London had had a private word with the proprietor of Crockford's, "suggesting" that he shut off John's credit at a certain reasonable point. The suggestion had been immediately accepted. Crockford's had a reputation it did not wish to have tarnished by having an angry, well-to-do, and influential father loudly proclaiming the establishment had taken advantage of his son.

It had never been necessary for the general manager of Crockford's to have a fatherly word with John Law, to suggest that a gentleman knows when the wheel, or the cards, or the dice, are going against him, and knows when to quit, so that he might play another day.

On each of his previous three visits, John had made money at the hazard tables. A little money on his first visit, a little more on his second visit, and a bundle on his third. He had, by then, confidence in himself. He *knew* that he could compute the odds for or against a dice thrower making his point with really astonishing speed and ease, and that he was able to judge those caught up in the hysteria of winning or losing and make wagers with the odds comfortably in *his* favor.

He had returned to Edinburgh from London over the

summer with a fat purse and a sense of self-satisfaction. And then he had gotten drunk (or *been* gotten drunk) and lost every farthing he owned, and sixty pounds he did not have, at an all-night whist game in Edinburgh. The cold truth was that he had been plucked like a chicken, and it had required every possible effort and humiliation to keep his plucking and his trips to several moneylenders from his father.

That had taught him, he believed, several lessons: one, don't gamble with your "friends"; two, don't gamble when you're tippling; three, don't *gamble* at all. Bet only when the odds were unquestionably in your favor.

He vowed that when he returned to London, he would go to Crockford's only on business. He would make money by betting against people, not against the dice or the wheel. He had done it before and could do it again.

Then he had had a thought that, he happily concluded, proved he was being entirely sensible about the matter. The management at Crockford's were not fools. They were aware that they got no percentage of wagers between spectators, and consequently would have banned such wagers if they could. He would have to be very careful to keep them from seeing that he came to Crockford's not to fill their pockets, but his own.

When he set out from Edinburgh, he was convinced that with the money he had in his pocket, plus the allowance that would be waiting for him at the Bank of London, he would have the necessary capital to go to Crockford's and make some money. Even after that outrageously self-important little officer of the watch had taken all that money from him for a jail bond, and he'd made the mistake of underestimating David's skill with the cards, he hadn't been discouraged. All he would have to do was make a small, purely business loan from the man at the Bank of England, and he would be in business.

But the otherwise usually helpful man at the Bank of London had refused to advance him any money. His father had issued strict orders against lending him money. David, of course, had turned him down, saying he needed his cash for his horse trading.

"I'll give you twenty-one pounds a month from today if you loan me twenty now," John had offered.

David had looked at him thoughtfully for a long time before replying. Then he said, "No, thank you."

"That's a lot of interest I'm offering you," John had said, very surprised that David had refused the offer.

"That's five percent a month," David had replied. "Sixty percent a year. If you can afford to pay me that kind of interest, what you're involved in is either crooked or risky." Then he smiled broadly and added, "Knowing you, John, more than likely both."

In desperation then, he had tried, with what little money he had and, in the tavern near their apartment to win at cards and at hazard enough of a nest egg to go to Crockford's. He had lost with unbroken regularity, playing against people he should have been able to easily part from their money. The frustration was maddening. He had resolved never again, when somehow, inevitably, money came into his hands, to be without funds again.

And there was time to worry about other things too: he became convinced there was a genuine risk that something would be said to him, or perhaps that he would even be asked to leave, if the management at Crockford's came to understand that he came there to make money for himself, not to enrich the club. He came up with the idea, to be put into action once he got back in business, of putting aside a certain figure to lose at gambling every time he went there, and to make himself extraordinarily visible when he did so.

The best way to be simultaneously conspicuous and to convince the management that one was the sort of club member they desired was to wager at the board of one of the wheels of chance. Whatever it cost him to lose there on a regular basis would be what the instructors at St. Peter's School called "normal business operating costs," defined as "necessary expenditures not directly related to the cost of merchandise acquired for resale."

Sometimes, he knew, if he planned things in great detail beforehand, when the time came to actually implement the plans, things looked differently than they had and plans had to be discarded. But that didn't seem to be the case tonight. Once he was actually inside Crockford's, his plans seemed better thought through than ever.

John Law entered the gaming room, walked directly to the wheel of chance, and rather loudly addressed the man standing with his hand on his wheel.

"I feel lucky tonight," he announced loudly. "Tonight I cannot lose."

He ostentatiously covered his eyes with his hands and dropped shilling coins totaling a pound on the wagering board. He was rather proud of himself that he had had the strength of character to go through with his plan to lose one pound a night at Crockford's even when that one pound represented precisely half of all his capital.

There were chuckles from both the players and the man at the wheel. It would be remembered that John Law had begun the evening's gaming at the wheel of fortune with a bet of a pound.

(He had even thought about that and concluded that twenty one-shilling pieces looked like more money than the one-pound piece they equaled.)

Some of the laughter was feminine and pleasant, and he peered under the fingers covering his eyes to see who it was.

She was as pleasant-looking as her laugh sounded. But old. Probably not far from thirty. And married. He smiled at her politely nevertheless.

He heard the wheel being spun, a sort of whooshing noise, accompanied by the clicking sound the pointer steel made passing over the nails.

The clicking sound slowed and then stopped. There were the expected groans and louder snorts and grunts of approval. Someone had won.

"I have lost *again*?" he said loudly, dramatically, as if this was beyond reason.

"On the contrary," the rather pretty older woman said, "you have won!"

She nodded at the wheel. The pointer was at seven. He looked down at the wagering board and saw that his pile of shillings had been blindly placed on number seven.

There was a splendid chance, he thought, to make a gesture that would not be forgotten. It was a question, he told himself, of remaining calm and collected when another, less-strong-willed man would be involved in the hysteria of winning.

He had come to the wheel-of-fortune wager board intending not to gamble, but to pay a pound as the cost of doing business. The fact that he had won, he told himself, was no reason to change that basic, sound, businesslike intention.

When the wagering-board attendant started to slide two stacks of gold pound coins, twenty-five in one, five in the other, a total of thirty pounds, toward him, Law raised his hand to stop him.

"Do it again," he said. "Tonight, I cannot lose!"

There were chuckles, and the rather pretty older woman applauded politely, smiling at him.

They will not quickly forget that I let my won wager lie, he thought, permitting them to recoup their loss on the very next spin of the wheel.

He gave the pretty older woman a smile, noting her firm bosoms with approval and regretting that she was both old and married and not one of the tarts.

He then covered his eyes again as the wheel spun.

What I should have done was take twenty of the thirty pounds, he thought. A wager of ten pounds would have made a sufficient impression of feeblemindedness. But then he decided that was the hysteria of winning speaking, not the calm voice of business, and that he had, in fact, made the right decision. The bottom of the ledger page was that he was going to be out only one pound.

"Seven," the wheel attendant called. "Mr. Law wins again!"

"I'll be goddamned! The question now is whether I will have the courage to carry this through to its proper ending, instead of taking my winnings, which is more money that I have ever had in my life, and getting out of here.

The wagering-board attendant was now sliding stacks of coins, each stack containing twenty-five pounds, toward him.

There should be thirty-six of them, he quickly calculated. Thirty times thirty is nine hundred. Twenty-five into nine hundred is thirty-six. My God, that's a lot of money!

A crowd was now gathering at the table as the attendant kept counting out the gold coins and then arranging them in neat stacks. Law felt the eyes of the older woman on him, and he looked at her and smiled. Then he looked back at the wager-board attendant counting out his money.

When he finished, there were thirty-eight stacks of coins, not thirty-six. And extra stack of twenty-five and a smaller stack of five.

It is inconceivable that Crockford's would make a mistake like that, he thought. There is obviously a reason someplace. And then he thought of it. I actually wagered thirty-one pounds, not thirty. I wagered the thirty pounds I won plus the original one-pound wager. That adds up. Thirty-one times thirty is nine hundred and thirty. That would give me thirty-seven stacks of twenty-five plus five over.

And now the question is, Will I have the strength of character to let that all ride? There is no way in the world that I could win a third time in a row.

He suddenly felt very calm and as if things were moving very slowly, half as fast as they ordinarily did, perhaps even slower than that. If I let the whole thing ride on number seven, the worst than can happen is that I will lose it. But I won't be losing nine hundred and thirty pounds, really, but just the one I intended to lose in the first place. And if I do lose, that would explain why I became a very cautious gambler. And if I win, if the immutable laws of logic should go beserk, my God, I'd have a lot of money!

"Let it stay," John Law said, in what he hoped was a calm and level voice.

The wager-board man looked at him in surprise.

"I'm afraid, Mr. Law," a voice said in his ear, "that we can't permit that."

He turned to see who was speaking to him. It was the manager. He had come up without Law noticing to stand between Law and the very attractive older woman.

"I beg pardon?" Law said.

"We have a two-hundred-pound wagering limit," the manager said. "House rules. I'm sorry."

Time seemed to be moving very slowly. He had time to

think, If I bet the two-hundred-pound limit, the odds are enormous against me that I will lose that bet, whereupon I will be expected to wage another two hundred, and when I lose that, another two hundred, and to keep betting until I lose all my money, or win again, which is about as likely as my sprouting wings. But what to do?

"Are you telling me, sir," he said somewhat archly and loud enough for the crowd around him to hear, "that I cannot let that nine-hundred-odd pounds lie?"

"House rules, Mr. Law, I'm sorry," the manager said.

He did that arithmetic in his head, too. If he had been allowed to make the wager and had won, Crockford's would owe him 28,080 pounds. That was an enormous sum. He could put it out at 3 percent and get back better than six hundred pounds a year *ad infinitum*. He could live very graciously indeed on six-hundred-odd pounds a year.

But money was relative. What was a fortune to him should not be a fortune to Crockford's. Since they wouldn't accept the wager, that meant they could not afford the wager. Crockford's obviously was not the cornucopia of wealth it tried to paint itself.

"Very well, sir," John said, "if you will not accept my offer to try to win all of your money back at one spin of the wheel, you leave me but one alternative."

"Excuse me, Mr. Law?" the manager asked more than a little nervously.

"I said you leave me with but one alternative," John repeated.

"And what is that, sir?" the manager asked, worry in his voice.

"To give you the chance to win it back a shilling at a time," Law said, and reached down to the wagering board and dropped a shilling on number seven. There was laughter, he noted with pleasure, at his wit, including a very nice laugh from the attractive older woman with the attractively swelling breasts.

"Spin the wheel," he ordered, smiling at her directly.

The wheel spun and came to rest on 00.

"You see?" John Law cried triumphantly to the manager.

"You had your chance and lost it. And now that I see my luck has broken, I will retire from the game."

There was applause now. The spectators enjoyed the manager's defeat, his humiliation.

The manager, with some effort, fixed a smile on his face. "The wise gambler knows when to quit," he said.

He got a little applause for that, and then he leaned close to John. "May I have a word with you, in private, Mr. Law?"

"Yes, of course," John said.

Now what? Is this bastard going to try to talk me out of my winnings? Perhaps hit me on the head and take them? Drug me?

The manager took him to the office, where he waved John into a chair and then seated himself behind a desk. He took a sheet of paper and a quill and dipped the quill in an inkwell.

"I'd like to make a suggestion, Mr. Law, if I may," the manager said as he wrote.

"Certainly," John said.

"May I suggest this," the manager said, sprinkling drying sand on the note he had written and handing it to Law, "would be a safer way of handling your winnings?"

Law looked at the piece of the paper:

London
16th Jany 1692

To the Managers, the Bank of London
Pay to John Law, Esq., on demand, from our accounts, the sum of
Nine hundreds and Thirty-Six of Pounds Sterling. On behalf of Crockford's Club, Ltd.,
Wm. Emmons,
Manager.

It was not the first bank draft John Law had ever seen. But it was the first time he had ever seen one for what it really was. It was not simply a piece of paper, instructing someone to do something. What it was was money. It was exactly the same thing as all those stacks of pound coins he had just left on the wagering board. It wasn't a piece of paper: it was nine hundred and thirty-six pounds. The good name of Crockford's stood behind it. It was just as good as gold. Better. It didn't weigh as much as gold, and if someone stole this from him tonight, it would be useless to them. It was made out in his name and the bank would not pay it to anyone else.

"We will be happy, of course, Mr. Law," the manager said. "To provide a carriage and several of our men to accompany you to your home if you would prefer to take the cash."

"Oh, no," John said, folding the draft and tucking it into his vest pocket. "This will do nicely. Thank you very much."

"And may I congratulate you on your good luck?" the manager asked.

"Thank you, very good of you," John said.

"Are you going back to the games?"

"I think not," John said. "I think I've had quite enough for one evening, and what I need now is a drink."

2

When he finally saw the attractive older woman with the firm breasts from the gaming room upstairs, John Law was a bit embarrassed. For one thing, only God and the woman knew for how long he had been sitting at the table in the bar room, staring at his untouched second cognac, lost in thought. He had not been thinking about his winnings, which would have been normal, but about the ramifications of the draft he had in his pocket, the piece of paper that represented money, that was as good as money. For another, he felt somewhat the country bumpkin for mistaking the woman for a lady. She was in here; ergo, she was a tart. Crockford's protocol forbade ladies in the bar room.

The wedding ring she was wearing was explicable in that context. He doubted that the older man with her was her husband. There was something about him that smelled of the pimp. His clothes were a little *too* good. Many tarts wore wedding rings in the belief it gave them the appearance of respectability. The jewelry was obviously not genuine. He should have suspected about her right off. The diamond pendant around her neck, resting against the swell of her bosom would, had it been real, have been worth a fortune.

There was something odd about her, and after a moment, he was sure that he had figured it out. She was certainly a tart, otherwise she would not be in the bar room. But she was not an ordinary tart, for regular tarts were not permitted to ply their trade, however discreetly, in the game rooms. That meant that she was a special sort of tart, a cut above the ones in here, who was permitted upstairs. That meant that she was expensive, and that would explain her presence here, now, with the too-well-dressed man, at the adjacent table.

She had seen all the money he had won, and he looked like a likely prospect for a very profitable evening's work. The thought rather pleased him. He had already more or less made up his mind to have a tart, and this one seemed to be the cream of the crop. Even if she was a bit long in the tooth, she was undeniably attractive, and if she was expensive, certainly she must have capabilities worthy of the premium price.

And then the man with her stood up and walked to John's table. "My wife and I noticed you were alone," he said, "and thought you might care to join us."

"How good of you," John said. He picked up his brandy glass and moved to their table and sat down.

"Good evening," she said, as if she was amused.

"Please don't take offense," the man said. "But the truth of the matter is, my wife was a bit concerned about you."

"Oh, really?"

"We saw your extraordinary run of luck," the woman said to him, looking in his eyes. "And I told my husband that I was worried about you carrying all that money about the streets."

I'll bet you were!

"Forgive me," the man said. "My name is Hambleden, and this is my wife."

"How do you do?" John said. "My name is Law."

They shook hands.

"Well, I appreciate your concern," John said. "But I had them give me a draft."

"That was very wise of you," the woman said to him.

"I nonetheless appreciate your thoughtfulness," John said.

"The other thing that concerned me," the woman said, "was that you would go out and celebrate, too much, I mean."

"A celebration had entered my mind," Law said.

"Why don't you come by our place," the man said. "I'd be delighted to open a bottle of champagne for someone who took Crockford's for as much as you have."

These people have class. They have made their proposition, except for the question of what it will cost me, with a certain undeniable and admirable finesse.

"That's very kind of you," John said. "Thank you." He looked around for a waiter. "Let me have the bill for all of this," he said.

"Put it all on mine," the man countermanded his order.

"Very well, milord," the waiter said. That struck John as the final touch.

"You are a very impetuous young man, aren't you?" the tart said to him. She spoke well, he thought. As if she had studied the manners of her betters.

"I suppose," he said. "I'm very glad to find you here."

"Are you indeed?" she asked.

"I noticed you upstairs," he said.

"Oh?"

"But under those circumstances, of course, I didn't dare speak to you."

"Of course not," she said.

He looked at her for a moment, wondering what it was going to cost him. Plenty, probably, but it didn't matter. Tonight he could afford any woman. He had never really had a tart like this one, although he'd heard about them, the very very expensive ones. He found her eyes, as well as her bosoms, interesting. Her eyes were wicked.

He would, he decided, do it just this once, no matter what it cost. After all, this was the night he had won all the money. It seemed fitting that he should also have a tart with an incredibly high price.

He thought of something else.

"They've offered me a carriage," he said. "I'll go see to it."

"We have our carriage," the man said.

Even a carriage!

"Shall we go," the man said, "or shall we have something else to drink here."

"Let's go," the woman said.

He went out of the bar room, spoke to the doorman, told him he would not be needing the offered carriage, and waited for them to claim their clothes from the footman. When she came down the stairs she was wrapped in furs, and he thought that it would take someone who really knew to be able to tell them from legitimate gentry.

There was a carriage, a landau, parked at the curb ten yards away. The coachman was looking at the door, obviously expecting them.

He followed them to the landau. There was a coat of arms painted on the door. That, John decided, was a bit much.

Then the coachman said, "Where are we going, milord?"

"Home, please," the man said to the coachman, and then motioned for John to get into the carriage.

My God, they were gentry!

The man sat across from them. John found himself sitting beside the woman. Her perfume filled the small enclosed area.

"It's not far," the man said. "Just several squares away."

"It's far enough," the woman said, "that I want the robe."

Her husband searched under the seat, found the robe, and spread it over his wife's lap and John's. He felt her thigh against his leg. He thought that it was entirely innocent, a result of the cramped carriage. And then her hand came to rest on his leg, first still rather innocently in the vicinity of his knee, and then upward until she had found what she wanted, and there was no way her touch could have been innocent and accidental.

"Where are you from, Mr. Law?" she asked conversationally.

"Edinburgh," John replied, keeping his voice under

control with a terrible effort. There was no way the husband could see in the dark carriage what his wife's hand was doing under the thick fur robe, but he was not used to being fondled the way she was fondling him.

And then the landau stopped, and as the coach sagged when the coachman climbed off his perch, she let go of him and pushed the robe over to her husband.

John got out first. They were before a white-stone-faced town house. He turned and offered her his hand to get down from the carriage.

The door to the town house opened and a liveried servant came out.

"Good evening, milord, milady," he said, and then to John, "Good evening, sir."

"Charles," the man said as the servant took their clothing, "would you bring a bottle of brandy to the drawing room, please? And see what else Mr. Law would like to have. I have to empty my bladder. Rather desperately."

"Richard!" the woman complained.

"It's the truth," he said. "How about you, Mr. Law? Or haven't you been drinking champagne all night?"

"I'm fine, thank you," John said.

"Then excuse me, please," he said, and went up the stairs.

He followed the woman into the drawing room. It was exquisitely furnished and a fire was burning in a fireplace.

"Are you hungry perhaps?" she asked. "Would you like Charles to bring you something to eat?"

"No, thank you," he said.

The servant was right on their heels with a bottle of brandy and three glasses.

"Thank you, Charles," she said to him.

"Milady," he said, and backed out of the room.

She poured brandy into a glass and handed it to him.

"This is a beautiful place," he said.

"Now that you know where it is," she said, "I hope you will come back. Timing your visit to coincide with one of the Marquess's frequent trips out of town."

"And who is your husband?" he asked very softly.

"The Marquess of Sprilley," she said. "You didn't know?"

"No," he said.

"Does that frighten you?" she asked.

"No," he said. "Why should it?"

She laughed. "He's going out of town, I believe, on Friday night."

"I see," he said.

"Have you made plans for Friday night?" she asked.

"I have now," John said.

Chapter Nine

1

Sally Ward had become aware, over the weeks, of the growing affection between her parents and David Gardiner. It was not hard to understand. David and her father were two of a kind: simple, hardworking men who knew, and cared about, horses. They even shared a droll sense of humor.

At first, for reasons Sally didn't understand, her mother had disliked him, been suspicious of him. But as she came to understand that David was exactly what he appeared to be—a simple, decent young man—even she had responded to him. Now, when he rode back to London early on a Monday morning, he usually carried with him a couple of loaves of bread and a bag of boiled eggs or something else to eat, a gift from her mother, who was not known for her generosity.

David had become, Sally thought, sort of the son her parents had never had. He spent practically every weekend at the farm, ostensibly to look after his animals or to try to make some deal with horses at the Saturday market or at some fair. But what he really wanted, Sally thought, was to be at the farm, with his own kind of people. He was uncomfortable in the city and had confessed to her that he didn't like St. Peter's School.

"What it's really for," David had told her, "aside from training the sons of the rich to run their family businesses, like John Law, is to train lawyers and bankers and clerks, and people to go to India for the Royal Indian Company, or North America, for the Hudson's Bay Company. Or to go into the government. It's really not a place for somebody who's going to be a horse trader in Scotland."

It had been clear to Sally from the first time she had met David that there was no sense in thinking about whether he might be the man she would marry. That was simply out of the question. David was a Scotsman, and when he finished St. Peter's School, he would go home to Scotland. She had learned from David that his father had raised himself from being a horse breeder not much different from her father to being a successful businessman. She had known, when David had told her father that "Edward Gardiner & Son, Purveyors of Fine Horses," was "one of the better" of such businesses in Edinburgh, that, if anything, he was understating the case. Like her father, he was incapable of boasting.

But despite the success of his father's business, she had heard David tell her father, he himself was just a horse breeder, and if had his way, he would have liked to have stayed on the farm, breeding and training horses. But he understood why that wasn't possible: he would, sooner or later, come into ownership of Edward Gardiner & Son, Purveyors of Fine Horses, by Appointment to the Crown. He might own a farm and a breeding operation, but he would not work them. He was going to have to work in the office in Edinburgh. The proof of that was that he had been sent to St. Peter's in London to learn about business.

Whether or not he liked to admit it, Sally thought, he was at St. Peter's for just about the same reason as John Law. He was already, she saw, more of a businessman than a farmer or horsebreeder. She had heard him talking to her father about how to figure the real price you had to get when selling an animal. It involved adding in the cost of feeding the animal, based on whether it had been possible to let him graze for his food or whether it had been necessary to feed him, and figuring in how long you had owned him. Sally didn't understand all of what he told her father, but she had seen that her father had paid close attention to David.

It never entered Sally's mind that she would spend her life anywhere but here on the farm on which she had been born. The only unknown was the identity of the man with whom she would share her life. The only thing she knew for sure was that it would not be David Gardiner, or anyone like him.

This had allowed her to come to think of David as a brother. She had never had a brother, so she knew she couldn't be entirely sure, but she thought it was logical that since brothers and sisters felt affection toward each other, the disappointment she felt when, rarely, he didn't show up sometime Friday afternoon or very early Saturday morning was the normal disappointment a sister would have felt if her brother had not come home as expected.

She had had, she thought, everything in proper perspective.

And then David had kissed her.

Her face flushed now as she thought of it. For the truth was that it had been more than a kiss.

It had happened on Monday last, about as early as it was now.

What she had planned to do that morning was get dressed, properly dressed, *modestly* dressed, and then see about giving David something to eat before he started back to London.

But what had happened was that when she opened the blinds in her room to let the first light of day come in, she had heard sounds from the barn that told her that Harriet, a four-year-old mare, was about to drop, or maybe had already dropped, her first foal. So she'd forgotten about modesty when she dressed, forgotten that it was likely she would encounter David, so she had just pulled a blouse over her head, wrapped a skirt around her

waist, and then run out to the foaling barn in a pair of
work shoes.

If Harriet needed help, Sally would run back to the
house and tell her father. Or David. David knew as much
about foaling as her father did.

When she had pushed open the door to the foaling
barn, however, she found that David was already there.
Stark naked.

He was standing beside the red-glowing stove with his
back to her in the act of pouring over his head a bucket
of water from the rainwater barrel.

He saw her when he shook his head to shake the water
off.

"Get the hell out of here, girl!" he snapped, a sort of
whispered shout, she thought, as if he was afraid somebody else would hear him. "What's the matter with you?"

Sally backed out the door, leaned against the barn,
and giggled. She had really embarrassed him. His face
had been bright red, even though she really hadn't seen
anything she wasn't supposed to, except his rear end.
And he had a funny-looking rear end. He was tanned all
over except for his rear end, and his legs down to his
knees. His rear end and the back of his legs had been as
white as a baby's. No wonder, she thought, he didn't
want anybody to see it. Anybody would laugh at it.

David came out of the foaling barn a minute or so
later, wearing an old pair of trousers, but bare from the
waist up.

"What the hell are you doing out here?" he had angrily
demanded.

For some reason, Sally had thought, he looked more
naked with his pants on than he had before.

"I thought I heard Harriet," she said. "She's about to
drop her foal."

When she spoke, she met his eyes. They seemed, she
thought, to be looking for something in hers.

"She's dropped it," he said, and turned his back to her
and went back into the foaling barn.

Sally followed him inside. Outside the big stall where
they put the mares in labor was a large pile of straw.
There was blood on it and other signs of the foaling, and

she knew that David had swept the stall and replaced the straw with fresh. He hadn't had to do that, she thought. There were hired men to do that. But it was the sort of thing she would have expected David to do, so the foal and the mare would have a clean stall.

She started to open the stall door.

"I wouldn't do that," he ordered. "She had a bit of a bad time of it, and she's lying down, and I think she should stay down."

The wooden sides of the foaling stall had been reinforced with straps of iron. Sometimes, often, hooves would flail and without the straps of iron the walls wouldn't have lasted long.

In front, one board had been removed, so that it was possible to look into the stall without opening the door. Since her father had removed the board, he had removed it at the level of his eyes. That placed the opening four inches above the level of Sally's eyes, even when she stood on the tips of her toes.

When he saw her jumping up to catch a fleeting glance into the stall, David had stepped behind her and put his hands on her waist and picked her up, lifting her high enough off the floor so that she could see in. Harriet was on her side, on a thick bed of fresh straw, with her gawky-legged foal standing straddle-legged beside her, as if wondering how to get at her teats.

Harriet, whinnying, very nervous, had struggled to her feet, so her foal could suckle.

"I wish she hadn't done that," David said. "He could have gone an hour without his breakfast."

He set Sally down and she turned to face him. Her eyes were at the level of his chest, of his nipples, and the thought ran through her head that that had probably been an oversight of God's. A nipple that wasn't able to suckle young was absolutely unnecessary.

"She's a mother," Sally had said, wondering why her voice seemed to be so faint and unsure. "Mothers'll endure pain for their young."

"Aye," David had replied, and it seemed to Sally that his voice seemed a little weak and strange, too.

She had been looking into his eyes. Then she dropped

them, not so much in modesty but because the way he was looking at her made her feel a little dizzy. When she looked down, she saw that his trousers were wet from the water he had had been pouring over himself when she had first come into the barn. And she saw that not only was the cloth clinging to the bulge at his middle, but that the bulge in the middle was larger than normal, that David was in the same shape the stallion had been just before he covered Harriet.

She looked away in embarrassment and then up at him, and all of a sudden he had his hands on her face, holding it at once as if he thought it was eggshell that he might crush, holding with enough strength that she couldn't have moved it a fourth of an inch.

And then he kissed her. When Sally had seen his face approaching hers, she knew what he was going to do, and she decided that the only thing she could do under the circumstances was suck her lips in so that all his lips would touch was skin, not the red sensitive part, and at the same time either kick him in his privates, as her mother had told her to do when a man grabbed her and tried to have his way with her, or slap and scratch his face. Or both.

But when she thought about kneeing him in his privates, there was a mental image of the bulge in his pants, and she thought that if she kicked him there, she might turn him into a gelding, and that would be a terrible thing to do; while she was thinking about that, she forgot to suck her lips in and press them tightly together, so that when his lips did touch hers, they got the soft, red sensitive part.

And then Satan had taken over, as her mother had told her he would. He didn't kiss her long, just a moment, just long enough to make her heart beat hard, and then he pulled his face away.

"*What* are you *doing*?" Sally demanded, not nearly half as sternly, as reprovingly, as she had intended, and he let go of her face. But then he kissed her immediately again, this time with his arms around her, and she could feel the hard muscles of his chest against her bosom;

then her own body, as if it had a mind of its own, pressed against the bulge at his middle.

Somehow her blouse came out of her skirt, and all of a sudden she felt his hand on her breast, the very first time in her life since she'd had them that they had been touched; and when he did that, she seemed to grow all weak in the middle, and her knees sort of caved in, with the result that her body was pressing hard against his.

And then he had stopped. He was quivering all over as if he had the influenza or something, and there was something strange happening with her too. She was afraid for a moment that she was going to faint right there.

"Don't!" she said, aware that at the moment she said it he wasn't doing anything at all, not even touching her.

He grunted, and by the time she could think that he sounded like a stallion about to cover a mare, he had pulled her blouse up and out of the way and bent his head and kissed her right on the nipple.

She had yelped then and pushed him away, and he backed away from her, his chest heaving, and groaned.

"Oh, my God," he said. "Oh, my God!" And then he backed away from her and fled from the foaling barn.

She had watched him go and then, wondering why she was out of breath, she leaned against the wall of the foaling stall and waited until the faint feeling had passed. She had difficulty accepting the reality of what had happened. She had been kissed, really kissed, for the first time in her life, and for the first time in her life, someone had touched her breast. Not only touched it, *kissed* the nipple.

And that someone was *David!* Whom she had thought of as a brother. And she really hadn't done anything to stop him! Satan had gotten in her and made her act like whores must act. And that was why he had backed away from her, because he thought she was a whore. She hadn't pushed him away, or kicked him, or anything, until he had actually raised her blouse and put his mouth on her bosom. *Was* she meant to be a whore? Was that why she hadn't pushed him away or kicked him?

She didn't know how long she had stayed there, leaning against the wall of the foaling stable, breathing as hard as if she had run a mile. But it was long enough for him to go to the other barn, saddle Wanderer, and mount him.

She had heard the sound of the hooves and gone to the door of the foaling stable and looked out in time to see him riding out of the barnyard. He'd put his shirt and his coat on, but he hadn't buttoned them or even tucked the shirt in his pants.

Then she had an entirely satisfying thought. He hadn't thought she was a whore. He was afraid, because of what he had done. He was afraid she would tell her father what he had done. She wouldn't do that, of course. If she did that, her father would kill him—or try to, anyway— and at the very least tell him to take his horses and go and never come back.

But, she had thought, it was going to be interesting to have David afraid of her, afraid of the power she held over him.

That good feeling had lasted about thirty seconds. Then she had thought that, as shy as he was, he would be so ashamed of what he thought he had done that he was liable never ever to have the courage to face her again. It was entirely possible, she thought, that he would send someone with a note to pick up his animals, and she would never see him again.

Sally understood that she had learned something else about herself in the five days since David had ridden bare-chested out of the foaling barn: the somewhat startling truth seemed to be that she was an accomplished and skillful liar, and lying didn't seem to bother her at all. She had not even felt ashamed of herself.

The first person she had lied to was her mother, just as soon as she walked back to the house after David had ridden off.

"Your blouse is out of your skirt," her mother greeted her. "What have you been doing?"

"I cleaned the foaling stall," she had lied without even thinking about it.

"Is Harriet showing signs?" her mother asked, accepting that lie without question.

"She dropped it," Sally had said. "David said she had a bit of a hard time, but that she'll be all right."

"And the foal?"

"Having his breakfast," Sally had said with a smile.

"Where was David going, riding off in such a hurry, without his breakfast and with his shirt and coat unbuttoned?"

"To London," Sally had replied. "He said he had things to do. He stayed until he was sure that the foal was all right, and then he left."

"Without his breakfast and with his shirt half off?"

"I don't know about his breakfast," Sally said. "What do mean, 'with his shirt half off'?"

"His shirt was half off, is what I mean, his shirt was half off," her mother replied.

"I don't know what you're talking about," Sally had lied. She was glad her mother couldn't see her face. She was sure she was as red as a tomato.

Her mother snorted. "You didn't notice that his shirt was half off?"

"No," Sally insisted. "I didn't."

"He didn't try to do anything to you, did he?"

"David? Don't be silly."

Her mother snorted again. "Let me tell you, miss," her mother said, "you're not fooling me for a minute."

"I don't know what you mean," Sally replied.

"I'll tell you what I mean," she said. "I mean that I'm going to tell your father to tell David to stay away from you, is what I mean."

"He wasn't doing anything to me that he shouldn't," Sally insisted.

Her mother snorted again. "I mean to have a word with your father," she said.

"Do what you want," Sally said insolently.

Her mother had turned around and slapped her.

Sally had run from the kitchen, her face smarting, her eyes filled with tears.

He didn't do anything to me he shouldn't have, she thought firmly. And then she wondered if she were losing her mind. Of course he had. He had pulled her blouse out of her skirt and kissed her right on the nipple. He

should not have done that. The shocking realization came
that she had really liked him doing that to her.

She had also lied easily and successfully to her father
when he came to her after her mother had "had a word
with him." She told him that she had no idea what had so
upset her mother, that if David's shirt had been out of
his pants, she hadn't noticed; and if it had been, and hers
had been, it was because they had been on their hands and
knees helping Harriet drop the foal and cleaning up
afterward, and that nothing had happened between them.

She even worked up a few tears, saying that it wasn't
fair that her mother should accuse her of doing something wicked when all she was doing was helping David
with the foaling.

The lies came easily, the more she did it. She complained that her mother was being unfair to David too.
Harriet wasn't David's mare. He had no obligation to
help her foal and make himself late to go back to London,
which explained why he had ridden away without his
breakfast.

Her mother, she said, now sobbing, had a nasty suspicious mind and it was unfair. Her father had put his
hand on her shoulder, told her to stop crying, and explained that the only reason her mother was that way
was because she loved her and wanted to make sure that
nothing happened that would hurt her.

He went on to say that he knew she was a good girl and
that he trusted her, and that David was a good lad and
that he trusted him. That made her feel like a sinner.

"I'll say the same thing to David when he comes on
Friday," her father said. "In case your mother says something to him."

"He probably even won't be here next weekend," Sally
said, dabbing at the tears in her eyes with her knuckles.
"He has an examination coming up that he has to study
for."

That was another lie that had popped into her mouth.
David had said nothing about an examination. But he
was likely to be afraid to come to the farm after what
he'd done to her, and there would have to be a satisfactory explanation for that.

"I feel sorry for him," her father replied, "having to go to school, studying things that he doesn't give a tinker's dam about and that he'll never use after he's learned them. It's clear he'd rather be working a farm."

And that had been the end of that. She had lied to her mother, who hadn't believed her, and to her father, who had; and she wasn't half as ashamed or afraid as she knew she should be. It was even worse. She had spent a lot of time thinking about what had happened, about what David's mouth and the bristles of his beard had felt like against her breast, the way his kissing the nipple had made it stand up. And she wasn't ashamed about that, either.

She hadn't been sure all week if David would appear as he usually did. Or been able to decide what it would mean if he didn't show up, whether he really had something to do in London or whether he was afraid to face her, or thinking she had told her father what he had done, afraid to face her father.

When he hadn't shown up on Friday, she thought he wouldn't be coming at all. She had spent a long time in bed before going to sleep, reflecting on what his not showing up had meant. It was possible that he just hadn't come on Friday, period, and that he would appear early Saturday morning, as he often did. Or it might mean that he wouldn't be coming this weekend at all. For perfectly ordinary reasons, having nothing to do with his pulling her blouse up and kissing her nipple. She told herself that if she knew that he hadn't come because of that, it would be better than not knowing. If she *knew*, she could think of some way to tell him that she hadn't told her father, and wouldn't if he promised to behave in the future.

Not knowing was the hard part, and thinking about that had kept her awake a long time.

She woke up a lot earlier than she thought she would, considering how long it had taken her to get to sleep. And when she started to open the shutter so that she could look out the window on the off chance that he just might be coming down the lane, she told herself that she was playing the fool and that there was going to be nothing on the lane but maybe a chicken.

But there he was, on Wanderer, riding slowly down the lane toward the house. That meant, she realized as she pulled the shutter closed again so that he wouldn't see her looking out, that he must have left London in the middle of the night.

The reason my heart is beating like this, Sally told herself, is because I was up half the night thinking and then got up long before I should have.

Sally took her time doing her hair before she started out of her bedroom. Then she had another thought: if he saw that she hadn't bound her breasts, he was liable to think that was an invitation to do again what he had done before. She couldn't let him think that; he would think she was a whore. She pulled her blouse out of her skirt and took her arms out of the sleeves and let it hang around her neck as she bound her breasts. She examined herself in the mirror. The binding didn't do much to conceal them, she thought, but at least they won't bounce around. Then she went out of her room and into the kitchen.

He wasn't in the kitchen, although he now habitually let himself into the kitchen if no one seemed to be around. She went to the window. Neither was he at the barns and stables with Wanderer, unsaddling him, to either turn him loose in a field to graze or put him in a stall.

That meant he was in front of the house.

She went to the main room and peered out the crack in the blind. He was in front of the house, standing by Wanderer's head, feeding him lumps of sugar. He was, she decided with something close to satisfaction, too afraid to come in the house.

She pushed open the door and feigned surprise. "I thought I heard somebody out here," she said.

"I didn't mean to wake you," he said.

"You didn't," she said. "You're early, aren't you?"

"My sister's getting married," he said.

"Huh?"

"I said my sister's getting married," he said. "There was a letter from her Thursday. She's getting married to an army officer and she's going to go to Hannover, in Germany."

"Oh," she said. It was all she could think of to say.

"I expect I'll have to go to the wedding," he said. "It's going to be grand affair, she says."

"That's nice."

"I don't know what I'll do about getting out of school," he said. "To go to the wedding, I mean. And I'll have to ask your father if he'll take care of my horses while I'm gone."

"I'm sure he will," Sally said.

He looked at her a moment, and then blurted, "Did you tell him?"

"Tell him what?" Sally asked innocently.

"Jesus, girl, you know what," he said.

"What do you think?" she asked coyly.

"Answer me, damn you!" he said furiously.

She walked back into the house. She had almost made it to the kitchen when he caught up with her, grabbed her arm, and spun her around.

"Answer me!" he said.

"No," she said.

What he's going to do now, Sally thought, is kiss me again, and then pull my blouse out my skirt and try to touch my bosom again.

Isn't he going to be surprised when he finds the band?

But David didn't kiss her and he didn't try to touch her breast. What he did was touch her face very lightly with the balls of his fingers.

"You have to understand, Sally," he said, "that I went crazy because just being near you makes me crazy. You'll have to try to forgive me. It'll never happen again."

That was her cue, she knew, to say something like "I forgive you, but if it ever happens again, I will tell my father."

What she did, instead, was raise her hand to his face. And then he lowered his face to hers and kissed her very, very gently on the lips.

The astonishing thing, Sally thought, was that that produced precisely the same effect, the weak sensation in the knees, the light-headedness, that she'd felt when he'd put his hand on her naked breast and then kissed the nipple.

2

Two minutes after John Law reached the home of Eleanor Hambleden, the Marchioness of Sprilley, at eight-thirty o'clock that Friday evening, it was quite clear to him that she had made a bloody damned fool of him.

She had, "now that he knew where it was," invited him to "come to see her when her husband was out of town." The marquess, she had told him, would be out of town on that night. He had drawn the logical conclusion from that that she would, under those conditions, bring to its natural conclusion the business she had started by groping him under the robe in her carriage.

When he reached their home, it was ablaze with candles and lanterns. That had puzzled him at first, until he was admitted by the butler and almost immediately learned that he was to be but one of a dozen guests the marchioness was entertaining at dinner and, afterward, with a string quartet.

The marchioness, an enormous diamond hanging at the division of her breasts, greeted him in the drawing room as if she barely remembered his name. At dinner he found himself at almost the opposite end of the table from her, between a fat woman of forty and a viscount who reeked of rose water and who looked at John Law in a way that made him distinctly uncomfortable. Over his lamb chops John Law, righteously indignant, decided that as soon as brandy and cigars were announced for the gentlemen and the ladies left, he would find his coat and leave. He would not, he decided, thank his hostess for dinner, and give her the satisfaction of smirking at him.

But then he felt her eyes on him and he looked down the table at her. When she saw that she had his attention, she wet her lips with the tip of her tongue.

That is clearly some wicked signal. But is she doing it

as a bona fide suggestion, or because it amuses her to tease me?

He did not leave immediately when brandy and cigars were announced. He smoked his cigar, had three brandies, and waited to see what would happen next.

The gentlemen were asked to join the ladies in the drawing room for the entertainment. He found himself sitting uncomfortably on a small chair directly before the string quartet, who demonstrated their repertoire for what seemed like hours. What with the wine and the brandy and the coffee, he was convinced that he would not make it to the conclusion of the entertainment.

He did, but his bladder was swollen to the point of pain, and even before the applause had died down, he was on his feet, looking for a servant who could give him directions to some place he could relieve himself.

"If you will be good enough to come with me, sir," the footman said, and marched ahead of him up the wide staircase to the second floor and then down a corridor and to a bedroom. He took a chamber pot from a bedside table and ceremoniously removed its cover.

"Will that be all, sir?" the footman asked. "Or would you like me to wait for you?"

"That will be all, thank you," John said, forcing a smile and waiting until the footman had closed the door behind him before tearing at his flap.

"Oh, my God!" he said aloud. "I was about to burst."

"I'm glad you didn't," Eleanor said, laughing in her throat. She had entered the room from an adjacent room. John was horribly embarrassed, but there was nothing he could do but finish the business at hand. Then he turned to face her.

"Are you having a good time?" she asked.

"I didn't expect to find the house full of people," he said.

"What did you expect? I could have hardly asked you here, alone. What would people think?"

"What happens now?" he asked.

"I've called for a carriage to take you home," she said. "It will be a few minutes before it's brought around."

And then she walked out of the room.

When he went downstairs, she was at the door to the drawing room, saying good night to her guests. He joined the others, whose ranks depleted as carriages were announced. When there were only half a dozen people standing there with her, a footman called his name.

"Thank you for coming, John," she said to him. "It's always a pleasure."

"Thank you for your hospitality," he said.

"We'll see you soon again," she said, and gave him her hand, and he bowed over it and kissed it.

The hell you will. You've made a fool of me for the first and last time.

In the carriage, a coupe, John Law opened the window in the ceiling. "Take me to Crockford's," he ordered.

There was no response, but the coupe jerked into motion.

What he was going to do, he decided, was go to the bar downstairs in Crockford's and pick out a tart. A tart that was a tart, not a marchioness who looked like a tart and who amused herself making a fool of young men.

By the time the coupe stopped he had managed to work himself into a rather fine pique. She had had no right to do to him what she had done. He had not made an advance to her beyond a smile. She was the one who had brought him to her table; she was the one whose hand had explored him so intimately under the robe in her carriage; and she had clearly implied that she had something other than dinner and a string quartet in mind when she had invited him to her house, "when her husband was out of town."

And then that business of the tongue.

He was the aggrieved party, all right.

He climbed down from the coupe. He had no idea where he was, but this certainly wasn't the front entrance to Crockford's. Then, seeing they were in a mews, he decided that this was the back entrance to Crockford's, where those who did not wish to be seen going in the front door could enter and leave the place in privacy.

"This way, if you please, sir," the coachman said to him, leading the way with a lantern.

They went down a ground-floor corridor, to a stairway. The coachman handed him the lantern.

218

"The second landing, sir," he said. "And I'll be here when you want me."

"You may go home," Law said.

"I have been instructed to wait, sir," the coachman said.

"Well, wait, then," Law said curtly, and started up the stairs. When he opened the door on the second landing, he found himself in the upstairs corridor of the home of the Marquess of Sprilley.

He went down the corridor, opening doors. The first two doors opened into bedrooms, including the one where he had relieved himself. He started to turn away from that room and then remembered that she had come into it from an adjacent room. He opened that door.

The Marchioness of Sprilley was in that room. She was in the bed, in the act of lighting a long thin cigar from one of the two candles that sat on the bedside tables. There was, he noticed, a bottle of brandy on the table and two glasses.

"I was beginning to think you were lost," she said. Then she got off the bed and walked over to him. Her hair was down and she was wearing some sort of chemise. For all it did to conceal the darkness of her nipples and the black patch at her groin, she might as well have taken that off, too.

"I've heard it said," she said, "that everything worth having is worth waiting for. Do you think that's true?"

She took a puff at the cigar and then handed it to him, and when he had taken it, she put her fingers to the buttons of his shirt.

He was trembling and his heart was beating furiously in his chest, and he did not trust himself to try to speak.

3

John Law told David Gardiner that he had won "a nice sum of money" at the wheel of chance and that he had met a very interesting lady, but he did not tell him how much money he had won, nor identify the lady.

To have won 936 pounds was nearly as incredible as having been taken into Lady Eleanor's bed, and he rather doubted that either would be within David Gardiner's comprehension. Stout fellow though he was, John reasoned, David Gardiner was simple, a man of the soil who could not be expected to possess the sophistication he did. Law told himself this was not a criticism of David, but instead simply seeing things as they were.

He had, he thought, seen David in his natural surroundings at the Ward farm. There had been absolutely no way to get out of going out there with him, although John could have easily come up with half a dozen more interesting ways to spend a weekend. David had said that it would do him good to get out of London for a bit. But what he wanted to do was show John the farmer's daughter.

Sally Ward was as pretty as John had remembered from the brief look he'd had at her in The Duke's Arms, and it was easy to understand why David was taken, indeed, smitten, with her. Under other circumstances, John would have loved to have a go at her himself. And she wasn't as dull as he thought she would be. She was actually far more clever than he would have thought possible. As David was far more clever than he would have guessed he would be.

That had explained a great deal to him, when he thought about it. He had made the assumption—understandably, since he knew so few of them—that all farmers were rather dull. That wasn't true in David's case, and it wasn't true in the case of Thomas Ward, or his daughter, either. It was logical to assume that David's "father" was much like Thomas Ward, a cut above the average dull farmer, and thus a bit (in the case of David's "father," a good bit) more successful.

This did not mean, of course, that any of them were nearly as intelligent or sophisticated as he himself was. The proof of this came, John believed, when he had handed David a draft for one hundred pounds, announced that figure as his winnings, and suggested that David invest it for him in animals, for a percentage of the profits, if any. It had been almost too much for David to handle.

He was convinced that David Gardiner would handle the

money with at least as much care as he handled his own, and one hundred pounds put out that way was going to return him a greater percentage than leaving it in the bank would have. And a hundred pounds, he judged, was about all the money that David could handle in his horse trading; a hundred pounds would buy a number of first-class animals. To buy any more would require stabling facilities beyond those available at the Ward farm and cause other problems.

So far as Lady Eleanor was concerned, the less David knew about her specifically, the better. His simple farmer's soul would be upset by the very fact that she was older ... and married. It simply would be too much for David to accept that he was having an adulterous affair with the daughter of an earl and the wife of a marquess.

It was a bit difficult for him to accept himself. Lady Eleanor had been astonishing in bed, a work of art without her clothing, as skilled as any tart he had ever known, and the most enthusiastic and appreciative female he had ever bedded. Immediately after their first tumble, which understandably had been excited and brief and nowhere near as extraordinary as the tumbles that followed, she had matter-of-factly raised the question of where they could meet in the future. For obvious reasons, they could not meet again as they were meeting now, she said. While she had paid the coachman well for his secrecy, it was simply too dangerous.

John confessed to Lady Eleanor that he shared his apartments with David, who was not really a gentleman, although the son of a successful family, and who was rather young, to boot. It was unlikely, he told her, that David would be able to understand their relationship, and he did not, in other words, think it a good idea for her to come to his apartments.

The other possibilities were to take a room in an inn, on a permanent basis, or to find a small apartment somewhere. They decided the latter course would be best, and he was smugly pleased that, with more money at his disposal than he knew what to do with, he could easily afford an apartment for his "mistress." He was thrilled with that, too, the idea of having a mistress at all being only slightly less thrilling than having a mistress who was a marchioness.

Eleanor said that her husband's circle of friends included a number of young men in the midst of which John would fit in inconspicuously, and that she could arrange for them to attend the same weekends in the country. It would pose no problems, she said. A modicum of discretion was all that would be required; her husband was not overly jealous.

On David Gardiner's part, he did not confide in John Law the incredible change in his life. It was likely, even certain, that if he told John that he and Sally had partaken of the physical joys Church and society restricted to the married state, John would assume that Sally was nothing more than any other farmer's daughter willing to raise her skirts to all comers.

It was, of course, not like that at all. He loved Sally, and she loved him, and what had happened between them in the barn on the fresh haystack had been a manifestation of the overwhelming size of the love between them, a love that would eventually, once they sorted things out, result in a proper marriage between them. Law would certainly make one of his sophisticated remarks, some comment about Sally that would enrage him and end their friendship. It would have been unreasonable of him to expect John Law to understand that what he and Sally shared was love, of a depth and purity that placed it far above what Law would think was simply a tumble in the hay.

In a way, he thought, he pitied John Law. What he had had—twice, once in the hayloft and then again when Sally had sneaked into his room very early one Sunday morning—was holy and sacred. All that John had had over the weekend was a spot of luck at the wheel of chance, followed by the tumbling of a tart paid for, David was sure, with his wheel-of-chance winnings. In other words, both sinful and sordid, sin paid for with the proceeds of sin. John could not be expected to understand that. He himself had never known the incredible difference between tumbling, which he now understood was nothing more than a human version of covering a mare, and the physical manifestation of the joining of souls, which is what he and Sally had.

And Sally had seen John Law for what he was. She had told David that while he might be a fancy gentleman, she didn't think he was really much of man. She told him that she didn't understand how they could be friends, they were so different. Although he could come up with no answer to the question, David took it as one more proof that Sally was uncommonly clever.

While David really had no interest in dealing in horses with John Law's money for a percentage of the profits, he accepted the notion and the draft with something of an ulterior motive. If he had more business to do, he would have to go out to the Ward farm more often than on weekends. If he was at the farm, it was possible that Sally would come to the stables while he was examining his animals, or perhaps, if he stayed the night, come to his room early in the morning to make sure he was awake.

There were several problems he was willing to face squarely. They all involved his parents or the Wards. His father had sent him to London to study business at St. Peter's School, not to court a woman. His parents thought of him as a boy, and boys do not get married. Furthermore, as his father had taken pains to point out, boys could not legally own property. There was no question whatever in David's mind that he could support Sally with the proceeds from his horse trading, but if his father wished, the law said that whatever David possessed was his father's, if he wanted it.

David knew that his father wouldn't want the horses, or the money, as such, but that it was entirely possible, to save him from "a boyish infatuation," that his father would clip his financial wings. In this, he would be encouraged by his mother. David was very much aware that his mother firmly believed him to be an innocent and helpless twelve-year-old; sending him to London was insanity, and was certain to result in some catastrophe. His mother was going to regard his plans to marry Sally as proof of her prediction.

That fact that Kate was to marry would have nothing

to do with it. Marriages were arranged all the time for girls younger than Kate, but men were supposed to be older—at least twenty-two, and better more—before they went to the altar.

So far as Sally and the Wards were concerned, they had often made it plain to him that they were pleased that he regarded Sally as a sister, and vice versa, for it would have been impossible to maintain their relationship if it were otherwise. It wasn't that they didn't like him, David understood, but rather that they knew he would be returning to Scotland and there was no chance at all of his becoming the man they needed on the farm and expected to acquire through Sally.

If he and Sally were to start feeling romantic, the Wards reasoned, they would be married and he would take Sally to Scotland; and they thought they would be left alone, to fend for themselves in their old age, and they certainly were not going to permit that.

He would somehow work out the problem of what to do with the Wards, as he would work out the other problems. The solution to all problems was to proceed slowly. The first thing to do was discreetly begin to inform his mother and father of Sally. The best way to do that would be to start mentioning her very casually in his letters home. Until now, the letters, promised for once a week, had not always been sent.

David began to make up for that now. He began to write twice a week, and in each letter, he managed to drop in some innocent aside about "the Wards' daughter," telling his father that it was really remarkable how helpful she could be to her father, since she was possessed of an unusual amount of useful knowledge, coupled with a desire to work.

He informed his mother that the Ward girl ("Have I mentioned her before? Very pleasant personality, refined, devout. Has well-washed blond hair and very blue eyes") had been learning from her mother how to bake pastry, and while it wasn't anything like his mother's, which he missed very much, it was really remarkably good for a young woman. And incidentally, "for a young woman, she is remarkably intelligent. Her parents have even taught her how to read and write."

Once he had to throw away a whole letter, which annoyed him greatly. In it he had written that, "so far as the Ward girl (whose name is Sally, have I mentioned that?) is concerned, looking down that long lane to marriage (still obviously far away from me, but on the hand, now that Kate has found a husband, perhaps not as far as one might think), a man could do a lot worse. She is honest, and sweet-tempered, and healthy and not bad-looking."

That, he had decided, was going a bit far. His parents would be liable to grow suspicious if he wrote anything like that. So he tore it up and wrote another, this time limiting his references to Sally to a brief comment that she had brought into the fields, where he had been helping Mr. Ward distribute oats and wheat to the horses, the best beef soup he had ever eaten, his mother's excepted.

He was convinced he was on the right path. The thing to do was let the Wards get used to him, and through his discreetly worded letters home, give his parents an appreciation of what a fine young woman Sally was. In the meantime, he could get out to the farm frequently when he had time off from school.

And then, of course, when he went home to Kate's wedding, he could act older, behave like a man, and demonstrate he had the maturity and the sense to marry. The more he thought of it, Kate's getting married was a splendid idea, even if it did mean she would have to go off to Germany.

Chapter Ten

1

The thought, Kate knew, had been born in anger.

It had been decided that David would not come from London for the wedding. Her father had made the decision and her mother had agreed. It would take him a month, more likely six weeks, to come from London and then to go back. For a day, *half* a day, of wedding celebration. There was no way he could just leave school for six weeks and expect to catch up with the others, which meant, when it got down to taking a close look at it, that he would pay for half a day in Edinburgh at her wedding with the loss of a whole year of school.

Not to mention the expense.

They told her David was a practical lad; she knew that. He would understand.

Kate, tight-lipped, had walked out of the kitchen, where the decision had been made.

Goddamm it! If David won't be there, I just won't get married!

The thought didn't, wouldn't, go away, even after she had been forced to admit the logic of her parents' argument.

It was the first time she had actually considered what was happening.

She had been caught up in the excitement of it all.

She'd thought all along, from the time she was not much more than a little girl, of getting married, and she'd thought a lot about it after David had been sent off to London. That seemed to be some indication that the time she would marry was a good deal closer than it had been before.

And there had been overtures from others, beside this thing with Thom Frazier. She knew she wasn't too bad-looking a girl, and then there was the dowry. She knew that her father would provide a more-than-decent dowry, and that meant a good husband, one close to her age, for one thing, and one from a decent family like her own.

But she had never dreamed of anything so grand as being an officer's wife, of meeting the man she would marry at a grand dinner in the home of Captain William Law. Not that Captain Law was behind it. The appearance of the Duke of Lauderdale had proved who was behind it.

She was unable to think of that drunken old man as her father. Her father was the man she had known all of her life. But neither was she able to entirely put from her mind that she was what she somewhat wryly thought of as being "the old bastard's bastard."

Clearly, that was behind the whole thing. The old bastard, for God only knew what reasons, had decided to see her well-married. It wasn't as if Thom Frazier had had to be propelled to the altar at sword point. He was as embarrassed by the duke's interest as Kate was. Maybe more.

But he really liked her, and that was of course very flattering, even more so because he was a good-looking fellow, and a nice one, and he wasn't chasing her because he couldn't catch someone else. Thom was a little stiff, but Kate thought that was probably because he was an officer, and that underneath he was the opposite. He even had a sense of humor.

But right after it had been decided that David would not be able to come to the wedding, and she'd had that thought born in anger that if David couldn't come to the wedding, there wouldn't be a wedding, she had another, terrible, unreasonable thought that just wouldn't go away: she didn't want to marry Thom Frazier.

She didn't want to go to Hannover and probably never see her mother and father and David for years. And she didn't want to have Thom Frazier's babies. Thom was a very nice fellow, and he was an officer and a gentleman, and he would probably be very kind to her in bed, but the very idea of being in bed with him with their clothes off, and doing that, when it wasn't funny, was frightening. She just didn't want to do it.

Kate tried to bring the subject up to her mother and got nowhere. Mary MacPhee Gardiner heard her out, but she said that she had herself found out that love wasn't what young girls thought it was, being swept off your feet by some handsome young man, but that it came later, after you were married, when you learned that your husband was a good and decent man and a good father to your children.

My father is not Thom Frazier, Kate decided. My "father" is not even my father. It may have worked out well for Mother, marrying a man because she had to and learning to love him later. God knows my "father" is a fine and decent man, and I love him dearly. But I don't *have* to marry Thom; I'm not carrying a child.

And because she knew and loved Edward Gardiner so well, she knew there was no sense in even trying to talk to him. He loved her, and because of that, he saw it as his duty to see that she was married well. The dowry he was going to pay to Thom Frazier, and with which Thom would buy a captain's commission in the Borderers, was twice, maybe three times as much money as Kate thought it would be worth. And more, probably, than he could really afford. He was making a sacrifice so that she could marry Thom Frazier, so that she could be an officer's wife and have a life far better than anyone he had known had ever had.

And then the thought that had been formed in anger because David wasn't going to be able to come from London to be at the wedding crystallized: I don't love

Thom Frazier. I don't want to go to the Court of the Elector of Hannover. I don't want to marry Thom Frazier and I don't want his babies.

She went again to her mother with this, and Mary MacPhee Gardiner talked for more than an hour to her, telling her that all girls have doubts before their marriage, that it was a perfectly natural thing. It would all pass, Mary told her, once she was married and came to understand what a fine young man Thom Frazier was and what a fine life they could build together.

"Once the babies come," Mary said, "you'll understand what makes a woman happy."

A week before the marriage was to take place, after the rehearsal in the church, Edward Gardiner and his wife gave their daughter some money. Some of it was half the money Mary had brought into the marriage. They also gave her one of the two two-crown gold pieces she and David had received from the Lord High Commissioner for Scotland when they were twelve.

At four o'clock the next morning, Kate Gardiner, carrying several changes of clothes and the Bible she had been given when she had been confirmed into the church, went quietly to the barn, saddled a horse and rode into Edinburgh.

She unsaddled the horse and left him where he would be seen right away in the fenced area behind the office. Then she went into the office and sat down at Edward Gardiner's desk and wrote a letter to her parents, saying that she was sorry for all the trouble and embarrassment she knew she was causing, but that she just couldn't marry Thom Frazier. She was going to David in London, and if David wouldn't help her, then she would go into domestic service.

Then she went down to the waterfront and boarded the royal mail packet *Prince David* for London.

2

An expensively furnished apartment near Lincoln's Inn Fields, John Law thought as he left Crockford's Club at half-past eight on a Saturday night, was a splendid thing to have, presuming your mistress was there. If that were not the case, it had little, virtually no, appeal.

He was five pounds richer than when he had entered Crockford's, and considerably drunker. Neither condition pleased him, as either should have. He had often thought, before he had come into his money, how delightful it would be to have enough so that it wouldn't matter if he lost a bit at the tables, or so that he could pick whichever of the elegant tarts in the bar room at Crockford's struck his fancy at the moment.

It hadn't turned out that way. Instead of becoming what he had always hoped to become—a devil-may-care gambler, easy-come easy-go—quite the reverse had happened. He was so afraid of becoming poor again that he gambled with great caution. The result of that seemed to be that he now won with just about as much regularity as he had previously lost, but with absolutely no excitement and very little pleasure.

The acquisition of a titled mistress similarly had not been what he had thought it would be. In a perverse way, it had been morally uplifting. It now never entered his mind to engage the services of one of the tarts at Crockford's. He realized both that it would be below him and that there was something essentially sordid about it. In one sense, he sometimes thought, it would be considerably cheaper to have one of the tarts on a regular basis than it was to maintain his relationship with Eleanor, Marchioness of Sprilley.

He liked to play mentally with numbers, and he had often simultaneously tormented and pleased himself with the cold mathematics of the affair. On a per-tumble basis, Eleanor, his "free" mistress, was costing him a good bit more than any of the tarts at Crockford's would have cost.

The apartment, for one thing, was outrageously expensive. There was the rent, of course, and that was bad enough. But it didn't end there. He had had to engage the services of a maid, to clean the place up. The landlord's definition of a "completely furnished apartment" had not included either linen or tableware, and the cost of that had been astonishing.

Then there was the cost of having a restaurant send around food and wine when Eleanor was there. That cost, compared to the others, was relatively minor, not because the thieves who ran the Golden Ram charged prices that bore any resemblance to fair and just, but because Eleanor was able to sneak off to the apartment so seldom.

And then the goddamned flowers! It was impossible for him, of course, to make her small presents as tokens of his affection. How would she explain a ring or a pendant to her husband? But flowers, lots of expensive flowers spread around the apartment, he had learned, satisfied the requirement of a gift without posing problems. Flowers in winter, he had learned, were as dear as diamonds.

There were other expenses. Livery, for one thing. Eleanor could not be expected to have herself driven to the apartment in a carriage with her husband's coat of arms emblazoned on the doors. And certainly she couldn't walk. That meant that every night her husband *might* be out of town and she could get out of the house for a couple of hours, he had to rent a carriage and circle the block on which her house was located. Sometimes, on the third trip around the square, she would be waiting on the curb at the corner. Whether she was or not, the livery had to be paid. And if they did pick her up, he had to pay to keep the carriage until it was time for her to return home, very early in the morning; which cost an outrageous price, to which had to be added a generous tip to the coachman to ensure his silence.

And he was still paying half the expenses for the apartment he shared with David. There had been an extraordinary letter from his father, informing him that David Gardiner, the son of the horse trader, was, in case John was not already aware of this fact, also a student at St. Peter's. Certain things had come to light, the details of which his father was reluctant to commit to paper, that caused him to suggest in the strongest possible terms that he seek out young Gardiner and take him under his wing—if possible to open his apartment to him.

For another reason, when he had mentioned to Eleanor that he was thinking of moving out of the apartment, she had flatly rejected the notion.

"It's much better," Eleanor had announced, "that it be known you are sharing an apartment with another student. And that we keep this place as quiet as possible."

It now rather frequently entered his mind that he would not be immobilized with grief were the affair to end. While Eleanor beyond doubt gave him the most interesting and satisfying tumbles he had ever experienced, they were damnably infrequent and, on a per-tumble basis, damnably expensive. Eleanor, however, gave him no indication that she was tiring of the relationship. Apparently, she was getting all that she wanted out of it. There had also been a growing suspicion in his mind that sometimes when he circled her house and she did not appear on the curb, this was because she really didn't want to make love with him that night, rather than because the marquess was at home, or expected to be.

When John Law got into the hired carriage outside Crockford's, he sensed that tonight was to be another of those nights when something "unexpected" would have come up that would keep Eleanor from being on the curb on his third or fourth trip around her square. Despite her assurances that very afternoon, when he had arranged to meet her for a moment on Bishop's Lane, that she was "as sure as she could be" that they could be together tonight, experience had taught him the odds were against her being on the curb.

He was right. After the carriage had made four trips around the square, it was obvious to him that tonight was going to be another night he would be billed for a cold roast chicken and three chilled bottles of champagne delivered to the apartment by the proprietors of the Golden Ram which would be consumed the next day by the maid. Another night that he would sleep alone.

"To hell with it," he said.

"You say something, gov'nor?" the coachman asked, opening the little window below his seat to look into the interior of the coach.

John told him to take him to the apartment he shared with David.

He paid off the coachman and looked up the windows of the apartment. They were dark. They were usually

233

dark on a Saturday night. On Saturday nights, David was in the country, counting the money he had made at some fair that day and staring with cowlike eyes at his beloved Sally Ward.

The only difference between David and me, John Law thought somewhat drunkenly, is that he rode farther than I did just to go to bed alone.

He headed for the tavern two squares away where they took most of their meals during the week. Infrequently (and certainly, he thought somewhat bitterly, not tonight, when a tumble is absolutely essential to my health and well-being) there were girls there who could be talked into bed. There were always girls there, however, who could be paid for their favors, and the thought entered his mind that tonight he just might make an exception to his rule about having become too mature to pay for it.

There were none of the girls who could be sometimes talked into a tumble in the tavern, and those who could be paid for their favors had already been spoken for. Painfully aware that a very good and very expensive dinner was going to waste in the other apartment, he had a rather poor supper in the tavern, washing it down with two bottles of wine. The wine was on purpose. Wine put him to sleep. He sensed that he was going to have trouble getting to sleep tonight.

Then he walked home, and as he neared the apartment, he saw the glow of oil lamps in the apartment. His spirits immediately soared. David was home. There had been trouble in Eden. Either he had had a spat with Saintly Sally, or Farmer Ward had finally begun to understand that David's interest in the farm was not limited to the welfare of his horses and had sent him home.

In either case, David would be available as a drinking companion, either back at their tavern or, if he were really crushed by his spat with Sally, on the town itself. They could drink until morning.

He went quickly up the stairs, found his key, unlocked the door, and went inside.

"I have a splendid idea," he called. "Let's go get tumbled."

There was no response.

Oh, hell! He's been rejected. Saintly Sally has told him to be gone, now and forever. He's sitting in there with his chin hanging to his knees, convinced that the world has come to an end.

"David?"

He went into their sitting room.

There was a female in there, standing in the shadows.

I'll be damned. He's got a girl up here. He must have had a really bad spat with St. Sally.

"Is that you, David?" the female asked.

"No," John cried. "But anything David can do, I can do better."

And then the woman said, "Oh, it's you. What are you doing here? Is David with you?"

"I live here," he said. "And David fortunately is not . . ." And then he stopped, for the woman had stepped away from the shadow of the drapes into the light. It was David's exquisite redheaded sister.

"What are you doing here?" John asked, genuinely surprised that Kate Gardiner was in London.

"Where's David?" Kate asked.

"In the country, I would suppose," he said. "Did he know you were coming?"

She shook her head no.

"How long have you been here?" John asked.

"About an hour," Kate said. "The landlord let me in. What are you doing here?"

"I live here," he repeated. "David and I share this apartment."

"Oh," she said, and he sensed that information, for reasons he could not imagine, did anything but please her. "Where did you say David was?"

"I don't know, but I'd wager he's in the country. At the Ward farm. He spends most of his weekends there."

"With that girl, Sally?" Kate asked.

"With her and her family," John clarified.

"And when will he come back?"

"Probably very early Monday morning," John said.

"Oh," she said.

"He didn't know you were coming?"

"No."

"Well, in the morning," John Law said, "I'll take you out there, if you like."

"Oh, that would be nice of you," Kate said.

"What are you doing in London?" he asked.

"I came to see David," she said.

Ask a dumb question, get a dumb answer.

"Would you like something to eat? Or drink?" John Law said.

"What I would like is a good wash," she said. "I was on that boat more than a week."

"There's a tub in the kitchen," John said. "You'd have to heat water."

"I didn't want David to walk in on me when I was in the tub," she said.

It took him a moment to take her meaning.

"Well," he said, "I was about to have a nightcap at the tavern. So why don't I do that while you have your wash?"

"I need a good wash," Kate repeated.

"I'll have to carry you some water up here," he said.

"If you show me where the well is, I'll carry it myself," Kate said.

"Don't be silly," John said. "You drag the tub out and I'll get the water."

Why the hell did you make that offer? She's perfectly capable of carrying her own water.

He took their two buckets and went down to the back alley and filled them at the well, and then, staggering under their weight, carried them back to the apartment.

"What we do," he said, "is heat that big pot to boiling, and then mix it with one and a half of these. That makes the water nice and hot."

"I know how to heat water for a bath," she said, and there was a suggestion that she was laughing at him. "How long have you been living with David?"

"Since we came to London," John said.

"He never said anything," Kate said.

"I asked him not to," John said. "I had the feeling, until recently, that my father didn't want me close to David."

"Yes, I know," she said.

"You do?" Her response had surprised him.

"I overheard what he had to say about us when we were at your house," Kate said.

It took John a moment to put that all together. Seeing his difficulty, Kate helped him. "When you were talking to your father in the library," she said, "I was exploring your house. And opened one of the doors to the second floor of the library."

It was a moment before John replied. " 'I was about to say something very clever," he said. "Eavesdroppers hear naught but ill,' something like that. But what I really want to know is whether or not it's true."

"I think it is," she said.

"But David doesn't know?"

"I'm sure he doesn't," Kate said. "And I hope he never finds out."

"I'll not tell him," John Law said.

"Thank you, Mr. Law, for being so considerate," Kate said.

Does that mean she thanks me for promising not to tell David that he's the duke's bastard, or that she wants me to go away so she can have her bath?

"I'll go down for my nightcap now," he said.

"A wash won't take me long," Kate said.

He looked at her and smiled, and the first mental image of Kate Gardiner naked in her bath popped into his mind's eye.

Damn, I better stop that! That is David's sister, and I'm drunk, and there is no doubt whatever what he would do to me if I simply said something out of line. If I tried anything with her, he would, quite literally kill me.

He smiled at her and went out of the apartment and back to the tavern, where he ordered tea, so that he would not get drunk and do something, drunk, he should not do. Then he told himself that he was being absurd. He wasn't an animal; he could control his lusts; he was a gentleman, and gentlemen did not make advances to their friends' sisters.

He had a brandy and then another, and finally decided that by now she could have given herself two thorough

237

washes. He paid the bill and walked back to the apartment.

There was a glow of a lamp this time. She had taken her wash and gone to bed. And he would, he told himself, very quietly let himself into the apartment and go to bed himself.

The first thing that went wrong was that Kate had apparently decided the smaller of the two bedrooms was used by her brother. They had flipped a shilling over that, and David had won. That had put John into the smaller of the rooms, and when he walked into it on tiptoe and sat down on the bed to find a match for the candle, he sat on Kate Gardiner.

"Christ!" he blurted. "What are you doing in here?"

"Isn't this David's room?" Kate asked. "Oh, I'm sorry. I just thought that this would be David's room . . ."

"No harm done," John said. "You just stay where you are, and I'll go sleep in David's bed."

"No, I'll move," she said. "You'll want your bed."

"It's unnecessary," he said.

"Just give me a moment to light the lamp," she said. "I'm in my nightdress."

He fled into the sitting room, found a candle, and lit it. In a moment the door to David's bedroom opened and she stood in the center of it. She had lit the lamp, but left it on the table. The light from it silhouetted the outlines of her body. He looked away as quickly as he thought about the decent thing to do, which did not happen immediately.

"In there," he said.

"Thank you," Kate said softly, and went into David's room.

John Law waited until she had closed the door, and then he exhaled audibly. Then he blew out the candle, and went to his room. He undressed, put on a nightshirt, and got into the bed.

It was still warm from her body, and the smell of her was in it, some of it the soap with which she had washed herself and some of it just the smell of a clean, warm, female body.

I will ignore this. I will put it from my mind. It is absolutely despicable of me to have lewd thoughts simply

238

because my best, my only friend's sister, in all innocence, happened to lay for a bit on my sheets and pillow.

He rolled on his side and tried to go to sleep, and when that failed, he rolled onto his back and put his hands under his head.

Then he heard her crying. At first he thought it was another of those goddamned cats that conducted their romances in the alley, but then he understood what it was. She was crying.

Because I sat on her? Or did she see me staring through her nightgown?

He listened to it for a minute or so, and then he got out of bed, lit the lantern again, went into the sitting room, and stood by the door.

"Miss Gardiner?" he called.

There was no answer, and the crying stopped. He was just about to turn away from the door when it opened again. She was standing there, looking as forlorn as anything he had ever seen in his life.

"What is it?" she asked.

"Is there something I can do?" he asked. "I heard you crying."

"I wasn't crying," Kate said. There were tears dripping down her chin.

"Of course you were crying," John Law said. "I know crying when I hear it, and you were crying. Now, you tell me what's wrong, and we'll see what we can do about it."

"It's none of your business," she said, half sobbing.

"Of course it's my business. Your brother is my best friend, and in his absence, it most certainly is my business."

She looked up at him. Tears were forming in her eyes.

"It isn't," he asked, "anything that I have said or done that's offended you?"

She shook her head solemnly.

"Then what is it?"

"Thank you very much, Mr. Law," she said. "But there's nothing that you or anyone else can do." Then she turned around, went to the bed and threw herself on it, now sobbing shamelessly.

"For Christ's sake, stop that!" he said a moment later.
"The one thing I can't stand is a caterwauling female!"

That seemed only to make it worse.

He walked to the bed, leaned over her, and gingerly
touched her shoulder. "Miss Gardiner," he said. "Kate,
please stop that."

She did not stop.

"At least tell me what's wrong," John Law pleaded.

She rolled over on her back and looked up at him.

"Please," he said.

She sighed, and she told him. She told him everything
that had happened, and how she had come to London, and
how she now knew that it had been a terrible mistake, but
that it was too late now to do anything about it, she had
already stood Thom Frazier up and humiliated him and
his parents, and even John Law's father, who had arranged the marriage, and she probably had gotten him in
trouble with the duke, because the old bastard was behind
the whole thing; and now she was in London, and she
couldn't live here because there was no room for her, and
now that she thought of it, she had been wrong, and David
would know that and be as furious as her parents.

That, John thought, explained the mysterious letter
from his father ordering him to be nice to David. The
duke was showing an interest in his bastards, and his
father was sensitive to the duke's desires.

He wondered if Kate knew how dangerous it was to
interfere with what the duke wanted done.

Somehow during this recitation of woe, as he thought
of problems that Kate wasn't capable of considering, John
Law sat down on the bed, and his hand, which had so gingerly touched her back, began to rub it to comfort her,
and then he'd put his arm around her back to hold her.
And then he'd laid down beside her and held her against
him.

And all of a sudden he could feel her warm breath on
his mouth and her breasts pressing against his chest,
and that had been too much for him and he'd kissed her.
He had intended to kiss her very gently, to comfort her,
but it didn't turn out that way.

When he finally pulled his face from hers and sat up and looked down at her, he said, "Christ, I'm sorry!"

To which, after a moment, she replied, "Why?"

And that was the way it had happened.

3

Kate said that it wasn't that she was afraid to face her brother, but rather that she didn't want to embarrass him in front of the Wards.

"To hell with the Wards," John Law said. They were having breakfast at the tavern.

"Would you ride out there and tell him I'm here?" Kate said.

"Yes, if you wish," John Law said.

"Thank you Law," she said.

"If he finds out what happened between us," John said, "he'll kill me."

"He'd kill both of us," Kate said. "So I don't suppose we'd better tell him, do you?"

"I'm sorry, Kate."

"No reason," she said.

"I'm a despicable bastard," he said. "If I had any idea that you . . ."

"Were a virgin?" she asked softly. "There has to be a first time for everybody," she said.

"Jesus Christ! " he said. He stood up, put the key to the apartment on the table, started to say something and then changed his mind.

Then he went to the stable and saddled his high-stepping mare and rode out to the Ward farm to tell David his sister had run away from home and her marriage and was in the apartment.

David and the Wards were off at a fair someplace, and it was half-past five before they returned to the farm. That gave John Law plenty of time for a number of disquieting thoughts.

Kate Gardiner was in a good deal of trouble, all right, all of her own making, and that wasn't especially surprising, considering what an independent mind she had. There were a lot of females—practically everyone he had ever met, to get right down to it—who would have woken up this morning figuring they had some sort of claim on him for what had happened.

If she told David what he had done to her, it was entirely likely that David would do something idiotic, like offer him the choice between being killed and making an honest woman of his sister. He couldn't marry her, of course; that was simply out of the question.

For one thing, he didn't love her. For another thing, she was who she was, and that meant that in addition to being a horse trader's daughter, which would give his mother and his sisters convulsions, she was the bastard of Lauderdale, which would give his father apoplexy.

Somehow, he believed her when she said she wasn't going to tell David what had happened. He didn't think that was entirely because it would cause trouble for him, or because it would make her look even worse in her brother's eyes than running away the way she had. He thought it was because she was honest enough to admit to herself that it had taken two of them to do what they had done. That sort of honesty was extraordinary.

When David finally showed up at the Ward farm and John took him aside and told him what had happened, David didn't say a word. But his face lost its color and his lips and the lines at his eyes tightened, and John recognized that as a sign of fury.

"For Christ's sake," John Law said. "Have a little understanding. Would you like to have to go to Hannover with some woman you didn't like?"

"I'll thank you, John," David Gardiner had said as icily as John had ever heard him speak, "to keep your nose out of my business."

And with that, he jumped on Wanderer and rode out of the yard without even saying good-bye to any of the Wards. Not even Sally.

"Well, will you stay to supper, John Law," Sally's father asked, "since we seem to have lost David to whatever it is you told him?"

"Yes, thank you, I will," John said, having instantly decided there was no reason he should do without his supper. But then he changed his mind. "I'd better go after him," he said. "And keep him out of trouble."

"Hah!" Sally snorted. He looked at her. "Sorry," she said, and then she asked, "Is he in trouble?"

"His sister ran way from getting married," John told her. "She's at our place."

"Why?" Mrs. Ward asked. "Why did she run away?"

"Because, Mother," Sally said angrily and impatiently, "she probably didn't like the man her folks had picked for her, and she had a brother to run to who would help her."

John Law put his heels to the mare's ribs. A family fracas was obviously about to begin here, and one family fracas per day was more than enough, thank you.

On the way back to Loondon, although he covered much of the distance at a canter, he was unable to catch up with David. There was time for him to consider his position. David had given him all the excuse he needed not to go to the apartment. He had been told to mind his own business. There was nothing he could do to help things between David and Kate at the apartment. On the contrary, in the heat of the argument, it was possible, even likely, that Kate would do something, or say something, even just look at him, that would give David an idea of what had passed between them.

The smart thing to do, obviously, was go to the apartment he had rented for Eleanor and stay there for several days, until the Gardiner twins had worked out whatever was to happen between them.

He rode, nevertheless, directly to the apartment where Kate was. He owed her, he told himself, that much. After all, he thought, he was a gentleman. He brightened when he thought that money might be a problem. If it were, he could help her there.

4

"I thought," David Gardiner said when John Law let himself into the apartment, "even knowing you as I do, that you wouldn't have the gall to come back here."

Now what does that outburst mean? That he suspects, that she's told him, or that he's simply upset?

David was sitting at a table with a mug of tea before him. Kate, who glanced only briefly at John, was sitting on the couch, leaning forward, supporting her chin on her hands and looking, John thought, quite desolate.

"For one thing," John Law said, "I live here. For another, I have been laboring under the impression that we're friends. And friends—"

"Friends?" David Gardiner said. "*Friends*? My God, you don't know what the word means."

He knows. Good God, she's told him!

"David," Kate said, artificially bright, "has the insane idea that something passed between us last night."

"Insane *idea*?" David said bitterly. "For the love of God, Kate!"

"You're berserk, David," John Law said.

"God*damn* the both of you!" David said furiously. He jumped up from the table and went into his bedroom and returned in a moment holding up the sheet from the bed. For a moment, John Law had absolutely no idea what the sheet signified.

"One of you, no doubt, cut yourself shaving," David Gardiner almost screamed. "You son of a bitch, Law!"

Kate broke down then at the visible proof of her lost virginity. She covered her face with her hands and started to cry. Without thinking what he was doing, Law started toward her.

"Stay away from her, you whoremonger!" David warned, stepping between them, his fists balled at his sides.

"I don't think that's quite the word," John Law said. "Your sister is not a whore."

"I was talking about you," David said. "A man who keeps an apartment for his whore is a whoremonger."

That called for a reply, but John Law could think of none to make.

"And a girl," David said, warming to his subject, "who gives to a whoremonger what properly belongs to her husband is a whore."

"She didn't give me anything," John blurted. "I took it."

David punched him then, the blow coming so quickly that John couldn't avoid it. It hit him square in the face, and he lost the focus of his eyes and his balance and felt himself falling backward onto the floor.

Kate screamed.

When John Law's senses returned and his eyes focused, he saw David standing over him, his fists balled, ready to punch him again.

"Get out of here before I kill you," David said in a voice that was surprisingly level.

"And what happens to Kate?" John Law asked.

"What happens to her is none of your business," David said, losing control of himself so that it came out an angry scream.

"Kate," John Law said, "do you want to come with me?"

David threw himself at John Law then, his balled fists opening to grab at John's throat. They rolled around the floor, smashing furniture, as John tried to break David's grip on his neck.

And then Kate threw herself on her brother's back and somehow succeeded in pulling him off.

"Get out of here, John," she said.

"And leave you with him?"

"I can handle him," Kate said. "You being here just makes things worse."

John got to his feet. There was something on his face. He put his hand to it. His mouth and chin were covered with blood.

"Get out of here, John," Kate repeated.

"My apartment is at Twenty-three Chelton Alley," John Law said. "Near Lincoln's Inn Fields."

"If she goes to your apartment," David Gardiner said, "with God as my judge, I'll kill both of you."

"For God's sake, go," Kate said.

Holding his hand to his face in a futile attempt to stanch the blood flowing from his nose, John Law turned and went out of the apartment.

Chapter Eleven

1

Gorley House, the country home of Stephen Winslow, to which John Law had been invited for the weekend, reminded him very much of his home outside Edinburgh. Elm View was about the same size as Gorley House, and both were stone buildings, three stories plus attics, built in the shape of a shallow U. The main building at Elm View was a bit roomier than Gorley House, but there were fewer and smaller outbuildings at Elm View than at Gorley House. Overall, aside from the furnishings (Elm View's furnishings were of a higher quality than these, John Law thought), the two houses were very much alike.

John Law thought that he would in no way have been embarrassed had the circumstances been reversed and his host here were his guest at Elm View. And, he thought, Stephen Winslow would have felt as much at ease at Elm View as he felt here.

The difference would be, of course, that at Elm View Stephen Winslow would have been the guest of John Law's father, not John Law's, and here Windslow was host in his

247

own house, although he was only two or three years older than John.

Mr. Samuel Winslow, who had operated a very successful business in the Indian trade, had gone to his reward a year before. He had left the firm—which exported ironwork and machinery to India, and imported silk and spices from India—and Gorley House to his only son, Stephen, whom John had met at Crockford's.

More important, Stephen Winslow was an acquaintance of the Marquess of Sprilley. And more important, separately, of his wife. Eleanor, Marchioness of Sprilley, had described Stephen Winslow to John Law as a "dear friend" who would do anything she asked. What she was going to do, Eleanor had told John, was have Stephen ask him for the weekend to Gorley House. She would also arrange for Winslow to invite her husband.

There would be, she told him, about twenty people in all at Gorley House, enough to provide the opportunity for them to be together without causing comment. When she told him what she had arranged, he had been pleased. He had been with Lady Eleanor only twice in the month since the day David had punched his nose and thrown him out of their apartment.

There had been eight planned rendezvous. Law had met Lady Eleanor seven times at the noon hour, near St. Peter's School, while she was ostensibly shopping, and five times at Crockford's, by loose prearrangement. He would walk down Fromm Street to St. Peter's Church, and if she was shopping, she would do the same thing. If she happened to be at Crockford's, they would look for each other in the bar. They had met a dozen times under such circumstances, and eight times she had told him she was sure she could "get away" that night or the next.

On six of the eight occasions when Eleanor had been "sure" he had rented a carriage and driver and made endless and fruitless trips past her house to the curb where she was supposed to wait to be picked up. Except for two times, what Lady Eleanor called "unfortunate circumstances" had kept her from meeting him.

248

Each time, after the first time he had circled in vain past the Sprilley house, he had angrily vowed that he would not again hire the carriage, nor again go through the frustration and humiliation of having her fail to show up. But each time his high resolve failed him: the apartment was lonely, and the prospect of getting her into his bed irresistible.

But even on the two times she had met him and they had gone to the apartment, what went on in bed wasn't what it once had been. Either he was becoming jaded, or she was becoming bored, or something. The last time they had tumbled, the most extraordinary thing had happened: at the pinnacle of his passion, so to speak, he had called a name. But he hadn't called out "Eleanor." What he had called out, uncontrollably, in that last intimate second was "Kate."

Lady Eleanor had been furious; she had slapped his face and demonstrated both a violent temper and a rather remarkable command of obscenity before she could regain control of herself. That, he had thought at the time, had put the cap on it. As he suffered her abuse, he decided he would never again walk to St. Peter's Church hoping to meet her at the noon hour, nor go to the bar at Crockford's, hoping to see her there.

And he had not.

But then one night, very late, as he left Crockford's, not entirely sober, he had run into them, and while the marquess was getting his coat, she took his arm and, her breath delightful against his ear, told him what she had arranged for them at the home of Stephen Winslow.

"Didn't Stephen wonder why you asked him to invite me?" he had asked.

She had laughed her wicked little laugh. "He did't wonder at all," she said. "I told you he's a *dear friend*."

"By which you mean a former lover," he had jealously accused.

"Yes, of course," Eleanor had replied matter-of-factly. "You're darling when you're jealous."

"I don't want to be around your husband," he had protested, "or one of your former lovers."

"Darling, don't be silly. Stephen's house will be much safer for both of us than that little apartment of yours."

"How?" he asked. "And what do we do with other people around?"

She had looked at him out of her fascinatingly naughty eyes and smiled wickedly.

"We will be," she said, "the picture of decorum. Nothing more than a discreet squeeze beneath the table." She demonstrated. "But after everyone has had dinner and gone to sleep, who knows?"

It was rather humiliating to learn how naïve he had been. He had believed that he had overwhelmed the lady, causing her to stray for the first time, in a burst of overwhelming passion, from the path of marital fidelity. The truth seemed to be the reverse; she had selected him to replace Stephen Winslow in her bed as David Gardiner would walk down a line of horses at a fair, selecting an animal that looked to have the desirable characteristics for its intended use.

It was possible, even likely, he thought, that he hadn't even replaced Stephen Winslow, but someone else in a long line of young lovers. He tormented himself with the thought that the truth probably was that Stephen was Lover Number Seven and he was Lover Number Twenty, and that Lover Number Twenty-one was just over the horizon, to be brought into play when Eleanor became bored with him. As she now sometimes seemed to be.

What he should do, he knew, was bow to her graciously as he left her life forever. But he had quickly recognized that this was to be another of those times when, fully aware of what he should do, he was going to be unable to do it. It wasn't that he was smitten with a violent passion for Eleanor, personally, but with the entire notion of having a mistress and of making a cuckold of a nobleman.

The closed end of the U of Gorley House faced the River Thames. For some reason the Thames here, near West Mosely, was by no means as impressive as it was in London, nine miles away. Here it was nowhere near as wide. He didn't understand that, but he wasn't going to make a fool of himself by asking.

Stephen Winslow, his host, came up to him as he was looking down at the river, which looked gray and unfriendly in the fading light of the December day.

"You're all alone," Stephen Winslow said to him. "Come, I'll introduce you to the others. The Marquess of Sprilley has just arrived."

The absence of a reference to Eleanor was obvious, and John Law looked at Winslow in curiosity.

"And Lady Eleanor, of course," Winslow said, smiling knowingly.

You're mocking me, you bastard. And I don't know what to do about it.

The dress Eleanor was wearing pressed her bosoms together against an enormous diamond-studded gold cross.

"I believe you know Mr. Law?" Winslow said.

The marquess did not offer John Law his hand.

"How are you, Law?" he asked.

"Good evening, John," Eleanor said, and extended her hand.

"How lovely you look tonight, Lady Eleanor," John Law replied with what he thought was just the right degree of smoothness. As he bowed politely over Eleanor's extended, gloved hand, he rather relished the mental image of the same hand lovingly encouraging him to a repeat performance.

"Mr. Law is the chap, you know, Winslow," the marquess said, "who took Crockford's for nine hundred odd betting twice on seven?"

"I've heard the story," Winslow said.

"I understand our host, Mr. Law, is going to let us play at hazard later on," the marquess said. "Perhaps you'll give me a chance to take some of it away from you?"

"I would be happy to afford you that opportunity," John said.

Others came to greet him, and there was a moment when he could look at Eleanor. She met his eyes and allowed her tongue to wet her lips. It could have been innocent or it could have been symbolic, John decided. In either case, he found it quite exciting.

He found himself, whether by design of Winslow or by coincidence, across the table from Eleanor at dinner. She removed the question of whether the lip-wetting was innocent or not by slipping her foot from her shoe and raising her leg high enough so that she could get her foot in his lap, when she was sure she had his attention, both wetting her lips again and signaling with her eyes for him to go upstairs after dinner.

There was brandy and cigars after dinner while the ladies retired, and he made a point to speak to the Marquess of Sprilley before leaving the dining room and making his way up the stairs to his room.

Eleanor was not, however, waiting for him in his room, and she did not show up in the half-hour he waited for her. *Damn her!*

Furious with himself, as well as with her, John returned to the dining room before the marquess and some others had left it for the drawing room, where card tables had been set up.

Law joined a whist table and played with great concentration, hoping to be excluded from the invitation to play at hazard when it was offered. The last thing he wanted was to find himself wagering large sums of money against the marquess, which was, he thought, what the marquess had in mind after that remark about his having won all the money at the wheel of chance.

He was enormously relieved not to be invited to gamble at hazard, and as soon as he thought he could, without causing undue attention to himself, he excused himself from the whist game. It was possible, he thought, that Eleanor might now be in his room, that he had misinterpreted her previous signal. In any event, he was bored with playing whist, and if she wasn't there, he could at least get some sleep. If she wasn't, he thought, he would make his excuses first thing in the morning and go back to London.

And that would be the end of it. Period. No more lapses in resolve.

He had just reached the first of the wide stairs in the foyer when someone called his name. He turned, smiling, wondering who it could be. It was the Marquess of Sprilley.

"Yes, sir?" John said politely, wondering what the hell he could want and then deciding that he was about to be invited to play at hazard after all. *Damn*! But there was nothing that he could do about it.

"A word with you, Law," the marquess said.

Stephen Winslow and a man to whom John had been introduced but whose name he had forgotten was with the marquess.

"Certainly," John said.

"I understand that you have an apartment near Lincoln's Inn Fields," the marquess said.

"That's right," John replied.

"And I also understand that you have been entertaining my wife in your apartment," the marquess said.

John's heart jumped in his chest, and it was only with a major effort that he was able to keep his smile on his face.

"I'm afraid I don't understand," John said as levelly as he could manage. I'll think of something. I'd better, otherwise this is going to be very awkward.

"I asked you, Law, if you have been entertaining my wife in your apartment," the marquess said.

"I truthfully don't recall," John Law said without much confidence.

"You don't recall?" the marquess replied. "Then you are a liar, sir, as well as a scoundrel." His voice was almost conversational.

Then he raised his hand, so slowly that the movement was not alarming, and John made no attempt to duck. The marquess held his right glove in his left hand, and he brushed it against John's cheek.

Only then did John pull his head back.

What the hell is that? John Law wondered, more curious than disturbed. And then he was chilled, and the skin at the base of his neck actually tightened, when the realization suddenly came to him. He had just been challenged to a duel!

But dueling is illegal. Doesn't he know that?

"If you are to be in your apartment," the marquess said, still conversationally, "my seconds will be pleased to call upon you."

And then the Marquess of Sprilley and the man with him walked up the staircase.

Stephen Winslow remained behind, looking uncomfortable.

"I do hope you'll believe," Winslow said, "that I had no idea whatever that he knew about you and Eleanor."

There was something in Winslow's behavior—the fact that he didn't seem excited about what had just happened—that gave John cause to think that perhaps things weren't as bad as they first appeared to be.

"I don't suppose that he will remember that little challenge to a duel in the morning, will he? After I'm long gone, with my profound apologies to you?" Law asked.

"I'm afraid he was quite serious," Winslow said as if surprised that Law should ask.

"But that's insane!" John protested. "One of us is liable to be killed, and the other, for certain, will be thrown in jail."

"Hung," Winslow corrected him as if they were talking about other people. "The king has made hanging the penalty."

"Well, I won't do it," John decided. "That's all there is to it."

"In his way, Law," Winslow said dryly, "he is treating you very decently. He's regarding you as a gentleman."

"And if he didn't?" John asked, excited and sarcastic.

"Then he would feel free to have you dealt with by footpads. Which would be what a nobleman would do if his wife were insulted by a member of the lower classes. He would not be expected to dirty his hands on someone who was not a gentleman."

"But the best he could expect, killing me, would be to be hung himself?"

"He doesn't have to kill you to make himself liable for hanging," Winslow explained. "Just go through with the duel. But what I suspect he thinks is that he would be freed at a trial by the House of Lords, no matter what the king has said."

Law had not until that moment considered those ramifications. If this came to the attention of the authorities—and he had no doubt that it would—the marquess would be tried by his peers in the House of Lords. His peers would probably decide that what he had done was something they would have done themselves, and set him free, or punish him with a fine or some other punishment designed to satisfy the king's decree but which would not cause him much, if any, inconvenience.

On the other hand, John Law, Esq., would be tried in court, where judges were not going to defy the law, and since the king had said dueling was a capital offense, that was the law.

"I have no intention of going through with this," Law announced.

"Oh?" Winslow asked somewhat contemptuously. "My dear fellow, I don't see where you have any choice in the matter. Not if you expect to be received in any home here, or for that matter, in Edinburgh, ever again."

"I'd rather take my chances explaining why I ran my sword through a footpad," John said. "Than why I was in a duel."

"And you think you can solve this by simply running off into the night?" Winslow asked, making no attempt now to conceal his contempt.

"That's exactly what I'm going to do," John said.

"I don't think the marquess," Winslow said after a moment, quite icily, "will be either surprised or disappointed."

John looked at him in mingled shock and anger but bit off the comment that came to his lips.

"You'll have to leave London," Winslow went on. "And I daresay the marquess will make this affair known in Edinburgh, so you won't be able to go there, either. Where are you going to go? What are you going to do with your life?"

"You miss the point, Winslow," John said, suddenly quite calm. "If I went through this insane duel with the marquess, I wouldn't *have* a life. He'd either kill me, or I would kill him, and then find myself waiting for the rope in the Tower of London. Taking that slut he married to bed may have been the great mistake of my life, but it's not worth either killing for, or getting hung because her idiot of a husband has some grotesque notion of protecting her good name."

Then he turned and walked out the front door of Gorley House and around to the back, to the stables, where he roused the stablehand and ordered him to immediately saddle his mare.

2

David Gardiner had spent that weekend night at the Ward farm and ridden into London very early in the morning. It was bitter cold, and he went to the apartment as much to get warm as to collect the books he was supposed to have read, and had not, over the weekend.

An hour after he had punched John Law in the nose, and then, without exaggeration, tried to throttle the life out of him, there had been a knock at the door of the apartment. Kate had spent most of the hour, all of it, after he had gotten control of himself, convincing him that John hadn't raped her, either by holding her down (of which he had already proven himself capable) or by getting her drunk. That she had, in other words, given herself to him. That if he wanted to be angry, he should be angry with her, not him.

She was simply incapable of understanding, he had thought, that a friend doesn't tumble a friend's sister or his wife, no matter if she leaps stark naked into his bed like a mare in heat.

"If that's John Law," Kate had said to him, "you tell him you're sorry."

If that's John Law, he had thought, if that bastard has the gall to come back here after what he's done to my sister, this time I will kill him.

He had jerked the door inward and found himself looking at Sally and her father.

David was literally speechless.

"If you'll not ask us in, David," Sally's father said, "we'll come in without it."

Sally pushed past him. "Has he been in one of his righteous moods?" Sally said to Kate. "You can tell by his face, most of the time."

"He's been in one of his righteous moods," Kate said, and chuckled. "Oh, has he been in one of his righteous moods."

"I'm Sally," Sally said.

"I knew that," Kate said, "the moment I saw you."

What had happened was the last thing David had expected. The Wards offered their home to Kate.

"Until this thing sorts itself out," Sally's father said. "You wouldn't want to leave here, now, would you? All by herself, most of the time."

By God, I would like to get her out of London. If she stays here, she's likely to run off after John Law like a mare in heat.

"My father's likely to send after her," David said.

"And?"

"If she doesn't want to marry this fellow," David said, "she doesn't have to."

"I told you, that's over. He wouldn't, he couldn't, marry me now that I've run off and practically everybody thinks I've played the whore," Kate said.

Sally's father looked at her. "Whatever happened," he said, "you're not the whore and you shouldn't even use the word."

"Sorry," she said.

"You stay with us, missy," Sally's father said. "Until you get things sorted out. As long as that takes."

David had understood at that moment what was behind their appearance. Sally had wanted to come because of him. The reason her father had come (he was slow, but shrewd) was because it had occurred to him that if David could no longer go home, that turned him into an eligible suitor for Sally. A son-in-law who could run the farm.

Sally's father thought that Kate's father was a fool for not keeping an eye on her, not catching her and giving her a good thrashing when she tried to run. But that was past now, and you didn't cry over spilt milk. You mopped up as much of it as you could and fed it to the hogs.

Sally obviously had her eye on David, and vice versa, and the only thing that Sally's father could find wrong with that was that David wasn't going to be near London. Now, maybe, *likely*, if they took in the sister, he would be. He had been surprised at how easily his wife had come to agree with him.

"It's not as if we'd have to support her," his wife had said. "David'd naturally expect to do that. I expect it's our Christian duty."

So Kate had gone out to the Ward farm that very night, and David had written a letter home, saying that she'd shown up in London and that she was all right and he was able to take care of her, so they should not worry. He didn't mention the Wards. If his father arrived in London, as he half-expected him to any minute, he just wouldn't tell him where she was. She was a god-damned fool, certainly, and the way she had thrown herself at John Law absolutely disgusted and enraged him; but she was his sister and he wasn't going to see her dragged home to Scotland to be mocked and ridiculed and then married off to whoever would have her, as a reject.

Two days after he had mailed the letter to his father, there had been a letter from his father, telling him that Kate had lost her senses and run off to London. If she showed up at his place, he was first to make sure she was all right (David hadn't known what he meant by "being all right," and then realized that his father suspected she had run off because she was pregnant) and then write immediately, so the problem "could be dealt with."

He hadn't written his father a second letter. He would wait until he had a reply to his first one, to see how furious his father was with *his* defiance. He had told his father how he felt about Kate going home to be married off to the first man who would have her.

In the meantime, he was content with the way things were going, except that, with Kate around, he never got to be alone with Sally. The more it looked like that when "things settled down," it would turn out that he would marry Sally and move onto the farm, the better he liked the idea. He had already had some interesting thoughts that he could do here what his father had done in Edinburgh, turn a small horse-breeding operation into a nice business. The Ward farm, was just large enough, if properly run, and close enough to London to make that very possible. In the meantime, however, he had decided to remain in school. There was a good possibility that when their father had time to cool down, he would forgive Kate and take her back home on her terms.

In that case, David thought, Kate's good luck might not be the same thing for him. He knew the Wards would fight his carrying Sally off to Edinburgh.

When he got to the apartment very early on Monday morning, it was as cold inside the apartment as it was outside. There was no fire in any of the fireplaces in the apartment. David, aware that it was a bit unfair, cursed John Law for having forced him to throw him out. If John were still living here, there would be fires in the fireplaces.

David had not of course *forgiven* John for what he had done to Kate, but he had calmed down about it in the past month to the point where he felt that John probably could no more have helped doing what he had done to her than Wanderer could help kicking down a fence to get at a mare. That didn't mean he wanted John anywhere near Kate or Sally. Just that he thought he had sort of acted the horse's ass about it. He would really have been in a mess if he had killed him, and if Kate hadn't pulled him off John, that could have happened.

He looked at the clock on the mantel. It had not run down. It was one of the new ones, from Germany, that ran four days on one winding. It was John Law's, and God alone knew what it had cost him. According to the clock, it was quarter to seven. Classes did not begin at St. Peter's until nine. That meant that even if he went somewhere for breakfast, he would have more than an hour to kill before going to school. And when he got to school, what he was likely to find was that the fires hadn't been laid there until a few minutes to nine, and the classrooms would be as cold as the apartment.

Clearly, the thing to do was light a fire, or fires, here, and at least get warm before going in search of breakfast.

He made three trips up and down the stairs, once to get wood from the wood bin, once to get coal from the coal bin, and a third time to borrow a shovelful of coals from the landlord.

When he returned from his third trip, John Law was leaning against the fireplace.

They looked at each for a moment before either of them spoke. David saw in John's eyes a genuine fear that he would throw him out.

"Splendid timing, John," David said to him finally. "What did you do, hide until you saw me coming with the coals?"

"Yes," John said, "as a matter of fact, I did."

David saw John's enormous relief at his reception, and was glad that he hadn't told him to get his belongings, which was obviously why he was here, and then get the hell out.

"I understand," David said. "Better to freeze your balls off than to be seen carrying wood and coal and like a member of the lower classes, right? Especially since David the Dumb will do it anyway?"

"I'm in a spot of trouble, David," John said. "I need your help."

"The lady's husband is after you, no doubt?" David said over his shoulder as he poked at the fire. "Waving his sword and threatening to carve you into little pieces?"

"As a matter of fact," John said, not quite succeeding to sound nonchalant, "the gentleman's seconds on are on my tail, so that they can arrange a date and place where he can carve me up according to the rules."

David, convinced both by the tone of John's voice and by the look on his face that John was telling the truth, stood up and looked at him.

"He's actually challenged you to a duel?" David asked.

"Slapped me gently in the face with his glove," John said. "Before witnesses."

"Don't tell me you were idiot enough to accept a challenge," David said. "They'll hang you for just dueling, even if you won."

"You will be proud to hear that I ran," John said.

"I'm surprised," David said. "And yes, proud. You've already been in jail once because they thought you were dueling. It might have been more difficult to get you out of the Tower of London."

David smiled at him.

"I'm in deep trouble, David," John confessed.

"Obviously," David said. "What are you going to do about it?"

"I'm going to have to leave the country for a while," John said.

"And how are you going to afford that?" David asked.

"With the the money I won at Crockford's."

"Well, then you're in luck. I sold the animals I bought for you. Two weeks ago. I've got your hundred pounds, which now comes to about a hundred and nineteen and six."

Flushing slightly with embarrassment, John confessed that wasn't the money he was talking about.

"What money, then?"

"I won nine hundred and thirty-pounds at Crockford's," he said.

"You told me a hundred," David accused.

"I didn't want one of your moralist's lectures," John replied

"You've got eight hundred and more pounds?"

"A little over a thousand," John said. "In the Bank of London. It should carry me for a while. If I can get it."

"You really think that the challenge was genuine?" David asked. "Or is your imagination running away with you?"

"It's genuine," John said with conviction. "People are looking for me. And they're perfectly serious people."

"Where will you go?"

"Paris, I think. Maybe the Lowlands. Maybe Germany. For God's sake, maybe even one of the colonies in North America. Anywhere but England or Scotland."

"Is it really that bad?" David asked. "Have you thought this through? If I were you, I'd go home and tell my father everything."

"I have been informed," John Law said dryly, "reliably informed, that the marquess will lose no time in making it known to his friends in Edinburgh what's happened. Which means that my father will shortly hear about it. My father will be nearly as angry as the goddamned marquess."

"He may understand," David said.

261

"One of the last things he said to me before I started out for London this time was that if I became involved with another woman . . ."

"*Another* woman?" David interrupted him.

"There was another incident," John said. "Do you want the sordid details?"

David Gardiner shook his head.

"He said if I became involved with another woman," John went on, "he would disinherit me. My father is a man of his word. I think he'd feel obliged to carry out his threat if I had put a baby in the belly of a whore. And even if I misjudge him, if he were to come loyally to my assistance . . ."

"What?" David asked.

"I don't think I have the right to bring my shame home," John said.

"You feel shamed?"

"*He* would," John said. "Before the people who are his friends."

David looked at him without replying.

"And, yes, damn you, David, I'm ashamed of myself," John said.

"How can I help you?" David asked softly after a moment.

"Go to the Bank of London for me. I'll give you a draft. Clean out my account and meet me somewhere and give me the money."

"Why can't you go yourself?"

"Because I think they'll be looking for me—there, I mean. I told someone that I would be leaving, and I wouldn't leave without my money."

"I would have to try to lose anyone who followed me," David thought aloud. "And if you're right—and I don't know if you are or not—and they were looking for you at the bank, they would know what I was doing."

"It's very likely that you can go to the bank, providing you are there when the doors open at eight, get my money, and no one will know anything about it. I'll make out the draft to the 'bearer,' so your name won't be involved."

"I'm involved," David corrected him. "If they come looking for you, they'll come here. And I live here."

"All you have to tell is the truth," John said. "That you never laid eyes on Lady Eleanor and that you have no idea where I have gone."

"And hope they believe me," David said.

"Well, then, go to hell, David," John exploded. "I'll take my chances on going to the bank myself."

"I'll get your money for you," David said patiently. "Where do you want to meet me?"

"You'll be doing this at some risk to yourself," John said. "I feel obliged to tell you that."

"Now you're letting your imagination run loose again," David said.

But when John insisted that David take his pistol with him, he didn't put up much of an argument. He remembered what his father had said about never needing a pistol until you needed one badly.

3

The moment David walked into the Bank of London and handed the clerk the draft for £1,020, he knew that John Law's concern that the outraged marquess would have sent people there to look for him was justified.

The clerk, mumbling, "Excuse me, sir," backed out of his cage with the draft in his hand. It would be pleasant, and dangerous, to believe that his obvious excitement, David decided, was caused by the size of that draft.

He turned to see where the clerk was going. He went to a closed door, knocked on it, went inside, and closed the door after him. In a moment the door opened a crack and it was obvious that someone, maybe several people, were looking at him through the crack.

Then the door closed again. The clerk didn't come out again for two minutes after that, and then he took a very long time to count out the money when he was back in his cage.

David was not at all surprised when someone came up to him outside the bank, on Threadneedle Street, as he was untying Wanderer's reins from the hitching post.

"Good morning," a rather pleasant voice said.

"Good morning," David replied civilly, turning to see who was talking to him. It was a young man, no more than three or four years older than he was.

"I'm the Viscount Whitten," the young man said. "I believe we have a mutual acquaintance."

"Who would that be?" David asked, wondering who Whitten was.

"Mr. John Law," the viscount said.

"I know Mr. Law," David replied. He looked beyond the viscount. There were two men on horses watching the encounter. It was obvious they were with the viscount. They were well, if simply dressed, and David did not think they were aristocrats. And then he understood who they were. Servants. Or something like servants. Masters of horse. Estate managers. Something like that.

"You don't happen to know where I could find Mr. Law right now, do you?" the viscount asked.

"Sorry," David said.

"It's really rather important to me," the viscount said.

"Sorry," David repeated.

"I think you're lying to me, sir," Viscount snapped.

"I don't give a damn what you think," David said. He pushed past the viscount and swung easily onto Wanderer. In a moment, before the viscount could return to his own horse and mount, he was in the thick traffic moving up and down Threadneedle Street. He headed down Moorgate toward the market at Billingsgate. Beyond that was the Tower of London, the most infamous prison in England, which John Law, in a sort of gallows humor, had picked as their rendezvous.

Threadneedle Street was crowded, but Moorgate was not, and once David had turned onto it, he was able to urge Wanderer into a brisk canter. Because of the large animal's long and easy stride, he made good time until he reached the crowded Billingsgate Market. With a little bit of luck, however, he thought, he could make his way through the shoppers and the jumble of tables and stalls of Billingsgate more quickly than the three men following him, and then gain even more on them the far side of the market, before he reached the Tower of London.

If his luck held, he would have to waste no time looking for John at the Tower. He could then give John his money, warn him that he had been followed, and then turn away from him. He would then allow the viscount and his friends to catch up with him. He would lead them on a long wild-goose chase around the outskirts of London before heading for St. Peter's. That way, he could probably give John a good two hours' head start, perhaps an even longer one.

When he got to the Tower of London, he thought that good luck was with him. John was grazing his mare on the sparse grass against the Tower's walls. When David saw that John had seen him, he turned Wanderer to begin to circle the Tower at a walk. He knew that John would catch up with him. In a moment, he could both pass him the money and warn him about the men who had followed him from the Bank of London.

It happened that way, except for two things he had not expected. First, he was nearly overcome with unexpected emotion as he handed John the money and realized that he was saying good-bye for probably the last time.

"I'm in your debt, David," John said. "Yet again."

"I'm being followed. Three men, one of them young. He said he was Viscount Whitten," David said.

John looked quickly over his shoulder. "I don't see them," he said. "You must have lost him. Thank God, I would hate to have to kill him."

"Who is he?" David asked.

"The lady's brother," John said wryly. "Defending her honor." He smiled at David, reached over, and affectionately touched his arm. "Relax, David. I'll be all right from here on." He touched his heels to his mare and rode off.

But a moment later, when David turned from taking a last look at John, he saw Viscount Whitten and the men with him. They obviously had been much closer on his tail than he had dreamed they would be. That probably confirmed, he thought, his guess that one of the men was a master of horse.

Then he saw that the viscount and his two men had seen John and were now following him. His plan of leading them on a wild-goose chase was going to be impossible.

David turned Wanderer's head and started to follow the viscount and his men. They certainly wouldn't do anything violent in town, he reasoned, and perhaps, if Law saw them on his tail, he would make an effort to get away. The mare was fast. It was possible that he would be able to lose them.

John headed down Lower Thames Street and then turned onto London Bridge. If he sensed that he was being followed, he gave no sign. He didn't even look over his shoulder.

London Bridge was a massive structure, huge cut stone pillars sunk into the river bottom supporting a base more than a hundred feet wide. The base supported a half dozen six-story stone buildings, with the cross-river passage cut through their first floors like a tunnel. Excepting cathedrals, it was the largest structure David Gardiner had even seen. There was nothing even close to it in Edinburgh.

The passage tunnel, like Billingsgate Market, was crowded with shops and shoppers. Constables of the crown and private policemen, hired by the merchants, patrolled the crowded passage. The viscount and his men would not dare try to do anything to John on the bridge. Once the bridge was crossed, however, and once they passed Southwark Cathedral, the closely packed buildings opened up, and ten minutes beyond Southwark Cathedral, they would be in open country.

At first, David couldn't make up his mind whether or not the viscount and his men knew that he was following them, or whether he should make his presence known to them. If they knew he was there, he reasoned, they might think twice about attacking John. And then they might not, since the odds would still be in their favor. Finally deciding that he could always make his presence known when he wanted to, if that seemed to be the smart thing to do, he kept a position as distant from them as he dared to without losing sight of them.

Twenty minutes past Southwark Cathedral all the questions were answered. There was a stand of elm, through which the Borough High Street passed, and then an open area perhaps a hundred yards square, and then a larger stand of elm.

When John reached the open area, he spurred his mare into a gallop. The viscount and his men speeded up to catch up with him. David put his heels to Wanderer.

Just before he was about to enter the second stand of trees, John reined in his mare, turned her around, and sat there, facing his pursuers.

The viscount and his men reined in their animals. The viscount said something to them and then dismounted. He walked toward John Law, drawing his sword as he walked. When he saw that the viscount had drawn his sword, John threw the reins over the mare's head, so she would stay where she was, and then slid off her. Then he drew his own sword and took several steps in the direction of Viscount Whitten.

David reined in Wanderer. The men who had ridden with the viscount turned to look at him, and he had the feeling they regarded the encounter much as he did, that it was really none of their business and should be settled between John Law and the viscount. David decided the best thing he could do was stay where he was and see what happened. There was no question in his mind that John was skilled with his sword and that he would not be at a disadvantage fighting the viscount.

So far as he was concerned, John had jumped into the woman's bed knowing that what he was doing was likely to get him into trouble, and now he was going to have to pay the price of her favors. So long as the fight was fair, he had no business involving himself. And from what he could see, it was going to be fair, one well-set-up skilled swordsman against another.

He didn't think it would end with John killing the viscount. John was no fool and had tried his best to avoid dueling the marquess. In that situation, like this, he had everything to lose and nothing to gain. If he lost the duel, he would be killed. If he won, he could be hung for murder. If the authorities heard about it, he could be hung for dueling.

What he hoped would happen, what he thought was

likely, was that John would prove the better swordsman and, having had time to consider his options, would use this skill to cut up the viscount without injuring him fatally, just hurt him enough so that he would be forced to quit.

After that, he could flee the country as he originally planned, leaving behind him a furious cuckolded husband, but with his reputation among the aristocrats as a bounder and scoundrel too cowardly to duel somewhat restored by his having carved up the viscount.More important, with a little luck there would not be a warrant for his arrest as a murderer or a duelist. He could claim that what was happening here was simply self-defense.

He might not, David thought, even have to stay away from England. There was no law against self-defense, only against dueling. John had refused a challenge to a duel, and Viscount Whitten had pursued him out here. There was no prearrangement. This wasn't a duel.

But as the viscount and John advanced slowly toward each other, their swords held loosely at their sides, David realized that what he had just thought was wishful thinking. The idiotic notion of honor among the aristocracy was so strong that the viscount would rather be hung than admit he had chased Law, and was not going to fight him. He would not dirty his hands by fighting. He would swear on the Bible that it had been a duel, a matter of honor, and would go happily to have his neck stretched.

The Viscount Whitten raised his sword and John raised his. They touched, the steel blades ringing like a bell, and then they began to fight. It was almost immediately apparent to David that they were more or less evenly matched. David was a little ashamed to realize that he was excited by their confrontation, even pleased by it. He had to remind himself that the viscount, despite his graceful movements, intended to run his sword through John Law.

And then John's greater skill as a swordsman became apparent. With quick, precise movements, his sword flicked at the viscount's face, his arm, and his chest. If he had lunged, he could have put his sword through him. He didn't lunge. It was his intention, and he succeeded, in drawing blood from the viscount's chest and arm, and slicing his forehead and then his cheek, with the sword, so that blood flowed, but there was no chance of a fatal or even serious wound.

But instead of discouraging the viscount, this served to enrage him. His thrusts became more violent, less controlled, which forced Law to defend himself with less grace (and thus less control) than he had at first.

And then the viscount made a violent thrust, almost throwing himself at John Law to give his blade the thrust the force it would need to run through John's chest. John, with an awkward movement, turned the viscount's blade at the last moment. The viscount went sprawling on the ground. David wondered if John had tripped him.

The viscount's sword was still in his outstretched arm. As he struggled to get to his feet, John ran to him and pressed his foot onto the viscount's wrist. Then he bent over and picked up the sword. He threw it as far as he could toward the treeline.

David let his breath out. There had been a genuine chance that John would have lost control of himself and done the viscount some serious harm. But he hadn't and now the fight was obviously over.

John walked back toward his mare. She hadn't run or walked away, but now (perhaps excited by the fight) she was acting up, staying just out of the reach of John's hands as he reached for her reins.

The viscount, after a moment, regained his feet. Blood streamed down his face from the cuts on his forehead and cheek. He ran halfway to the men who had ridden with him.

"Shoot him," he screamed, pointing at John and then wiping at the blood on his face with the same hand.

Neither of the men with him made a move.

"Shoot the bastard," the viscount screamed. "Or, by God, I'll kill you myself."

When there was no response to this, he ran, staggering, the rest of the way to them and demanded their pistols.

There was some hesitation, but finally first one of the men and then the other handed him their pistols.

David put his heels to Wanderer and galloped across the opening.

The viscount raised one of the pistols and fired it at John Law. David saw the mare stagger, then fall on her side, blood gushing from a wound in her neck. The pistol ball had struck an artery.

John looked at the viscount in surprise and rage.

The viscount ran toward John, stopped ten feet away, and leveled the pistol.

"Stop!" David called, and put his heels to Wanderer as he awkwardly drew his pistol from the pouch hanging from the saddle. It was primed, he remembered, if the powder hadn't been jarred from the pan.

The Viscount Whitten heard David shout and heard the pounding of Wanderer's hooves. He spund around, took a quick look, and raised his pistol.

The shot that rang out, however, came from the pistol Edward Gardiner had given his son just before he left home, the pistol that was intended to protect him from brigands and footpads on the High Road. And by then David was too close to Viscount Whitten to miss.

The viscount staggered and looked in total surprise at his leg, now flowing blood, then at David Gardiner, and then crashed heavily to the ground.

David reined in Wanderer and turned him around. He saw that one of the viscount's men was attempting to prime another pistol. He spurred Wanderer again and cantered toward the viscount's men. Out of the corner of his eye he saw John Law trying to control his terrified and badly injured mare.

The viscount's man primed his pistol and cocked it and aimed it at David. David reined in Wanderer, stopped, and met the man's eyes.

"This has gone far enough," David said. "If anything else happens, they're going to hang us for sure, and this is none of our business."

The man looked hesitant, but after a moment he lowered the pistol and then, with some difficulty, lowered the hammer, and slipped it into its holster. David turned Wanderer toward John and the viscount.

The viscount was in agony. He was holding his wounded leg with the both hands.

"You'll die for this, you bastard!" he said.

"You'd better thank God you're alive," David said.

He saw John coming to them. John had found his sword and had it in his hand, and for a moment, David was afraid he intended to use it. But then he stopped walking long enough to find the mouth of the scabbard with the tip of the sword, and to put it away. David let his breath out in relief, only to suck it in a moment later in even greater fear when John found the viscount's pistol and picked it up.

"John," David cried, "for God's sake!"

John looked up at him with both contempt and tears in his eyes. Then he walked over to the mare and shot her. He walked over to the viscount. "All you succeeded in doing, you stupid bastard," he said, "was killing a fine horse. I'm sorry he missed killing you." Then he spat on the viscount and went to David and Wanderer.

"Give me a hand up," he ordered.

David, ever practical, asked, "What about the saddle and the tack?"

"Let whoever buries her have it," John said. "I couldn't bear to have it."

David leaned over and gave John his hand. John heaved himself onto Wanderer's back behind David. David put his heels to Wanderer and the stallion began to walk.

A moment later, as they entered the forest at the far side of the clearing, David became aware that John's chest was heaving against his back. For a moment he thought that perhaps John had been injured. And then he understood what it really was.

John Law was weeping for his lost high-stepping mare.

Chapter Twelve

1

Sally Ward and Kate Gardiner were shelling peas with Mrs. Ward in the kitchen when Sally saw David and John Law riding down the lane, both on Wanderer. Sally had immediately sensed that something was seriously wrong, but she resisted the temptation to run to the door as they approached. She was certain that if something were wrong, she would immediately be sent away. Kate might be permitted to stay, but she would be sent away. She had noticed that her mother had recently been treating her more like a child than she had in years.

Instead, giving no indication that she had seen John and David, Sally set the bowl of peas on the table and left the kitchen by the rear door. Her mother would think she had need of the outhouse. When Kate looked at her, Sally put her finger in front of her mouth as a signal for silence and then moved her head, to tell Kate to follow her when she could.

In the month Kate had been at the farm, they had become like sisters, Sally thought. They really under-

273

stood each other, and for the first time in her life she had someone her own age to exchange thoughts and confidences with. To a point, of course. After first swearing Kate to secrecy, she had confessed that she thought David was the finest young man she had ever known, and if it ever came down to that, she would jump at the chance to marry him.

She stopped short of telling her what she and David had done together, telling each other they loved each other and doing what you weren't supposed to do, if you were a decent girl, until you were married. That was sort of a *sacred* secret, Sally had decided, between her and David. Sally had hoped that Kate would tell her everything about why she had run from getting married, but she either hadn't, or the truth ("I didn't want to go to Hannover with him") was terribly dull to be responsible for all the trouble it had caused her.

Kate had said nothing about another young man and had professed contempt when Sally had asked her about John Law. A little too much contempt, Sally had thought. She thought it was entirely possible that something had happened between John and Kate. David had told her if he "never saw the son of a bitch again, it would be too soon," and Sally could think of no reason—save if John had tried something with her—that would make him that angry except that he'd done something, or tried to, with Kate.

She was pleased that whatever it was that had happened between David and John was over, the proof being that they were here together. She knew there was a strong bond between them, however different they were from each other.

Once Sally was inside the small wooden outhouse, she stood up so that she could look out one of the holes her father had drilled, in a star-shaped pattern, into the door to provide some light for the interior. She could see her mother's cap, bent over the bowl of peas in her lap, and then Kate's cap. Kate, again, had probably decided that it was not right for her to fool Sally's mother, because the Wards had taken her in. Kate was as straight-sided as her brother, most of the time, even if she had run away and humiliated her parents and ruined her reputation.

She watched as David and John rode up to the front of the house and slid off Wanderer and walked out of sight, but obviously to knock at the door. A moment later, Sally saw her mother and then Kate stand up and leave the kitchen.

Sally then quickly left the outhouse and ran back to the side of the house. She got there in time to hear her mother tell David and John that her father was in the field by the stream. Then she ran away from the house, taking a circuitous route to the field. Her mother would be furious when she didn't return from the outhouse. She would instantly conclude that Sally was being both "slothful" for avoiding the work in the kitchen, and "deceitful" in the way she had left the kitchen. The least she could expect was to have her mother grab her by the hair and slap her face. More likely, her mother would demand that her father whip her. Sally hated that more, not because her father hurt her any more with a harness strap (her mother's slaps were delivered with far more force) but because he was so unhappy when he had to do it.

She had recently thought she had been getting more beatings lately, not because she had deserved more, but as sort of a lesson in advance, so that she would not get any ideas, like Kate had had, about running away if things didn't go her way.

However her mother decided to do punish her, she would just have to take it. The important thing that had to be faced was that David was in some kind of trouble and she had to know what it was.

Luck was with her when she made her way to the field by the stream. Her father, who had been turning the soil behind a pair of Percherons, so that he could get in some late-winter oats, was quite by chance close to the stone wall that separated the field from the stream. Sally saw that she was going to be able to make her way up the stream to where her father was with no danger of being seen, so long as she ran bent over. Furthermore, when she got there, she would be able to conceal herself behind the stone wall close enough to be able to hear what was being said. If her father had been in the middle of the field, she would have been no better off than if she had stayed in the kitchen.

"Can we speak to you a moment, Mr. Ward?" David asked when he and John rode up to her father.

Her father, too, sensed immediately that something was wrong.

"What kind of trouble are you in, David?" her father asked levelly. "Or is it you, John Law?"

"You don't have to know about it, Mr. Ward," David said. "It'll be better if you don't."

"But you want something from me?"

"Only that you care for Kate, and for Wanderer and the other animals, until I can make arrangements for them," David said. "We're going to take two other horses. I think it would be best, if anyone should ask about us, if you were to say that you didn't even know we were here."

"Is there trouble with your father, lad? Has he come after Kate? Is that what it is?"

"I wish it was my father," David said.

Ward waited expectantly for David to continue, and when he didn't, said, "We're friends, lad. I'll do what you ask of me, but you owe me an explanation. Is somebody else coming looking for Kate? Who's liable to be asking questions about you?" David didn't reply, and after a moment, Ward asked, "The Law?"

"Maybe," David said. "I don't know."

"Goddammit, you tell me what's happened!" her father demanded angrily.

"The mess we're in," John said, "is my fault, Mr. Ward."

"That don't surprise me none," Ward said. "What exactly is it?"

Alternately, David and John told Ward about the Marquess of Sprilley, and his challenge to a duel, and the reason why. Sally was not particularly surprised to hear what John had been up to. From the way he had looked at her the first day, she had known that he had a hunger for women, even though, she thought, that had been before she had really understood what went on between men and women.

And she held her breath waiting for David's reply when her father asked the obvious question: "And what married woman's skirts have you been lifting, the queen's?"

"I haven't been raising any married woman's skirts," David protested.

Just mine, Sally thought wickedly.

"Then why are you running?" her father asked.

John Law answered for him. "The lady's brother came after me," John said, "after I'd taken his sword from him. He got pistols from his men and tried to shoot me. He killed my mare with his first shot, and then, when David tried to keep him from shooting at me again, he aimed his pistol at David. And David shot him. He had to."

"Shot him?" Ward asked evenly. "Did you kill him, David?"

"Unfortunately, no," John said.

"I shot him in the leg," David said. "I don't think I killed him."

"But if he dies?" her father asked.

David didn't reply.

"If he dies, it's murder," her father said. "Lord, what a fool thing to do!"

"If he hadn't shot him, he would have killed him. Or me," John said.

"It would have served *you* right, Ward said angrily.

There was a moment's silence.

"Your mare was killed, you say?" Ward asked.

"She took the ball intended for me," John replied softly. "I had to put her down."

"Damn!" Ward said, then he turned to David.

"And what are you going to do?"

"John's going to France," David said.

"I asked about you," Ward said.

"I guess I'll have to go with him," David said.

"Once you start to run, you can never stop," Ward said.

"David," John said, "they may not be after you. The marquess may be willing to take his chances with the House of Lords, but I don't think the viscount will. If he charges you with shooting him, the circumstances will come out."

"And who do you think will be believed?" David asked resignedly.

"What the devil would you do in France?" John said.

"What are *you* going to do in France?" David countered.

"*I* know how to make money," John said. "You can turn an honest pound here, dealing with Englishmen, but I don't think you'd be nearly as successful in France."

"What do you think I should do?" David asked defiantly. "Since I am so helpless?"

"You wouldn't be the first Scot to take to the Highlands when the king's sheriff was after him," John said. "And we don't know for sure that he will be after you."

"He's right, John," Ward said.

"And I'll see that you have enough money so that you won't have to ask your father," John said. And then he groaned.

"I've got money," David said. "Enough to take care of myself for a while, and to pay for Kate here . . ." Then he stopped. "What's the matter with you?"

"Goddamn me for a fool," John said. "The money is in the saddlebags."

"Oh, God," David said.

"What money?" Ward asked.

"The money I was going to use to go to Paris," John said. "Now what the hell am I going to do?"

"You can't go back and get it?" Ward asked, looking at David. David shook his head.

"To answer your question, Mr. Ward, after I see John off to France, I'll go home to Scotland and make myself hard to find in the Highlands for a while."

"Didn't you hear what I said?" John said. "I'm without a farthing."

"I've got your hundred pounds and some," David said. "And about a hundred of my own. You can have half of that. You can go to France. Not quite as luxuriously as you thought you could, but you can go."

"Maybe what I had better do," John said, "is go back and face the music."

"Don't be a fool," David said. "You can't go back and neither can I."

"What I am going to do in France without any money?"

"A minute or so ago you told me you were able to make money," David said. "So make it."

There was a pause after that.

"And what about your animals?" Ward finally asked.

"We've been riding double on Wanderer, and riding hard," David said. "I don't want to kill him, and I wouldn't want anything to happen to him if we should be caught up with. So I'd like to leave him with you and Kate. We'll take two of my other horses."

"If Kate decides, after this, that she'd best go back to Edinburgh," Mr. Ward said, "she could take Wanderer and the others with her. There's a cart here she can use. Or we could tell her father where she is."

"No. We won't tell my father anything until we have to," David said. "Kate can go back the way she came, by herself."

"Whatever you say," Ward said.

"I was hoping for something like that," David said. "A cart, I mean. But I was afraid to ask."

"I'm pleased to do it," Ward said.

"If I only hadn't lost the goddamn money," John said, "we wouldn't be in this mess. I could have given you enough to take Kate and the animals back to Edinburgh, and I could have paid Mr. Ward for his trouble."

"I wouldn't do it for money," Ward said coldly, and added, "Nor for you."

"How have I offended you?" John asked, taken aback.

"Don't you really understand what you've done to David?" Ward asked. "To my girl? To everybody?"

"He would have done the same for me," David said, coming to John's defense.

"You can believe that if you want to," Ward said.

"I left my saddle on my mare," John said. "I'll need a saddle. Will you sell me a saddle? I have at least that much money, and I'll need a saddle."

"No," Ward said bluntly. "I don't want your money. You know where the tack is. Take a saddle if you need one. Just don't put me in the position of having given you one, or sold you one."

John and Ward looked at each other for a moment, and then Ward turned to David and put out his hand. "God go with you, David," he said. "And if you think someone may be after you, you'd better go with Him now."

"Yes, sir."

"Put Wanderer into a stall," Ward said. "There's a wind, and if he's hot, he's liable to take a chill. I'll turn him into a pasture when I finish here."

"Thank you," David said.

"And if you haven't said anything to the wife or Sally, don't," Ward said. "I'll think of something to tell them later."

"I hope I don't see her," David blurted. "God knows what I would do."

"Then maybe it was time for you to leave, anyway," Ward said coldly.

David met his eyes and then started back across the field to the farm buildings.

"Whether or not you wish it, sir," John Law said, bowing to Ward, "you have my gratitude."

Ward looked as if he were going to say something, but in the end he said nothing. His head inclined just enough to qualify as a nod. And then he went back to his plow, picked up the Percherons' reins, and clucked the huge animals into motion.

2

Sally knew she had two choices: she could return to the stables by the same route she had come to the fields, in which case she could avoid being seen by either her father or her mother, and she might be able to make it to the stable before David and John left; or she could run after him now, take a chance on cutting across the field between here and the house. In that case she could certainly get to the stable before they left, but it was almost certain that she would be seen. By now her mother was sure to be looking for her, and it was more than likely that her father would keep looking back toward the stables to see when David and John left. It really wasn't much of a choice. She would have to return the way she came.

As she ran, she thought that the worst thing that could happen was that David and John would have picked out the animals they were going to take with them, saddled them, and started back out the lane by the time she got to the barn. In that case, she would run after them, cutting across the field by the road. Her mother and father would probably see her, but that wouldn't matter. By that time, she would be with David, and they could do what they wanted to her afterward.

But David and John ran to the stables, and more quickly than Sally would have thought possible selected two of David's animals and saddled them. She was still two hundred yards from the main stable building when she saw first David, and then John, already astride, duck their heads as they came out of the stable door, and immediately urge the animals into a canter, then a gallop as they went back down the lane.

There was no way she could catch up with them now. They were gone.

And her mother found her.

"God will punish you, you slothful child," her mother screamed at her.

There was nothing to do but go into the kitchen and face what was going to happen to her.

"You're not going to get off that easy," her mother said when Sally had crossed the field to her. "You go into the barn and wait for your father."

Sally dumbly complied. A whipping now didn't seem nearly so important as the realization that actually gave her a pain in the belly that she might have seen David for the last time in her life. That possibility was so terrible that it was difficult to accept. She had had two lives, one before David and one since. Since the first time he had kissed her. Since *that* had happened between them. It was inconceivable that *that* was over, that she would never see him again, that they would never do *that* together again.

Wanderer's head came out the stall where David had

put him. His ears perked forward when he saw her, and he whinnied. She went to him and put her hand on his nose.

She knew how much David loved Wanderer. He had no right to just run off and leave him, either. A flash of anger ran through her, and then a crazy idea came to her.

It was such a preposterous idea that it actually chilled her and made her shiver. But if the idea was unthinkable, so was the thought that she would never see David again, that she would not share his life.

She saw Wanderer's bit and bridle where David had laid it across the gate to an open stall. When she picked it up, it was still warm from his body. He whinnied again when he saw her with it, and obligingly lowered his head to let her put it on him. She opened his stall and led him to the tack room. She would need a saddle. But if she took a saddle, that would be the same thing as stealing one. She wasn't stealing Wanderer, she was taking him to his owner.

She thought about it a moment and then led Wanderer beside a rainwater barrel. She put the cover on the barrel and then climbed onto the barrel. She hoisted her skirts and straddled the large stallion. She kicked his ribs with her heel and her sandal fell off.

To hell with it, she thought defiantly and kicked the other sandal loose. Then she bent low against Wanderer's neck and started to ride him out of the stable. There was no point in trying to hide from her parents anymore.

But then someone came up beside her and grabbed the reins.

"What in the world are you doing?" she demanded. It was Kate.

"I'm going after your brother and John Law," Sally said. "Let go of the reins!"

"Where are they going? What's going on?"

"Let go of the reins!" Sally said, but Kate didn't.

"Tell me what's happened," Kate demanded.

Still on Wanderer's back, Sally told Kate what she had heard.

"And you're going to run after them? Is that what you're saying?"

"I love him," Sally said. "And if he leaves now, I'll lose him."

"And if you leave now, bareback and barefoot, on a tired horse," Kate said, "you'll kill yourself. Get off of there."

"And just give up, is that it?"

"Help me hitch up the cart," Kate said, pointing. "We'll take that large piebald to pull it, and tie Wanderer up behind."

"You're going, too?"

"I want to hear from David himself what's happened," Kate said. She felt something of a hypocrite. She was as unwilling to see John ride off forever out of her life as Sally was to lose David. But she couldn't say that out loud. David and Sally were going to be together. There was no chance that she and John could.

But she wanted to see him one more time.

When they had the large piebald hitched to the cart and had put robes and even two buckets of feed into it, they tied Wanderer's reins to the back of it, got in it, and drove it out of the barn.

Kate stood up and put the whip to the piebald, and frightened, he broke into a gallop.

They heard Sally's mother screaming at them, but they didn't stop, and when they looked at each other, they giggled. By the time Sally's mother could get to the field to tell her father what had happened, and by the time he could set out after them, it was unlikely that he could catch up with them. He would be traveling much faster on a horse than they could move in the cart, but when he reached the first crossroads, he wouldn't know which way to turn.

3

An hour later, the feeling of joyful insanity was gone. They had galloped ten minutes, until the piebald was heavy with sweat, before reining him in. Wanderer was already tired, she knew, from carrying David and John to the farm; and even without a rider, running was too much exertion for him. And Wanderer would kill himself trying to deliver what she asked of him.

Sally took the reins from Kate and walked the piebald at a slow pace, while Kate, walking beside him, rubbed Wanderer down. Sally had time now to calm down and think. She had no idea where they were going because she had no idea where David and John were going. She knew nothing of France except that it was across the English Channel, and she knew nothing of the English Channel except a vague notion of its direction.

John and David would have to board a boat, she understood that, but she had no idea where that could be done. Certainly at a number of places, but which one?

When they came to the first fork in the road, Sally realized she had absolutely no idea which fork David and John had taken. She took the right fork, her only reason a vague notion that the English Channel was to the right. She hoped her father wouldn't reach the same conclusion. If he caught up with them, he'd make them go back.

When she same to the second fork, she turned right again, very much aware that she wasn't even sure that the men had come this way. They just as easily could have gone left at the first fork.

Once, she reined the piebald in and turned to Kate.

"What do we do? We don't know where they are, or where we are."

"Do you want to go back?" Kate asked.

"Do you?"

"Not yet."

Sally reached up and cracked the piebald on the rump with the loose end of the reins.

It had been a hollow gesture, she thought sometime later, but on the other hand, what else was there to do but press on? What would happen now was out of their hands. The option of returning home was obviously open, but it seemed out of the question. It wasn't because what she had done so far would obviously earn her a whipping (and this time her father would whip her willingly, not simply because her mother insisted) and probably one for Kate too. Or Kate would be told to go, which would be far worse than a whipping. It was because turning back would sever the spider's web of a connection she still had with David. She was unwilling, perhaps unable, to break that connection.

By the time an hour had passed, she refused to permit herself to think of anything but the chances of catching up with David and John around the next bend in the road, or watering their horses at the next stream. She wondered, since she was defying God's holy commandment about honoring thy father and thy mother, whether God would hear her prayers, and ultimately decided that all He could do would be to ignore them, and she prayed that David and John would be in sight when she came to the next bend.

There was no sight of either of them, and she became aware that as the sun sank lower, the cold, already bitter, would grow worse. They had shawls around their heads and had wrapped the blankets and robes around them, but they were still cold, and finally they got under the blankets together, to warm each other. But they didn't get warm, it was entirely possible that they would freeze.

But there didn't seem to be anything for them to do but ride on. Darkness fell more quickly than Sally thought it would. It was very dark and she could barely see the road. She couldn't have seen David, she thought, if he were twenty yards ahead of her.

There were faint lights, from time to time, from farm-house windows, and that, she thought, offered her some chance. She could go to one of the farm houses, say she was lost, and pray that they would put them up overnight. If she had money, it would be different, but she had no money.

If she didn't catch up with him by the time she counted to a thousand she would turn in the next farm lane.

After she had counted to a thousand five times, with tears running cold down her cheeks, she pointed Wanderer into a lane, at the end of which she could see faintly glowing rectangles, the light from a fire coming through the cracks in the shutters.

"I'm sorry, Kate," she said.

"Me, too," Kate said. And then added, "Damn them, anyhow, running off like that."

We will probably, Kate thought with resignation, be raped and murdered and Wanderer will be stolen from me.

To the left, Kate saw an open fire in a copse of trees. She thought first of the warmth a fire would give, then that it was a strange place for an open fire to be.

Without quite knowing why, she nudged Sally. "Look," she said.

"So what?" Sally replied, her teeth chattering.

"Let's look," Kate said. "What have we got to lose?"

Sally turned the cart off the road and toward the fire. When they got closer, Kate thought they would be able to see who was near the fire. Probably gypsies. Maybe even footpads and highway robbers.

Whoever it was, there were horses, for Wanderer raised his head and stiffened his ears and whinnied behind her, and there was an answering whinny.

But as they came close to the fire, she could see neither horses nor people, and for a moment she had a pleasant idea. It was just a fire, and Kate thought they could take advantage of it witout having to face anybody. But just as the foolishness of that got through to her, someone stepped in front of the piebald and cried, "Hold in your tracks, or by God, I'll put a ball through your forehead."

It took her a moment to find her voice, and a moment longer before she was able to say what she wanted.

"Put the pistol down, John, it's me, Kate."

4

"Good God!" John Law said, and walked to the cart and looked at her. He shook his head. "I'll be damned," he said, and then he raised his voice and shouted for David.

"By God," John went on when David came up from somewhere behind the cart. "Look at this. This is all we need!"

Kate wondered why he was so furious.

"What the hell are you doing here?" David asked, and then without waiting for a reply, went on, "Goddamn, you must be frozen!"

He reached out and put his hand on Sally's face, and then worked it under the robe, searching for her ankle and then her foot.

Without quite knowing how it happened, she swung her leg over the side of the cart, got off, and wound up in David's arms.

He scooped her up in his arms.

"Bring the cart," he said to John, and then he carried her to the fire. He set her down on blankets and then began to rub her feet and ankles. She realized she desperately had to relieve herself. This was hardly the time for that, but it became imperative.

"I've got to go," she said, and struggled to her feet.

When she returned, John was warming his hands by the fire. Kate had been standing next to him, but when she saw Sally, she followed her into the dark.

When they came back, David started questioning them.

"Is anybody after us? Is that what this is all about?"

"I don't know," Sally answered.

"Her father will probably come after us," Kate said. "But I don't see how he can hope to find us."

David glowered at her, but didn't respond. "What the hell do you think you're doing here, Sally?" David asked.

"I'm going with you," she said.

"What the hell is the matter with you?" David snapped at Kate. "Why didn't you stop her?"

"It was as much my idea as hers," Kate said.

"I don't doubt that for a second," David said angrily. "Well, you damned near froze to death for nothing. You're going back first thing in the morning."

"I am not," Sally said.

"You are."

"Oh, for God's sake!" John said angrily.

"We cannot," Sally said.

"Why?" David said.

"Because my father will believe that something has happened between us," she said. The words had just popped into her mouth. "And because, after this, my father and mother would send Kate away. They'd think she was responsible for my running."

"Did you tell your father that something happened between us?" David asked.

"By God," John said. "Saint David just fell from grace."

"Shut up, John," David said automatically.

"I didn't tell him anything," Sally said. "But that's what he's going to think. Otherwise, why would I run after you?"

David looked into Sally's face. "This is a stupid thing you've done," he said.

"Not if I want to be with you," she said. "Staying would have been stupid."

"How did you find us?"

"God directed us," Sally said with conviction.

"I don't believe what I'm hearing," John said. "In five minutes, a horde of angry farmers, led by her father, is going to come raging down that lane with blood in their eyes."

"You have any bright ideas?" David challenged. "There's nothing to be done about sending them back tonight. The piebald is worn out. Wanderer will die without rest. And these two females would freeze."

"Probably," John said. "So what do wo do with them?"

"We'll make sort of a cave out of the cart," David said. "Open to the fire. So we all won't freeze."

He moved the cart around with the piebald and then unhitched and hobbled him. Then he hobbled Wanderer.

"Kate, damn you," he said bitterly. "You knew better than to bring him."

Kate did not take the rebuke. "He's not hurt," she said. "And I thought you'd want him." Then, seeing what he was doing, she helped him arrange some of the blankets around the cart to break the wind. She had spent nearly as much time as he had in the Highlands and knew how to keep from freezing to death. She and Sally were, Kate thought, probably suffering less from the cold than they had. David and John had been sleeping on the ground.

Sally began to arrange the remaining robes and blankets under the cart.

"You realize, of course," John said, "that what you are doing, Sally, is preparing to sleep with David."

Kate and Sally looked at David in alarm. The last thing they needed was for them to start fighting.

"You're right," Sally said. "I've never *slept* with him before."

David looked between them and then, to everyone's relief, laughed.

"I don't think your father would make much of the distinction," he said, and crawled under the cart and turned on his back. One by one, the others crawled in after him. When they had finished arranging themselves, David and John were in the middle, with Sally beside David and Kate beside John.

"Curiosity overwhelms me," John said. "Sally, how long has this shameful behavior been going on between you and David?"

"Oh, shut up, John," David said resignedly. "Just shut up and go to sleep."

"Forever," Sally said, and laughed.

"And your father knows?" John asked.

"I guess he does now," Sally said.

"You *guess* he does now?" John replied, and laughed heartily.

Despite himself, David had to chuckle. The chuckle turned into laugh, and the laugh was contagious.

David put his arm around Sally. "God forgive me, I'm glad you're here," he said.

"If you insist on bringing the Almighty into this," John said, "entreat Him not to direct her father here, as He directed her."

Kate lay stiffly beside John, aware that he was carefully keeping his body from touching hers.

"Would you please put your arm around me?" she asked. "I'm freezing."

She sat up so that he could get his arm around her.

"Don't say one damned word, David," Kate said.

He didn't.

This wasn't, Kate thought as John pulled her close to

him, and she felt the warmth of his body against hers, exactly all she had hoped for, but it was all that she was going to get.

5

Sally felt someone shaking her. She was instantly awake, but it took her a moment to remember where she was. She was lying in a field somewhere, under a cart, wrapped in blankets with David. John Law had shaken her.

"Forgive the intrusion," he said wryly.

David, she saw, was still asleep. She pushed him. He didn't respond at first, and his face was flushed and hot. But then he sat up suddenly, alarmed.

"What's the matter?" he asked, and then he groaned. "My whole damned arm is asleep."

Sally saw that it had started to snow, a fine, powdery snow that had put a white dust over everything.

"Kate and I have decided that we would rather face the marquess or her father, or both, rather than freeze to death here," John said. "Get up."

David was now on his feet, grimacing, rubbing his upper arm. Snuggled close to him, Sally had been warm, but she felt the chill coming on.

David coughed, a deep, unpleasant hacking sound.

"Let's get out of here," John said. "And find someplace warm and something warm to eat."

David nodded his head in agreement and, coughing again so that his whole body shook, walked almost staggering, to where the horses were hobbled. When Sally stood up, she was suddenly reminded that she was barefoot. The ground was wet and cold under her feet.

David hitched Wanderer to the cart. That made sense, Sally thought, for Wanderer was the most powerful animal of the three. David would ride the piebald. But when they were ready to leave, David got in the cart.

"I'm a little under the weather," he said. "I'm going to ride in the cart for a while."

Kate was more alarmed than Sally. She knew David best, and she knew that there had to be more than a little something wrong with him to make him get in a cart. She mounted the piebald, John mounted his mare, and the little procession moved away from the embers of the fire back to the farm lane, and then back to the highway.

Sally was aware of David's being sick. She would have had to be deaf and blind not to be aware of his flushed face and his steady coughing. It was clear that he had caught a chill from sleeping on the ground. She was surprised that he had caught it, and not John.

Once, her eyes met Kate's as David was hacking. Kate shook her head.

A little more than an hour on the highway, they came to a tavern. The door was closed, and there was no answer to John pounding on it, but smoke coming from a chimney told them someone was inside. Finally John went around to the rear of the building, and a minute or so later, the door opened and a grumpy middle-aged woman waved them inside.

Both Kate and Sally were sensitive to the look of disapproval they got from the woman. It was understandable, of course, that the innkeeper's wife would conclude that two strange, simply dressed young women who arrived at her tavern's door very early in the morning after obviously having spent the night in the company of two young men—one of them obviously a gentleman, and thus certainly not a husband to either of them—were traveling whores.

The fireplace in the public room of the tavern held still-glowing remnants of the previous night's fire. Without asking for permission, John loaded it with fresh wood and adjusted the damper. Then he went into the kitchen and returned with a bottle of brandy.

"Take a couple of large swallows of this," he said to David. "It'll burn the chill out of you."

David drank from the neck of the bottle as if the brandy was water. He coughed painfully when he was finished, but smiled.

"If that doesn't do it," he said, "nothing will."

In a short time, flames crackled around the fresh logs,

and Sally was able to warm her backside from the heat. Kate saw what she was doing, and joined her.

Sally was surprised at the quality of the food they were served. She had expected cold meat and bread. There was, instead, fried ham and eggs, even fried potatoes and onions. There was also hot milk liberally laced with honey. And she was starved.

Kate noticed the same thing and had been equally surprised, considering the initial reception they had been given. Then it occurred to her that John looked as if he would have money. The innkeeper's wife was willing to overlook their being wandering whores so long as they had a swell with them to pay their bills.

David continued to cough and to blow his nose, but he didn't seem to look or feel as bad as he had before. The brandy, Sally thought, and the food had restored him.

"I have been thinking," David announced as he ate the last of his slice of ham.

"About what?" Sally asked.

"The best thing for you to do is go home," he said. "The both of you, I mean. I'll take Kate home in the cart, and you take the piebald back and tell your father to take it out from what he'll owe me."

The good feeling immediately left here. There was no question in her mind at all that he had, as he said, been thinking, and that what he said was the conclusion he had reached.

"And you'll send for her later?" John asked. "Is that what you're thinking?"

"Yes," David said.

"Sometimes you're really an ass, David," Kate snapped.

"I'm not going back," Sally announced in a soft but determined voice.

"If you send her back, after this," Kate said, "she'll be in the same disgrace with her neighbors as I am in Edinburgh. Is that what you want for her?"

"What else, dammit, Kate?" David said.

"One may presume, I presume," John said dryly, "that your intentions with regard to the lady are honorable? That the absolute pinnacle of your ambition is to take Sweet Sally to wife?"

David had to smile at John. "Yes," he said, "that is the 'absolute pinnacle' of my ambition."

"And you," John said to Sally, "are apparently willing to spend the rest of your life with him?"

"Yes," Sally said softly, wondering why she wasn't angry that he was mocking her.

"Then the logical thing for you two to do is marry, John pronounced.

"Now you're the ass," David said, sounding more disappointed than angry. "That's impossible."

"Why?"

"Because getting married requires . . ." He stopped and turned to Sally. "I thought about all this," he said, and then turned back to John. "Getting married requires, first of all, her father's permission, and right now we have as much chance of getting that as we do to fly; and second, it requires the publishing of banns at the parish church, and that takes six weeks. You're not as smart as you think you are, John."

"We shall see," he said, and got to his feet. "Don't send her back until I return, all right?"

David spent the next thirty minutes, until John returned, explaining to Sally and Kate why it was going to be necessary for Sally to return home until such time as he could go to Scotland and arrange to return for her. "After things have settled down," he said.

She knew what he meant by that: until he knew for sure that he wasn't going to be arrested and hanged for shooting the viscount.

As Sally knew it would be, his reasoning was inarguable. There was simply nothing else they could do, given the law requiring a father's permission for a girl to marry, and the Church law's requirement concerning the publishing of banns. She would just have to return to face her parents, as he and Kate were going to have to go face theirs. But she was not to worry, He loved her and nothing on God's earth was going to keep him from marrying her.

John returned, wearing a self-satisfied smile.

"It's all arranged," he said.

"What's all arranged?" David demanded suspiciously.

"The priest will see you right away," John said. "He wants to have a little talk with you."

"If it's all the same to you," David said, "I'm in no mood to have a little talk with a priest."

"After which, he will marry you," John said. "Bind you for all eternity to Sally. For better, for worse. You know how it goes."

"Goddamn you," David said. "This better not be your idea of a joke, John!"

"I don't deserve that," John said in a hurt voice.

"You've seen a priest?" Sally asked. Hope had just been born again in her.

John nodded. "And he will see you now," he said.

"And he said he'd marry us?" Sally asked. Without thinking what she was doing, she reached out and took David's hand.

"Presuming his talk with you goes well," John said.

"What does he want to talk about?" David asked suspiciously.

"I would suppose he wants to reassure himself that you both are sure you know what you're doing," John said. "Now, do you want to see him or not?"

When they went back outside, Sally saw that the snow had increased. Everything was covered with white. But the snow fell softly and there was little wind. The snow, she thought, covered the ugly ruts in the road, and the manure piles. It seemed a very nice thing for God to do on the day she was to be married.

The church, surrounded by a stone-walled cemetery, was a three-minute walk from the tavern. Behind the church (St. John's, Sally saw, which seemed nice, too, since John, who took his name from St. John, had arranged this) was the rectory, a small stone building with a slate roof, in contrast to the thatch roofs of the other buildings in the village.

A woman who was almost certainly the priest's wife opened the door to John Law's somewhat imperious knock. She gave Sally a gentle smile and then glowered at David so ferociously that David was startled.

"Be so good as to inform the good father that I have brought them to see him," John said.

"Yes, milord," the woman said. "He expects them."

When she had gone out of hearing, John put his arms around David's and Sally's shoulders and motioned Kate to come to him.

"Now, what I had to tell him," he said, "was that Sally's with child, but that, presuming he will marry you, I have decided to forgive you and continue you in my service."

"You told him what?" David exploded.

"Do you want to get married or don't you?" John replied. "Just remember that you're my stable hand and Sally is a scullery maid. Kate is her sister."

"And who are you supposed to be?" David demanded, his anger having given way to sort of an amused fascination.

"Viscount Whitten, of course," John said, visibly pleased with himself.

"This way, please," the priest's wife said, motioning to David and Sally.

For the next fifteen minutes, while David squirmed uncomfortably, the priest talked to them both of the sinful lusts of the flesh and told them the story of Christ and the Fallen Woman, how Christ had said, when they were about to stone her to death that he who is without sin should cast the first stone.

There was no reason, the priest told them, presuming they begged God's forgiveness with an open and contrite heart, that their sin should plague them for the rest of their lives. They could start afresh. The proof of that, the priest said, was obvious: the Viscount Whitten had graciously seen it as his Christian duty to give them a second chance and not to order them off his estates.

"Both of you should thank God for a kind and Christian master like him," the priest said, "who has found it in his heart to forgive you."

Sally was very much afraid that David would blow up at that, but he managed to keep his mouth shut.

An hour after they entered the rectory, Sally and David knelt before the altar of St. John's Church and heard themselves pronounced man and wife.

John explained to the priest that under the circumstances he could not, of course, permit himself to be listed as a witness. He had to think of the other servants and how they would react. The priest understood and said that under the circumstances he was sure God would forgive them for listing any name at all on the certificate of marriage. "The Viscount Whitten" suggested "John Law, Esq.," and signed that name.

He gave the priest two pounds, "for the poor," and they returned to the tavern.

"You'll have to teach her to cook, of course, and scrub floors," John said, now really enjoying his role. "But with a little effort on your part, David, she may turn out to be a decent wife."

"I just hope it's legal," David said.

"Of course it's legal," John said. " 'Whom God has joined together, let no man put asunder.' "

"Thank you, John," Sally said, and kissed him on the cheek.

"John, me too," David said, and emotionally shook his hand.

"Your plans are firm, then? You're going to take the cart and go to Scotland?"

"Right," David said.

"That brings us to my plans," John said, and David looked at him curiously.

"How much money do you think it's going to take to get you home?" John asked. "I mean to say, how much can you loan me?"

"More than I want, less than you think you'll need," David said. "You probably won't believe this, but we can probably get home on a pound. Or a pound and six."

"You'll need more than that," John said.

"I'll keep out three pounds," David said, and counted out three pounds and gave the rest of his money to John.

"I wish you'd take the mare," John said as he counted the money. "And turn her over to my father."

"Sure," David said.

John Law put out his hand. "I'm going," he said.

"Go with God, John," David said.

John looked at Sally. "You are a lovely bride, Mrs.

Gardiner," he said, and leaned over and kissed her. Then he looked at Kate. "You're just lovely," he said.

"Take care of yourself, John," Kate said, and then she found herself hugging him.

He pushed away from her after a moment, looked at her again with a strange look on his face, and then turned and walked out of the tavern without saying another word to anyone.

"Go with God, John," Sally said softly after the door had closed after him.

The woman came into the room with the slate with their bill.

"You have a room for my wife and my sister and me?" David asked.

The innkeeper nodded.

"Don't you think," Kate said, "that we should be going?"

"Kate," David said, "the brandy's worn off. I don't know if I'm going to be able to walk across the floor or up to a room. I can't go anywhere just now."

"You should have said something before he left," Kate said.

"He would have stayed," David said. "And he couldn't afford to do that." Then he hunched his shoulders in and started to shake.

"He's got a bad chill, he has," the woman announced. "You'd better do something about it."

"I think we'll spend the day and the night," David said. "And see what the weather brings."

The weather was fine the next day, but it was three days before David was well enough to have the girls help him down the stairs and into the cart.

Chapter Thirteen

1

Once he was alone, John Law was forced to face the fact that he had no idea where he was going, how he was going to get there, or what he would do when he got there. He spent the next three days making his way on backroads in a wide circle around London. He didn't stop for the night until after dark, and he rose from beds in inns in small villages very early in the morning to resume his journey. And he spent a good deal of time looking over his shoulder to see if anyone seemed to be chasing after him.

He would not have been surprised to have seen a squad of dragoons galloping after him, nor to find the law blocking every crossroads he came to. There was more than enough time for his imagination to paint in fine detail his arrest, his being thrown in jail, his trial, and his being taken from a cell and hung from a gallows.

And when he was not thinking about this, he found himself thinking about Kate. The memory of being with her, of her naked body next to his, of the smell of her hair against his nostrils, was so real that it was painful.

There were no soldiers on the roads looking for him, and no roadblocks at any crossroad, and that made it possible for him to consider that perhaps things weren't as bad as they had at first seemed. It *was* possible, he told himself, that when the men with him had taken the seriously wounded Viscount Whitten back to London, or wherever they had taken him, he and the Marquess of Sprilley had had second thoughts.

Despite what Stephen Winslow had said about the marquess not been very much concerned about what would happen to him if he were tried by his peers in the House of Lords, he very well might have concluded that pursuing the matter further wasn't going to be worth the cost. For one thing, he no longer could send Eleanor's brother to do the dirty work. David's pistol ball was going to keep the viscount in bed for some time. And that was clear proof that dealing with John Law wasn't going to be as simple as finding him, killing him, and making it back in time for tea.

So far as they knew, he was still traveling with David, and that raised the question of just who would get killed in a second encounter. The marquess was a cuckold, but he wasn't a fool and he didn't want to get himself killed or wounded.

Besides, the marquess had, aside from the satisfaction of killing John Law, what he really wanted: if John Law were gone from London, the Marchioness of Sprilley could no longer pop into his bed.

By the time John ultimately made his way to Southend-on-Sea, he had been able to talk himself into thinking it was likely, even possible, that the danger had passed, that he had been hiding from pursuers who existed only in his imagination.

The relative peace of mind he had talked himself into vanished, however just about as soon as he reached Southend-on-Sea and began to make inquiries about passage to France. The tavernkeeper of whom he asked questions seemed a bit too helpful and far more friendly and curious about John Law than seemed natural.

He was sure, he told John, he could arrange comfortable and cheap passage for him in the morning, and in the meantime John could have a good meal and a good night's sleep right there in the tavern.

This bastard's clearly up to something.

"Second things after first," John said.

"Sir?" the tavern keeper asked.

"First thing, I'll visit your little building, and then I'll have something to drink," John explained.

The tavern keeper smiled at him.

John went out the back door toward the outhouse, then climbed a fence and ran around to the front and jumped onto the piebald. He saw the tavern keeper's son running down the street.

There was no conclusive proof, of course, but John thought it was more than likely the boy was running for the watch, or some constable, to tell him that the young gentleman they were looking for was in the tavern. A little embarrassed that he hadn't thought of this before, he was now sure what was really happening: the law was not going to dispatch hordes of soldiers or officers of the crown to gallop wildly up and down country roads on the off chance that they would find him. What they would logically do, what he was sure they had done, was visit taverns and inns and offer tavern keepers a reward for turning him in if he should show up.

I got out of that place just in time. Another ten minutes, and I would have been in chains.

He rode ten miles farther, to Shoeburyness, and by the time he got there, he had still another change of mind. For all he *really* knew, the tavern keeper's son's running down the street could have been a simple and innocent coincidence. He could have been running home or on an errand that had nothing to do with John.

And he thought, it was more than likely that his imagination was running away with him. He had certainly been under a great deal of stress, and he was tired almost to the point of exhaustion. That would make him think there was an officer of the crown lurking behind every tree.

The thing to do, he decided, before he did anything else

301

was to put to the test his theory that a reward had been offered to anyone who reported his presence.

There were two taverns in Shoeburyness, one of which was conveniently, for what he had in mind, located twenty-five or thirty yards from a thick stand of elm trees.

He went to the tavern, drank a quick beer, asked for and paid for a room, and even went so far as to make sure the tavern keeper learned his name. Then he went to the room, closed the door, climbed out the window, reclaimed his horse, and went and hid in the stand of trees. If two or three men wearing the king's badges and carrying pikes showed up at the tavern, he would be able to see them and simply ride farther into the forest and get away.

He waited for what seemed like forever but was actually no more than two hours before deciding that no one was going to come to the tavern to throw the fleeing criminal into irons.

He went back to the tavern, put his horse in the stable, ate a late supper, and went to bed.

In the morning, he thought, he would arrange for his passage to France. But with morning came the idea that perhaps that wouldn't be necessary at all. That, in fact, considering his financial position, would probably be a very bad idea.

What the hell can I do in France without being able to speak the language, and more important, without any money?

He didn't have to go to France. Anywhere out of London would do nicely. Particularly if he could get his hands on some money. And he thought he saw the solution to that, too. He had property in London, in both apartments, things like clocks and tableware and even clothing that could be turned into cash.

Everything seemed to fall into place. If he went back to London and carefully got into the apartments and removed from them what he could take to the pawnbrokers on London Bridge, he could then head for Scotland. If David felt safe hiding from the law somewhere in the Highlands, there was no reason he couldn't do the same thing, provided he had some money. Not only for himself, but for David. He was ashamed that he'd taken almost all of David's money.

That idea seemed sweeter when he thought that if he was holed up in some shepherd's cottage in the Highlands, with someone periodically bringing food to him, that someone was liable to be Kate. There were a lot worse things in the world, obviously, than being alone with Kate Gardiner in a shepherd's cottage in the Highlands.

When he went downstairs in the tavern in Shoebury-ness, the first question he asked the tavern keeper was which was the road to London.

2

There was a good deal more in the apartment he had shared with David Gardiner that could be turned into cash than he remembered. He made three trips to London Bridge loaded down with items to be put up as security for a "loan" from pawnbrokers, and as many to the used-clothing dealers at Billingsgate; and when he was finished, he had nearly twenty-five pounds to show for it.

The apartment he shared with David, he knew, was a different matter from the apartment he had rented to be with the Marchioness of Sprilley. For one thing, she only knew of the former, not where it was, and therefore could not possibly have told her husband.

The apartment near Lincoln's Inn Fields was something else. The marquess knew about that. It was possible that he had not yet given up the idea of making John pay for the marchioness's favors with his life, and would have left men to watch the apartment in case he returned to it.

The smart thing to do would be simply take what he had and start out for Scotland. With a little bit of luck, he might even be able to catch up with David and the girls. They were traveling by cart, and he would make much better time.

On the other hand, the things that he could convert to cash in the Lincoln's Inn Fields apartment were far more valuable than the things he had had in the other apartment. And the idea of just giving them up without making an effort to reclaim something was distasteful. In addition to everything else, John was still smarting over the fortune he had left in the mare's saddlebags after that bastard brother of Eleanor's had shot his mare. He realized that he was incapable of simply abandoning property for which he could get at least a hundred pounds, and probably more, in that apartment.

He was cautious, however, and watched the streets around the apartment carefully before he went close to it. Finally satisfied that no one was watching it, he went inside and loaded himself down with what he thought of as samples of his wares. A sterling table setting, two crystal glasses, and a silvered mirror.

What he would do, he decided, rather than carry everything to either London Bridge or Billingsgate Market, was show the buyers there what he had to offer and then get them to come to the apartment and haul it away themselves.

That idea worked, too. He wasn't offered a third of what he had paid for the silverware, but the London Bridge silversmith was perfectly willing to come to the apartment right then and to pay with cash. The used-linen dealer paid him even less a share of what it was worth for the Irish linen he'd bought to impress Eleanor, but he too paid in cash.

While the dealer in crystal was in the apartment examining John's crystal and explaining how bad the market was, and how little he could hope to make selling the crystal, there was a knock at the door. When John opened it, there was an officer of the watch, a very young officer of the watch, John Law noticed despite the sinking feeling in his stomach, standing there. Beside him were two watchmen holding pikes.

The young officer respectfully lifted his hat. "I'm sorry to trouble you, sir," he said politely. "But I'm looking for John Law."

"Indeed?" John asked.

"We have been furnished information that he might turn up here," the young officer said.

"What do you want with him?" John asked. Immediately,

he thought: What I should have said was that he sailed two days ago for the Massachusetts Colony.

"You do know him, then, sir?" the young officer asked.

John nodded. "What do you want with him?" he repeated.

"I'm afraid that he's in a good bit of trouble, sir, to get right to the heart of the matter."

"What sort of trouble?"

"He's charged with robbery and assault with a deadly weapon on the king's highways, I'm afraid. He and another fellow."

"That's absurd," John said.

"I'm afraid not, sir," the young officer said. "The charges have been brought by Viscount Whitten."

"The viscount is a liar," John said angrily.

"Excuse me, sir," the young officer said, "but how do you know that?"

"Because I'm John Law," John said indignantly. "And I'm not a highway robber."

The young officer looked distinctly uncomfortable. It wasn't hard for John to understand why. He had come here looking for someone who was not a gentleman. Viscount Whitten, unwilling to admit that he had been cut up in a fair fight by a gentleman, had turned John and David into highway robbers who had wounded him while trying to rob him.

When the young officer had seen John and the apartment, which, even though most of the readily movable furnishings were gone, still was clearly the sort of place only someone with a very large amount of money could afford, he had naturally assumed that John Law was a servant here.

"Obviously, sir, some sort of mistake has been made," the young officer said uncomfortably.

"Obviously," John firmly agreed, aware that the more indignant he looked and sounded, the better his position in the eyes of the young officer.

"But I'm afraid," the young officer said, "that I'll have to ask you to come along with me to the watch office, so this can be straightened out."

"That's preposterous!" John said.

The young officer took a sheet of paper from his waistcoat and handed it over to John.

"There's this, I'm afraid, sir," he said.

John took it and read it. It was a warrant for the arrest "of John Law and John Doe on charges of highway robbery and assault with deadly weapons, to wit, a sword, rapier, saber or similar weapon, and a hand-held firearm.

"I don't even know anyone named Doe," John said, handing it back to him. "And I am not a highway robber. I'm a last-year student at St. Peter's School, and I am fortunately in a financial position where it is not necessary for me to rob anyone."

"They put the name 'John Doe' on warrants," the young officer explained, "when they don't know the true name of the accused."

"Well, you just go back where you came from and tell whoever it is who sent you that a mistake has been made," John said.

I have the strangest feeling that I'm not going to be able to get away with this.

"I'm sure," the young officer of the watch said, "that once we bring this before the captain, we will be able to straighten it out in short order. But I'm afraid, Mr. Law, that you are going to have to come with us."

The only chance I have to get out of this now is to explain what happened to someone in authority. If I run now (and with those two draft horses with the piles, I don't think I could run, anyway), it would be the same thing as confessing that I had indeed tried to rob Whitten at sword point.

Rob Whitten? That miserable bastard! He's got my thousand pounds!

"Very well," John said. "I suppose the thing to do is get this settled once and for all as quickly as possible."

"Yes, sir," the young watch officer said, visibly relieved, "I'm sure that's the best thing to do."

3

Things did not go well with the captain of the watch, although at first he was courteous and seemed to be sympathetic.

"God's truth, Mr. Law, you don't look like a robber along the highway."

"The charge is ridiculous," John said.

"But Viscount Whitten signed the warrant, naming you," the captain said, "which puts me on the spot, you see."

"Well, get the bastard in here," John said, letting his indignation run wild.

"At the moment, that's out of the question," the captain said.

"I was under the impression, Captain," John said, "that I am entitled to face my accuser."

"That's not possible just now," the captain said.

"Why not?"

"You . . . or whoever . . . damned near killed him," the captain said. "From what I hear, he still may lose his leg. I mean, they may have to take it off. And if that happens, that might kill him. And if he dies, that would make this thing murder."

"A moot point, I would say," John said.

"I don't understand what that means," the captain confessed.

"Highway robbers are hung just as high as murderers," John said.

"I take your meaning," the captain said. "I think the best thing you could do right now, Mr. Law, is get the other fellow in here, and I'll listen to what he has to say."

"What other fellow?"

By God, I'll hang before I get David involved in this.

"John Doe," the captain said. "The fellow who was with you."

"I have no idea what you're talking about," John said.

"There was nobody with you when you had the run-in

307

with the viscount? You do admit having a run-in with the viscount?"

This fellow is more clever than I at first thought he was. I have no intention of answering that question.

"You are charging me with highway robbery," John said. "And I demand my right to face my accuser."

"I told you," the captain said, considerably less friendly, "that you can't do that. He's in St. Mary's Hospital, and damned sick."

"Then I suggest we go to St. Mary's Hospital and face him there," John said.

It was a moment before the captain replied.

"I'll ask about that," he said. "It's possible, I suppose. But in the meantime, Mr. Law, I'm afraid I'm going to have to hold you."

"May I speak to you as a gentleman, Captain?" John said.

"Sure."

"You understand, of course," John began, "that I am admitting nothing."

"I understand," the captain said.

"Viscount Whitten's injuries are not limited to a pistol-ball wound, are they?"

"He's been pretty bad cut up," the captain offered.

"Have you considered the possibility that he got into a fight over a woman, and after he was cut up, tried to shoot the other man? And was himself shot?"

"That's a duel," the captain said. "And I thought of that right off."

"But the man he went after is not automatically a duelist. I mean, if he was chased by Whitten and then forced to defend himself, that isn't a duel, is it?"

"That would make his Lordship guilty of assault, if not dueling," the captain said. "Which would take the whole matter out of my hands and put it into the House of Lords."

"Precisely," John said.

"You get this friend of yours in here to say something like that, Mr. Law, to swear that you neither robbed the viscount nor agreed to duel with him, and we can put this matter to rest right off. The other fellow, I suppose, is like yourself, a gentleman?"

Very clever, Captain.

"There was no one else, Captain," John said.

"I'm growing tired of this, Mr. Law," the captain said, and there was no longer any suggestion of friendliness in his voice. "So I'm going to ask you one more time: where can we find the fellow with you?"

"I'll tell you one more time," John said. "There was no one else."

"Have it your way," the captain said flatly. "Right now, the way things are, you've been charged with highway robbery and assault by the viscount. You're right about having the right to face him. But until he's up to that, or until he dies, whichever, I'm going to have to hold you."

"In the Tower of London?"

"No, Mr. Law," the captain said. "The Tower is only for the nobility or people charged with treason. You'll go to one of the hulks."

"I don't know what that means," John said, and he was now frightened.

"When the Navy is finished with a ship—I mean, when it's not safe to take them to sea again—they tie them up on the banks of the Thames, and we use them as prisons. Not real prisons, but sort of holding prisons."

"And how long do you intend to hold me?"

"Until the viscount either dies or is well enough to face you, or until you decide to give me the name of the man who was with you."

4

In a dark and foul-smelling office in what had once been the quarterdeck of the *Valorous,* John Law was relieved of his purse and his boots and issued a moldy blanket, a pewter plate and mug, and an object that was somewhere between a dull knife and a spoon and that he understood was the implement with which he was supposed to eat.

His money—he now had something over one hundred

pounds—was carefully counted to the last halfpenny, and a receipt issued. The receipt was then put in his purse, which he would receive when he was released.

He was told the reasons for taking his boots. For one thing, in the middle of winter, a man could not run far barefoot. For another, the boots would soon be ruined in the prison holds, the decks of which were constantly under at least an inch of water, most often more.

"We want you to have boots when you get out of here," the warder told him cheerfully. "No matter where you're going when you do."

He was then taken out onto the icy deck. A pair of warders hauled on a block and tackle that raised a heavy iron gratework over a hold. When the gratework was raised high enough for him to pass under it, he was motioned to the edge of the hatch and then signaled to descend a steep ladder to the hold.

The stench was incredible and there was a heavy haze of smoke in the hold. It took a minute or two for his eyes to adjust to the darkness and to find a place free to sit on. There was an inch of water on the deck so cold that it was painful to his feet.

I won't be here long. The law is the law, and they have to let me face my accusers. I could be out of here in an hour if I gave them David's name. But that, of course, I cannot do.

There were fifty or sixty men in the section of the hold that he could see, and the hold obviously stretched much farther in both directions. Here and there small lamps glowed, and three open fires, in cut-off barrels filled with sand, gave off some light. As his eyes became adjusted to both the darkness and the smoke, he saw the other amenities. There were water barrels, barrels serving as toilets, and a table at standing height down the middle at which, he realized, he would be eating. The bunks were, in no apparent order, built wherever they could be raised off the deck.

He wrapped the blanket around his shoulders, tried to arrange the straw on his bunk to cushion his body, and tried to sleep. He had just dozed off when something bit his bare ankle. He reached down quickly and caught a bug. It was too dark to see it, but between his fingers it seemed enormous, and when he squashed it, it was full of a sticky liquid that he thought was more than likely his own blood. He rubbed his fingers on his trousers and shuddered.

An hour after that, a tallow candle seemed to float to him through the darkness. It was no more than six feet away before he could see the hand that held it, and a moment after that, the face that went with the hand.

The face was large, scarred, and frightening. The hair on the head was about as long as the beard on the cheeks and chin, through which could be seen both scars and suppurating sores. The eyes were large and sunken, and when the face smiled at him, he saw a good many rotten and as many missing teeth.

"Good evening to you, sir," the man said.

Good God, now what?

"Good evening," John replied as civilly as he could. This was obviously no place where he could tell the man to be gone.

"It's an awful place, ain't it, for the likes of a gentleman like yourself?" the man asked.

"It's awful, all right," John agreed.

"And some of the people in here is really rotten, they is," the man said. "Steal your food right out of your mouth, and worse, just for the meanness of it."

God, I hadn't even thought about food. What manner of slop are they going to feed me in here?

"Is that so?"

"When I first got thrown in here, they even tried it with me," the man offered. "And as you can see, sir, I'm considerably larger and better able to protect myself than you are."

"What exactly is it you want?"

"When I saw you coming in here," the man said, "I thought maybe we could be friends, so long as we're both in here together."

John suddenly remembered a conversation he'd had two years before, when he'd first come to London. One of the upper-classmen had found himself locked up in a hulk like this after a drunken fight, and he had reported what John had thought of at the time as unbelievable stories of men having sex with one another.

Was that what this fellow was after? And if so, what could he do?

As if reading his mind, the man said, "Some of them that's been in here long sometimes can't tell the difference, or don't want to, between a man and a woman, if you catch my meaning."

"I think I would rather be killed, first," John said as much to himself as to the man.

"So long as you've got some money and are willing to be friendly, it won't get to that."

"What makes you think I've got money?" John asked.

"You've got more than a hundred pounds in the warder's office," the man said.

"Exactly what does being 'friendly' mean?" John said.

"A friend would share what food, and candles, and firewood he could afford to buy with a man what has no money to buy it," the man said.

"And how much would that cost?"

"A pound a day would do two men just fine," the man said.

"A *pound* a day?"

"The thing is, you have to buy such things from the warders, and they price things according to how much money they know you have," the man said.

"And a pound a day would buy food and candles?"

"And firewood, and even a little soap and water, if you're of a mind to wash from time to time. And my friendship."

"Which means exactly what?"

"That I would stand by your side in case you got into a tiff or something with some of the others."

"And what are you in here for?"

"They say I murdered a man," the man said.

"They say?"

"They don't seem to be able to find the body," the man said. "And why are they holding you, sir, if you don't mind my asking?"

"They say I'm a highway robber," John said. "And

they're waiting to see whether a man they say I robbed dies."

The man didn't say anything for a moment, then he stood erect.

"So what you're saying is that you don't think you need somebody to stand with you."

"Not at all," John said, and put out his hand. "Not at all. I'm very happy to make your acquaintance."

What the hell, what choice do I have? And I have a hundred pounds. That's nearly three months of "friendship," and I don't think I'll be here that long.

"My name is Arthur Carter," the man said, and reached out and shook John's hand. "And if you don't mind my saying so, I never met a highway robber before. I ain't never ever been on a horse."

5

John's fears that Arthur Carter was going to be a problem quickly disappeared. It soon became apparent that he was, in his relations with John, an honest man. He had no money whatever, and what he wanted was food and tallow candles, and he was offering the bulk of his body in exchange for them.

Aside from the slightly discomfiting thought that Carter was entirely capable of killing one of the others in living up to his side of the bargain, which would cause other problems, John realized that Arthur Carter was a godsend in his present predicament.

He was willing to please to the point where he tried valiantly, at John's request, to learn how to play chess. He succeeded in making a rather crude set of pieces from wood scraps whittled with a sharpened piece of metal, but the rules of the game proved beyond him and served only to make him think of John as a creature of extraordinary intelligence.

It was nearly three weeks before anything happened. And then one day, just after the noon meal, the heavy metal grate was creakingly opened again and a warder came after John.

He was taken first to the warder's office, where his boots were returned to him, and, surprisingly, he was provided with hot water, soap, and a razor. He was then carried, in a barred cart, back to the watch office. As it became apparent to him where they were going, he wondered why. The worst possible thing that could have happened was that Viscount Whitten had died and he was to be charged with his murder. The best thing that could have happened was that the viscount, informed he would have to make his accusations in person, had withdrawn them, and he was to be set free.

The real reason, John decided, was probably going to be somewhere between the two extremes.

In the captain's office were two somewhat familiar men. It took just a moment for John to identify them as the men who had been with Viscount Whitten the day of the fight.

He was taken into a room where he was alone with the captain and a man in an ill-fitting wig, who was not identified to him.

"Mr. Law, I want to tell you again that if you will give me the name of the man who was with you," the captain said, "you have the right to have him here with you now, during these proceedings."

"I don't know who you're talking about," John said firmly.

"Well, it's up to you," the captain said. "Now, you saw the men outside. Do you know either of them?"

"So far as I can recall, I never saw either of them before in my life," John said.

"The men are servants of Viscount Whitten," the man in the badly fitting wig said.

"And where is the viscount?" John asked.

"Still in hospital," the captain said. "Under the circumstances, the judge has said that if the men outside properly identify you, we can hold you until the viscount has recovered sufficiently to make his own accusation."

"If those men work for the viscount," John protested, "what do you expect them to say?"

"We hope, the truth," the man in the wig said. He

314

gestured to the captain, who went to the door and motioned the viscount's servants inside.

"You," the man with the wig said, pointing at one of them, "have you ever seen this man before?"

"Yes, your Lordship, I have," he said.

"And you?" the man in the wig asked the other one.

"That's him, your Lordship," the other one said with more certainty.

"You're telling me that's the man who shot Viscount Whitten?" the man in the wig asked.

"No, sir," the second man said righteously. "This is the one his Lordship was dueling. The other one was the one who shot his Lordship."

"Dueling, you say?" the man in the wig asked.

"Yes, sir," the self-righteous servant said. "And this one cut his Lordship up something awful before the other one shot him."

"If he was cut up badly, why did he shoot him?"

"I couldn't answer that, your Lordship," the servant said, "but that's what happened, as God is my witness."

"A duel," John said, "requires two willing participants—"

"I know what a duel is," the man in the wig said. He gestured impatiently for the servants to leave his presence.

"What happens to you now, Mr. Law," the man in the wig said, "is that you go back to the hulk until such time as we can lay our hands on Mr. David Gardiner, and get him here, and hear his version of the events."

He was momentarily surprised that they had learned David's name. But then he realized that all they would have had to do was ask at the school for a man fitting the description given by the viscount's servants. Obviously, he was not going to be able to keep David out of this completely.

"Milord," John said, finally realizing that the man who looked like a clerk was obviously someone of much greater importance, "if I were willing to state that I accepted the viscount's challenge to a duel, would it be necessary to involve anyone else?"

"I'm afraid so," the man in the wig said. "Seconds, you see, Law, are considered quite as guilty as the duelists."

"I didn't duel that bastard," John said, losing his temper.

"Now, I'm beginning to wish I had. If I'd have dueled him, I'd have killed him."

The man in the wig looked at John Law as if he were some kind of strange insect.

"That is all, Captain," he said after a moment, "that I shall require of Mr. Law at this time."

6

Edward Gardiner said nothing when he opened the door of his house and found Kate standing there. It had started to snow again and her shawl was wet with melted snow. He looked beyond her and saw a good-looking horse and idly wondered where she'd gotten her.

"I'm not here to ask forgiveness," Kate said.

Mary MacPhee Gardiner, who had been, as was her custom, standing by the door in the kitchen, out of sight, but where she could hear, ran to the door when she heard her daughter's voice. Something stopped her, perhaps the look in Kate's eyes, from doing what she wanted to do, which was wrap her in her arms.

"David's in trouble," Kate said.

That tipped the scales. Mary pushed her husband out of the way and put her arms around Kate's shoulders and led her into the kitchen.

"You're soaked," she said. "You'll catch your death."

Edward Gardiner followed them into the kitchen.

There was tea, and Mary filled a mug and added both honey and whiskey.

"What about David?" Edward said after a moment.

"He's in bad trouble," Kate said.

"You said that," Edward said coldly.

"The law's looking for him," Kate said. "If they catch him, they'll hang him."

"Where is he?" Edward asked.

"And he's bad sick," Kate went on.

"What's the matter with him?" Mary asked.

"And he's married, and she's sick, too," Kate finished.

"Married?" Edward asked incredulously.

"The Ward girl?" Mary asked.

"Yes," Kate said.

316

"I asked where he is?" Edward repeated. "I suppose the girl is with him?"

"Why is the law after him?" Mary asked.

"He shot a man," Kate said. "Viscount Whitten."

"How in the hell did he get involved with a viscount?" Edward demanded angrily. "Was that your doing, too, Kate?"

"For God's sake, shut up!" Mary suddenly shouted at her husband.

He looked at her in anger and surprise. "I have a right to know," he said somewhat lamely.

"This chills me," Kate said, looking with surprise at her shawl and taking it off.

"No wonder, it's soaked," her mother said, and then she took the shawl from Kate and led her into the bedroom.

"What are you doing?" Edward said.

"I'm going to take her clothes off and put her to bed," Mary said. "What did you think?"

Twenty minutes later, Mary went back into the kitchen. Her husband was there, sitting at the table with a glass and a gray pottery mug of whiskey before him. He looked at her, but said nothing.

She went to the cupboard and got a glass and filled it half full of whiskey. He looked at her curiously.

"This is for Kate," she said. "God willing, it'll burn out her fever."

She left the kitchen, to return in a minute. She looked at her husband and then got another glass and filled it.

"One's not enough?" he asked.

"This is for me," she said, and tipped it up and drank half of it.

"I didn't know you used it," he said, as much surprise as disapproval in his voice.

"You don't hold with women drinking," Mary said. "But yes, I use it."

"Is David's trouble that bad?"

"Bad enough," she said. "But why I took it is because for the first time, Edward, tonight I'm afraid of what you're going to do."

"You better tell me what you know," he said.

So, not looking at him, she told him what she had

learned from Kate. That David had shot, possibly killed, Viscount Whitten in order to save John Law's life; that the authorities were looking to arrest him, and if they succeeded, they would take him to London and probably hang him; that the Ward girl had run off with them and they had been married; that David had taken a chill from sleeping on the ground the first night he'd been running, and was very sick; that John Law had fled to France; that the three of them had been almost three weeks on the way to Scotland, keeping to back roads to avoid the law.

"So what it boils down to," Edward said tiredly, "is that your daughter ran away from a marriage that was more than she had any right to expect, subjecting us to humiliation before the whole damned city, and your son is a criminal on the run from the law, married to another runaway girl."

"That's about it," Mary said.

"And will you tell me where they are?" he asked.

She looked at him.

"You owe me that, Mary," he said.

She didn't respond for a long time. She looked at him, then at her whiskey glass, and then at him again; finally she drained her glass and looked at him again.

"They're in the shepherd's cottage above Lyekill," she said.

He stood up and walked to the door, where his great-coat hung on a peg.

"Where are you going?" she asked softly.

"Where do you think, Mary?" Edward asked.

She looked at him.

"I'm going to David in the Highlands," he said. "Where the hell else would I go when the law's after my son to hang him?"

Mary started to cry.

"Goddamn it, stop that," he said, and then he was out the door.

318

Chapter Fourteen

1

The Honorable Percival Hyatt, Captain of the Life Guards of Horse, had rather expected to be received by the Lord High Sheriff for Scotland when he and his detachment of cavalrymen arrived in Edinburgh. Captain Hyatt bore with him a warrant commanding the Lord High Commissioner for Scotland and any and all officers under him to take into arrest and to turn over to Captain Hyatt one David Gardiner, a fugitive, believed to be in Scotland.

Gardiner was to be returned to London and placed in the custody of the Lord High Sheriff of London and held for trial on charges of highway robbery; criminal use of a deadly weapon, specifically a firearm; and criminal assault upon the body of Viscount Whitten.

Hyatt's father was the Marquess of Deal, a rather influential man sure to be known by reputation, if not personally, by the Lord High Sheriff. Captain Hyatt did not expect to be received by the Lord High Commissioner himself, although the warrant was directed to him personally. The Duke of Lauderdale, to Hyatt's personal knowledge through his father, had not received the First Lord of the Admiralty during that dignitary's most recent three-day visit to Edinburgh. He hadn't even sent regrets. He simply hadn't received him. He could hardly be expected to personally acknowledge a warrant delivered by the hand of a lowly captain of the Life Guards of Horse.

The Lord High Sheriff for Scotland, however, acknowledged Captain Hyatt's presence, and the signature of the king's keeper of the seal on the warrant by sending word that he would receive Captain Hyatt at half-past two o'clock. That rather surprised Captain Hyatt, who thought that the combination of his father's rank, his own position as a captain of the Life Guards of Horse, and the importance placed upon the warrant would be enough to ensure an invitation to take lunch with the second most powerful man in Scotland.

When he got to Holyroodhouse Palace, the former Augustinian abbey that, enlarged, now served as the administrative headquarters for Scotland and the royal residence, Hyatt found that the Lord High Sheriff was an old man, which he decided was the reason he had not been invited to lunch. Old men with power had a tendency to be crotchety.

The Lord High Sheriff did offer him a glass of wine and then read the royal warrant.

"You know the particulars of this case?" the Lord High Sheriff asked after he had read the warrants.

"Is there some question in your Lordship's mind about something specific?" Captain Hyatt asked.

"Surely you have heard more than is written down here," the Lord High Sheriff said impatiently.

"There have been certain rumors, milord."

"Let's hear them," the Lord High Sheriff said.

"I am reluctant to repeat them, milord," Hyatt said uncomfortably.

The Lord High Sheriff didn't say a word. He simply looked at Hyatt through eyes that were at once bloodshot with age, contemptuous with power, and cold with anger, for he had not immediately received an answer to his question. Hyatt remembered his father's warning: "Be careful with those people, Percy. Lauderdale answers only to the king, and sometimes not to him."

"Viscount Whitten, who brought the charges," Hyatt said, "is brother to the Marchioness of Sprilley. It is being whispered about that the marchioness became involved with a commoner—"

"With the son of a Scot horse trader?" the Lord High Sheriff asked incredulously.

"With a student, a Scot, at St. Peter's School," Hyatt said.

"I suppose," the Lord High Sheriff said after a moment, "that that's possible."

"And it is whispered that after he refused the challenge of the marquess, the viscount felt obliged to seek satisfaction for his sister's honor. And that this one shot him when he was about to run his sword through the other one."

"What *other* one?"

"The other student. The one they have in a hulk on the Thames," Hyatt said. "His name is Law, I believe."

"It was Law, then, who was riding this marchioness— what did you say—Sprilley?"

"Yes, milord."

"Never heard of them," the Lord High Sheriff said. "But it was Law who was riding the marchioness, is that what you're telling me?"

"I am repeating what is whispered about, at your Lordship's command," Hyatt said.

"If what is being 'whispered about' is true," the Lord High Sheriff demanded, "what's this business about highway robbery?"

"Viscount Whitten has apparently made that accusation, your Lordship," Hyatt said.

"I can believe that Law was riding the marchioness," the Lord High Sheriff said. "And I can believe that he cut up some other young pup, but I can't believe this charge of highway robbery."

"You know these fellows, milord?" Captain Hyatt asked.

"Help yourself to more wine," the Lord High Sheriff said, not responding to the question. He heaved himself with a grunt to his feet and walked out of the room as if movement were painful.

In ten minutes he was back.

"Captain Hyatt," he said, "his Grace will receive you at midday tomorrow."

"I am honored, sir," Hyatt replied. "Please inform his Grace that I will be honored to attend him at that hour."

The Honorable Percival Hyatt was not a fool. He knew that the invitation of John Maitland, Duke of Lauderdale, Lord High Commissioner for Scotland, to luncheon had nothing to do with the duke's desire to pay his respect to the Marquess of Deal by having his son to luncheon.

Whoever this Gardiner was, he was not a simple highway robber. The Lord High Sheriff had instantly recognized the name of the other one, Law, and knew enough about him to instantly accept that he had been having an affair with a marchioness. Hyatt realized that he was not surprised. He had thought it odd that the keeper of the seal had been willing to order a detachment of the Life Guards of Horse to Scotland with a warrant for the arrest of a common criminal.

The Lord High Sheriff nodded.

"Milord," Hyatt said, "it was my intention to round this Gardiner chap up straight off—"

The Lord High Sheriff snorted. "God!" he said, shaking his head in disbelief.

"Sir?"

"Your confidence in your ability, Captain," the Lord High Sheriff said, "is astonishing. If I sent the Borderers after him, the entire damned regiment, I would be surprised if *they* could lay their hands on him in a month. *Six* months."

Captain Hyatt colored.

"Milord," he said, "I was going to say that, if you would prefer, I will put off placing this man Gardiner under arrest, until—"

The Lord High Sheriff interrupted him. "Pray let me tell you something, Captain Hyatt. What I prefer is of no more consequence than what you prefer. This is Scotland, where the only preferences which count are those of the Duke of Lauderdale."

"And what are his Grace's desires in this matter?" Captain Hyatt asked.

"His Grace has asked you here at noon tomorrow," the Lord High Sheriff said. "If I were you, I'd try to be early. Is that clear enough for you, Captain?"

"I meant, certainly, no offense, milord," Captain Hyatt said quickly.

"None, so far, has been taken," the Lord High Sheriff said. Then he walked back out of the room in which he had received Captain Hyatt.

2

The Honorable Percival Hyatt was also in possession of a letter from the colonel commanding of the Life Guards of Horse addressed to the Colonel Commanding the King's Own Scottish Borderers. It requested the latter to provide for the troopers of Hyatt's detachment and their mounts, and expressed the hope that the president of the Borderer's Mess would offer Captain Hyatt its hospitality.

When he presented himself to the colonel, Hyatt's initial reception was more than cordial. The colonel commanding warmly shook his hand and told him that he had the privilege of the acquaintance of the Marquess of Deal.

"I'll see that you're made as comfortable as possible, Hyatt," the colonel said.

"Most kind of you, sir," Hyatt said.

"And you have arrived just in time for a fine party," the colonel went on. "I feel quite sure that Captain Lord Davies of Icomkill would wish me to extend the most cordial invitation to a visiting Life Guards officer to dine with him and the officers of the Borderers tonight."

"Again, sir, that's most kind of you."

"It's liable to be a bit of a drunk, frankly," the colonel said. "Lord Davies has quite a bit to celebrate."

"And might I ask what, sir?"

"Three days ago, Lord Davies was Subaltern Frazier, who had a bit of trouble paying his own mess bill, much less trying to entertain the officers."

"I don't quite understand, sir," Hyatt said.

"His Majesty," the colonel said expansively, "no doubt at the suggestion, or at least the request, of the Duke of Lauderdale, has graciously seen fit to restore the estates and the title that were forfeit by Captain Davies's late father during the rebellion."

"Oh, I see," Hyatt said. "I wasn't aware there had been an amnesty."

"There hasn't been," the colonel said. "It's really quite extraordinary."

"And you don't think I would be a bit out of place, sir?"

"To the contrary," the colonel said. "Everyone of importance will be there. I wouldn't be a bit surprised if the duke himself made an appearance."

"Well, then, thank you again," Hyatt said. "I'll look forward to it."

"Lord Davies," the colonel said, "will, I am sure, be honored to have you, sir."

They smiled at each other.

"Might I ask the nature of your assignment in Edinburgh, Captain?" the colonel asked. "Perhaps the Borderers might be able to be of some small assistance to you."

Percy Hyatt wished that the colonel's hospitality would have stopped with the invitation to Captain Lord Davies dine in. He was extremely reluctant, even unable, as an officer and a gentleman to lie to another officer and gentleman by telling him that it was, for example, a "confidential mission." On the other hand, from his session with the Lord High Sheriff and his summons to meet with the Duke of Lauderdale tomorrow, it was clear that he was in a delicate, perhaps even dangerous position.

"I will have to rely on your discretion, sir," Hyatt said. "It's a matter of some delicacy."

"Indeed?" the colonel asked with anticipation at becoming privy to something interesting.

"I'm here to arrest one of your local young men," Hyatt said, "who is charged with either dueling with Viscount Whitten, or robbing him on the highway, depending on which version you care to believe."

"One of our local young men?"

"A chap named Gardiner," Hyatt said.

"Gardiner?" the colonel asked, surprised.

"He and a fellow named Law, who's now being held in London—" Hyatt went on, only to be interrupted by the colonel, who held out his hand, palm flat, to stop him.

"I don't think that you and I should be discussing this," the colonel said. "You will forget my question and I will forget the matter entirely."

Hyatt knew when he had made an error. He came to attention.

"With the colonel's permission, sir," he said, "I will withdraw."

"Granted," the colonel said.

Hyatt saluted, took a step backward, did an about-face, and marched toward the door.

"Hyatt!" the colonel barked, and Hyatt stopped, did another about-face, and faced the colonel.

"Sir?" he barked.

"Should you happen to meet Lord Davies tonight, for God's sake don't mention any of this to him."

"Perhaps it would be best, sir, were I to decline Lord Davies's kind invitation."

"I've considered that," the colonel said. "It's best that you go. If you can avoid a conversation with him, do so. If you cannot, mention nothing of your mission. Lie, if necessary."

"I understand, sir."

"I hope so, Captain Hyatt," the colonel said. "I do indeed hope so."

3

The ducal carriage, preceded by and trailed by four silver-helmeted cavalrymen of the Horse Guards under the command of a captain, made its way slowly down Canongate past the toll booth and the prison. The guards at the prison snapped to attention when they saw the carriage contained the Duke of Lauderdale.

The procession made its way up the incline known as the Royal Mile into the city itself, past St. Giles' Cathedral and then turned into Princes Street. Near the end of Princes Street, the carriage stopped under a sign that read "EDWARD GARDINER & SON, PURVEYORS OF FINE HORSES."

The Duke of Lauderdale's aide-de-camp started to get out of the carriage. The duke laid a hand on his arm. "You understand," he said, "that you are to ask for Mr. Gardiner first?"

"Yes, your Grace," the aide said.

"Only if he is not there are you to send the woman to me."

"I understand, your Grace," the aide said. He understood his instructions, but was baffled by what was happening. The Duke of Lauderdale ordered people to come to him, he did not go to them, and that is what he was doing now.

The aide returned in several minutes to report that neither Edward Gardiner nor his wife was at their place of business. The chief clerk in charge in their absence had told him that Edward Gardiner was in the mountains and the wife at the horse farm, ten miles from Edinburgh.

"You got directions to the farm?" the duke asked.

"I did not, your Grace."

"Please be so efficient as to do so," the duke said icily.

The aide-de-camp believed he was about to be dispatched on a twenty-mile ride to the country. He erred. When he returned to the carriage with a hastily drawn map, the duke impatiently ordered him to give it to the driver. He was headed into the country himself.

The Lord High Commissioner's aide-de-camp was further surprised when they reached the Gardiner breeding farm. Mistress Gardiner, a fair-skinned, trim woman whose red hair, tied at the neck, nearly reached her waist, did not react as the aide-de-camp expected the wife of a horse trader being called upon by the Lord High Commissioner to react.

She was frightened, of course, and that showed. But she was not stricken mute with terror, nor did she seem surprised.

"Madam," the aide-de-camp said when she came to the door of the stone cottage, "the Lord High Commissioner commands your presence." He gestured toward the carriage, and then was mildly embarrassed that he had done so. The Lord High Commissioner of Scotland had gotten out of the carriage and was relieving himself.

Amazing old buzzard, the aide-de-camp thought. At an age when he should be in his grave or confined to his bed, he looked at Mistress Gardiner as a man half his age would look at a still physically attractive woman.

Mistress Gardiner walked up to him. But she did not curtsy or even bow her head.

And the conversation was not at all what the aide-de-camp expected between his Majesty's Lord High Commissioner and the wife of a horse trader.

"Mary," the Duke of Lauderdale said.

"John," she replied.

"I understand your husband is in the mountains," the duke said.

"What is it you want, John?"

"You know what this is about."

"Then you have come for him?" Mary asked.

The Duke of Lauderdale did not reply to that, but his face grew white with anger.

"I had to ask," Mistress Gardiner said.

"You would think that of me?" he asked. "Even that?"

Mistress Gardiner did not reply to the question. "He has been ill," she said.

"Wounded?"

"A very bad chill," she said.

"From which you have helped him recover?"

"His wife," she said.

"He has a wife? I didn't know about that."

"She brought him, she and Kate, in a cart, from England."

"That's where Kate was? She ran to England to be with her brother?"

"Yes," she said. "And then when she needed to, when there was no place else to go, she helped bring him back."

"Where are they?" the duke asked.

"In a shepherd's cottage," Mary said, gesturing toward the mountains.

"I will see them," the duke said.

"You can't go there in a carriage. And he's still too weak to leave his bed."

"This is a horse farm, isn't it, Mary?" the duke said. "Certainly, there's a spare saddle."

"Are you up to riding a horse into the Highlands?" she asked.

"Don't argue with me, Mary," the duke said. "Just get me a saddled horse."

She nodded and turned from him and walked toward a horse barn. The duke watched her a moment, and then, stiffly, painfully, walked after her. When the aide-de-camp started to follow, the duke held up his hand to stop him.

"You'll stay here with the guard," he said. "See if you can get them something to eat. But you will not let them, or your imagination, wander."

Then he followed the horse dealer's wife into the horse barn. A minute or two later, they came out of the barn, the horse dealer's wife riding astride a high-stepping mare, the duke on a high-tempered stallion. They rode off side-by-side straight up the mountain.

4

The shepherd's cottage was built into the side of the mountain, so that only the thatched roof, the thatch held in place by large flat rocks, was exposed to the wind. There was a fenced area behind the house, woven of saplings and stuffed with thatch against the wind. There were three horses in it. Smoke rose from a chimney, blown immediately horizontally away by the icy wind.

The Duke of Lauderdale got stiffly down from his horse and almost staggered to the door, which he pushed open.

He found himself face to face with Kate, who was holding a pistol, aimed right at his middle, with both hands.

"You know who I am," the duke said. "Put that thing away."

"Yes, I know who you are," Kate said, not lowering the pistol.

There was more in that reply than an admission she recognizes me as the Lord High Commissioner.

"Put that down, Kate," Mary said to her daughter. "You'd not kill him."

"What is he doing here?" Kate asked, still not lowering the pistol.

"I don't know," Mary said. "But killing him would only make matters worse."

Kate thought that over and then laid the pistol on the table.

The duke waited until she had turned back to face him before he spoke. "We already know you're arrogant and disobedient," he said. "But I didn't think you were stupid as well. Raising a pistol to me could cost you your life."

"I don't think you're here as the Duke of Lauderdale," Kate said, "your Grace."

"You have a tongue like your mother," the duke said.

Kate didn't reply.

"How is your brother?" the duke asked.

"He is weak and I don't think seeing you here would do him any good."

"Hasn't your mother taught you to pay due respect to your betters?" he snapped. "Just who do you think you're talking to?"

"I know who I'm talking to, your Grace," Kate said, meeting his eyes.

By God, now there's no question about it. She knows.

"This is the woman he married?" the duke asked, looking at Sally.

"Yes," Kate said.

"What's your name, girl?" the duke demanded.

Sally was terrified to the point where she was physically unable to speak.

"Where did he find her, in a tavern somewhere?" the duke said to Kate.

"She comes from as decent a family as I do," Kate said. "She's frightened by you, is all."

"But you're not?" he asked.

"No," Kate said after a minute, "I'm not."

"Why not?"

"Because now that I've seen you twice, I know my mother is right about you."

"And what does your mother say about me?"

"That you're not the complete bastard most people think," Kate said.

"Goddamn me," the duke said after a moment, "if you're not your mother's daughter."

"And my father's," Kate said, meeting his eyes.

"Kate, for God's sake!" Mary said.

"It's a good thing for him that you didn't marry young Frazier," the duke said. "He'd not have been able to handle you." He looked at Sally again. "Found your tongue, girl?"

"My name is Sally, your Grace," Sally said, and managed a quick curtsy.

"And you're married, properly married, to this fellow the king wants to hang for being a highway robber?"

"A highway robber?" Kate asked. "What do you mean by that?"

The duke ignored her. "Sally," he said, "I asked you if you were properly married."

"Yes, your Grace," Sally said.

"In a church?" the duke asked, of Kate.

"In a church," Kate said. "We have the certificate. Do you want to see it?"

"I don't think either of you would lie to me," he said. "She, because she's afraid of me. You, because of what you are."

"I'll not lie to you."

"We'll see," he said. "What I'm going to do is ask you what's happened, and you're going to tell me. And then I'm going to ask the same thing of your brother, and by God, I better get the same story."

"David's liable to lie to you, to keep us out of it," Kate said.

"I had considered that," he said, and there was a touch of approval in his voice. He turned and started to say something to Mary. But he stopped, when their eyes met, and it was a moment before he spoke.

"If there's whiskey here, Mary," he said, "I would like some."

"There's whiskey, and food," she said. "I'll fix you something to eat."

"There won't be time to eat, if I'm to get off this godforsaken mountain by dark."

"You'll spend the night here," she said. "It's already too late."

"And I am too old?" he asked.

"That, too, John," Mary said. "I don't want you dead because of me."

He walked to the table and sat down. It required an effort. He saw Kate looking at him.

"Years ago, I gave you a coin," he said.

"I remember," she said.

"You still have it?"

"I spent it."

"Running away?"

"Bringing David home," she said.

"I see."

"David still has his," Kate said. "He believes the Duke of Lauderdale gave it to him."

"What are you saying?" he asked.

"He will probably try to pull his forelock to you," Kate said, "and he'll wonder what you're doing here."

"I take your point, Kate," the duke said. "I can see now why your mother takes such pride in you."

Kate managed a smile.

"And your father, too," the duke added.

5

Partly because of personal curiosity and partly because he knew that the more he knew about the situation, the less chance there would be that he would get in trouble, Captain Hyatt decided that he would, if given any opportunity at all, ask a few discreet questions.

The opportunity came as soon as he walked into the officer's mess of the King's Own Scottish Borderers. There were half a dozen officers at the bar, and they had apparently been told to expect him, for as soon as he handed his sword and helmet to the servant at the door, three of them came quickly across the room to greet him.

"I have the distinct honor and privilege," one of them said formally, "to offer you the hospitality of our mess."

"Thank you very much," Hyatt replied, and shook hands with each of them.

"And now that's out of the way," the same man said, "let us give you a glass of ale. We're saving space for tonight, when we're being entertained."

"So I understand," Hyatt said. "I've been invited to dine in with you."

"Splendid," the young officer said. "And now, since the colonel has made it quite clear that we are not to ask polite questions about what brings you to Edinburgh, we'll get straight to the important things, like women and horses."

Five minutes later, Hyatt was able to bring up John Law's name.

"I met a chap from here in London," he said. "Named Law. Anyone know him?"

"That would be young Law, I expect," one of the officers replied. "He goes off all year to some school in London."

"And who is 'old' Law?" Captain Hyatt inquired dryly.

"One of us, as a matter of fact," a middle-aged, florid-faced captain said. "Served with the duke during the rebellion. And then went off to more important things."

"I don't quite understand," Hyatt said.

The captain tapped Hyatt's mug of ale. Hyatt raised his eyebrows in question.

"That's Law's Pale Ale you're drinking," the captain explained. "Young Law is the heir apparent, in a manner of speaking."

"Oh, I see. A *prominent* citizen?"

"Prominent and rich," the Scot replied.

That reply seemed to answer a number of questions. Law was known to the Lord High Sheriff because his father and the duke had been comrades-in-arms. His being rich explained the Lord High Sheriff's remarks about his being willing to accept any story about young Law—what was it he had said, riding the marchioness? —but that he didn't think it was likely that he would be a highway robber.

But then Hyatt remembered that the Lord High Sheriff had known the name Gardiner just about as well as he had known Law's. He decided that he would take the chance of asking about him, too.

"And what about a chap named Gardiner?" he asked. "I have a vague idea he's a friend of Law's."

"That would probably be young Gardiner," one of them said.

"Probably?" another snorted. "Certainly!"

"We don't mention that name in here," the middle-aged captain said firmly. "Sorry."

"All Hyatt's asking about is the boy," one of the young lieutenants protested.

"Another rich and prominent family?" Hyatt asked.

"I will tell you, sir," the middle-aged captain said, "that the young man of whom you speak is the son of a horse dealer. I would not describe them as either rich or prominent. Edward Gardiner and Son holds an appointment to the crown as purveyor of horses. They supply most of ours. For the regiment, I mean. And for the government. I have never met either father or son, and can therefore tell you nothing about them. And now, sir, I would be grateful if we could change the subject."

"I'm terribly afraid I've offended," Hyatt said. He would have loved to have learned more, but asking even one more question would be impossible.

"Not at all," the captain said. "Perhaps I might ask you to sign our guest book, Captain Hyatt?"

"I would be honored, sir."

And that, Hyatt thought, is all I'm going to be able to find out from anyone here. Or, for that matter, from anyone else, unless either the Lord High Sheriff or the Duke of Lauderdale himself said something. Everyone else was obviously afraid to discuss David Gardiner.

6

The dining in at the Borderers' officer's mess was unlike anything Captain Percival Hyatt had ever before seen. It had some extraordinary things, from a rather foul-smelling substance called haggis and a march through the room, at least six times, of brawny bagpipers playing their extraordinary music.

It began decorously enough, but soon the officers were in various stages of drunkenness. They seemed particularly pleased when they were able to get three young subalterns very drunk, and even more delighted when one of them fell unconscious to the floor.

Hyatt tried to make himself as inconspicuous as possible, and he refused as many drinks as he possibly could. There was simply no telling what these barbarians would do if they found a drunken officer of the Life Guards of Horse helpless in their midst.

When the Borderers' captain leaned over the chair in the dark corner of the mess to which he had retreated, Hyatt took a moment to recognize him as his host.

"I would be grateful, Captain Hyatt," Captain Lord Davies of Icomkill said to him, "for a private word with you."

Hyatt got somewhat uneasily, if immediately, to his feet. If they could put their young officers to bed for the night on the manure pile behind the stables, there was no telling what they had in mind for him.

"I am at your Lordship's pleasure," he said.

Lord Davies alarmed him further by leading him out of the mess through the kitchen, which made Hyatt worry that half a dozen others would be waiting for him in the alley behind the kitchen to manifest upon his person some insane Scottish idea of humor.

But there was no one in the alley. Lord Davies of Icomkill led him across the parade ground to one of the watchtowers and told the soldier on duty there to admit them. He then preceded Hyatt up circular stairs to the top of the watchtower itself, where he relieved the soldier on duty by telling him to wait below until summoned.

"I wanted to be sure no one overheard us," Davies said to him.

"I confess to being a little confused, milord," Hyatt said.

"I want you to tell me about David Gardiner," Lord Davies demanded.

"I'm not sure what you mean, milord," Hyatt replied.

"You've come here with a warrant for David Gardiner," Lord Davies said. "I know because your man told my man all about it. I want to know what it's all about."

"Do you know Gardiner?"

"I know his sister," Davies said.

"You are putting me in a very embarrassing position, milord," Hyatt said.

"I was engaged to marry Gardiner's sister," Lord Davies said.

"I was not aware of that, milord."

"She ran to London, to her brother, rather than marry me."

Hyatt made no reply.

"I am unable to believe that Kate's brother is a highway robber," Davies said.

"There seems to be some question that he is, milord," Hyatt said.

"In any event, I wish to do whatever I can to help him. Last week, that would have been impossible. But this week, as you keep reminding me, Hyatt, I am Lord Davies, and perhaps there is something I can do."

"I regret, milord," Hyatt said, "that I am unable to discuss this matter with you."

"You have two choices, Hyatt," Lord Davies of Icomkill said matter-of-factly, "you can either tell me everything you know, and have heard, or I will throw you from this tower."

The Honorable Percival Hyatt, Captain of the Life Guards of Horse, decided that the logical thing to do was tell Lord Davies what he wanted to know. It was eighty feet, perhaps more, to the ground, and there was no question whatever in his mind that Davies fully intended to throw him off if he didn't tell him what he wanted to hear.

7

Captain Percival Hyatt was admitted to the private offices of the Lord High Commissioner of Scotland by the Duke of Lauderdale's personal aide-de-camp at precisely noon the next day. He was informed that the duke was not available and that he should return the next day.

He did, and received the same message.

On the third day, however, when he presented himself, the aide-de-camp showed him into an interior room. The duke was behind a worktable, on which, to one side, were the plates and remnants of the meal he had obviously just eaten.

Captain Hyatt respectfully bowed his head.

The duke nodded. "Hyatt, isn't it?"

"Yes, your Grace," Hyatt replied, and bowed again.

"You will please offer your father, when you go back to England, my best regards," the duke said.

"I will be pleased to do so, your Grace."

The duke nodded, and then said, "Read it to him, Andrews."

The aide-de-camp, who wore the uniform of the Horse Guards, took a large sheet of parchment from the duke's table, and read aloud, "Holyroodhouse Palace, Edinburgh, seventh March 1686."

Hyatt, at first having no idea what the document was, decided that the Lord High Commissioner was about to issue a warrant of his own for the arrest of David Gardiner. Hyatt had learned that the Duke of Lauderdale was highly jealous of his royal prerogatives, and by issuing his own warrant, he would maintain his position as master of Scotland.

"Your Majesty," the aide read on, and that surprised Hyatt. It was not a warrant, but a letter to the king. Was the old buzzard going to cause him trouble because he had been sent here with a royal warrant? Had some step in protocol been overlooked that had enraged the old buzzard's sense of self-importance?

"I have received Captain Hyatt, of your Majesty's Life Guards of Horse," the aide-de-camp read on, "who came hence bearing a warrant issued in your Majesty's name for the arrest of one of your Majesty's subjects, David Gardiner of Edinburgh."

Now what? Hyatt wondered.

"Your Majesty will doubtless be pleased to learn that by the grace of God, a miscarriage of justice has been prevented. The matter was brought to my attention by your Majesty's Lord High Sheriff for Scotland, who is also aware of the facts in this case—"

What the hell is he talking about?

"While the man named in the warrant issued in your Majesty's name was in fact in London, his taking ill led to his wife's bringing him home from London at least a week, possibly more than a week, before the assault upon Viscount Whitten took place. Of this there can be no doubt, for when the illness of Gardiner came to my attention, as a token of my appreciation of Gardiner's father's long and faithful service to your Majesty's Lord High Commissioner for Scotland, I called upon Gardiner to visit the son and offer the family the services of my physician.

"Your Majesty's Lord High Sheriff for Scotland suggests to me that whoever made the assault upon Viscount Whitten, being aware that Gardiner had departed London, used his name.

"I remain your Majesty's most loyal liege, Lauderdale."

John Maitland, Duke of Lauderdale, Lord High Commissioner for Scotland, raised his rather bloodshot eyes to meet those of Captain Hyatt.

Their eyes held for a moment, and then Lauderdale gestured to his aide-de-camp, who laid the letter on the table before him.

"I wanted you to witness my sealing this, Captain Hyatt," the Duke of Lauderdale said. "In case any question might arise." He folded the document, rubbed the crease, dripped sealing wax on the edges, and then stamped his crest into the soft wax.

He handed it to Hyatt. Their eyes met again.

John Maitland, Duke of Lauderdale, Lord High Commissioner for Scotland, had just given the King of England and Scotland the choice between believing Viscount Whitten or him. There was no question whose version the king would accept. Why the Lord High Commissioner had decided to intercede in David Gardiner's behalf was an interesting question, but Captain Hyatt was well aware it was a question only the king would dare ask.

Chapter Fifteen

1

Captain Lord Davies of Icomkill arrived at the Gardiner house shortly after nine the next morning. A stablehand told him that the master and the mistress were in the country and were not expected back until the next day. He had no idea at what hour.

Davies returned to the house shortly after noon the next day, where another stablehand told him they had not returned and that he had no idea when they would. After some delay he produced another stablehand who was able to draw a map for him to find the horse farm. Davies had then to ride back into town, to the Borderers' barracks, and obtain permission to be absent from duty the next morning if that should prove necessary. It was after three before, having changed out of his uniform, he was able to set out from the barracks for the horse farm.

He was riding down a narrow portion of the road—a defile with a stream to his right and a rocky outcropping, above which was a stand of elm—when he encountered the Horse Guards trooper. The defile at that point was

339

wide enough only for two riders or a carriage. The appearance of the trooper, moving at a canter, was not surprising. He was obviously preceding a section of horse or perhaps some sort of a supply detachment, possibly even a carriage, and he had been dispatched ahead by his corporal to clear the defile of single riders coming the other way.

Davies had already begun to tense his reins, to turn his mount, when the trooper called out to him.

"Make way! And quickly, you clod!"

It was one thing to be asked to wait, even another to be ordered to make way for a body of troops. It was something else entirely, particularly to an officer of the Borderers, to be curtly ordered about and called a clod.

Davies turned his mount again, this time back in the direction he had been traveling, and he touched his heels to the animal.

"Watch your goddamned tongue, trooper!" he called harshly. "Who do you think you're ordering about?"

He was past the surprised trooper and around a corner of the defile before the trooper could even shout again after him. It had just occurred to him that the trooper was vaguely familiar when he found himself riding almost into a captain of the Horse Guards, three more troopers, and a carriage. Behind the carriage were four more troopers, and he recognized the carriage.

The captain raised his hand, ordering the procession to stop, and then rode up to Davies. By that time, the trooper who had attempted to stop him had turned and come after him.

"I told him to make way, sir!" the trooper called.

"Make way, sir," the Horse Guards captain ordered icily, "for the Lord High Commissioner."

"My apologies, sir," Davies said, trying to turn his animal on the narrow crowded defile. "I will always make way for the Duke of Lauderdale."

"Then apparently your hearing is bad, sir," the captain said.

"My hearing is fine," Davies said. "I was under the impression I was being rudely ordered to make way for a detachment of Horse Guards."

"Do I understand you, sir, that you would not make way for the Horse Guards?"

"The Borderers give way only to his Grace and the King," Davies said, and by then he had his animal turned and he gave him his heels and cantered to the end of the defile, went off the road, and stopped to let the procession pass him.

His temper had momentarily gotten the best of him, and it was only when he was waiting for the carriage to pass that he began to wonder what the duke was doing so far out in the country.

He respectfully removed his hat as the carriage approached and then bowed his head as it passed. He saw a scowling face, that of the duke's aide, in the carriage window, and then it disappeared. A moment later, the carriage door opened and the aide stepped out and called to the coachman to stop.

When the carriage had stopped, he jumped to the ground, unfolded the step before the footman could reach it, and held out his hand to offer the duke assistance to demount.

The duke walked to the side of the road and began to relieve himself. Then he looked up at Davies.

"My Lord Davies," he said sarcastically.

"Good afternoon, your Grace," Davies said, and bowed again.

"Pray tell, My Lord Davies," the duke said with sarcastic courtesy, "what brings you here at this hour, to interfere with the smooth passage of my carriage?"

"I humbly beg your Grace's pardon," Davies said. "I thought it was simply a detachment of the Horse Guards."

"I'll bet you did, you arrogant bastard," the duke said, chuckling as he rearranged his clothing. "What are you doing out here, Thom?"

"Milord, I'm—"

"Got some well-teated farmer's daughter out this way, have you?" the duke interrupted. He looked at Davies and saw his face flush. "Specifically, Thom, where are you going?"

"As a matter of fact, your Grace, I am on my way to see Mr. Gardiner."

"Mr. Edward Gardiner?" the duke asked. "No doubt to seek satisfaction for the insult his daughter paid you?"

"No, sir," Davies said.

"You didn't consider yourself insulted, Davies?" the duke asked.

"Milord," Davies said. "It has come to my attention that David Gardiner, Miss Gardiner's brother, is in some sort of trouble."

"And?"

"I came to offer my services, if they should be of value," Davies said.

"First she runs off instead of marrying you, making you look like an ass, and now you're rushing to help her?"

Davies did not reply.

"Well, you heard right. David Gardiner damned near got himself hung as a highway robber," the duke said.

"Your Grace, I find that hard to believe."

"So did I," the duke said. "Consequently, Thom, your services are not required. So there's no sense you going up there."

Davies looked uncomfortable.

"Ride back with me," the duke said. "Turn your horse over to one of the troopers and get in the carriage."

"Milord, I had hoped to see—"

"Get in the carriage, Davies," the duke said. "I wish to speak with you."

"Yes, milord," Davies said. He dismounted and handed the reins of his horse to the trooper who had initially blocked his way. Then he climbed into the carriage, sitting beside the duke's aide, riding backward, facing the duke.

"I am getting the odd feeling that you are still taken with the Gardiner wench," the duke said after a moment. "Despite what she did to you, despite the proof she's given you that she is wild and disobedient and everything, save perhaps a slut, that can be wrong with a woman."

Davies, coloring, did not reply.

"God," the duke said, "I'd forgotten what it was like, to be so eager to get under a woman's skirts that nothing else matters."

"My intentions toward Miss Gardiner are honorable, your Grace," Davies said stiffly.

The duke laughed. "Nothing to do with getting your hands on her, right? It's pure and noble, My Lord Davies?"

"Milord," Davies said uncomfortably.

The duke laughed again. "Very well, Thom, if you're determined to give her the chance to make an ass of you again, I'll not stand in your way. But not today. Today would be a bad time and I want to talk to you about Hannover."

"I am, of course, at your Grace's command."

"Yes, My Lord Davies," the duke said, "you are."

2

John Law had been in the hold of the prison hulk *Valorous* for nearly two months when the grate was opened unexpectedly in midmorning and he was summoned onto the deck.

He was taken forward by two warders and half-pushed against the bulkhead of the forecastle and ordered to strip. The prospect was frightening. It was cold enough on the icy deck clothed. But he had long before learned what he thought of, in a paraphrase of the Prayer Book, as the First and Great Commandment: "You do what the warders tell you to do, when they tell you to do it, for otherwise, you will be whipped, or beaten, or starved, or all three, and then you will do it anyway."

He stripped off his clothes and stood naked, wondering what was going to happen next. He had no idea what it would be or what he had done that had put him where he was, but he was prepared for just about anything. Even with the protection of Arthur Carter, he had been subjected to more humiliation, and for that matter, pain, in the hold of the *Valorous* than he had ever before considered possible, much less experienced.

What happened, however, came as complete chock. First, without warning, he was doused from the forecastle deck with two bucketfuls of a whitish, foul-smelling substance. Shivering, he looked up in surprise in time to see prisoners coming down the ladder with more buckets of the stuff they had thrown down on him.

He had recovered enough by then to realize that what had been thrown on him was the concoction they used to kill the bugs in the hold. He had been debugged, he realized, and wondered why. Was he to be brought to trial?

He had actually received only the first step in the routine delousing process. That was being drenched with the stuff. The second step was less pleasant. The two prisoners, part of the dozen or so prisoners who had wormed their way into small extra privilege by taking over the dirtier jobs of the warders, now began to scrub him with stiff-bristled brushes, paying particular attention to the hair parts of his body, his scalp, his underarms, and his crotch.

Finally, he was doused again, this time with "clean" water from the Thames and pushed into a room in the forecastle, where he was permitted to dry himself with bundles of rags and then to dress himself in clothing he had paid the warder who provided his and Arthur Carter's food to bring from his apartment. He was even provided with a razor and soap and a glass so that he could shave. When he'd finished that and saw what his face looked like, he regretted shaving. He had been bitten by God alone knew how many bugs, and his scratching at the bites had caused festering sores, which, with his beard gone, made him look, he thought, like a leper.

When he had finished, he was led to the side of the hulk and taken ashore; then he made another trip through London, past the eyes of spectators who seemed delighted with his predicament, in an open, barred cart to the watch office where he had first been arrested.

There he was out into a small windowless room and left to wait for several hours before being taken from it and led into the watch officer's office.

The man with the ill-fitting wig was there again, and by now John Law knew that he was either a judge or a man who liked to be treated as one.

"Good afternoon, milord," John said politely.

The judge sniffed and grimaced. "I gave specific instructions," he said, "that you were to be given the opportunity to clean yourself up."

"Your Lordship's instructions were executed with a will," John said. "Perhaps what your Lordship smells is what they bathed me in."

The judge looked at him a moment, as if he was going to reply to that, but then he changed his mind.

"We seem to have made a mistake, Mr. Law," he said. "And fairness seems to dictate that I inform you we did."

My God, are they going to let me go?

"The man," the judge said, "whom we believe to be your accomplice in the assault upon Viscount Whitten is not the man we thought him to be. It is not David Gardiner of Edinburgh."

John said nothing. He had no idea what was going on.

"You don't seem very surprised, Mr. Law, to have me tell you that."

"Milord, I was taught that the truth will come out in the end," John said.

The judge laughed. "The reason we are so sure is that we have it from the Lord High Commissioner for Scotland himself that Mr. Gardiner was in Scotland when Viscount Whitten was assaulted," the judge said.

Wouldn't you be surprised, milord, to hear that David Gardiner is the Duke of Lauderdale's bastard?

"Nor does that, I notice, Mr. Law, surprise you."

"I confess, milord, that it does not," John said.

"Captain Hyatt, of the Life Guards of Horse, who carried the warrant to Edinburgh, returned with all sorts of interesting information," the judge said. "Among it that you are the son of Captain William Law, who rose with the duke during the rebellion. Is that true?"

"Were it true, I would deny it to spare my father the humiliation of having a son in these straits," John said.

"Very noble, I'm sure, Mr. Law," the judge replied dryly. "What I found interesting, personally, considering your father's apparent friendship with his Grace was that his Grace did not have personal knowledge that you, too, were in Scotland at the time of the assault. I would not, nor would others, have questioned the duke's recollection of events in that case any more than I would question it regarding Mr. Gardiner's remarkably rapid trip from here to Scotland."

"Excuse me?"

"We have witnesses who place Mr. Gardiner at the Bank of London on the very same day Viscount Whitten was assaulted. If we are to believe them, *and* the Lord High Commissioner, he was almost immediately after leaving the bank miraculously transported to Scotland."

"Obviously, the witnesses who saw him at the Bank were mistaken," John said.

"Obviously," the judge agreed. Then he went on, "A solution to your predicament, Mr. Law, has been proposed."

"Oh?"

"Lord Sprilley was approached and asked if he really thought it possible that the son of a man who had ridden with his Grace the Duke of Lauderdale was capable of a robbery and assault upon the person of Viscount Whitten. Did you know that the viscount is the marquess's brother-in-law, Mr. Law?"

"I'd heard that, yes," John said. He was growing excited. The attitude of the judge was considerably different than it had been previously. He was being treated as more of a social equal than simply the son of a well-to-do merchant. The influence of Lauderdale was apparently as great and as wide-ranging as his father had suggested.

"In a few words, the marquess said that he would be willing to have a word with his brother-in-law on this matter, perhaps suggesting to him that he had made an error of identification in your regard."

"That's most gracious of the marquess," John said. I am going to get out. I'll be damned!

"The marquess said that he was sure that in the case of someone from a fine family such as yourself, who had, moreover, just taken the king's commission as an ensign in the Royal Navy and was about to embark for the Caribbean and the Pacific on a three-year voyage, Viscount Whitten would realize that he had made an error, because of his injured condition, and would be prepared to swear to that effect."

"What did you say about the Royal Navy?" John asked.

"I think you heard what I said, Mr. Law," the judge said. "Those are the marquess's conditions."

"That's absurd!" John said. "A commission in the Navy? I get sick in a boat on a river."

"Perhaps Lord Sprilley is aware of that," the judge said.

"I beg your pardon?"

"Lord Sprilley, Law, is not going to forgive you easily for making him a cuckold. . . ."

"If you know about that, then you know what's behind this whole thing!" John protested.

"The only two things I know for sure, Mr. Law," the judge said, "are that Viscount Whitten is in hospital with a leg he may yet lose because there is a pistol ball put in it by a friend of yours. And that that friend is not, because Lauderdale says he is not, David Gardiner."

"I was simply defending myself," John said. "Whitten came after me and I defended myself."

"That's called dueling," the judge said. "The penalty for dueling is death by hanging."

"For God's sake, make Whitten tell the truth!"

"In the eyes of the law, if he told the truth as you see it, he would be confessing either to offering a challenge to a duel or to assault. *He* would hang, and I rather doubt that he would say anything that would put his neck in the noose."

"My God!" John said in exasperation.

"The favors of Eleanor, Marchioness of Sprilley, Law, are going to cost you three years in the Royal Navy."

"The hell they are!"

"Three years in the Royal Navy is much preferable, I would think, to three years in the hold of the hulk of the *Valorous*," the judge said.

"You can't keep me there forever," John said defiantly.

"We can keep you there until you come up for trial. And I don't think that Viscount Whitten, whose testimony of course would be required at the trial, will be physically fit to appear for a trial for some time. Perhaps even years."

"You mean as long as that bastard stays in bed, he can keep me in the *Valorous*?"

"I wouldn't phrase it quite that way," the judge said, "but that's about right."

"I would die in the Navy," John said. "I'll wait the bastard out."

"You're being very foolish," the judge said.

"I have no damned intention of going off to drown in the Pacific!" John said.

"I'll give you some time to think it over, Mr. Law. I'll send for you again in several weeks or a month."

"Milord, may I ask one question?"

"You may *ask* whatever you like."

"Does my father know where I am?"

"I really don't know," the judge said. "You would be better able to judge that than I am. But if he does know, if I were you, I would go on the premise that he has already sought the good offices of the Duke of Lauderdale. And that the duke has decided that one miraculous transport to Scotland at a time is all the king will believe."

"I was hoping that he did not know," John said.

"I suggest to you that your father would be less distressed to hear that you had extricated yourself from this mess by taking the king's commission in the Royal Navy, than to hear you were in the hold of the *Valorous*, waiting trial."

"How soon do I have to make up my mind?" John asked after a moment.

"As I said, Mr. Law, I'll give you some time to think it over," the judge said. "I'll send for you again in several weeks . . . or a month."

The temptation to take the offer now, so that he would never have to return to the cold and the filth and the rats and vermin of the *Valorous* was never overwhelming. But John resisted it.

"Thank you, milord," he said.

3

"Captain William Law, your Grace," the aide-de-camp announced.

John Maitland, Duke of Lauderdale, had been reading with the help of a large magnifying glass. He laid it down and looked at the door as William Law stepped inside and respectfully bowed.

"Thank you for receiving me, your Grace," William said.

"I won't say I'm glad to see you, Willy," the duke said, motioning him into the room and then into a chair beside the table at which he was reading. "I damned well know why you're here."

"I regret, your Grace, that I had to come," William said.

The duke pushed a gray pottery bottle across the table toward William.

"Pour us one," he ordered. "You look sick."

William stood up, took the jug, and poured whiskey into two glasses. The duke reached over and took one of the glasses.

"Old times, Willy," he said. "They always seem better than they were."

"Old times, your Grace," William said. Both men drained their glasses.

"How did you find out?" the duke asked.

Obviously he knows. How long has he known? Have I overestimated the intimacy of our relationship by being surprised that he didn't tell me himself?

"I had a letter yesterday from my man at the Bank of London," William said.

"Bastard took his time telling you, didn't he?" the duke said. "I wondered why you hadn't been here before this."

"I come before you shamed, your Grace," William said.

"Worse than that, Willy, it won't do you any good," the duke said.

"I am prepared to beg for my son's life, your Grace," William said.

"Please don't, Willy."

"I dared presume that you would at least hear my plea," William said.

"We're old friends, Willy. I know what you want to plead."

"Surely you can't believe that my son is a highway robber," William said.

"What your son is, Willy, is a spoiled, irresponsible, hot-blooded young pup who tumbled the wrong woman," the duke said. "One married to an ass with friends in high places."

Then the duke saw the look of confusion on William's face. "Good God, Willy, don't you know what's happened?"

"I have been informed that John is charged with highway robbery and assault with a deadly weapon."

"Then your banker is either an ass or a friend of Sprilley, or both," the duke said. He paused a moment, and then went on. "What happened, Willy, is that your son got caught jumping the Marchioness of Sprilley. Sprilley challenged him to a duel. To his shame, your son refused the challenge. He was apparently planning to run home."

"I had heard none of this, your Grace," William said.

"The marchioness has a brother, Viscount Whitten. When he heard that your son was running, he went after him, caught him, and started to carve him up, whereupon David Gardiner put a pistol ball in his leg."

"David Gardiner shot the viscount?"

"Involving David Gardiner in his mess was hardly the gentlemanly thing for your son to do, was it, Willy?"

"No, sir, it was not."

"What you should have done with him, Willy, was buy him a commission in the Borderers, instead of letting him run wild."

"I thought he would get in more trouble as a young officer in the Borderers than he would elsewhere," William said.

"If he was in the Borderers, I probably could have helped him," the duke said. "I can't help him where he is now."

"But what about David Gardiner?" William asked. He knows that I am asking about his bastard son.

"I lied to the king about him," the duke said. "Nothing's going to happen to him. All he did was what I would have done. Come to the assistance of a friend who happened to be a damned fool."

"I had hoped," William said, his voice strained, his face red with humiliation, "that I could beg you to come to the aid of an old friend, who has also been a damned fool."

"Good Christ, Willy! If I could have helped you, I would have. Don't you really understand?"

"No, milord, I do not."

"Then you are, in fact, a goddamned fool. I would have thought you would have known better. Every commander, right up to the king, indulges his lieutenants. Sergeants indulge corporals. Captains indulge lieutenants. Kings indulge lord high commissioners. But only to a point. Only to a point, Willy, only to a goddamned *point*. After that, you start looking around for lieutenants who won't ask so many indulgences. And I have crossed that point. My credit with my king is expended."

"Because of your protecting David?"

"That may damned well have overdrawn an already empty account," the duke said. "How much do you think it cost me to get Icomkill's title and estates restored? Christ, Willy, you don't think our beloved sovereign did that out of Christian charity, do you?"

"For the girl," William said softly. "You did that for the girl."

"And then the ungrateful bitch's goddamned brother has to shoot the goddamned viscount to protect your goddamned son, Willy. I thought that you of all people would know that the Lord High Commissioner for Scotland is not God."

"Milord, I am shamed."

"Why the hell should you be shamed? You neither jumped the marchioness nor turned coward and refused a fair challenge when you were caught with your hand up her skirt."

"For not realizing that you would have helped me if you could," William said softly.

"What that goddamned son of yours needs is the discipline you didn't see that he got by putting him in the Borderers," the duke said. "Well, he'll get it now, I suppose."

"What's going to happen to him?"

"If it were up to me, I'd have the bastard flogged, just to start," the duke said. Then he saw the look in William

Law's eyes and stopped. "I don't know, Willy. Sprilley's after his ass. And Sprilley probably knows that I can't go back to the king."

"I understand, milord," William said.

"Oh, God, Willy!" the duke said. "You know that if necessary I'll go to the king personally. If necessary means that if they start to hang him . . ."

"Thank you, milord."

"But only then. You understand that, Willy. Only then will I do what I can to keep him from being hung. But anything they do to him short of that, he deserves."

"I understand, milord. I'm grateful."

"Pour yourself another drink, Willy," the duke said. "And then leave me."

4

A week after the Duke of Lauderdale's visit to the shepherd's cottage in the Highlands, Sally Ward Gardiner, who was curled up in sleep beside Kate before the hearth, was wakened by her husband.

"What are you doing out of bed?" she asked.

He put his finger in front of his mouth as a signal for silence and motioned for her to come with him. She got up and he took her hand and led her out of the cottage and to the side of it, where there was a small enclosed shed used to store feed for the animals.

"What is it?" she asked in a whisper.

He repeated the sign for silence and carefully made a base for the candle he had brought with him by dripping wax onto one of the timbers of the building and then sticking the candle base into it.

"What is it, David?" Sally asked.

He leered at her.

"You're crazy!" Sally protested. "You shouldn't even be out of bed!"

He advanced on her, his hands, fingers extended, held at the level of his shoulders, like a monster, his eyes wide.

"David, no!"

"Sssh," he said. "You don't want to wake Kate, do you?"

He pushed her back onto a bale of hay. "I wonder if it's going to be as much fun now that we're married and it's not a sin?" he asked as he pulled his nightshirt over his head.

"David!" Sally protested. Not very much, she thought. Just because she thought she should. Not because she really wanted him to stop.

The next morning, over the objections of his wife and sister, David Gardiner saddled the horses and then, with a visible effort, hauled himself onto Wanderer's back and started to ride down out of the Highlands and back to Edinburgh.

Sally's and Kate's predictions to the contrary, David did not fall in a swoon from his mount, but the trip did exhaust him, and once he got to Edinburgh, he went to bed and slept for eighteen hours.

He was awakened by his father, and when he pulled himself into a sitting position, he saw that there was a young man in the room.

"David," Edward Gardiner said, "if you feel up to it, Lord Davies wants to talk to you."

"I am not yet comfortable with that," the young man said. "I think of myself still as Thom Frazier."

"What can I do for you, milord?" David asked.

"Can you not call me Thom?" Lord Davies asked.

"That would make me uncomfortable," David said.

"If I were your brother-in-law," Lord Davies said, "perhaps it would not."

"I don't think I understand," David said.

"He's still willing to marry Kate," Edward Gardiner said. "Even after everything."

"You make it sound more patronizing than is the case, Mr. Gardiner," Lord Davies said. " 'Willing' isn't quite the word. I hope that she will agree to marry me."

"Have you asked her?" David asked.

"I wanted to talk to you first."

"Why?"

"Because the last time, she ran to you, is why," Edward Gardiner said to David.

"And you think she might again?" David asked.

"You took her in once," Lord Davies said.

"After what she did to you once, you're going to give her another chance?" David asked.

"I want her for my wife."

David looked at Captain Lord Davies of Icomkill intently for a moment and liked what he saw. For some reason, he had pictured him in his mind as an icy-faced, much older aristocrat.

"Then you're a fool," David said. Lord Davies turned white in the face. "I know something of that myself," David went on. "There's no reasoning with a fool, is there? I mean, if a man figures he cannot live without a particular female, he can't, can he?"

"No. And I have concluded that is the case with Kate."

"You'll probably regret it the rest of your life," David said. "When she's driven you out of your mind, you'll remember you had your chance to get out of it and threw it away."

"Then you won't let her run to you again?" Lord Davies asked.

"I'll go further than that," David said. "I'll try to talk some sense into her. Sometimes, not always, she'll listen to me."

5

Kate had taken Sally shopping in Edinburgh, in the shiny carriage, behind two jet-black horses, and had had a good time. The idea had been hers, but her father had made it a more pleasant event than she had imagined.

"I've got a really fancy pair of matched blacks I'd like you to show off," he said. "Two pretty girls should do that nicely."

When he'd hitched the team for her, he put money in her hand. "Get her whatever she needs," he said. And then when she'd seen how much money he'd given her and looked at him in surprise, he added, "For one thing, she's earned that and more, and for another, it's really David's. So far, he's put a good deal in the business and taken damned little out."

That meant, she realized, several things. Most important for her, that she had been forgiven the humiliation she had caused him by running. And equally important, that he approved of Sally. She realized again how much she loved the man who had been father to her.

When they came back from town, Sally's shoulders wrapped in what she had said, before Kate had bought it for her, was the "prettiest shawl she had ever seen," there was another black horse tied to the rail before the house. He was a fine, massive animal, his hooves blacked, his glistening saddle resting on a black-and-gold saddle blanket on which was embroidered in gold and silver thread the royal crest. It was the mount of an officer of the King's Own Scottish Borderers and she knew which one even before she followed Sally into the house and saw Thom Frazier sitting with her mother and her father and David. They were at the table in the front room, a clay jug of whiskey and glasses before them.

"Should you be out of bed?" Sally asked David. Kate told herself that it wasn't Sally asking David, it was a wife asking her husband, with proprietary right.

Thom Frazier stood up and his face flushed. "Kate," he said.

"Milord," Kate said.

"I had hoped it would be Thom," he said.

"Thom, then," Kate said, and smiled at him.

Sally looked at Kate with a question in her eyes and Kate nodded.

"Thom," David said, "this is my wife, Sally."

Kate thought, Thom? So they've become instant friends? Why does that surprise me? They're both good men.

"Lord Davies of Icomkill," Kate's mother said, and added, with pride in her voice, "My father was master at arms to Thom's father when he was Lord Davies of Icomkill."

Sally didn't know how to respond. She wasn't used to being around the nobility, and the situation was awkward enough as it was.

"I hope," Lord Davies of Icomkill said to Sally Gardiner, "that you will be inclined to call me Thom, Mistress Sally."

Sally colored and gave him a nervous smile.

"Say something about her shawl, David," Kate said.

David looked at Sally, and the shawl, and shrugged his shoulders. "Is something wrong with it?" he said, and then, finally, he understood. "That's quite nice. Where did you get it?"

"We just bought it," Sally said.

"Very nice," David said.

"Thom has come for a word with you, Kate," Mary said.

"Oh?" Kate asked. She had known from the moment she had seen the black stallion, much less Thom, what he wanted here. "I was about to unhitch the team."

"Your father will unhitch the team," Mary said quickly.

"I'll do it," Thom said, and walked quickly to the door and held it open for Kate.

They walked to the stable, leading the team, saying nothing.

And nothing was said until the animals had been unhitched and stripped of their tack and put into stalls and Thom had pushed the carriage into its shed.

"You know why I'm here, Kate," Thom finally said.

"I think so."

"I want you for my wife."

"I know," she said.

There was an awkward silence.

"The duke has been telling me that I won't be gone to Hannover for long. I mean, he will be wanting me to come back every six months or so. And that assignment won't be for long. No more than three years. If that's what's bothering you. Leaving your family, I mean."

"I don't love you, Thom," Kate said. "Not the way that Sally loves David." Nor the way I love John Law.

"Oh," he said, and she was truly sorry that she had hurt his feelings.

"I wish I did," Kate said. I also wish John Law hadn't had to run to France, but that's the way things are.

"Sometimes it comes later, I hear. I mean, love. I mean I . . . I don't know what I mean."

"I know what you mean," Kate said, "but I don't think that would be enough."

356

"It would be enough for me," he said quickly. "I can make you learn to love me, Kate."

She looked at him but didn't reply.

"I didn't mean the way it sounded," Thom said. "I sounded as if I could order you—"

"I know what you meant, Thom."

"Is there another man, Kate? Is that what this is?"

There is another man. But there is no chance in the world that he would marry me. "No," she said.

"It is humiliating for me to beg this way, Kate."

"I would not humiliate you for the world," Kate said. "You're a good man, Thom, and I'm very fond of you."

"But you don't love me and you won't marry me?" he said bitterly.

"That's two questions," Kate said. "I've only answered one of them."

He looked at her in confusion for a moment. "Then I'll ask it straight out," he said. "Will you marry me, Kate, or no?"

"If, understanding the way things are, you want me to," Kate said.

His face brightened and his eyes lit up. "I'll be good to you, Kate, I swear," Thom said.

She smiled at him.

He danced around a little, and for a moment she thought he was going to kiss her. But he didn't.

"Let's go tell them," he said, and took her hand.

Kate wondered if it was a sin to marry a man you didn't love, a man you didn't want to kiss. Then she thought that it probably happened all the time. It had happened in her own family. Her mother had married her father, not because she loved him, but because she was carrying the Duke of Lauderdale's bastard twins. The love, and there was no question that now her mother loved her father as deeply as Sally loved David, had come later.

Thom was a good man.

Catherine, Lady Incomkill, Kate thought as she walked with Thom back to the house, would probably learn, in time, to love her husband. She would try.

Chapter Sixteen

1

David Gardiner left Sally in his bed very early in the morning, not responding to Sally's protest that there were hired men about to do the early-morning work. It was better to let her think he was headed for the stables or the fields.

He saddled Wanderer, was furious with himself when he couldn't find the strength in his legs to leap onto his back, and made up for it when he had finally pulled himself into the saddle by immediately putting his heels to him, causing the stallion to first rear back and then take off at a gallop across the fields. He sailed effortlessly over the stone fence and started down the highway toward the city.

David reined him in, aware that he had acted childishly.

Thirty minutes later, he was between the twin rows of ancient elms at Elm View. No one came out from the house when he rode up to it. He wondered whether it was because no one had seen him or because he wasn't dressed as someone calling at the front door of the Law house would be dressed.

He slid off Wanderer's back and waited for a moment, and twice called, "Hey!"

When there was no response, he walked up the shallow flight of stairs, leading Wanderer behind him. Wanderer was trained not to wander far when his reins were let loose. But his training wouldn't have kept him from grazing in Elm View's flower beds. For reasons David didn't pretend to understand, Wanderer regarded Dutch tulip beds and roses somewhat more highly than he regarded grass.

David twice lifted the heavy brass knocker and let it slam back.

A full minute later the right of the double doors was pulled inward, and he found himself facing the butler he remembered. The butler, to judge by the puzzled look on his face, did not remember him.

"Yes?" he said.

Not "Yes, sir?" Well, what did you expect, the way you're dressed? "See to my horse," David said.

"Sir?"

I learned that from John Law, that tone of arrogance, when dealing with servants. It obviously works: now he calls me, "Sir."

"Mr. David Gardiner to see Captain Law," David said.

"Sir?"

"Are you deaf, man?" David snapped.

"I don't believe the master is yet up and about, sir, but if you would care to step inside a moment, I will inquire," the butler said.

He called a name over his shoulder and a footman appeared. When the butler nodded, he went to David and took Wanderer's reins from him. The butler bowed David into the entrance foyer.

"If you'll be good enough to wait, sir," he said, and then went quickly up the wide staircase.

It took Captain William Law about five minutes to waken, to get out of his nightshirt into trousers, a shirt, shoes, and a dressing gown, and to comb his hair and begin to descend the stairs. By that time, David Gardiner was beginning to grow impatient. He stalked back and forth on the marble floor of the patio, and when he heard footsteps on the stairwell, his hands were on his hips and his impatience showed on his face.

William Law thought, My God, he's the duke as the duke must have looked at twenty. The hands on the hips, the head cocked to one side in anger. The flashing eyes. "You caught me in my bed, Mr. Gardiner," he said. I called this boy "mister." Not by courteous intention. It was the natural thing to do.

"I thought it best to come here, rather than to your brewery," David said.

Not a word of apology. Not even a hint of it on his face or in his voice. And he's treating me as an equal. If that. "Come into my library, Mr. Gardiner, I'll have someone get us some tea."

David nodded and followed Captain Law into the library. The butler appeared in a moment, and Law ordered tea right away; then he ordered the butler to set the breakfast table.

"I understand you've been ill," Captain Law said to David. "I'm glad to see that you are recovered."

"I was under the impression until a few days ago that John was in France," David said, not acknowledging what Captain Law had said with so much as a nod. "He is, in fact, in the hold of the prison hulk *Valorous*."

"I have been apprised of the situation," Captain Law said.

"Then will you be good enough to tell me what you have done to get him off the prison hulk?" David demanded.

"There's not much I can do about that, I'm sorry to say," Captain Law said.

The response angered and surprised David. He waited for an explanation, but none was forthcoming. "If there is some question in your mind . . ." David began and then stopped. "Thom Frazier told me he is charged with highway robbery and assault. I am here to tell you that John is guilty of nothing more than bedding a whore who happens to be an aristocrat, and that there is no truth whatever to the charges leveled against him. *I* put the pistol ball in the viscount."

"So I have been informed," Captain Law said. "I am indebted to you for John's life."

"If I had been thinking," David said, "I would have ridden the bastard down, and we wouldn't have had all this trouble."

"As I understand the story, Mr. Gardiner, John's troubles are of his own making. He had no right to involve you."

"He is my friend," David snapped, as if that explained everything.

"Then John is indeed fortunate," Captain Law said. "I think you're the first friend he's ever had."

"As I understand it, Captain Law . . ."

He's just like the duke. If he doesn't like what is said to him, he is able to dismiss it as if it hadn't been said at all.

". . . you have a friend to whom I suggest you should turn."

"I beg your pardon?"

"Or do you intend to let John be hung?"

"He won't be hung," Captain Law replied. "You're talking about the Duke of Lauderdale, aren't you?"

"I understand you and the old bastard are old friends," David said.

"I understand that his Grace has been a rather good friend to you, too," Captain Law said.

"I am forced to choose between believing the duke is interested in justice, or that he felt sorry for my father," David said. "The question in my mind, Captain Law, is what kind of a father are you? If my father was willing to beg the old bastard for my life, why won't you do the same thing for John?"

He doesn't know. He doesn't have any idea, Captain Law thought.

"I have been to the duke. Not on my knees, but the next thing to it."

"Then go all the way," David said. "I'm sick to death of the way the aristocracy, and those who ape their manners, will cut off their own balls before they'll lose their *dignity* and *honor*."

"David," Captain William Law said gently, "I would gladly exchange whatever dignity and honor I may have to get John home. It's just not that simple."

He felt the eyes on him, the eyes of Lauderdale, looking out of this boy's face, and felt the chill he had felt so many times before when the duke had been making up his mind. And then the eyes softened and were those of a boy again.

"If I had gone on my knees, David, it would have made things worse," Captain Law said. He was aware that the butler had rolled a cart to the door of the library. He motioned him in.

"I'm not hungry," David said petulantly.

"Whether or not you eat here won't change John's situation a bit," William Law said. "Don't be a fool."

"What did Lauderdale tell you?" David asked, again ignoring what Law had said as if the words had never been spoken.

"That if it was up to him, he'd start with a flogging," Captain Law said, chuckling and wondering why he did. "And that he'll do what he can to keep him from the noose."

"He said that, that he'd keep him from the noose?"

Captain Law nodded.

"He's apparently not the friend of yours everyone believes he is," David said. "Who does he think he is . . . God? He gets me out of this mess, and it was me who shot the viscount, and he won't help John. And all that John really did was not kill the bastard."

"John fought him?" William Law asked. God forgive me, I'm hoping that he did, that he wasn't a coward.

"Fair and square, and he could have killed him if he wanted to," David said. "The fight was over when the viscount got the pistol."

"Have you calmed down enough to listen to me?" Captain Law asked.

There was a flicker of fire in David's eyes, and then it died. "I owe you an apology," he said. "I'm sorry."

"You owe me nothing," Captain Law said. "The reverse is true. But listen to me. There is nothing that can be done for John right now. We have to let events take their course. Do you understand that?"

After a moment, David nodded. "It's just that *I* shot the bastard," he said softly.

"Have some breakfast, David," Captain Law said.

"I might have a small piece of that ham," David said.

2

"The astonishing thing," David Gardiner announced to his wife, "is that it keeps getting better."

He was on his back, and Sally had just turned to him, throwing her arm and her leg over his body. She didn't reply, but slid her hand up his chest and pulled at one of the hairs around his nipple.

"There's probably a reason for that," she said.

"Practice makes perfect?" he replied.

"No," she said, and gave the hair a painful tug.

"You're not the only one whose hair can be pulled, wench," he said.

"That's not what I meant," she said.

"Oh, you mean because I'm over the being sick? A gift from God, certainly. You're not suggesting it's your cooking that's got me back in shape?"

"I notice that you clean your plate," she said.

"That's the mountain air," he said. "I'd do the same with a plate of beans."

They had been living at the horse farm for nearly a month. David had often thought that, if it were not for John being in the prison hulk waiting trial, he had heaven on earth. He had Sally at his side (and of course in his bed) and he was doing what he liked best to do: tending the animals and dealing with them.

He knew that it wouldn't last, and he was determined to enjoy it while he could. The polite untruth being told was that he was still "recovering from the chill," and that Kate was with them to "help Sally take care of him." The truth was that he was long over the chill and felt better than he ever had in his life. And Sally needed Kate to help her as much as she needed a third leg. The truth there was that Kate was with them to make sure she didn't have second thoughts, again, about marrying Thom.

Their parents believed that the chances of that—or of her doing something crazy, as she had the last time—were far less if she were with them. David was convinced that Kate had come to her senses and knew what a good catch she had in Thom. Thom as a man, much less Thom as Lord Davies of Incomkill. He didn't think she'd run, but he was glad she was here with them. She and Sally got along like sisters, and it was something like old times, when he and Kate had been left alone at the farm, when their parents had gone into Edinburgh.

"God, David, sometimes you're really stupid!" Sally flared at him, and sat up in the bed.

Now what the hell did I say to her? "There's no question of that," he said. "Look who I married."

"Look who you put with child," Sally said, and jumped out of bed.

"Jesus Christ!" David said, sitting up. Sally had opened the shutters and was looking out into the night.

"Is that all you've got to say?" Sally asked softly.

"Are you sure?"

"It's three months now."

"I wondered about that."

"I'll bet you did!"

"Well, what do you think?"

"What do I think about what?"

"About . . . being in that condition?"

"What do you think?"

"What do I think, or what do I think about what you think?" he asked.

"What do you think about it?"

"I wonder if it'll be twins," he said.

"Oh, God, David!" Sally said. "You would bring that up."

"Two boys," he said. "You have two boys, wife."

"We'll have what God gives us," she said. "And considering your relations with the Lord, that'll probably be two girls."

"Well, Jesus Christ," he said as the realization that he was going to be a father really set in.

"Jesus Christ had nothing to do with it," Sally said. "It was all your doing, you wicked man."

"Well," he said, "if you hadn't run around in your skin the way you are now, showing everything off in the moonlight, nothing would have happened."

She slammed the shutter and the room was dark. He sensed her coming toward the bed and put his hand out. She caught it and squeezed it, and then put it on her stomach.

"It doesn't feel like twins," he said.

"You can't feel anything yet, silly."

"Huh!" he snorted.

"David," Sally said, "we just did it!"

"You were the one went and stood in the altogether in the moonlight," he said. "*I* was perfectly willing to go to sleep."

3

David rode into Edinburgh every four or five days, taking the girls with him on about every other trip. Today, he had risen very early, before dawn, and started out in the darkness alone, with three horses in trail behind him. He'd made a good deal for them, and unlike most of the animals he bought, these hadn't required what he thought of as "freshening" before they were ready for sale.

Most often, when he bought animals, he would keep them at the farm for two weeks or a month, fattening them up with feed and good grazing, letting them run in the fields to strengthen their muscles, and getting them in as good a shape as possible before taking them into town to be offered for sale.

These animals had come to him in top shape and there was no sense keeping them at the farm when they could be sold the way they were.

He saw the man sitting across the road, just at the far side of the lane to the house long before he got to him.

A bum, he thought, a beggar. Although the man looked about as tough as they came, David didn't think he posed any danger, although sometimes you couldn't tell.

He was a little disturbed when the man got to his feet as David approached. David seldom gave anything to beggars, at least those who looked capable of work, but refusing them always made him uncomfortable.

He was about to be accosted. The man stepped into the road.

"Could I ask, sir . . ." the beggar began.

"Begone," David snapped.

". . . if you're Mr. David Gardiner, sir?" the beggar finished.

David reined Wanderer in and took a close look at the man. Up close, he appeared even rougher than at a distance.

"I'm David Gardiner," David said.

"I thought you might be, sir," the man said. The man reached into his waist and for an insane moment David thought he was reaching for a knife. But what the man came up with was a sheet of paper, folded in quarters.

"If you'd take care of that for me, sir, I'd be grateful," the man said, and then turned and started walking toward Edinburgh.

Wanderer was nervous and tossed his head, causing the hand in which David held the sheet of paper to jerk. He dropped the paper, and then, the moment it touched the ground, Wanderer's hoof stepped on it.

"Damn," David said. He was tempted to just forget the whole incident. The paper had been torn and ground into the earth and probably couldn't be read anyway.

But curiosity got the best of him, and he slid from Wanderer's back, pushed the animal out of the way, and retrieved the sheet of paper. It was wet and torn. He shook it, and then unfolded it. It was a letter and the salutation was "Dear Father."

The handwriting was familiar, and suddenly David recognized the hand as that of John Law. He turned the sheet of paper over, and there, in one corner, was the address: "Captain William Law, Elm View, Edinburgh."

He turned it over again and started to read it.

"Dear Father, If you receive this letter, it will come to you by the hand of Arthur Carter, whom I have promised ten pounds for the service."

David stopped reading.

The large, ugly, and somehow menacing man who had handed him the sheet of paper was striding determinedly toward Edinburgh.

"Hey, there!" David called.

If anything, being called after made the man walk faster. He did not look back.

David climbed back aboard Wanderer, urging him and the string of horses in trail into a fast walk. He caught up with the man, who looked up at him with mingled fear and defiance on his face.

"Where did you get this?" David demanded.

"John Law give it to me," the man said.

"Where did he give it to you?"

"In London," the man said.

"Where in London?"

"If you've got to know, on the prison hulk *Valorous*," the man said.

"Why didn't you take it to Elm View?"

"I did, and got myself beat by three servants," the man said.

"This says you are to be given ten pounds for delivering it," David said.

"That's what John Law said it said, but it didn't make no mind to them men what works there."

"You showed it to them?"

"I tried to. They didn't seem to care none."

"They probably couldn't read either," David thought aloud. "Well, come with me, I'll get you your ten pounds."

"I figure John Law done enough for me," the man said. "I can do without the money. You'll get the letter to his father."

"How do you know that?"

"John Law told me that if I had trouble, I was to look for you."

"And how did you find me?"

"The hired men said you would be coming in this morning, so I waited."

"Then you haven't eaten?"

The man didn't reply.

"What's your name?" David asked.

"Arthur Carter," the man said after a moment's hesitation.

"Well, climb up on the mare in the back, Arthur," David ordered. "And I'll get you some breakfast and your ten pounds."

"I can't do that," Arthur Carter said uncomfortably.

"Why not?"

"I ain't never been on a horse."

"Well, then," David said, "walk along beside me. It's not that far."

"I don't want no trouble," the man said.

"I'm a friend of John Law's," David said. "Didn't he tell you that?"

"I know all about you," Arthur Carter said matter-of-factly.

"Then you know I'll see that you come to no harm."

Arthur Carter thought that over for a moment and then said, "I'll cut across the field and meet you at your stable."

And with that, he started to trot toward the stone fence, leaped it nimbly, and ran across the field toward the stable.

4

Captain William Law wondered why David Gardiner had gone to the loading dock of the south settling room seeking him, rather than to the main building of the brewery. When he saw the man standing beside David Gardiner, he understood why. They would never have made it inside the front door of the administration building.

"Good morning, David," Captain Law said. "What's all this?"

David handed him the sheet of paper. "I read the first couple of lines before I understood what was going on."

Several heavy muscled handlers, the men who loaded kegs onto wagons, had by now noticed that the very rough man was speaking with the Captain. As much to protect him as from curiosity, they moved and stood behind the brewery owner.

Captain Law read the letter and then handed it to David. Then he turned and saw the handlers behind him.

"Dick," he said to one of them, "would you do me a service?"

"Aye, Captain, you name it," the man said, glowering at Arthur Carter.

"Go to the office and ask my clerk to give you ten pounds . . . make it twenty . . . in gold, please?"

"Aye, sir. Sir, is there any trouble?"

"No trouble at all, thank you, Dick," Law said, smiling reassuringly at him.

David read the letter:

Dear Father,

If you receive this letter, it will come to you by the hand of Arthur Carter, whom I have promised ten pounds for the service. I owe him a great deal for his kindnesses to me in my present circumstances. If I did not know that I have forever forfeited by my actions any further claim on you as your son, I would ask that you give him employment at the brewery. Despite his past trouble with the law, I have learned that he is honest, and believe that, given a chance, he would prove to be a faithful and law-abiding worker.

I was enormously relieved to learn that David Gardiner is no longer being held responsible for any of the problems I have caused. His sole offense was to be a friend when I needed one, and I owe him my life. I should be very grateful for any kindnesses you might be able to do for him and his family in the future.

As to my own future: two alternatives have been offered me. I can stay here and wait for trial. Although I am quite innocent of the charges of highway robbery, et cetera, Whitten has lodged against me, a trial would necessarily bring further shame upon the Law name, and the least I can do is spare you that. It has also been proposed to me that I take the king's commission in the Royal Navy and almost immediately embark on a three-year voyage to the Orient. I am wholly convinced that I would not live through such an undertaking, not only because of my tendency to *mal-de-mer*, so this, too, is out of the question.

There is a third alternative of which I have only recently learned, and that is to permit myself to be impressed into military service when the recruiters make their periodic visits to the prison hulk. It is my understanding that charges are dropped against men being held for trial upon their entering military service, and I have concluded that this is the best, indeed the only, solution. By the time you receive this, I will be a private soldier in the king's service, under another name.

I deeply regret the anguish I have caused you, and hope that in time you will find yourself able to forgive me.

John.

"My God!" David said, handing the letter back to Captain Law.

"If he thinks he wouldn't live through three years as a naval officer," Captain Law said, as much to himself as in reply, "what does he think will happen to himself in ten years in the ranks as a soldier?"

"Is that what he says?" Arthur Carter asked. "That he's going to get himself impressed into the army?"

Law nodded.

"You haven't read this?" he asked.

"No, sir," Carter said. "I can't read."

"Has he discussed this with you?" Captain Law asked.

"I told him he was a damned fool," Carter said. "I told him that."

"How often do the recruiters come to the prison hulk?" Captain Law asked.

"Every couple of months," Carter replied. "They was there just before they turned me loose. That was what give him the idea, I expect."

"Well," Captain Law said, "we've got to talk him out of

371

this insane notion." He paused. "Goddamn him," he added in exasperation.

"Ten years!" David said.

"He wouldn't last ten months, much less ten years," Captain Law said.

"I don't think a letter would do much good," David said.

He's reading my mind. "Obviously, I'll have to go to London," Captain Law said.

"He wouldn't want you to do that," David said.

"I should have gone when this first happened," Captain Law said.

"I'll go," David said. "If I hadn't shot the goddamned viscount, he wouldn't be where he is."

"I can't ask you to do that, David," Captain Law protested.

"You didn't," David replied simply.

"I would forever be in your debt," Captain Law said.

David held up his hand deprecatingly.

"At least, let me give you money," Captain Law said.

"Yes," David replied almost immediately—so quickly that Law was surprised.

"The only place I could get any money would be from my father," David said. "And I don't want him to hear about this until I'm gone."

Captain William Law was more than ashamed of himself for the effort it took him to ask his next question. It had to be asked, even if it would mean that David Gardiner would change his mind about going to London.

"You're not a single man any longer, David," Captain Law said. "What is your wife going to say about this?"

"I don't know," David confessed.

"You'd better think that through."

"My father, Captain Law, offered me a bit of advice when he was at the whiskey. He said that when a man knows that a wife is going to say no to a question about something he knows he has to do, he shouldn't ask the question." David paused. "At the time I didn't understand what he was talking about."

"And you do now?"

372

"She's with child," David said. "I know what she'd have to say if I asked her about this."

"You don't have to go, David," Captain Law said.

"Yes, I do."

God forgive me. I'm glad he's the duke's bastard. If he was Edward Gardiner's blood son, he would have done the practical, logical thing: he would not have gone.

There was a tug at Captain Law's sleeve. Dick, the barrel handler he had sent to get money for Arthur Carter, was standing beside him, ready to drop the money into his hands.

"Thank you very much, Dick," Captain Law said, and smiled at him. Then, looking at David, "But I'm afraid I underestimated how much I'll need. Why don't you take these fellows into the settling room and give them a taste, while I go get the rest?"

5

Arthur Carter had heard somewhere, from a sailor, who he reasoned should know what he was talking about, that so long as you were able to stay a little drunk, you didn't get the seasickness.

He related this story to David Gardiner as they were being rowed out to the coaster *Princess Mary*. The *Princess Mary*, bound for London and Amsterdam, had been halted by signal flags hoisted by the master of the port as a service to Captain William as she had been about to clear the breakwater.

David Gardiner, whose nautical experience was about as deep as Arthur Carter's, and whose stomach was already feeling very strange, was overjoyed to learn there was a solution to the problem. He had heard of the horrors of seasickness from John Law, and the only question in his mind when Carter told him about staying drunk was why John Law hadn't heard about it.

A ladder was put over the side of the *Princess Mary* when the small boat was rowed alongside, and David and Carter, terrified, made their way up it. At the top of the ladder, sailors hauled them over the rail and onto the pitching deck, where they found themselves facing an angry captain.

"What the hell is all this about?" the captain demanded.

David gave him the letter Captain Law had hastily obtained from the *Princess Mary*'s owner. It directed the captain to render all courtesies to the bearers, who were on important business for "my close friend, Captain William Law."

"Delighted to have you aboard, gentlemen," the captain said with an effort. He turned his head slightly from them and bellowed, "Get her underway, Mr. Lord!" And then he lowered his voice, "I'll have to arrange a cabin for you. Is there anything I can do for you in the meantime?"

"I wonder if you have any whiskey?" David asked.

"Whiskey?" the captain asked.

"I have been told that it quiets the stomach," David explained.

"Oh, you've heard that, have you?" the captain said. He seemed pleased. "Just as soon as I can get you settled in your cabin, I would be delighted to send you a jug."

"That's very kind of you, Captain," David said, smiling at Carter.

"My pleasure, I assure you," the captain said. "And now, if you'll excuse me . . ."

The captain was as good as his word. As soon as they had been taken to a cabin hastily evacuated by two passengers who were not on important business for a good friend of *Princess Mary*'s owner, a steward delivered two gray pottery gallon jugs of whiskey.

"The captain said to tell you, when you need more, just ask," the steward said.

David Gardiner and Arthur Carter each reached for a jug and tipped it to their mouths.

They'd gotten it just in time, David thought. The way the ship was bobbing in all directions at once, it was clear that without the whiskey, he was about to succumb to the seasickness.

The nostrum worked, for about fifteen minutes. David grew sick first, throwing up before he could get the chamber pot from beneath the bunk. When he saw David throw up, the nausea was contagious for Arthur Carter.

They were sick, continuously, for the next four days. David became convinced beyond any doubt that he was going to die and leave his unborn child, or children, fatherless.

Very early on the morning of his fifth day at sea, when he woke from another fitful hour's dozing, the incredibly foul stench in the cabin was so bad that he decided that at least he was going to die in the fresh air. He rolled out of the bunk and crawled across the deck, which was moving in odd directions under him, and down the passageway and onto the deck.

He would, he thought, find some quiet corner and there expire.

He was astonished that his stomach didn't heave. It had been heaving at no more than one-hour intervals since he'd come aboard the *Princess Mary*, although there had been nothing in his stomach after the first time. It was probably the cold, he decided, and the chilling effect of the spray that came over the deck.

He lay there fifteen minutes and had just begun to consider what he was going to do about the chill that had him shivering when two large sailors suddenly appeared at his side, lifted him to his feet, and half-carried, half-pushed him onto the quarterdeck.

"Sit him up over there," the captain ordered, indicating a place where there was a sort of bench behind the wheel, "and go get the other one."

David, shivering, hung on to the seat of the bench with both hands as the *Princess Mary* dipped her bow into enormous seas, and then, shuddering, recovered. Despite everything, there was something fascinating about all that water, towering one moment far above them and then sinking from sight, only to reappear a moment later.

A sailor appeared and wrapped a heavy blanket around his shoulders. David nodded his thanks. A minute or so later, Arthur Carter was brought up. It took three large sailors to get him in place beside David on the bench. He was, David saw, not surprised, as white as a ghost.

Two young boys appeared, holding steaming mugs in their hands. David hated them. They were as surefooted on the tilting deck as Highlands goats, and they were smiling at him tolerantly.

"Drink this," one of them said, holding the mug to David's lips.

"No, thank you," David said, violently shaking his head.

"Drink it, goddamn it," the captain ordered. "Or you will die. Right now you only think you will."

David was too tired to resist. He moved his head close enough to the cup to get a mouthful of its contents. It was so hot that it painfully burned his lips. And he had no idea what it was. It tasted salty.

"That's clam juice," the captain said, not unkindly.

The very thought of a clam made David's stomach wrench.

"After you hold a bit of that down—it'll give you strength, you'll be surprised—we'll try a cracker or two."

A half-hour later David felt light-headed, but his stomach had not tried to turn itself inside out again and the dry crackers he was nibbling tasted incredibly good.

The captain stood over him. "If you get your strength back, you can really kill him," the captain said, chuckling.

"Kill who?" David asked.

"The man who told you that whiskey works against seasickness. It's probably the worst thing you could have done."

"Why the hell didn't you tell us?" David snapped.

"You didn't ask," the captain said.

Thirty minutes, two mugs more of clam juice, and a dozen crackers later, David looked over at Arthur Carter.

"Feeling a little better, are you, sir?" Arthur Carter asked.

"You, too?" David asked.

Carter nodded. "I'd like to get my hands on the bastard what told me that about the whiskey," he said. "I'm true sorry about that."

"I'd like to get my hands on John Law," David said icily. "I think right now I'd kill the bastard."

"You know, when they offered him the chance to get

off the hulk by joining the Navy, I couldn't see why he didn't jump at it," Carter said.

"I do now," David said.

By nightfall, the two of them were able to make it to the dinner table in the wardroom. They were even able to eat a bowl of the soup they were offered, but neither of them was able to take more than a bite of the boiled salt pork and beans that were offered next.

And the captain took further pity on them.

"I was just in your cabin," he said, "and smelled the mess you made in there."

David, who did consider the mess made his personal responsibility and did not wish even to be reminded of it, glowered at the captain.

"I'll have it cleaned," the captain said. "But I can't open the port in these seas. If you two want to sleep on the deck here tonight, that'd be all right. With a little luck, it'll calm down enough before we make London for me to have the cabin aired out proper."

It was that night, on the floor of the wardroom, that the subject of getting John Law off the prison hulk *Valorous*, rather than just visiting him there and talking him out of going into the Army came up.

"I'm different from you and John Law," Carter opened the subject.

"Oh, I don't think we're much different," David said.

"If I had as much money as Captain Law gave you, I'd do different," Carter said.

David didn't reply.

"How much did he give you?"

"All there was in the strongbox," David said. "A little over two hundred pounds."

He did not volunteer the additional information that he carried a letter in his pocket from an officer of the Bank of Edinburgh to the Bank of London, authorizing them to give him what funds, to a thousand pounds sterling, he asked for.

"With the twenty he gave me," Carter said, "there'd be more than enough to take care of the guards."

"More than enough to do what?"

"To take care of the guards," Carter explained.

"You mean to help him escape?"

Carter nodded. "It can be done. What goes on the records is 'Killed attempting to escape, body lost in river.' "

"But then what would happen to him?"

"What he should have done in the first place, he goes to France."

"Oh, I don't know," David said. "I think that we'd best just tell him to stay where he is until we can get him out."

"He means it about the Army," Arthur said. "He don't know what he's doing, so he'll do it. That's what I mean about you and me being different. I'd rather be a fugitive in France with money in my pocket than a private soldier in the King's Own Whatever."

"All I have is the two hundred pounds," David said, not only replying to Arthur Carter, but also thinking aloud about what Captain Law would say if he returned and told him that he'd cashed the letter of credit and given the thousand pounds to John.

"Ah, the captain would give him all the money he needs," Carter said. "You saw his face."

"Yes," David said, "I did."

The thing to do, obviously, was go see John and then make what other decisions had to be made.

"I wonder what the penalty is for helping a prisoner to escape?" he asked.

"Hanging," Arthur Carter said matter-of-factly. "Hell, hanging's the penalty for practically anything."

Chapter Seventeen

1

If the Lord High Sheriff had not at that precise time of day elected to leave Holyroodhouse Palace by a side gate, on a personal errand, on horseback, accompanied by only three members of the Horse Guards, rather than his usual practice of entering and leaving the palace in his carriage, accompanied by a full section of the Horse Guard, under the command of an officer, Kate Gardiner would have never gotten inside the palace, much less seen the Lord High Commissioner.

The Lord High Sheriff of course recognized her immediately. She was standing with her hands on her hips, defiantly demanding of the officer of the guard that he send word to the duke that she was here. She had cowed the guard and the sergeant of the guard to the point where they had not felt secure in dealing with her as they would deal with any crazy female: that is, with the point of a pike. Before or after, they "interviewed" a good-looking young one, like this one, in the guard barracks.

The Lord High Sheriff rode to where Kate Gardiner stood facing the officer of the guard.

"What's this?" he demanded.

"A crazy girl, sir," the officer of the guard said, more than a little embarrassed. "I'll have her gone in a moment."

"I know her," the Lord High Sheriff said. "What is this, Miss Gardiner?"

"You know me, milord?" Kate asked, surprised.

"What do you want here?"

"I want to see the duke," she said.

"About what?"

"About my brother, milord,"

"The duke will not see you."

"He will not see me if he does not know I'm here, milord," Kate said.

"It is not fitting that you come here," the Lord High Sheriff said.

"Is that for you to decide, milord?" Kate challenged.

"If you were my daughter," the Lord High Sheriff flared, "I'd have you whipped."

"But I am not your daughter, am I, milord?" Kate challenged.

The Lord High Sheriff met her eyes for a moment, then turned to the officer of the guard.

"Present yourself to his grace with my compliments," he said. "Inform his Grace that the daughter of Gardiner the horse trader is here, demanding an immediate audience, and that I await his command in the matter."

"*Demanding* an audience, milord?"

"Is there something wrong with your hearing?"

Visibly surprised, the officer of the guard nodded, said, "Immediately, milord," and walked quickly across the courtyard to one of the rear doors.

He came back at a run.

"Milord," he said, "his Grace commands your presence and that of the girl."

"I hope," the Lord High Sheriff said as he got off his horse, "that you know what you are doing."

Kate didn't reply.

The Duke of Lauderdale raised his eyes from his magnifying glass and glowered at both of them. "What in Christ's name is this?"

"She was trying to enter the palace as I was leaving, milord," the Lord High Sheriff said.

"Just who do you think you are?" the duke snapped.

Kate audibly sucked in her breath but did not reply.

"Leave us," the duke ordered. The Lord High Sheriff left them. "Well?" the duke demanded when they were alone.

"My brother's wife is with child," Kate said.

"What has that to do with me?"

"And he has gone to London," Kate said.

"I asked you a question," he said.

"To which you well know the answer," Kate said.

"You push me too hard," the duke said menacingly. "Why has he gone to London?"

"Captain Law would not tell my father. But it has something to do with John Law, obviously."

"And your mother sent you here?"

"My mother does not know I'm here," Kate said.

"Your mother knows her place," the duke said. "I would that you did."

"My mother is her father's daughter," Kate said. "As I am *my* father's."

"That gives you no privilege," he snapped.

"I ask none from you. It is my brother's life with which I am concerned."

"You have no cause for concern," he said. "I am aware that your brother has gone to London. Captain Law was here yesterday on his behalf."

She raised her eyebrows in question.

"I'll be damned if I know why I am bothering to explain things to you," he said.

"Why was Captain Law here?"

"Because he received a letter from his idiot son informing him he was about to enter the ranks," the duke said. "Which means for ten years. Which is a bit much, I agreed, to pay for taking some other man's wife to bed. Your idiot brother believes that he is responsible for young Law being in trouble in the first place. So he has gone to London, risking his fool neck, to talk young Law out of letting himself be impressed into service." The duke paused and looked at her. "Do you follow all this?"

"Yes, I follow it."

"So I told Law, as I am telling you, that I will interfere one last time for whatever reason."

"That I don't follow," Kate said.

"I dispatched a team of couriers to London. They will be there before your brother's ship arrives," the duke said.

"I still don't quite understand—"

"By the time David gets to London, John Law will have been impressed into the Royal Grenadiers," the duke said. "David can turn right around and come home."

"For ten years?" Kate asked, horrified.

"So he will believe," the duke said smugly. "If he behaves himself, in six months in the ranks, he'll be allowed to purchase a commission. His father and I are agreed that six months in the ranks is just what that pup needs."

"Yes," Kate said thoughtfully.

"Oh," the duke said sarcastically, "I'm enormously flattered that you approve."

Kate smiled at him.

"Your coming here was very stupid," the duke said. "I hope you realize that."

"You received me," she said. "You didn't have to."

He looked at her, and as was his custom, ignored what he didn't want to hear as if it had not been said.

"But since you are here," he said, "perhaps you would take lunch with me."

"I would be honored, your Grace."

He looked at her shamelessly now, from top to bottom. "You must have that red hair from your mother," he said. "There's none that I know in my family."

Kate Gardiner, the horse trader's daughter, leaned forward and kissed John Maitland, Duke of Lauderdale, Lord High Commissioner from Scotland, on his bristly bloodshot cheek.

2

"Well, he's gone and done it, the goddamned fool," Arthur Carter told David Gardiner when he returned from his "look-around" at the prison hulk *Valorous.*

"Damn!" David said. "Did you find out what regiment?"

"The Grenadiers," Carter said.

"Where are they? Can we get him away from them?"

"If we're lucky, we may not have to," Carter said. "He's still on the *Valorous.* They're going to come fetch him, and the others, day after tomorrow."

"Is it desertion, do you think, if we could get him away before he actually joined the Grenadiers?" David asked.

"You mean, would the Grenadiers come after John Law to hang him for desertion?"

"Yes," David said, "I guess that's what I was asking."

"I don't know about that," Carter said. "But if he gets to the regiment, he would desert. The ranks of the Grenadiers are no place for a gentleman like him."

"Why are you so sure?"

"The Grenadiers are still looking for a deserter named Carson," Carter said. "Ernest Carson. I understand he looked something like me."

"Then you think we should get him . . . *try* to get him?"

"For him, it's the best thing," Carter said. "For you and me, I don't know. Helping prisoners escape is a hanging offense."

"Hell," David said after a moment, quoting what Carter had said to him on the *Princess Mary,* "hanging's the penalty for damned near anything."

3

The metal grating over the hold of the *Valorous* creaked open shortly after dawn. A warder stood at the top of the ladder and called out the names of those who had accepted impressment into the Royal Regiment of Grenadiers in lieu of a trial.

Those accepting impressment were given to understand that on successful completion of their military service, they would be returned to civilian life with a certificate of discharge giving their name. It was suggested that any possible trouble with law-enforcement officials in the future could be positively avoided if the name on that certificate was not the name under which they had been arrested.

They were then asked to give their names.

One of the names the warder called out was Whitten.

John Whitten got to his feet and walked toward the ladder, steeling himself for what he knew would be the first humiliation he would experience on the first day of his military service. He would be deloused, as he had been deloused on his visits to the judge.

He climbed the ladder and found himself being examined, and obviously found wanting, by a corporal of Grenadiers. The corporal, literally sniffing in disapproval, examined him for a moment and then pointed to the bulkhead rising from the deck at the forecastle.

John was familiar with the procedure. He walked to the bulkhead and began to take off his clothing.

"Wait till yer told!" a warder said to him, enforcing the admonition with a jab of his club.

John Law stopped undressing and stood to attention.

"Eyes front!" the warder snapped when he saw John looking over the side of the *Valorous* to the dock, where a barred wagon and a detachment of troops stood waiting for the volunteers.

John moved his eyes to the center of his head and looked back down the deck as the other volunteers made their way up the ladder from the hold and then to the bulkhead.

And then he felt a rough hand clap around his mouth. He lost his balance and felt himself being dragged backward into the darkness.

"Sssssh!" a foul breath hissed in his ear. "Nothing to worry about. You're about to be shot trying to escape."

I am losing my mind.

He was set on his feet, and a strong hand grabbed his upper arm and pushed him down a corridor and down a flight of stairs, and then down a second corridor. A door creaked open and he was pushed into a small cabin.

He turned around in time to see the door slam, and then he heard a bolt being slammed into place. He looked around the little room and saw an opening, barely large enough for a man to pass through, at the level of the deck. A rope, tied to one of the ship's timbers, passed through the hole and down.

He went and looked down the hole.

There was a boat there and two faces he had never expected to see again. Arthur Carter's and David Gardiner's. Both gestured frantically for him to descend the rope.

He slid down it so quickly that he burned his hands and nearly swamped the boat when his weight hit it. Arthur Carter grabbed his shoulders, knocked him to his knees, and then put his foot to John's back, flattening him in the bottom of the boat. Immediately a pile of netting dropped over him.

He felt the boat being pushed away from the ship and heard the noises as the oars were put into their locks; then he felt the surging movement as David and Arthur put their backs to the oars and the boat began to move through the water of the Thames.

A minute or two later, as he had begun to consider the ramifications of this escape, for himself and for David and Arthur as well, there came the sound of musket fire.

He tried to get up. A heavy foot and then another pushed him into the cold water slopping around the bottom of the boat.

"What the hell is that shooting?" John asked.

"That's them killing you as you tried to escape," David's voice said, and for some insane reason he and Arthur thought this was funny. Both of them laughed.

Fifteen minutes later, John felt the pile of netting being pulled off him. He sat up, shivering from the cold water in the bilge. They were under a pier, surrounded by pilings. A ladder nailed to one of the pilings led to a trapdoor. David was already halfway up it. Arthur, holding the boat steady, motioned for John to climb.

4

"Captain Seale, Willy," the Duke of Lauderdale said, "is one of the officers I sent to London."

"How do you do, sir?" Captain Seale said politely.

Captain Law had been summoned to Holyroodhouse Palace by another officer of the Horse Guards half an hour after Captain Seale had made his first report of his trip to the Lord High Sheriff. The Lord High Sheriff had decided that it was sufficiently important to wake his Grace the Lord High Commissioner.

"Tell Captain Law precisely what you told me," the duke commanded. "Leave nothing out."

"Yes, your Grace," Captain Seale said, and bowed to Lauderdale before reporting what he knew.

"You must understand, sir, that I was not present personally. What I have to report is what I learned from officers of the Grenadiers and from a visit to the *Valorous*."

Captain Law felt sick to his stomach.

"It was the decision of the board of inquiry, sir, that the prisoner in whom we were interested was killed by musket fire in the act of attempting to escape and that the body was washed downriver; recovery is unlikely."

"And what of the men who assisted in the attempted escape?" Captain Law asked, keeping his voice under control only with a massive effort.

"According to the officers of the *Valorous*, sir, several of those involved in the escape attempt were also known to have been struck by the musket fire of the guards and presumed to be killed," Seale said.

"I see," Captain Law said levelly. "Thank you very much, Captain Seale."

"That's all, Seale," the duke said. "Do I have to tell you I don't want a word of this spread about? Not a god-damned word?"

"I completely understand, your Grace," Captain Seale said. He bowed and backed out of the room.

Captain William Law looked at the Duke of Lauderdale. Their eyes held for a moment.

"I had best go see Mr. Gardiner," Captain Law said after a moment.

"Yes," the duke said.

"I'm terribly sorry about David," Captain Law said.

"David died," the duke said, "doing what he thought was right. A lot of men have no idea why they're being killed."

"That's not much, is it?"

"It's all we have," the duke said. "If the opportunity presents itself, Willy, would you privately . . . if you can think of anything to comfort Mrs. Gardiner, would you do it for me?"

"Of course," Law said.

"Goddamn the both of them!" the duke said bitterly.

5

It was three in the morning when they got to the farmhouse.

They were dirty and tired. It had taken them seventeen days to ride from London, for they had avoided the main highway in the belief that if anything had gone wrong, it would be best if no king's constable or member of the watch remembered three men traveling together.

They had left Arthur Carter on the outskirts of Edinburgh, telling him to find a place to stay and to leave word where it was at the office of Edward Gardiner & Son, Purveyors of Fine Horses.

There had been lights on in the Gardiner house in Edinburgh, but they had not gone in. They had been delighted to see that Kate and Sally were not at the house. That meant they were at the farm, and the farm would be a good place for John to hide until it was decided what he was going to do.

"Well, we made it," David said as he slid off the horse he had ridden from London.

A dog, growling deep in his throat, shot out of the darkness and was almost on David when he suddenly recognized the smell of him and began to whimper with pleasure.

The animal, however, was not similarly pleased to see

John Law. No sooner had he swung half out of the saddle and put a foot on the ground than the dog, a very hairy shepherd, rushed from David's side and fastened his teeth in Law's leather boot over his heel.

John kicked himself free of the ferocious animal and regained his seat, but the dog continued the attack for a couple of minutes, while David, who found the whole thing very amusing, tried to catch him and wrestle him to the ground.

David finally caught the animal, picked him up by his hair, and carried him toward the house.

The door flew open and David could see the women, Kate with a shotgun at her shoulder, in the light from the fireplace.

"Don't shoot," he called cheerfully. "We're very friendly people."

Sally screamed.

"For God's sake it's me!" David called.

"Oh, sweet God, it is!" Kate said. "Sally, it's him!"

Sally rushed out of the house, knocked the dog, who was apparently afraid of her, out of David's hands, and threw herself at him, sobbing, nearly hysterical.

It was pleasant, he thought, but unnerving. Is she always going to react like this after I've been away a month?

"You're supposed to be dead, damn you," Kate said. "Who's that with you?"

"Oh," David said as if he suddenly understood everything. "How did you find out?"

"It's me," John Law said, sliding off his horse. "I'm the one who's officially dead."

"Oh, my God," Kate said, "it *is* you!"

What a strange voice she has, John thought. Deep, as if she's singing, or something. It gets right to your bones.

And then Kate ran into his arms and put her arms around him. "You bastard!" she said. "You're supposed to be dead."

"I am," he said. "Dead as a doornail. Don't forget that."

And then they were kissing, not passionately as he would have expected—their lips grinding together, their teeth bumping—but rather oddly. She was kissing his neck and he was kissing the top of her head.

The dog jumped up on them, growling.

"Goddamn that animal!" John said.

"You are really a son of bitch," Kate said to John. "How could you do that to your father?"

"You mean my father knows?" John replied, surprised.

"Your father came and told my father," Kate said, "that you were both dead."

"Oh, hell," John said. "Well, I expect we'd better straighten that out right off."

"And you thought I was dead?" David said to Sally.

That set her off crying again.

"Yes, she did," Kate said.

"But why me?" David asked. "And how did you hear so quickly, anyway?"

"Captain Seale told Captain Law," Kate said.

"Who the hell is Captain Seale?" John demanded.

"He's the man who was sent to see you into the Grenadiers," Kate said.

"I don't understand any of this," David said. "And right now I don't give a damn. What I want right now is a stiff drink of whiskey and something to eat and then I want to go to bed."

6

The various stories all came out over supper, of course.

"Well, you did it to me again, goddamn you," David said to John. "You made me get you into deeper trouble than you were already in."

"Well, I, for one, have had enough of the whole affair," John said. "In the morning, I will ride back into Edinburgh and present myself to my father, and if he wants me to go into the ranks of the goddamned Grenadiers, I'll go."

"I don't even want to hear about it," David said. He got up abruptly from the table and walked into one of the bedrooms. Sally followed him.

In a moment, her hair undone, she came back out.

"David wants a drink to help him sleep," she said, and poured a mugful from the jug.

"Somehow," John said when she had gone back in the bedroom and closed the door behind her, "I don't think David is going to have any trouble sleeping at all, tonight."

"Sometimes I really hate you," Kate said.

"But not always," he said.

"Especially when you remind me of things I'd rather forget," she said.

"Like my welcome tonight?" he asked.

"Goddamn you, John," Kate said, and went into the other bedroom and slammed the door.

She came out a minute or two later, with blankets in her arms.

"You'll have to make do on the floor," she said. "At least it's by the fire."

"The height of comfort compared to what I've had lately," he said.

He took the blankets from her and she went into her bedroom. He laid the blankets on the floor, sat down on them, and started to pull his boots off.

She surprised him by coming out again with another blanket. "You'll need this more than I," she said. "That floor is cold."

He reached up and caught her hand. "There is another alternative," he said.

There was something in her eyes that made him drop her hand quickly.

"Just a jest," he said.

"That's the trouble," she said.

She went into the bedroom. She didn't close the door completely. He thought this was to take advantage of the heat from the fire. She could leave the door open safely now that she had made it quite plain to him that she didn't want him.

He lay down and turned his face from Kate's door.

"John," Kate's clear voice called softly, a moment later.

"What?" he called back.

There was no reply.

He lay there a moment, wondering what she wanted, afraid to think it was an invitation. It couldn't be. She wasn't that type, and David had told him that she was now willing to go through with her marriage to Frazier, now Lord Davies.

He forced the mental image of Kate in her marriage bed with Davies, whatever he looked like, from his mind.

And then Kate was on her knees beside him.

He sensed her and then heard her breathing, and after a moment he rolled over and looked up at her.

"What the hell are you doing?"

"Ssssh," she said, and then she crawled under the blanket with him.

"Are you mad?"

"Probably," she said. "I'll marry Thom, and I'll be a faithful wife to him and do the right thing."

"Then what are you doing here?"

"Don't you want me?"

"That's got nothing to do with it," he said.

"It wasn't very good for us the first time," she said. "For you, I mean. But it was my first time and I didn't know."

"What the hell are you talking about?"

"Before I marry him, before I do what's expected of me, I want to do it with you again. Because I want to. Not because I have to."

"You get back in your room," he ordered.

"Because you don't want me?" she asked.

"That's right."

She moved her hand under the blanket. "Liar!" she cried triumphantly.

"What did you expect?" he said.

"I didn't expect you'd be a hypocrite with me, John," she said. Then she let go of him and started to slide out from under the blanket.

He reached out for her, found her hand, caught it. Their fingers locked for a moment and then he pulled her to him.

"Now that that's decided," Kate whispered in his ear, "don't you think it would be nicer in the bed?"

7

John Law rode down the graveled road between the twin rows of Elm View. There was a carriage parked in front of the house, and then he saw that there was a guard of six or eight helmeted soldiers taking the shade by the road. That could mean only one thing: the prodigal had timed his return home with consummate finesse, to coincide with a rare visit of the man who had spared his life.

Well, to hell with that. I will sneak into the house from the side, and not let my father know I'm alive until after the Duke of Lauderdale has gotten back in his carriage and gone away. That problem can be dealt with later.

But a footman saw him, and when he approached the house, ran out to take the horse, confusion all over his face.

"Master John," he said, "there was talk you were dead."

"Obviously not," John said as he slid off the horse. "Loosen the cinch, but don't unsaddle him. I may not be staying."

"Yes, sir," the footman said. "Your father and his Grace are in the drawing room, Master John."

"I'll be in my room," John said. "When the duke has gone, will you fetch me?"

"Yes, sir."

The footman was in error. When John went into the library, planning to make it to the second floor, to his room, via one of the library ladders, as he had done as a child, he backed through the curtains into John Maitland, Duke of Lauderdale and Lord High Commissioner for Scotland, who was standing with his back to the curtain.

"Oh, my God! John!" John's father exclaimed.

"Good Christ!" his Grace exploded. "You son of a bitch, you're supposed to be dead!"

John bowed. "I am terribly sorry to disappoint you, your Grace," he said.

The duke slapped him, a violent blow, with his glass

held in his hand. John fell to the floor. The duke glowered at him.

"And David?" the duke said.

"David is well, your Grace," John said, afraid to get up. "I just left him."

"Goddamn Seale to hell!" the duke said.

"I had hoped not to interrupt you and his Grace, Father," John said.

"Just sneak in the house, is that it?" his father said angrily. "As if nothing had happened."

"I had planned to ask you what you wanted me to do about his Grace, Father," John said.

"What do you mean, 'do about me'?" the duke said. "Get off the floor!"

"I know what you tried to do for me, your Grace," John said, getting off the floor, putting his hand to his face, and then looking at the blood on his fingers. "It was my intention to present myself to you once I let my father know I was alive."

The duke glowered at him.

"I know what you tried to arrange for me with the Grenadiers, your Grace," John said.

"What are you talking about? Who told you that?"

"Kate, sir."

"Then goddamn her, too!" the duke said.

"I intend to marry the lady, your Grace," John said.

The duke's face turned blotchy with rage. "Sir?" he demanded.

"I intend to marry the lady, your Grace," John repeated.

"She's to marry Icomkill," the duke said. "Has it occurred to you that if one word of you being near her, much less proposing marriage to her, reaches Davies, he'll come after you with his sword?"

"Then I should be obliged to kill him, your Grace," John said.

"You're insane, that's all there is to it, you're insane," William said.

"You'd fight Icomkill for this woman, would you?" the duke said, raising his hand to quiet Captain Law.

"I would, your Grace."

"You have a reputation for running from a fight, you know."

"If I had killed the marquess, I would have hung. I am not a fool."

"Then why didn't you fight the viscount?"

"I did," John said, and it was evident that he was telling the truth. "And if I knew then what I have learned since, I would have run the bastard through."

"I believe him," the duke said to Captain Law. "I found it hard to believe that your son could be a coward."

"He's a fool, I'll grant," Captain Law said. "But he's not a coward. David told me about the fight with Whitten."

"You fancy yourself in love with the Gardiner wench, is that it?" the duke asked.

"Yes, sir, I do."

"And if your father disapproves, how would you support her?"

"I'll support her," John said, "as a laborer, if necessary. Or working for her father."

The duke snorted. "That brings us to your trouble with the law. Are you now considered a deserter from the Grenadiers?"

"I never took the king's shilling, your Grace," John said.

"How so?"

"David got me off the *Valorous* as they were preparing to haul me off to the Grenadiers."

"He had no idea that when they catch him, they'll hang him for helping you escape?"

"He was aware that if they caught him, we'd all be hung, your Grace," John said. "But they didn't catch us. The law's not looking for David."

The duke looked as if that was the first time he'd thought about that. "That's right," he said. "All David is guilty of is being a goddamned impetuous fool. Twice that I know of."

"He had the mistaken notion that he was responsible for me being there."

"In your eyes, doesn't that make him a fool?"

"No, sir," John said. "It makes him a courageous friend."

The duke did not like to be corrected. He glowered at John.

"I don't much give a damn what you do to me, your Grace," John said, "but I would be grateful if you would leave David out of it."

"All right," the duke said icily. "Leaving David out of it: you are one of two things, either an escaped prisoner or a deserter from the Grenadiers."

"Yes, sir," John said, "I suppose that's it."

"Your Grace," Captain Law said, "there is a third thing. They think John is dead, killed while escaping."

The duke looked at him.

"And what you're suggesting is that we leave it at that? That you give him money and let him run to France? Or North America?"

"Yes, your Grace, I beg you for that," Captain Law said.

"I could not do that," the duke said. "For several reasons. For one thing, I am the chief law-enforcement officer in Scotland. The law is the law." He met William Law's eyes. "And for another, Willy, I couldn't do that to you. Be responsible for your son not being able to carry on your name."

Captain Law was confused. He opened his mouth as if to speak.

The duke turned away from John Law and his father, pushed the drapes through which John had entered the room aside, and stepped out onto the veranda.

"You there!" he called to the officer in charge of the section of Horse Guard troopers. The officer, startled, came running.

"Yes, your Grace?"

"You will kindly present my compliments to the colonel commanding the Borderers," the duke said.

"Yes, your Grace?"

"You will ask him to prepare for me, at his earliest convenience, the necessary papers, whatever they might be, for the commissioning of Mr. John Law as a subaltern in the Borderers. Tell him I would be pleased if this could be arranged today."

"After I escort you back to town, your Grace?"

"No, goddammit, right now," the duke snapped. "I rode the highways of Scotland when every other bastard here would have loved to have run a sword through me; I don't need you to protect me between here and town today."

The officer bowed his head and hurriedly backed through the curtains.

"I trust," the duke said sarcastically to John, "that this meets with your approval?"

"I'm very grateful to you, milord," John said.

"I wouldn't be surprised," the duke said, "if you turn out a decent officer. Blood tells. Your father was a fine officer."

"Yes, sir, I know."

"And if you do marry that redheaded wench," the duke began.

"I *will* marry her, your Grace," John said firmly, almost defiantly.

The duke glowered at him. "There's soldier's blood in her veins, too," the duke went on. "She will make a good officer's wife."

John Law locked eyes with John Maitland, Duke of Lauderdale.

"I presume, Mr. Law," the duke said after a long pause, "that you will be discussing your plans with the Gardiners?"

"Yes, your Grace."

"Please pass onto them my best wishes," John Maitland, Duke of Lauderdale, said.

ABOUT THE AUTHOR

Allison Mitchell was born and raised in New Orleans, Louisiana, and is currently at work on a second novel about the Gardiners that takes the family to Louisiana.

More Bestsellers from SIGNET

More SIGNET Fiction

Buy them at your local

bookstore or use coupon

on next page for ordering.

Fabulous Fiction from SIGNET